Praise for *When*

"Julie Cantrell's *When Mountains Move* is a classic American novel of risk taking, struggle, renewal, and redemption. This book took my breath away. If you loved Ms. Cantrell's debut novel, *Into the Free*, you will treasure this sequel."

—Amy Hill Hearth, *New York Times* bestselling author of *Having Our Say* and *Miss Dreamsville and the Collier County Women's Literary Society*

"Julie Cantrell hits another home run with *When Mountains Move*—a gripping story of the uneasy trials of a new marriage and the hardships of ranching in the rough terrain of the Rockies. The biggest threat, though, is not the mountain lion that prowls in the shadows, but a harrowing secret from the past. Julie's storytelling talents took me to the brink of emotion, and I came out on the other side cheering! Don't miss this stunning sequel to *Into the Free*!"

—Carla Stewart, award-winning author of *Chasing Lilacs* and *Sweet Dreams*

"Cantrell is a wise and beautiful storyteller. Readers will be instantly drawn to Millie—secrets and all—and will savor her grace-filled journey toward truth and freedom."

—Beth Webb Hart, bestselling author of *Moon Over Edisto*

"Julie Cantrell is a born storyteller and her talent shines in *When Mountains Move*. This inspiring novel beautifully captures a time and place that will leave readers feeling that all is well in the world. It's a journey into the western frontier, young marriage, and unresolved pasts, but above all, it's a journey into the human spirit. Fans of *Into the Free* are sure to devour this magical and heartfelt story."

—Michael Morris, author of *Man in the Blue Moon*, *Slow Way Home*, and *A Place Called Wiregrass*

"If, like me, you are an armchair adventurer, you will love this beautifully written story about a young woman who treks to Colorado in 1943 to start a ranch with her new husband. Plagued by hardships often found in that era and a deep secret with the power to destroy everything, Millie's journey culminates on a mountain where she faces an impossible choice. Julie Cantrell's lyrical writing and engaging story captivated me for days. I loved *When Mountains Move*!"

—Kellie Coates Gilbert, author of *Mother of Pearl*

"Julie Cantrell is a masterful storyteller. *When Mountains Move* is a gripping tale, full of charm and heart. Because the novel is true to Millie's point of view, the reader is pulled at once into her world, her difficult decisions, and her reasons for choosing as she does. Each of her choices leads to another, and each ending brings a new, unexpected beginning. Reading *When Mountains Move* is like experiencing the Rockies in late spring: each peak exposes the reader to new heights, amazing beauty, and unexpected adventure. The result is a riveting tale that captures the reader's attention and holds it long after the last page. This is an engrossing, drama-packed novel about forgiveness and second chances. Millie is a heroine readers young and old will believe in."

—Michel Stone, author of *The Iguana Tree*

"Once again, *New York Times* bestselling author Julie Cantrell delivers a rich and moving story that pulled me from page to page. *When Mountains Move* explores the many facets of faith that are tested in the fires of betrayal and reminds us that even our deepest pain can be transformed. It is a beautiful novel that lights up the page and whose characters took up residence in my heart."

—Shelly Beach, Christy Award–winning author and speaker

"A lyrical, engaging story about a young woman overcoming a rocky start to her life. Millie is a spirited, complex character who must discover that the path to love and peace is paved with forgiveness. I enjoyed this novel immensely."

—Margaret Dilloway, author of *The Care and Handling of Roses with Thorns*

"Julie Cantrell's characters challenge the landscape, both internal and external. *When Mountains Move* is a beautiful journey of hope, healing, and triumph against the odds. Set against the stunning backdrop of the American West, it's one for your keeper shelf."

—Lisa Wingate, bestselling author of *The Prayer Box* and *The Sea Glass Sisters*

Praise for *Into the Free*

"Cantrell's exquisitely written story immerses readers in a world that is as cruel as it is beautiful. From the opening lines to the very last sentence, the book's magnetic prose bewitches and enthralls on every page. A visceral and gripping journey of a young woman's revelations about God and self, this novel will surely excite any reader who appreciates a compelling story about personal struggle and spiritual resilience."

—*Publishers Weekly*

"In this lovely novel, author Julie Cantrell shows us how our heart's desire can intersect with God's plan no matter how many times we deny it, or how blurred the lines between good and evil can sometimes be, and how we can sometimes see the existence of angels in disguise in our lives if we just look hard enough. . . . Exquisitely written. Julie Cantrell has created a haunting story that will linger in your heart long after you've turned the last page."

—Karen White, *New York Times* bestselling author of *The Beach Trees*

"Cantrell's words paint vivid pictures that bring Millie's harrowing story to life. Riveting you to your chair, this story is a reminder that sometimes faith—real faith—is slowly built during the darkest moments of your life."

—*Romantic Times*

"Julie Cantrell beautifully renders a vivid past, but her subjects are immediate and eternal—family secrets, love's many losses, revenge and revelation, and finally redemption. Her characters may buck and brawl and bray against the notion of God in their lives, but there's no denying He continues to send them into each other's paths, and Cantrell masterfully introduces them to one another in her wonderfully woven narrative. This book is full of insightful detail and wondrous turns, with an ending that moves in all directions through time like God's grace."

—Mark Richard, author of *House of Prayer No. 2*

"A lyrical, moving, haunting, wise, brutal, warmhearted, and ultimately freeing and inspiring coming-of-age tale told with poetic honesty. Julie Cantrell is a wonderful writer. She doesn't just tell a story, she invites you right into it so that you don't just read it, you live it. *Into the Free* swept me up and swept me along, and the story and the characters stayed with me—in the very best way—long after I turned the last page."

—Jennifer Niven, bestselling author of *The Ice Master*, *Velva Jean Learns to Drive*, and *Velva Jean Learns to Fly*

When Mountains Move

Julie Cantrell

Thomas Nelson
Since 1798

Published in Nashville, Tennessee, by Thomas Nelson. Thomas Nelson is a registered trademark of HarperCollins Christian Publishing, Inc.

Published in association with the literary agency of WordServe Literary Group, Ltd., 10152 S. Knoll Circle, Highlands Ranch, CO 80130.

Cover Design: Faceout Studios, Jeff Miller

Cover Photo: Trevillion Images

Thomas Nelson titles may be purchased in bulk for educational, business, fund-raising, or sales promotional use. For information, please e-mail SpecialMarkets@ThomasNelson.com.

Daniel 6:22 and Matthew 17:20 verses taken from the King James Version of the Bible. Public Domain.

Other citations are located in the Notes section at the end of the book.

ISBN: 978-0-7180-8127-0 (repack)

Library of Congress Cataloging-in-Publication Data

LCCN 2013943843

Printed in the United States of America

16 17 18 19 20 21 RRD 6 5 4 3 2

For those who matter most,
with hopes I live my life in such a way
you already know who you are.
And for Heather and Jeff,
who taught me there is no such thing as an ending,
only new beginnings.

Chapter 1

Friday, May 7, 1943

Church bells strike to announce the hour. My body quakes from the force of the sound, and again from the force of the man, uninvited. He pushes me down, nails his elbow into my throat. I fight, kicking, clawing. Screaming.

Someone calls my name. "Millie?"

I throw my fists into the night, lunging white-eyed toward the voice.

"Millie! Stop! It's me." Bump wraps his arms around me, and I jerk back, pushing against him. He withdraws, asking, "You okay?"

I don't answer. Instead, I stare at the pitch of the darkened ceiling and pull myself from the depths of the dream.

Bump slides close again and touches my hand. "You always sleep in your boots?" He smiles, trying to make light of the dark. He doesn't know I've spent the last six weeks fully dressed, even through the nights, always ready to run or to fight. I try to measure my breaths, slow my pulse. *It was only a dream, Millie. Calm down.*

"Storm's got me a little edgy." I offer Bump an apologetic

smile. I don't tell him how every time I'm alone, I stay on full alert. How strange sounds and shadows and even the wind can make me look behind and check for danger. I wasn't always this way, and I hope I can feel safe again someday, soon. For now, I leave the cot in the corner of the foaling room and walk across the red dirt floors of the Cauy Tucker rodeo barn, still trying to emerge from the haunting nightmare.

"Was I screaming?" I ask Bump. I'm always fighting and screaming in the dream. If only I could have done that during the actual assault. The one that left me frozen and numb. Silenced on the steeple-room floor.

"Nope." Bump's footsteps follow my own. "Not a sound. Just mean as a wolverine." He smiles. Even now, weeks after the event, my dreams are the only place I have a voice.

Bump tries again to cheer me. "Didn't mean to scare you." He wraps his arms around my waist and turns me toward him, delivering a strong kiss, pumped with passion. I try to let him ease my fears, but when he moves me against the coarse wooden slats of the barn, my shoulder hits the wall a little too fast. A little too hard. I flinch. A rising panic tenses my throat. My body ebbs and flows between desire and disgust. *It's not his fault, Millie. You can do this.*

There's no debating whether I love Bump; I do. But there is too much he doesn't know about me. I want to give him the truth right now, before we say our vows. Then maybe he could understand why he's found me frightened like this in the middle of the night.

"It's after midnight." I struggle to find words to start. "What are you doing out here?" I reach for a towel to dry him. He's walked in the rain all the way from the back barracks where he stays with the rodeo hands, a mixed bunch of cowboys stopping by between ranch jobs.

"Missed you is all." He pulls me back to him, moving his fingers from my shoulders, down to my waist, then below. At seventeen, I should want this, and not long ago I did. But now everything is different. Now I am afraid of what a man can do, even one as good and kind as Bump.

I pull away gently and hope Bump knows I don't want him to leave. I just want him to slow down. Give me time. *I'm not ready.* "Bad luck to see me before the wedding." I smile.

"No such thing." Bump catches my ear in his mouth and whispers, "How's that cot holdin' up?"

"Oh, the cot." I run my fingers around his drenched collar, beneath his stubbled chin. "I don't know what I'll do without it." I try to match his playful mood. "Think there'll be room to take it with us?"

"No room at all. In fact, I'm thinkin' we'd better give it a final farewell right now. Somethin' to remember us by."

Thunder clashes, and the paint mare in the back stall releases a loud, guttural response. Two others yell back to her, and the barn is suddenly a symphony of horse talk. I tap Bump's chest with my finger and softly scold, "I think we can wait, Mr. Anderson."

"Impossible." He brushes my dark curls behind my ear and kisses my neck, then my collarbone. Just six weeks ago, a kiss like this would have sent me into flame. But that was before. Before Bill Miller caused my body to react with panic every time it is touched. Bump struggles to remove my shirt in the dark, the small buttons proving difficult for his strong fingers. "Was hopin' I'd find you undressed at this hour." One button slips through.

I pull from him and move toward the hay room, flipping

a light switch and drawing louder reactions from the horses. Bump stays behind and watches me walk. I glance back long enough to catch his crooked smile, the one that tugs my heart in its tender corners and makes me cling to the possibility of happy-ever-after.

As the radio warms from a soft buzz to a heavy hum, I spin the tuner. Between cracks of static, the final few notes of an unfamiliar song seep out from the speakers. Then a pause, before Harry and Trudy Babbitt give voice to the Kay Kyser hit from last year. *"Who wouldn't love you?"* they sing. *"Who wouldn't care?"*

With a flick of my wrist, I toss Bump a pair of leather gloves. He catches them without looking, both in one hand. "Gettin' cold feet?" Worry lines his voice.

"Not a chance." I try to sound positive as I haul hay to the row of stalls. "I just figure we might as well get a jump on the morning jobs. We've already got the horses all confused." Bump follows with some old winter carrots, giving one wrinkled stalk to each horse. "How about you?" I ask. "You ready to back out?"

"You kiddin', Millie? I would've married you the first day I saw you."

Outside, the moon has sunk behind swollen clouds, and the stars have been swallowed by storm. In here, the fan blades spin, as the bright bulbs buzz like strange mouths shouting from the heavens. "Tell him, Millie," they yell. "Tell him the truth!" Bugs swarm the lights, as if even they want to stop all the noise.

I take a carrot from Bump and move back to offer an extra one to my favorite horse, Firefly. She takes it in three bites while I pet her soft bay coat. "I'll miss you, sweet girl." I trace the white blaze that lines the bridge of her nose. "But you'll be joining us in Colorado soon. I promise." She nickers. I hope she understands.

Bump runs his fingers along my spine, then pulls me to him again. I try to let the truth surface, but no matter how much I want to tell him everything that's happened, the deep, black force of fear gets in the way.

~

Between Bump's repeated attempts to take me to the cot and my stubborn resistance, we spend the hours filling feed bins and topping water pails, grooming the mares and mucking the stalls. By the time we cross the final job from our daily list, the rain stops and the sun creeps in.

We're just cleaning up the last of the brushes when a wave of nausea slams me, one of many I've been dealt in recent days. I bolt for the door and Bump follows me, concerned. "You all right?" He moves closer, speaks softly. I bend behind the pines and try not to let him see me get sick. With all that's happened in the last year, it's no wonder my gut is a wreck. But life is better now. Much better. I hope this is the last time I ever let worry get the best of me.

"I'm okay." I wipe my mouth with the back of my shirtsleeve, mortified. "Nerves, I guess."

"Nerves?" Bump seems stung. "Thought you weren't gettin' cold feet."

"Not about the marrying part." It's not a complete lie. "But yes, to be honest, I am a little nervous about the rest of it."

"What rest of it?"

My voice grows quiet. It's the old Millie coming through again. Yellow. Weak. The truth is . . . I'm not sure I deserve Bump, and I wonder if others are thinking the same thing.

"What I mean is, your entire family is coming. I have to stand up there in front of everyone we know and . . ."

"And what?" Bump's jaw sets. His shoulders stiffen.

"And . . ." I look away. "Pretend I'm good enough for you." I step around a mud puddle and make my way back into the barn, hoping the smells don't get to me again.

Bump tromps right through the puddle. "Good enough? For me? Millie, the guys can't believe I ever got you to talk to me, much less marry me. I still keep expectin' you to make a run for it." Then he adds, "Please don't." There's a sound in Bump's voice I've never heard. Doubt.

I give him my full attention again and exhale. Bump's blue eyes hold my own as he waits for my answer. That same color that first reminded me of hydrangea blooms. "I won't, if you won't," I say. And suddenly, I mean it. No matter how unsure I've been feeling, a promise is a promise. And it's one I want to keep. I move closer, rest my head against his sturdy chest, and allow myself to find safety in his long, lean frame. Bump lets the music move us while Sinatra croons.

A peaceful sky, there are such things
A rainbow high where heaven sings
So have a little faith and trust in what tomorrow
brings

Chapter 2

"There's something romantically hopeful about having a wedding in the middle of a war." Janine is speaking before she enters the barn. I met her six months ago, and she's been talking ever since. When she turns the corner and spots Bump with me, her pitch jumps two octaves.

"What in heaven's name are you doing here, Bump?" Janine swoops her arms in big circles and begins to shoo. "It's bad luck! Get!" She gives Bump a frisky nudge, but he manages to plant one last kiss on my cheek before darting for safety.

"If I catch you back in here again before the ceremony, you'll be sorry!" Janine's chirp is less painful to me now than when I first met the spitfire secretary, but I still pinch my ears when she hits certain notes. "He just can't wait, can he?" Janine giggles, and her entire frame, barely five feet high, springs with glee.

I swat at Janine, laughing. We head out to the pasture as a bicycle bell dings from behind us. "Sis! Sis!" Camille's called me this for months. Since the day her mother, Diana, took mercy on me and brought me home to live with them. Camille greeted me that day with an enthusiastic hug and announced she'd "always wanted a sister," as if Diana had just brought home a stray puppy from behind the corner store.

Camille drops her bike onto the wet grass before bouncing her way toward us, making Janine laugh. "Mornin', Camille," I say, lifting my hand to block the sun from my eyes.

"For the record, I no longer answer to Camille. Call me Ann." She lifts her cotton dress and curtsies. Camille always acts years beyond her age; she's only ten.

"Ann?" Janine feeds Camille the attention she craves. "Oh, please, do tell me, why Ann?"

"After Ann Sheridan, of course. Didn't you see her on the cover of *Motion Picture Hollywood Magazine*? Mabel thinks I look just like her." Camille tilts her chin up and to the right, striking a pose, then spins in circles, making her light pink dress flare. For the moment, every bit of anxiety breaks away and I want to keep feeling like this—hopeful, believing I really can forget the past and that everything is going to be okay.

Janine and I lean against a magnolia tree and watch Camille spin herself dizzy. "How *did* Diana Miller end up with such a sweet kid?" Janine whispers under a smile. Thank goodness Camille doesn't hear.

"Diana's not as bad as she seems." I shrug.

Janine rolls her eyes. "If you say so, honey."

"Well, she did take me in when no one else offered."

"Then why in heaven's name did you move into the horse barn, Millie? Everybody thought you'd plumb lost your mind."

I don't dare tell Janine the real reason I left the posh Miller home, or how even the Millers couldn't give me the only thing I ever wanted: a loving family of my own. I think back to the sudden shift in Diana, after she learned that her husband had once been engaged to marry Mama. How quickly her kindness waned and her protective walls went up. How Bill Miller would stare me down at the supper table. Right in front of his wife. "I guess I needed things to be a little more predictable."

"Predictable?" Janine shakes her head. "Honestly, Millie, wouldn't you rather sleep on soft sheets and bathe in a porcelain tub?"

"It's hard to explain, Janine. I admit, life with Mama and Jack sure wasn't perfect. Wasn't even good, most of the time. But at least I knew what to expect. When I moved in with the Millers, lots of things surprised me. Make sense?" I keep my eyes on Camille.

"Well," Janine says, laughing before lowering her voice back to a whisper, "to tell the truth, as tempting as that gorgeous house might be, I'd choose a barn over Diana Miller any day."

I nod, trying to think of a better way to defend Diana.

"Where's the dress?" Camille asks, finally getting dizzy enough to plant her feet. "Can I see it?" She wobbles as if she's about to fall. This makes her giggle.

"The dress? Oh no, Millie. I forgot the dress!" With that, Janine runs toward the rodeo office calling for Mr. Tucker.

"Not a good sign." Always dramatic, Camille sighs as if there may be no chance of saving this wedding. Anything to stop me from moving to Colorado.

"Worse things could happen," I say, waving it off. "Now let's go check on the most exciting part of the whole day."

"The groom?" Camille blows kisses to make fun of me.

"No, ma'am." I tickle her ribs and remember her obsession with Mabel's iced desserts. "The cake."

By nine a.m., Bump's relatives are already arriving from the Delta. The pasture is a steamy mess from last night's storm, so Bump spreads straw to protect everyone's shoes from the mud.

"I sure am glad Kenneth found him a good girl," Bump's mother says, offering me a hug before kissing her son on the cheek. She removes his Stetson and tousles his hair.

"I can't believe I got so lucky," I tell her.

Mr. Anderson doesn't say anything, which worries me, but he shakes my hand and Bump's too. When Bump pulls his father into a hug, the serious elder cracks a rare smile. Mrs. Anderson clasps her hands to her mouth as if this is the sweetest scene she's seen in years. Then she puts her arm around me and says, "Part of the family now, Millie."

Bump winks at me, and it's all I can do not to cry. One of the reasons I fell for Bump in the first place was because of his family. "We ain't got much, but we're good people," Mrs. Anderson teases. And she's right. They may be poor, but they are the kindest, most genuine people I've ever known. Now they consider me part of this family. My gratitude swells.

"You sure you don't want to move this wedding inside the arena? Drier ground?" Mr. Tucker joins us, puffing his cigar and filling the air with a sweet-tinged cloud of tobacco smoke. It's one of the many smells I've gotten used to in the time I've spent with the rodeo crew, but today the odor makes my stomach churn. Must mean my worries have come back in full force. I think of Mama being taken to East, labeled a "nerve patient," never again to leave the hospital for the mentally insane. *Get ahold of yourself, Millie. Don't overreact. This is a good day.*

Bump goes back to spreading hay, his polite way of letting Mr. Tucker know this is exactly where we want to have the wedding. Outside, under the trees, where we're most ourselves. No fancy church. No big rodeo production. Just a simple gathering of those we love.

"It'll be beautiful," Janine jumps in, out of breath. She holds a long white garment bag in her hand, and I'm guessing the wedding gown is hidden safe inside.

"But the pasture—" Mr. Tucker protests.

Janine tugs on Mr. Tucker's suit with confidence and stops him before he can finish his thought. "What a bride wants, a bride gets." As usual, she flirts shamelessly.

Releasing two more puffs of smoke into the air, Mr. Tucker winks at me and says, "What *Janine* wants, *Janine* gets." Then he offers a deep base chuckle that makes me wonder how long it'd take him to propose if he could realize Janine loves him.

I move to help spread straw, but Janine whisks me into the rodeo dressing room, chatting the entire way about everything from keeping my palms dry in the heat to the importance of keeping my eyes off the ground. When she points me to the bathtub, I tell her it's the best idea she's had yet. I sink beneath the warmth of the water and rest my head against a rolled towel. Slowly, I inhale. Exhale. Willing my stomach to settle.

Janine catches me just before I slide under the surface when she yells, "Don't wet your hair. We won't have time to dry it." A few minutes later, she's banging on the door. "What's taking you so long in there, Millie? We've got a wedding to attend!"

"Where do you want me, my queen?" I tease, tying a thick cotton robe at my waist and following Janine's pointed finger to a seat. Before I scoot into the chair, she's already at work, painting my nails, powdering my nose, and raving about how I'll "knock Bump's socks off." I let her have her fun.

I'm blowing my nail polish dry when three light taps hit the door. It opens. Diana enters. My breath catches. Since sneaking my suitcase out of her house in March, I haven't seen Diana at all. Not once. Now that she's here, I'm not sure how to react. There is so much that needs to be said before I leave Iti Taloa. So many loose ends that need to be tied. I stay in my chair and let Janine fasten fake pearl clip-ons to my ears. "Come on in," I say, the sounds falling heavy on my tongue.

Diana hesitates. I fear she's here to criticize. To tell me what she has ranted about to Camille many times: "Millie's way too young to be doing this." Or "Bump's parents are nothing but tenant farmers. He'll never be able to provide for her."

It's easy for Diana to judge. While she didn't come from old family money, I'm betting she had other options besides marriage. College. Travel. But for girls like me, the choices are few. I can catch up with my first love, River, and live on the road with the gypsies or head to Colorado and launch a ranch with Bump. If Diana's here to question my decision, I don't need her to make me doubt myself even more than I already do.

I love Bump. But the choice wasn't easy, and I regret not giving River the kindness he deserved. It was unfair for me to send him on his way with no explanation at all. I wish I could see him one more time, so I could give him a proper good-bye. Tell him I'm sorry. Let him know I care and that I never meant to hurt him. Maybe then I wouldn't feel as if I'm hurting River by letting Bump place a ring on my hand. I try to convince myself River doesn't care. That he left without looking back. But somewhere deep, I know it isn't true.

"I'm glad you're here," I tell Diana, hoping to ease the rift between us. My voice quavers even though I try to sound upbeat.

Janine snaps the case of rouge shut and drops her makeup brushes back into a cotton bag. I turn to the mirror and sneak a peek. "Wow! I hardly recognize myself."

"Gorgeous," Janine says, leaning into view of the mirror. Then she jumps back and pulls up the white lace dress she's letting me borrow. Only Janine would keep a wedding dress in her closet "just in case." She wiggles the hanger as if to ask, *You like it?*

"Oh, Janine," I gasp. "It's beautiful."

Janine smiles proudly as she removes the delicate gown from its hanger and motions for me to follow. I move behind a screen to step into the dress. Its long sleeves are unlined floral lace. The rest has a silk white lining and hangs loosely to my ankles, like something for a queen. Nothing like anything I've ever worn.

Diana perches stiffly on a stool, and I can't help but feel sorry for her. She's completely out of her element here in the world of cowboys and roughnecks. As Janine finishes zipping me up, Diana serves her a practiced smile. "You've been kind to provide help this morning." Her tone stretches a tad too high to be sincere, as if Janine is just another of her domestic servants, like Mabel.

"Where's Mabel?" I ask, surprised she hasn't shown up yet to wish me well.

"She still had thirty sets of silverware to polish, not to mention preparing the food." Of course. When Janine told me Diana had offered to help with the reception, I should have known it would be Mabel doing all the work. And polished silver? So much for a casual outdoor event.

"Somebody helping her?" I worry. The last thing I want to do is cause Mabel any trouble.

Diana's face tightens as if I have no right to question the way she handles her help. "I'm sure she'll manage. You'll see her at the reception." In her pristine day suit, her brand-new Carlisle heels, and her designer clutch shipped up from New Orleans, Diana turns to Janine and says, "Now, if you'll excuse us, I have a few things I need to discuss with Millie." Diana moves her glance from Janine to the door and back again.

"It's okay," I tell Janine. "You don't have to leave." It's not only that I don't want Diana treating Janine as if she's a low-class nobody; it's also that I'm afraid to be alone with Diana. Afraid of what she might know and of what she might say.

But Diana stares at Janine until she breaks. "I should go . . . check on the preacher," Janine says, making up an excuse and tugging her skirt into place before closing the door behind her.

I know Diana well enough to guess she's thinking Janine's dress is a little too tight for good taste, but she doesn't say this. Instead, she clears her throat and begins. "I hope you understand why Bill Miller won't be attending today." She still calls her husband by his first and last name, a habit she's formed to remind everyone that she married into the family who founded our town. "It's difficult for him to leave the bank on Fridays."

"Yes, ma'am. I understand." She doesn't need to know I purposely scheduled the wedding on a Friday morning for that very reason. I stretch my fingers and try to begin a conversation we've needed to have for weeks. "Diana, I want you to know . . ." She looks away, as if she's still not ready for this. I continue anyway, knowing it's now or never. "I had no idea Mama had been engaged before she married Jack. She never once mentioned Bill Miller." It's the first time I've said his name out loud since the incident six weeks ago. The words leave a sting.

Diana waits for more.

"I would never have moved in with your family if I had known. I wouldn't have put you in that position."

"I know," Diana says, pulling the brown plaid curtain so she can look out the window. Her voice is almost a whisper. "Things didn't turn out exactly as we hoped they would, did they?"

I shake my head. "I'm sorry."

"It's not your fault, Millie." Diana turns to look at me again, but I drop my chin before her eyes can catch hold of mine. "None of it is your fault."

The way she says this makes me wonder if she's figured everything out. Does she know what her husband did to me? Does she realize why I ran away from her house without saying good-bye? Does she know why I've spent six weeks living in a barn and doing everything in my power to avoid Bill Miller?

Diana puts her hands on my shoulders and I feel no anger from her, only affection. Slowly, she turns me to the mirror and begins to pin my veil in place. It's a tender gesture, one that helps my resentment fade away. I tremble when she puts her hands in my hair, remembering the love I felt from her when she sat on the edge of my hospital bed, told me the story of Pandora, and offered me hope. "You look beautiful, Millie."

Inside, I struggle with a storm of emotions. I know I should tell Bump the truth about Bill Miller, but what would he do if he knew? Things could get out of hand. Diana could find out. That would likely affect Camille. The thing is, as much as I love Bump, as much as I don't like hiding this from him, I also care about Diana and Camille, and I don't want anything to hurt them. I will focus only on that. The rest, I will try to forget.

Diana smoothes the layers of tulle with the tips of her fingers.

Then she puts her arm around me, as a mother might, and I let her hold me.

Just as I start to say "Thank you," Janine pops her head back into the rooms and squeaks, "It's time." She enters with Camille skipping behind.

"Ooh, I love it!" Camille says, flipping the veil with her hands.

"Maybe you can wear it someday." I lean low so Camille can get a better look at the pearly trim.

"Not a chance," she says, moving her hands to her hips in a stubborn stance. "I'm never getting married."

Janine laughs. "In that case, you'd better go save your seat, Mrs. Miller. This may be the only time you'll see Camille walk the aisle."

Camille waves her mother out toward the other guests, saying, "Yep. That's the truth!" As soon as Diana leaves, a big exhale fills the room and everyone relaxes again.

"You look so pretty," Camille raves. "Just like Hedy Lamarr."

I laugh at her comparing me to the most beautiful actress in Hollywood. "Only thanks to Janine. She's spent a good hour working her magic." I give Janine a hug. "I honestly don't know how to thank you."

"You just did, sweetie." Then she makes her way out the door, saying, "Camille's right. You do look gorgeous. So don't touch anything. Don't sit down. And don't you dare mess with your hair."

Camille closes the door behind Janine, spins back in my direction, and sighs as she lets all her weight fall against the door. "Finally, I get you to myself!"

I fumble through my bag to find a simple square package tied in a blue bow. Then I offer the gift to Camille.

"For me?" Camille acts the part, full of drama, and takes two happy leaps to reach me. She removes the paper lid and examines a crown of clovers tucked in cotton.

"I made it just for you, the way my mother taught me."

"What is it?" Camille touches the delicate white blooms with care.

"When I was a little girl, I could be having the worst day ever, and all I'd have to do is put on my crown. Suddenly I'd become the most powerful princess on the planet."

I pull the circle of stems from the box and arrange it atop Camille's blonde curls. "Now, anytime you feel weak, I want you to remember this crown. I want it to remind you that you are very, very smart, and absolutely beautiful."

"I am?" Camille asks.

"You bet you are. But that's not all."

Camille looks at me and a tiny tear drops from the corner of her eye.

"You're also brave and strong. But you know what's even more important than all of that?"

Camille shakes her head.

"You are loved. Loved bunches and bunches! And no one can ever take that away. You understand?"

Camille turns to look in the mirror. She stands in her expensive dress with her clover crown, I in Janine's long white gown and veil. "I don't want you to go," Camille says.

And this is what finally breaks me. Tears track the margins of my face, and I fight to hold back sobs. After years of watching trains and gypsies come and go, longing and praying for someone to take me with them into the free, I'm now undone at the thought of leaving Iti Taloa.

"I'll write. And you'll visit." I roll my fingers through Camille's soft curls. "We'll come back soon. I promise."

"From what I hear, it doesn't really work that way." Camille wipes a tear from her cheek.

"You read too many magazines." I kiss the top of her head, and we both struggle not to cry too hard. That's when Janine peeks back in and shouts, "Patience is spreading thin out here." Then she notices my tear-streaked makeup and sighs. "Millie! You can't cry!" She rushes through a frenzied touch-up, and I'm back to perfect in no time.

I smile at Camille, who has also dried her tears. "You ready?"

Camille looks in the mirror and straightens her crown. "I was born ready," she says, leading me out the door to meet my groom.

Chapter 3

Camille walks in front of me down the aisle of straw. She bounces each step, so full of spunk hardly anyone notices I'm walking behind her. I'm grateful all eyes are on her. With each peppy hop, she drops yellow wildflower petals. Most of the blooms catch the wind like sails, and their delicate dance brings me back to my childhood, when I roamed the forests in search of every yellow bud I could find. I was certain the bright blossoms were gifts sent directly from God, proof that I was never alone.

Now I follow the golden trail to Bump, standing proud and handsome in his sturdy gray suit. His light-almond hair, usually tucked beneath his cowboy hat, snatches sunlight, like God Himself has chosen this man for me. When Bump's eyes meet mine, my nervousness subsides. I straighten my spine, pull my shoulders back, and move beneath the boughs of the shagbark hickory, past rows of smiling friends and family members, directly to Bump's side.

As I turn to face the preacher, a wisp of wind twists my veil. Bump reaches gently to fix it. Mabel sings, "I Was Made to Love

You," and all thoughts of Bill Miller fly away. Before I know it, I am swallowing all doubt and saying "I do."

"I now pronounce you man and wife," the preacher says. "You may kiss the bride."

Bump offers me a respectful kiss. Then he whispers, "The real one comes later." His uneven grin stretches high to the left, and I know I have made the right choice.

We turn toward our guests, the first time as a married couple. I take my time to notice each person who has joined us here under this shade tree. Mr. Tucker, Janine, Camille, Mabel, and every member of the expansive Anderson clan all looking at us with open acceptance. Even Diana gives me a smile.

Camille passes out dandelions, and Janine instructs everyone to "Make a wish for the happy couple." Then she shouts, "Blow!" We smile under the sun, surrounded by a beautiful band of floating, feathery seeds. Each tiny plume skirts across the horizon representing a wish for Bump and me to succeed, a reminder that plenty of people will love us even if we fail.

By noon, the heat is building. The rodeo boys are barbecuing, and several members of Bump's family have pulled out a stash of guitars, banjos, and fiddles. Like folks from the Delta often do, they have somehow managed to scramble together a decent band. Mabel joins in, entertaining the crowd with her astounding vocals, and Camille is dancing up a storm.

Bump pulls me to the patch of straw-covered grass we are calling the dance floor. "Play somethin' special," he tells the band.

The crowd circles around the two of us, and everyone claps

as the musicians launch into "Dearly Beloved." Camille passes out cardboard fans to help everyone cope with the heat, while Mabel sings with enthusiasm, dancing and smiling through every perfect note.

Dearly beloved, how clearly I see
Somewhere in heaven you were fashioned for me
Angel eyes knew you, angel voices led me to you

Bump's skin smells of leather and hay and of all things real and comforting. I close my eyes and try to pretend no one is watching, that it's just Bump and me.

When the song is done, I don't want to let go of my husband. I want to continue holding my hands against the muscular rows of his back and leaning my nose into the tight curves of his neck, but Mr. Tucker surprises me by cutting in for the next dance. I nervously follow his lead and look back at Bump as the band shifts into "As Time Goes By."

Bump follows suit by choosing his mother. He stands a head and a half taller than her, but he bends down to let her kiss him on the cheek. I can't take my eyes off him, the way he treats his mother with such kindness, moving slowly and cautiously with her, tilting her back just enough to let her drift in delight.

"Mr. Tucker," I begin, talking near his ear so he can hear me above the music. "We're both really honored you chose us to run your ranch. You've done too much."

"Aw, shucks, Millie. I ain't done much." Mr. Tucker nods at the guests, who watch us dance. He's never one to shrink from a spotlight, and I laugh at him putting on a show. He sends me into a spin before I can remind him how much he's done. Putting

Bump through vet school, letting him do a year of training here with the rodeo, and now choosing Bump to launch a ranch in the Rockies. He convinced Bump to take the job by saying, "You're as ready as you'll ever be." Just like that, Bump was set on a new course, and now, I am too.

Mr. Tucker even bought Bump's parents a tractor, plus all the implements they'll need to help them finally purchase land of their own. According to our arrangement, we have three years to turn a profit. If all goes well, we'll develop a top breeding line of stock horses and a quality supply of beef cattle, Bump's family will keep the expensive farm equipment, and Mr. Tucker will help Bump establish a veterinary practice at any location of our choosing.

If we fail, we will be responsible for repaying the costs of the farm equipment, and we'll be grateful to keep any job Mr. Tucker assigns us. That's *if* Mr. Tucker can remain in business if the ranch goes under.

When the song ends, Bump's mother switches partners. As her husband, the tall, quiet leader of the Anderson tribe, takes her hand, Bump pulls Janine to the floor, and she cheers to be chosen. As soon as she's in Bump's arms, she calls for other couples to join the fun, and before I know it, the entire area is packed with twosomes, young and old, dancing along to a lively swing tune. Mr. Tucker stays right with me.

By the end of the first stanza, Bump cuts in. "'Bout time you figure out who your partner really is 'round here, Mr. Tucker." Bump passes Janine to our boss and takes my hand before either can protest.

At first, Mr. Tucker and Janine stand there, awkwardly looking at each other as if they don't quite know what to do. Then

Mr. Tucker extends his arm and Janine looks at me for advice. I wrinkle my brow as if to say, *What are you waiting for?* She gets the message and moves in to dance with the man she loves. Before the end of the song, they are so close I couldn't slip a sheet of paper between them if I tried. Four songs later, they are still hip to hip, and Janine is beaming.

Within an hour, Bump has danced with all of his young, giggly nieces, and I've been spun dizzy by every rough-cut cowboy on the lot. Mabel takes a break from singing and spreads a bright smile across her face. When she holds her soft arms open wide, I rush in for a hug.

"I'll never forget when you first sang for me," I tell her, remembering the day I followed her with my wagon of pecans and a three-legged stray dog named BoBo.

Mabel steals a fan from a passing child and starts to hum the tune of "Sometimes I Feel Like a Motherless Child." Her voice still soothes me.

"How in the world am I supposed to make it in Colorado without you?"

"You're ready, baby girl." She kisses my cheek, then turns me toward the shade and says, "But first, there's somebody I want you to meet."

Mabel leads me to the magnolia, where her friend moves to join us. The woman looks familiar, but I can't place how I might know her. I'm guessing she's in her sixties, about as old as Mabel but with a bit more wear and tear. Her hair is braided, and she wears a simple cotton dress with a faded floral pattern.

She reaches to tuck a loose strand of graying hair behind her ear as I say hello.

"I hope it okay for me to come." Her accent is not much different from anyone I know in Mississippi, a slow drawl with soft consonants and long-stretched vowels, but even in this opening sentence I hear a definite sprinkling of the Choctaw tongue, with a missing verb and a sharper clip to her speech.

"Millie, this is your grandmother, Oka." My heart nearly stops at Mabel's words. "Remember I told you she was my friend from back home?"

Of course I remember. This is Jack's mother, a woman I've wanted to meet ever since Mabel told me she was alive and well in Willow Bend. I hadn't known anything about her until I moved in with the Millers. It's just one of the many blanks Mabel filled in for me after Mama and Jack died. "No such thing as coincidence," Mabel once told me, and after so many pieces fell together, I'm inclined to believe she's right.

I smile at Oka. "I'm so glad to meet you." An understatement, to say the least. Mabel grins proudly, knowing how much this means to me.

Oka moves slowly, touching my hair, my face, then my shoulders. When she finally wraps her arms around me, I don't want her to let me go. I am drawn to her in a way I've never been to anyone, and I can't help noticing all the ways we are alike. The color of our eyes, our hair, our skin—darker than Bump's, even though he spends every day in the sun. She bites her bottom lip and pulls back, closing her fists against her side, perhaps to keep her hands from shaking.

Mabel steps behind me and holds my shoulder. There may be children playing and fiddles tuning, but I hear nothing but the rush of my own blood as it pumps boldly through my chest, a deep, tense echo of *being*.

"How 'bout we move to a table?" Mabel suggests. She motions for Oka to take a seat, and I follow suit. I've never been allowed to share a table with Mabel, her skin a shade too dark for that. But today, I make the rules.

"I always want to meet you," Oka says. "I was . . ." She pauses and shifts her eyes to a group of children throwing pebbles at trees. "I was afraid."

"I didn't know about you," I explain to Oka, leaning with my elbows on the table the way Diana never allowed me to do. "Not for a long time."

The silence stings, as if neither of us knows how to bridge the seventeen years that sit between us. I turn my attention to Janine, who is now leading all the kids in a silly rendition of "Bump and Millie sitting in a tree. K-I-S-S-I-N-G."

Oka speaks again. "I always care about you, Millicent." It is strange to hear someone call me by my given name. I can't shake the sound of Jack's voice: "The name fits. She ain't worth a cent." I try to remember River's voice instead. "Millicent means *strength*."

I struggle to match this real-world Oka with the grandmother I've imagined. The only clue I've had about her is a faded photograph and a letter written when Mama married Jack. But the letter was so formal, with perfect grammar and polished penmanship. I hadn't expected her to use such broken English. I have so many questions. So little time.

Bump returns before I can ask anything at all. He passes a plate of barbeque chicken to Oka and another to Mabel. "Bump, this is my grandmother, Oka. Jack's mother," I say. Oka watches Bump cautiously as he greets her with a warm smile.

I whisper, "Thank you" as he leaves to find tea. He makes three trips, serving the women, and then bringing cups for himself and for me. Mabel and Oka soak up the special attention. I figure they're thinking the same thing I am, how Bump is so different from Boone and Jack, the violent men Oka and I have known.

As we eat, I watch Oka from the corner of my eye, trying to learn everything I can about her in the short time we have together. I note the way she struggles to use a fork, how she prefers her tea without sugar, and how she makes the sign of the cross before she eats. Catholic. We've barely finished our meal when Bump's father stands and taps his fork to a half-empty glass.

"Let's bow our heads," Mr. Anderson begins, and everyone follows his lead. He starts by asking God to be with us as Bump and I begin our new lives together. Then he prays for our success on the ranch, that we won't see a repeat of the dust bowls, and that the cattle won't get black leg. Then he ends with words so tender, I struggle not to tear up again.

"When times get hard," Mr. Anderson says, "as they will, and when marriage becomes strained, as it will, and when Kenneth and Millie are so desperate they want to give up and walk out, may they find strength in You, Lord. May their faith draw them back to one another, and at the moments when they need it most, may they remember the love they feel today."

Chapter 4

By three, we've tied down everything we can fit into the back of Jack's truck. Bump's father checks our tires. "Don't forget the new restrictions. You'll need to stay under thirty-five," he says, reminding us to conserve rubber. "I'd hate to see you two get pulled over."

Mr. Tucker gives Bump a set of keys. "Did you pack some spares? Bound to have a flat or two on that stretch."

"Yes, sir." Bump nods. "Got three, actually."

"Smart." Mr. Tucker seems proud. "Last chance to change your mind." He passes a plump sack of money through the driver's window.

I give Bump an "Are you sure about this?" look, half hoping he'll take this opportunity to stay here, in Iti Taloa, with Camille and Mabel and Janine and Mr. Tucker. Or that we'll move to the Delta and help the Andersons farm their way out of poverty. Or that he'll convince Mr. Tucker it's crazy to start a cattle operation so far from home. Especially on the tail of the Depression and the dust bowl, let alone in the middle of a war. Half of me wants to jump out of the truck and shout, "What on earth are y'all thinking? Betting it all on a couple of desperate kids!"

"You'll need this." Mr. Tucker hands me a letter signed by Governor Johnson, along with a temporary X tag for fuel. "Got special permission for you to exceed your weekly ration. Fill up as much as you need until you get there. I know you won't abuse the privilege."

"What kind of bribe did this take?" Bump teases.

"No bribe," Mr. Tucker insists. "The governor just wants to see the ranch succeed, so we can bring all that money right back here to Mississippi."

I fold the letter and tuck it under a sack of sandwiches Mabel has prepared for us. Mr. Tucker bangs his thick fist on the top of the truck's roof. "Three years," he says. The keys click together in Bump's hand, a reminder that time is ticking.

Bump slides the key into the ignition and pushes the starter button. The black 1939 Ford truck we inherited from Jack roars to life. With that, Bump drums the steering wheel with his rough hands and says, "Here goes nothin'." From what I can tell, he is completely sure everything will work in our favor.

I've always wanted to leave this town and set off on some grand adventure, but as the engine turns, a deep fear spins inside me. Sharp and heavy, it slices away the joy and tells me I'm not ready for this. There's too much on the line.

I try to silence my doubts and remind myself how lucky we are. But the truth is, I am still struggling with my new reality. Not only that we are taking a big gamble with a three-year time line, but also the fact that I am now married, one half of a *We*. What will it mean, this belonging to another?

I rub the ring looped around my fourth finger, a shiny symbol of infinity. It's hard not to imagine how Bump thinks of me now. Is it my duty to love *and* to obey, as the preacher said? Does Bump expect me to surrender and submit, like Mama?

"Awful quiet," Bump says.

Everyone is waiting for us to pull away. I take a deep breath and send the words out quickly, before I swallow them down. "I guess I'm just thinking I'm not the kind of girl to obey, in case you don't know that about me." I smile, trying to ease the blow.

"Don't worry." Bump laughs. "I already know." He leans over to kiss me, and I let his lips meet mine. "Besides," he adds, "I ain't one to want a girl who obeys. I only want a girl to kiss me. Want *you* to kiss me, Millie. Every morning. Every night."

And with that, Bump honks the horn and steers our pickup away from the cheering crowd. I am all twists and tangles, waving farewell. Bump's nieces and nephews chase our tracks until the road tugs thin between us and their shadows bend in the sun.

Behind us, the church bells ring. The same church bells that have chimed every hour throughout my childhood. The same ones housed in the steeple where it all happened. A hollow, haunting reminder that they know the truth. They know my secret, and my husband doesn't.

I don't know if I'll continue trick riding, or if I will ever again perform with Firefly in front of cheering crowds. I don't know if the trees will sing in the Rockies, as they do in Iti Taloa, or if the dirt will be red, or if the creek beds will be heavy with clay. All I know is, I do not want my husband to know Bill Miller held me down beneath those steeple bells and cracked my core. I do not want that event, that one brief moment, to enter into our marriage.

We're barely out of town before Bump eases my worries. He's good at that. He turns up the radio and welcomes the hopeful harmonies of the Benny Goodman Orchestra. Singing along with a static-laced Helen Forrest, Bump hits every note and invites me to join him. I give in, and sing along: *"I'm riding for a fall again; I'm gonna give my all again. Taking a chance on love."*

Bump doesn't seem to mind that I'm way off-key. He only wants to have me with him, which is exactly where I choose to be. After stopping to fill the gas tank and to grab boiled peanuts and root beer at the Arkansas state line, we ride in silence for a while. I let my body bend into Bump's and feel the steady rhythm of his pulse as the nose of the truck pitches up and down across green hills.

"I wonder if the mountains will be as high as I imagine." I close my eyes and picture slim silver spires stretching into sky. I slip right into sleep and dream of two mountains, side by side. They are stuck in place, unable to bend, and hardened by forces much greater than either understands. Within reach of each other, they try to touch. The sun rises. Sets. Rises. Sets again. Two proud beacons of belief, green with the birth of spring, too young and hopeful to understand the sorrows to come.

I wake to Bump asking, "Sleep good?"

"I did," I confess. "Want me to drive for a while?"

"I got it," he says. "You were talkin' in your sleep."

"Was not!" My face feels four shades of red.

"Sure were."

"What'd I say?" *Please don't let him find out this way.*

"Never gonna tell." He smiles. I exhale.

"Tell me!" I nudge him.

"You kept sayin', 'Come with me, come with me.' Now what I need to know is, who do you wanna come with you?"

"Don't be silly." I pat his leg. "I was dreaming about mountains."

"Sure you were."

"No, really. You ever wonder if the mountains get tired of being stuck in place?"

"Never thought much about it." Then he adds, "Mama used to say faith could move mountains. Even just a little bit of faith. Small as a mustard seed."

"You believe that?" I am not convinced.

"I do." Bump says this without hesitation. As if nothing could ever weaken his faith.

I pull his rough hand into mine, move it up against the wild thrums of my heart, and say, "Thank you."

"For what?"

"For bringing me with you."

"Never planned it no other way." Bump leans his head out the window to look up at the darkening sky. "Need to find a place to stay the night. Any ideas, Mrs. Anderson?"

We are surrounded by humble hills, swelling and falling in deep, green waves. There's not a single light in the distance. "We have a tent, right?"

"You betcha!" Judging by the grin on his face, you'd think I've just told him we've won the war.

It may not be the honeymoon most girls dream of, but if I am going to face this night with my husband, I can't imagine any place I'd rather be. Someplace private, peaceful, away. I need to figure out who this new Millie Anderson is, and how much of this marriage situation I can handle. One quiet step at a time.

Soon we find a field of wildflowers and pitch the tent near a lake. Bump gathers a bundle of clovers. "For my bride," he says with a kiss. The water shifts from the color of smoke to a dark green moss, as the slim banana moon lends little light. I lean back to watch the stars swim in the black ocean above us.

"No rain tonight," I say.

Bump looks up and smiles.

The songs of spring peepers, crickets, and owls give rhythm to the rapid wings of black bats scooping bugs from above. All is peaceful. Balanced. Lovely. *He is not Bill Miller,* I remind myself. *I am safe here.* With the man I love.

Bump spreads a blanket for us in the tent and crawls back out beneath the stars. I've started a small fire, more for light than for heat, and unwrapped the sandwiches Mabel tucked in the truck for us. "Ham or roast beef?" I hold out the choices, hoping he'll choose beef. He does.

"Maybe we should save supper for later," Bump says smoothly, setting his sandwich down and removing his hat.

My body tenses. I unwrap the ham and take a bite. "I'm starving," I say. I don't know how much longer I can stall him. We sit under the stars and eat, but Bump can't keep his hands off me. His excitement is building, and I am running out of excuses to avoid going into the tent.

He hurries to finish his sandwich in three bites. "There. Done!"

I can't help laughing, but I continue to chew slowly. As I finish my own supper, I collect the clovers Bump gave me and begin tying stems together to make a crown. When he reaches for me again, I say, "I'm exhausted."

"Well then, we'd better not waste another minute." Bump lifts the cloth flap of the tent and shifts his eyebrows, an invitation for us to move inside.

I can't match his excitement. I want to, but I'm still stuck, somehow, in the steeple, when Diana's husband locked the door behind him and forced me to the floor beneath those bells. When light bled through red stained-glass windows, and I bled through my torn yellow dress. When Bill Miller pushed himself hard into me, calling out my mother's name, "Marie, Marie, Marie." Afterward, he stood, fastened his pants, and said, "Don't be late for supper." Then he turned the lights out behind him, leaving me there alone under the holy spire.

I sit all night in silence, not knowing how to leave the steeple. How to move past the pain and the shame, but knowing I will not leave this church as the same weak girl who entered. I carve a promise into the steeple-room floor. "Never again." And then I wait, in darkness, until I find the strength to climb down those same steps that took Bill Miller away. I don't leave the church, though. Instead, I step into the quiet sanctuary.

I slip into the baptismal waters, angry and broken. Desperate for a sign that God does exist and that I'll have His help getting through this.

And then it happens. A miracle. The sun rises and the light shines through the stained-glass windows onto the wooden cross. I hear the voice of God, and I know, I know, I am not alone.

I leave the church and meet the band of gypsies. Babushka wraps a red scarf around my head and says I am no longer yellow. "Red now," she tells me. "Krasnaya. *Strong."*

And by the time Mabel helps me sneak my suitcase out of the Miller home, I know what I have to do. I join the rodeo crew to compete in the Texas Stampede. I will survive. I will prove to Bill Miller, and every man like him, that I will never be hurt again.

Bump moves back to where I have rooted myself to the

ground. He begins to unbutton my dress. Right here, under the moon. The fabric falls against my shoulders as Bump kisses me down the center line between my ribs, leans me back into the grass, and rubs his hand gently across my bare stomach.

A trace of Bump's breath mint hits me, and I try to block the Sunday smell. A trigger.

Bump's hands move below my waist and explore me. I am numb. He moves down, kisses my knees. He slides off my shoes, one at a time, kisses my feet, moves his fingers between my toes.

I pull myself up and place the crown of clovers on my head. I hear a voice, my own voice, before it was taken from me. I am a girl in Sweetie's limbs, wearing clovers in my hair to protect me from Jack's wrath and Mama's distance. "I am brave," the young child in me tells herself. "I am strong." I answer, in the silence of my own thoughts, *Yes, yes. I am in control.* I enter the tent with my husband, and I *choose* to give myself to him, praying Bill Miller won't get in the way.

Chapter 5

For more than a week, Bump and I have made our best attempts to harmonize our way through cornstalks and hay fields, prairies and plateaus, right across the broad, flat waistline of America. I am hoarse, but every time I try to sit out a song, Bump encourages me to jump back in. "No fun without you," he says. His voice is still pitch perfect. Now he stops singing. A guilty grin spreads across his face, and he looks like a boy with his hand caught in the cookie jar.

"What?" I ask, trying to figure what he's thinking.

"Well, I know you don't like surprises . . . but . . . I got a good one for you."

The last time Bump surprised me, he announced his plans to leave Mississippi. It was the first time I'd met his family, and he told us the news as a group. "Colorado," he said, and it hit me like a punch. I had no idea he was planning to leave town, and—until that day—I had no idea I'd care if he did.

"So, what is it?" I hold my stomach, which is still turning, and hope it settles soon.

"Guess."

Playfully, I roll my eyes, but then decide I'm game.

"Jewelry?"

"Nope."

"Horses?"

"Negative."

"Books?" My voice reaches a hopeful peak.

"You're ice cold."

"Saddle?"

"Forget it," he says. "I'll just tell you."

"Finally!"

"I invited Oka to come visit us. In Colorado."

My heart jumps. "Oka? No way she'd be able to do that."

"Wrong again, Millie. That's the surprise. She *is* comin'. And not just for a visit. She wants to live with us for a while, to help us get settled. Maybe stay for good."

"You're kidding." I roll my eyes, certain Bump thinks me gullible.

"Not at all," he insists. "I suggested she wait a month or two and then come up by train. Janine said she'd help with the arrangements. She and Mr. Tucker might even come with her."

I can't break the smile from my face. We drive for hours, and all I can think about is Oka. Six months ago, I was an orphan with no family to call my own. Now I've got a husband who loves me and a grandmother too.

I'm just about to ask Bump what he thinks of Janine and Mr. Tucker when he points west. "Welcome to the Rockies, Mrs. Anderson. Home sweet home."

The truck's narrow window wears a coat of thick dirt, making it difficult to see much across the flat, stark horizon. "Pull over?" I request. "I want to remember the first time I see the mountains."

Bump laughs and steers the truck to the side of the road. I open the door and jump out before the wheels can fully stop their spinning. The mountains are barely visible, just cloud-shaped formations rising above the dry, dusty prairie. Nothing majestic or glorious yet, but still, they signal hope. Change. A new life. And suddenly, I think I might be ready.

"Look," I tell him. "Two peaks, standing together. Just like in my dream!"

"Can barely see 'em." He laughs.

I stretch my stiff muscles. "Bump? You really think we can move mountains?"

"No doubt," my husband answers, full of confidence as usual. He walks back to remove tumbleweed that has just blown under the truck and then tosses the tangled ball of vines into the wind.

"Wait!" I run to grab the prickly sphere. "I want to mail it to Camille. She'll never believe me otherwise." Bump laughs again, watching me spin the twisted treasure until it fits in the cab of the truck.

"You're lucky it's a small one," he says. "I've seen 'em much bigger than that!"

In the distance, a thin patch of trees trims the edge of a shallow riverbed. Most are covered in bright, new heart-shaped leaves. A number of seed pods cling to their limbs, but some have already popped open. Those that remain wait stubbornly for the right pitch of wind. With rough, gray trunks, the trees stretch more than twenty feet into the sky.

"From what I hear, most folks chop those," Bump says, following my gaze. "They're cottonwoods. Make good firewood, won't spit, but I don't think they'll grow up by our place."

"Why not?" I ask. We walk out to see the snowy seeds, the river.

"Too high. They like the lower elevations. Flat land with good water."

As a child, I protested Jack's threats to chop Sweetie, a tree that always offered me refuge and friendship. Now I'm in awe of these feathery swells and the way the leaves blow in the wind. They make a sound I imagine is not so unlike ocean waves. I'm glad I can still hear the songs of the trees. "Why cut something so beautiful?"

Bump smiles. "And that, Millie, is why I love you."

"That's why?" I ask. "Because I like trees?"

"That's one reason. Sure."

"What are the other reasons?" I give him a playful grin, fishing for compliments.

"Because you're real, Millie. Like no other girl I've met."

His words are sweet, but they carry weight. Even though Bump's given me no reason to think he wouldn't understand, I'm still too afraid to tell him about Bill Miller. We're worlds away from Diana's husband now, too far for him to hurt me anymore, and still he has this power over me. Every time I think of him, I cower in fear. I wish, more than anything, that Bump already knew the truth. That I didn't have to haul this heavy history. Then maybe he wouldn't have to wonder why I am the way I am. Why I have woken every night, clawing my way out of the horrible dream. Why I'm sometimes distant, when I should be close.

With each mile, the mountains grow taller and my excitement stacks with them. Before we know it, we are pulling into Lewiston, our new town. As Bump promises, it is burrowed into the eastern

Front Range of the Rockies, a quiet valley deep beneath the steep rise of Longs Peak. The roads are rough, mostly dirt with small sections of rock to prevent washout. Glowing red canyons have stretched along the last leg of our route, but now rocky crests top slopes of aspens and evergreens. The land is greener than the parched prairies we've spanned for days, and a large lake sparkles at the bottom of the valley, its rim dotted with families enjoying the day.

A row of wooden buildings stands straight and square against the picturesque backdrop, with false fronts to make the stores look taller and more significant than they really are. Cowboys in boots and spurs are gathered in front of a rustic diner, and a few mothers visit near the post office while their children play tag. An older woman, coughing, comes out of a building marked Doc's Place. It fronts a large pasture filled with horses and stands next to a barbershop, where three men sit on a bench and smoke. One with a pipe. The others, cigars. Next to them, a few customers move in and out of the general store where another sign reads Justice. A faded American flag waves in the wind.

"It's like all the Wild West towns I read about in those Zane Grey books from the library." I look around for dust-coated outlaws at odds with men who wear shiny badges on buttoned vests. This could be a town from a century ago, not 1943.

"Hardly seems real, does it?" Bump parks the truck in front of the store and comes around to open the passenger door for me. I press the wrinkles out of my dress and signal Bump to tuck in his shirt. He adjusts his hat and gives me a confident grin.

The altitude is already having its way with me. Mr. Tucker warned me about altitude sickness, but I never expected the change to affect me this much. At least not here, where still higher peaks pierce the sky above me. I try to extend my shallow breaths and will myself not to be a wimp, as I pat my curls for any unfamiliar clumps. "My frizz feels halfway tamed." I smile. "This low humidity might be good for me."

"You're beautiful, Millie. These mountain men won't know how to handle the likes of you. In fact, come to think of it, it might be best if I leave you in the truck." Bump takes my hand and pretends to pull me back toward our vehicle. I playfully resist until he starts laughing. Then we walk toward the store, entering together, hand in hand. He's not like other men who expect their wives to follow behind. Like a servant. Or a dog.

When we step into the store, Bump nods at an old man behind the counter whose thick, bristly hair looks as if it has never been combed. Two white sideburns frame his face, and he looks like a character from a Hollywood Western. As if he's just playing a part rather than running a general store in the actual wilds of Colorado.

"Help you?" More of a challenge than a question. His guarded look—deep burrows plowed across his face—warns he might not take well to strangers. One corner of his lips pinches a toothpick as he surveys the new couple in his town.

"Kenneth Anderson." Bump introduces himself properly, extending his hand for a steady shake. "And this here's my wife, Millie."

I blush at Bump introducing me as his wife, proud to have this title and grateful for the security it brings, the permanence of our partnership. I will never again be alone. I hold my head a little higher.

The storekeeper stands and offers a hairy hand to Bump, nods his head to me. I smile. He doesn't.

"First day in town," Bump explains.

"What brings you to these parts?" With his teeth still set around the toothpick, I can barely understand what the shopkeeper says. He still hasn't bothered telling us his name.

"Plan to run a ranch. For our boss, Cauy Tucker. A breeding facility. Beef cattle. Stock horses."

"So you're nesters, are you?" The man eyes a customer who has just eaten a nut from the bin.

Bump looks at me as if he isn't sure what the man means. Then he continues. "I guess so. Mr. Tucker bought a place out on Lone Ridge Road. It's been abandoned for a while, from what I understand."

"Old Fortner place?" the shopkeeper asks. I try to read his expression, but his emotions are masked.

Bump scratches his chin before he nods. "Name sounds familiar. That might be the one," Bump says. "Know anything about it?"

"Do, indeed. That's where I got me this beauty." The man points to a stuffed mountain lion mounted behind the counter. I can't believe it's not the first thing I noticed. It's huge, more than a hundred pounds, certainly big enough to take down a calf or a colt. Or me. My stomach twists into knots again.

The lion has been set as if it's about to pounce, with front legs bent, ears perked, and head stooped. Two shiny yellow beads glare out at me, cold and hard in the sockets where eyes should be. I take two steps to the side to avoid the feeling that I might become the animal's next meal.

When I was a young girl, my neighbor Sloth taught me to slay roosters, squirrels, rabbits . . . pretty much anything we could cook and call supper. But it was a solemn act. Sloth always said, "Best take time to thank God *and* your food. Both be keeping you alive today." Unlike this shopkeeper, Sloth never displayed the hide to gain bragging rights, even when he took a sixteen-point buck and all Mr. Sutton's hands came to see. I stare at the lion, and I'm not sure what to make of it. I never considered hunting an animal as a trophy. Never knew anyone who did.

By now, a half-dozen shoppers eye us with curiosity. With the shelves a messy disarray of goods and the walls lined floor to ceiling with everything from furs and traps to fabric and flour, I'm surprised the store can hold all of us.

I offer smiles to the ladies, careful not to look the men in the eye. As I lean into my husband, an excited redheaded kid comes running through the crowd with a lollipop stick poking between his lips. His mother reaches out to grab him. "I'm Katherine Fitch Garner," she says, moving closer to me, her long red hair falling loosely beneath a tan Stetson hat. She might be the most beautiful person I've ever seen: flawless pearly skin, sharp green eyes, and straight white teeth that form a smile so perfect it's hard for me not to stare. Plus, she's nearly as tall as Bump. "This is Henry." Her son pulls the green lollipop from his mouth and holds it out to me.

I smile. "Well, hello there, Henry. I think I'll let you keep that one, but thanks for the offer." He pokes the candy back into his mouth and extends a sticky greeting my way. I shake his hand and laugh, relieved to find kindness after the storekeeper's intimidating greeting.

"Friends call me Kat," Henry's mother adds as she pulls her sugary son back into place. He must be about six years old, with curls that cap his frame like wildfire. The same color as his mother's.

"Millie," I say. "Short for Millicent."

"I heard you mention the old Fortner place. My father's ranch isn't far from there," Kat says. "Mind if we swing by sometime?"

"That'd be great." I try to contain my excitement. I never expected it'd be this easy to make friends here. It's not something that ever came naturally for me.

Others fall behind Kat and introduce themselves to Bump and me. They are polite not to shower us with questions, but they also offer little information. It's different here than at home. In Iti Taloa, folks would have asked about my family, my church, and my husband's line of business. They would have already made their minds up about our status in the community, and we would never be able to cross the line they would have drawn for us. Here, I get the feeling they don't care one bit about where we've come from or where we're going. They are simply welcoming us to town. It's up to us to define the rest.

The grumpy store owner seems to be enjoying the commotion. His smug expression has loosened into a look that could almost be considered a smile. "Let me help you find a few things." He winks at Kat, and the crowd shuffles their attention back to bins of dried beans, horseshoes, and onions. I'm hoping he's not as gruff as he first seemed.

"We'll just grab a few necessities for now," Bump says, filling a sack with flour. I move to scoop oats, accidentally knocking down a sign that reminds shoppers to use ration coupons when purchasing sugar, coffee, and kerosene.

The shopkeeper eyes the sign as I quickly reset it. He then prompts us to buy bullets, new boots, canning jars. "How about some rope?"

"We'll be back once we get a good look at the place," Bump promises. "Got no idea what's in store for us yet."

A big-boned woman cackles from the back corner. Then a silence wraps the room, and the only sound remaining is a caged bird squawking. A chilling warning. Even Kat's son, Henry, stands still. There is something the locals aren't telling us, and Bump seems to sense it too. He looks around at the shoppers. Looks back at the store owner. "Sorry," Bump says, suspicion in his tone. "I never did catch your name."

"Halpin," the man says. "Sheriff Halpin." This surprises me, and I nearly laugh. How can this old man run a store *and* serve as sheriff? Must not be much crime here.

Bump doesn't react the way I do. Instead, he holds eye contact with the sheriff, and the long pause causes a woman next to me to shirk away awkwardly. I tug on Bump's arm, hinting for him to move with me through the store. I've never seen him act like this, and I'm afraid we're getting off on the wrong foot with the sheriff. Finally, Bump clears his throat and looks at me. "Find everything you need?"

We work together, quickly selecting a few more staples before paying for the goods and carting our supplies to the exit. Just as we open the door to leave, a tall, sun-leathered man enters the store alone.

"You've got no business in here," the sheriff tells the new customer, more of a growl than a greeting.

Others shift their attention to the man at the door. One of the younger women whispers something to her friend. Sheriff Halpin rustles his way from the back but stops halfway, as if he doesn't really want a confrontation. The man stands in the entrance, leaving the door wide open. He looks to be about Oka's age, early sixties maybe, with gray eyes and a rugged brown beard that matches a head full of thick brown waves. A worn hat is in his hands.

Around his neck, a collection of animal teeth has been strung with leather, and he wears a pair of buckskin pants. His skin is as pale as Bump's, but he dresses as if he belongs to a native tribe. I count two pistols, each holstered on a hip, with a line of bullets wrapped around his middle. I try not to stare at the bone-handled knife attached to that belt. This strange man has probably been living in the wild for decades, but he offers a warm smile and shakes Bump's hand, ignoring Sheriff Halpin's warnings.

"You the ones here to run the ranch?" It's obvious this fellow has come to meet us. We've been in town a matter of minutes and word has already spread.

Bump introduces us and repeats our plans to operate a breeding facility. "Plan to handle a little veterinary care for the region too." Most people are surprised to learn Bump has completed vet school. It's on account of his poor Delta roots that still shape the way he talks. His thick southern accent makes this man smile.

In return, the stranger speaks with a soft, hollow voice, one of an old man with cloudy eyes and tired lungs, but nothing about him looks tired or weepy. "You're bound to need some help out there."

"Might," Bump agrees.

"Well then, I'm the man for the job." He looks at me with a charmer's grin.

"I'll keep that in mind," Bump answers, apparently not ready to decide if he needs more help than I can offer. I give him a glance to imply that yes, we will definitely need help.

The man catches my look. "I know horses," he says. "And cattle."

"What can you do?" Bump asks.

"I do it all. Roping. Branding. Sorting cattle. Can do some light vet work too, stitch a wound, foal out mares."

Bump listens. "You break colts?"

The man says, "Sure I do." Then he adds, "I also braid reins, ropes. Some metal work too, shoes, bits. Nothing fancy, but they'll do the job."

Bump looks at me as if he doesn't believe all of his claims.

The man continues. "Also know my way around the milking station, and I can handle crops pretty good too. Believe me, weather could wipe you clean in no time if you don't know what you're doing."

Bump and I both smile politely, but Sheriff Halpin pounds heavy steps toward the man. "I'm warning you!" I tug Bump's arm, suggesting we leave too. Bump offers Sheriff Halpin a final farewell, trying to leave on a positive note. "Appreciate your help, sir."

The sheriff doesn't respond. Instead, he keeps his eyes set on the man, who continues to completely ignore him.

I nod back to Kat and her son, Henry.

"We'll swing by in a few weeks," Kat says. "Give you time to get settled."

"Please do," I tell her, hoping she'll keep her word.

When the man follows us out, Sheriff Halpin shouts, "Don't come back!" I'm not sure if he means the strangely dressed man, or all of us.

I climb into the truck, and Bump hands me the two small sacks of supplies we've purchased in hopes of getting off to a decent start with the sheriff. Before Bump can close my door, the man questions Bump again. "Mind if I follow you out and take a look at the place?"

"We ain't even seen it for ourselves yet." Bump laughs, closing the passenger door. The man waits, as if he knows Bump will give in. Sure enough, he does. "I do suppose we'll need help eventually. But I gotta ask, what's all the fuss about? With the sheriff in there?"

"It's personal," the man says. "I'm no danger."

Bump doesn't answer, so the man continues. "I have my own tent, teepee of sorts, so I won't require boarding. Just a spot to pitch."

Bump has moved to his side of the truck where he opens the driver's door. He doesn't yet sit.

The man continues. "I hunt. Fish. You won't have to feed me." Now he waits while Bump assesses the situation.

Finally, my husband extends his hand. "How can I reach you, if it turns out we do need the help?"

"Just send word around town. Ask for Fortner. It'll get to me." The man shakes Bump's hand with confidence.

"Fortner?" Bump asks.

"Right," the man answers. And with that, we leave him standing in front of the general store, his arms crossed, and his eyes planted right on us.

"Well, that was interesting." I adjust in my seat and try to read Bump's thoughts. "What's his story?"

"Got no clue. But I wouldn't be surprised if he shows up tomorrow ready to work."

"Sounds like he's on the sheriff's bad side." Not a place I want to be.

"That's for sure," Bump says.

"And what did he say his name was?"

"Fortner." Bump's brow twists as if he's trying to solve a puzzle. "Like the ol' Fortner place, the ranch we'll be runnin'. Kind of strange, don't you think?"

"I do. But from the way those shoppers reacted when they heard we planned to fix up the place, I'm bettin' we could be in over our heads. Might not be the worst thing to have some help."

"No doubt it'll be a lot of work for us, Millie, but to tell you the truth, I'm lookin' forward to havin' you all to myself for a while. Won't be long before Oka arrives, and I ain't ready to share you quite yet."

I smile and give Bump a kiss. Then another. "Well then, I guess it's official," I say. "We're ranchers now."

Chapter 6

Within minutes, our old Ford truck is bouncing along, running parallel to the stretch of mountains. We turn and follow a rough and narrow road that winds alongside a river. Heavy with snowmelt, the river surges around boulders and rocky crevasses, twisting and bubbling away from the mountains above. There is a power to the mountains, and while the river flows toward lower ground, I am drawn to the peaks. I'm glad the road ahead will take us higher. I lean my head out the passenger window and let my hair blow in the breeze.

We drive more than twenty minutes outside of Lewiston, navigating wicked switchbacks and narrow turns, until, finally, Bump slows the truck and turns onto a dirt driveway.

"Is this it?" I ask as he weaves around deep ruts in the lane.

"Yep. Nearly five thousand acres."

The land spans like a skirt around us, holding a mix of towering evergreens, thin-leaved aspens, and pond-dotted pastures. "All to ourselves?"

"Yep," Bump says again, smiling like a kid with a new toy.

I imagine herds of horses galloping across the skyline,

dipping their soft noses into the ponds and foaling in pastures. I lean up toward the dash to get a better view. "I can't wait to see Firefly's reaction." I miss my horse with a sudden sharpness. "When can we bring them out here?"

"Soon as we ready the pastures," Bump promises. "Shouldn't take more than a couple months." We pass an old, rusty windmill, missing a few blades. The fencerow is badly damaged too. Nothing but barbed wire strung between splintered wooden posts, many of which have been knocked down by snow, wind, or animals.

"Manure seems to have held up just fine," I tease. Dry white piles pepper the landscape. As Bump turns a curve, my excitement plummets. I catch sight of a dilapidated cabin. He parks the truck, and we get out to find our new home is a slanted and wind-battered shell of rough-cut logs. It's been patched together with a mixture of mud and grass and what appears to be horse hair, but most of the chinking has worn away, leaving large gaps along the exterior of the crooked structure.

L shaped, the house holds a sagging porch across the longer side. The shorter stem has a second floor, its exterior made of unpainted milled slats, as if it were an afterthought. Windows line each level, but every glass pane is broken and the wind thrashes across the shards of glass with a high-pitched howl.

Bump and I walk together around the property, carefully surveying the home's exterior. He's the first to speak. "Watch your step." He points to the worn wooden planks as we make our way across the porch. We find one spot where rainwater has dripped over the years. Or maybe snow. Either way, it's rotted clear through. "Gotta replace these boards."

"Fine place to put a barrel," I say, trying to find the good. I struggle to open the warped front door and am met with a cloud of dust. We both fight coughs and sneezes, but soon the particles settle and we step carefully into the house.

"Looks like the Jerries beat us here." Glass crunches beneath Bump's boots as he walks ahead of me through the clutter. "It's a war zone." Rough, uneven planks make up the floor, with gaps as wide as a fist in some parts where piles of dirt seep through. Feed sacks whip from the broken windows in shreds. Newspaper scraps and gunnysacks have been stuffed between logs. Bump opens a wooden cupboard in the kitchen. A mouse runs out. I jump.

"Anything else in there?" I ask.

"Nothin' you'd want to see." He closes the cupboard and continues through the house.

I jiggle the handle of a woodstove and peek inside to find a heap of old white ash. I'm hoping it's hardwood. Then I can boil it down to make soap the way Sloth taught me. "We did come for adventure, right?" I move into the bedroom to find another space without furniture. I was looking forward to a real bed, but I don't dare complain. Bump seems sad enough without my pointing out the obvious.

"One heck of an adventure, all right." I can almost see Bump's spirit sinking as he kicks at a loose pile of dirt. Even though we expected it to need work, turning this house into a home will be a bigger challenge than either of us had bargained for.

"At least the fireplace looks good." I move back to the living area where a large stone hearth centers the room. Between that and the woodstove, we shouldn't have to worry about heat once winter hits.

Bump nods and makes his way up the stairs without saying a word. I follow. We find two small rooms, both with floors that slant at awkward angles. The glass windowpanes are broken, like the ones downstairs, but these rooms are cleaner, and aside from a few birds' nests, the top floor doesn't seem to be nearly as infested with wildlife.

As we walk around the house, we compose a list of tasks to be done: replace the windowpanes, rid the house of rodents and insects, scrub everything inside and out, repair doors and floors. The list grows longer with each step.

"We got no business here, Millie. What was I thinkin'?" I've never seen Bump so full of doubt. "I shoulda given you a choice. I never offered you a way out of this deal, did I?"

I move toward him, but he steps away and paces the floor. I stay still and watch him. The noise of creaking boards and booted steps pounding the wooden planks is nearly more than I can handle. I am reminded of my father, Jack, and the sounds that made me hide in fear every time he returned home to deliver wounds Mama called bangers and stamps. Is this how it starts? Something goes wrong, an unexpected disappointment, and anger begins to swell inside a man? I shudder.

After a long stretch of silence, Bump turns toward me again and says, "Here's your chance, Millie. If you wanna toss in the towel, no one would blame us. We'll go right back to Iti Taloa, and we'll be fine. I promise. Mr. Tucker will understand." He has seemed sure of this plan from the start, never hinting to the tiniest fleck of hesitation. Yet now he sounds as if he's full of fear. Could it be that he is as afraid as I am? His blue eyes hold my own and I begin to soften.

"Well, I have to admit, it *is* nice to be asked." I kiss him, so he knows I'm not bitter. I walk back downstairs and out to the backyard. Bump follows me to the edge of the river, waiting for an answer. We are shaded by slim clumps of wimpy willows that bow to an army of water birch trees, standing proud and wearing their dark bark like armor.

"What do *you* want, Bump?" I lean against a sturdy spruce and breathe in the evergreen smells that remind me of Christmas. I think of all we've left behind in Mississippi. The good, and the bad. "I mean, what do you *really* want?"

"I just want you to be happy." He takes my hand. "Stay here? Or go back to Iti Taloa? I'll do whatever you want, and we won't have no regrets. Either way."

"Promise?" My eyebrows peak.

"Promise." He still sounds deflated.

I take my time to answer. I look out at the weedy pastures and the crumbling house. I let it all sink in. "You really think we can turn a profit in three years?"

"No way of knowin'." Bump looks around doubtfully.

"You think we stand half a chance?"

He's quiet for a moment. Then, slowly, almost if he's trying to fight it, a smile creeps in. "More than half," he says with a hint of optimism again.

I'm encouraged. "And you think we'll be able to bounce back if we don't succeed?"

"No doubt about that." His smile spreads.

"You really think I have what it takes to be a rancher's wife?"

"Not just a rancher's wife," he says. "A rancher."

"Well, how can I not take that dare?" I manage a genuine smile and say, "Let's go for it."

"You sure?" Bump asks.

I nod, remembering Mr. Tucker's words of encouragement. "Ready as we'll ever be."

My husband's smile can no longer be hidden. He almost darts across the grass when he turns his attention back to the list of jobs. "At least the coop is in decent shape."

I follow Bump to the chicken house and open the door to the roosting area. Bad move. The stench is unbearable, and raccoons have claimed the shelter. The mother stands upright, hissing and baring her sharp teeth as her three kits curl behind her. I figure they've only had their eyes open a few days, so I hurry to close the door and leave them be.

"It won't take much to get a flock started in there," I say, grateful Sloth taught me how to manage a coop before he died. "Can probably find some hens in town that are already laying."

"I reckon so."

"The pasture has potential." I move back toward the fence. "And the barn is still standing." I ignore the bleached-white bones of cattle scattered across the land.

"Attagirl." Bump winks.

"It really is beautiful here," I say. The wide, shallow river curves behind the house, and I've already spotted at least two fresh springs bubbling across the property. "We shouldn't have to worry about a water source."

"Bound to be full of trout." Bump dips his hand into the clear river water, then tosses a rock to make a splash. He looks up at the mountains stretching above us and adds, "There'll be plenty of game to hunt too. Elk. Mule deer. No tellin' what else."

Thick blackberry bushes climb a long stretch of fence, and signs of a large garden remain on the side of the house beside what appears to be a creamery. "Woodshed seems sturdy enough, and I'm betting we can save this outhouse too," Bump adds.

"Outhouse . . . ," I mumble. I'm just realizing there are no luxuries here. In my head, I tick off all the other things we'll be doing without: running water, electricity, telephones . . .

There's no use complaining. I direct my attention instead to another outbuilding that looks to have been used as a smokehouse. There's a fair-sized root cellar as well. It's got dirt floors but seems to be a sturdy log structure dug into the ground. Certainly a good place to store preserves, root vegetables. Another useful skill I learned from Sloth.

"At least the weather's nice," I say. The wind is blowing straight and strong. The sun dots the cloudless sky with a brilliant blur. And a peregrine falcon paints the blank blue canvas, his yellow claws tucked tight against his speckled tail feathers. Bump curls his hands around my waist and pulls me against his chest. Then he points to a back corner of the right pasture where black charred trunks stand naked in the sun.

"Fire?" I ask.

"Looks that way," Bump says. Then he adds, "But that wasn't what I was showin' you. Look closer. Underneath."

At the base of the leafless trunks, at least five acres continue to burn bright yellow with wildflower blooms. Their color a stark contrast to the ashen remains. I'm brought back to the blooms of my childhood, the ones that always delivered hope. It's as if God has sent a message, just for me. A reminder that life can renew itself.

The sun stands proud above us, and sky stretches blue into forever, and I am wrapped in my husband's arms. Here, in this moment, I am completely at peace.

"We can do this, Bump."

"We can?" He still sounds doubtful.

If ever Bump needed me to be strong, to be sure, it is now. I look him in the eye and make another promise. "We will."

I hammer stakes into the ground, helping Bump make camp in the yard. "I sure hoped to have more to offer you than this," he says, looking at the tent as if it's a disgrace.

"Bump, stop it. Look at this place." I point to the river rushing beside our tent, the majestic mountains rising up behind it, the open-aired pasture where our horses will foal, and the lush green valley deep below in the distance. "Who could possibly ask for more?" I gather wood and clear a firepit, forming a ring of stones around the ground I've scraped bare. Bump strings a hook and begins fishing for supper. There isn't anyone around for miles, and no matter how far I look in any direction, I can't spot a single car, or home, or steeple, or shop. It's just Bump and me.

"First thing tomorrow, I'll start on the house." Bump pulls an empty line from the water and casts again.

"*We'll* start on the house," I correct him.

"Should be able to make a good bit of furniture with the scrap wood in the barn," he promises. "Tables, shelves. Most of what we need. But we'll have to order a mattress."

"Told you we should have brought that cot," I tease. I stack a triangle of small twigs, strike a match, and light the fire.

"You deserve better," Bump says. "Sheriff Halpin gave me a Sears and Roebuck for any big items we need delivered from Denver. I'll drop an order in the nearest mailbox tomorrow. Think I spotted one about ten miles down the road. Why don't you take a look at the form, see if there's anything else you want to purchase."

"Can't think of a thing," I say. "We've got all those wedding gifts in the truck. Dishes, pots and pans. Some linens and utensils. You packed every kind of tool we could possibly need. Oka stocked us with seeds, and Diana gave me a set of stationery. Mabel has us all set with preserves. Let's stick with a mattress for now. That sounds like a good place to start."

"Got one!" Bump yells, pulling a trout to the surface. "Grab that stringer, will ya?"

I manage the fish while Bump baits his hook for another catch. "One more, and we'll be set."

After supper, I pat my bedroll and call Bump closer. "You take good care of me, you know that?" He smiles and pulls me onto him. I unbutton his shirt, tug at the sleeves, gently undressing him. He falls back, beneath the stars, and I kiss his neck, his chest, trying again to distance myself from that steeple. He wraps his arms around me and starts to turn me under him. I resist. Maybe someday I'll be able to rest in my husband's arms without feeling Bill Miller force me down against the wooden floor. But for now, I keep my back to the moon and my spirit guarded.

Chapter 7

We have been living at the Fortner place for less than a month, and we've already managed to get the house in fairly decent shape. As promised, Bump built some tables and shelves from the wood in the barn. We salvaged some chairs from the clutter, but we did splurge on ordering a brand-new bed. Mattress too. It was delivered yesterday from Denver. After sleeping on a cot in the rodeo foaling room for more than a month, followed by nearly three weeks of tent camping and then a pallet on the living room floor, our new bed is a blessing. So soft, and clean, and comfortable. I don't want to climb out of it.

I am awakened by Bump's kiss, as I have been each morning since the wedding. He's already dressed and ready to work. "How do you do it?" I mumble, closing my eyes and rolling into my soft pillow. "I always thought I was a hard worker. Then I met you."

He laughs and says, "Sleep as long as you want."

I pull the pillow over my face and try to will myself out of bed. Like me, Bump's a doer. We've both worked ourselves to the bone and already the windows have been repaired and the doorknobs all function as they should. The house is clean from top to bottom, and except for a few spiders, nearly all the critters who made our house their home have realized they're being booted out, including the coons in the chicken coop and a colony of bats in the barn who had no desire to leave and caused quite a fuss. Now Bump rattles dishes in the kitchen, and I can't ignore the day any longer. The smell of fresh coffee moves into the bedroom and guilts me out of bed. I don't know if it's the thin air or the endless work, but I am tired beyond belief.

"It's not like me to feel this way. I can't keep up with you." I smile, shuffling into the kitchen with lazy feet. "What's your plan today?" I'm certain he has a long list of tasks to accomplish before we even break for lunch.

"Prep the cistern and the water pump. Hope to run pipes into this house before winter. But first I gotta clear that back corner where the fence has gone missin'." He grabs a day-old biscuit from the bread bin and heads outside, taking his coffee with him.

"I admit, I look forward to tearing down that outhouse," I say behind him. "Think we could tackle the water pipes first?"

Bump laughs again but doesn't stop walking. "It's on my list," he yells back. "I promise."

Before moving outside, I clean the kitchen, make the bed, and find the book I was reading as the sun slipped away, *Tender is the Night*. I open to chapter four for one last taste: *"You're the only girl I've seen for a long time that actually did look like something blooming."*

I can't help myself. I think of River. If he were here, we'd likely spend the entire day in this new bed. He'd play his harmonica and quote Fitzgerald. We'd read aloud—poetry, classics, the Bible, it wouldn't matter. The words would warm our blood, and we'd tumble back together between verses, and the sun would leave without us ever greeting the day.

Bump walks by the window, carrying a roll of barbed wire. He's already worked up a sweat. I mark my page and save the book for later.

By ten, the sun is hot and I am covered in dirt, a pile of weeds to my right and a hoe in my hand. I look up to see Katherine Fitch Garner riding a copper sorrel—her son, Henry, managing his own chestnut a few steps behind. I squint to get a better look and wave hello. They ride closer before halting the horses. "Hi there," I say. "It's Kat, right? And Henry?"

"That's right. Hope we haven't caught you at a bad time." Kat reaches for her son's reins.

"No, not at all." I remove my work gloves and dust my hands on my jeans. While tying my hair back in a knot, I offer them a drink of water from the well pump.

Kat holds up a canteen and declines the offer. "Think I can tear you away from your Victory Garden long enough for a ride?"

My heart sinks. I can't begin to explain to her how much I want to join them on the trails, but our horses are still in Mississippi and we haven't purchased any new stock. "No horses yet."

Kat's lips spread into a bright smile. "Why do you think Henry rode this one over here?"

She couldn't have said anything better. I throw the hoe in the yard and try to keep myself from running, startling the horses. I help Henry move from his saddle to his mom's. Then I lead my mount to the river. Kat and Henry follow.

"Had any time to get to know the area yet?" Kat asks.

"Not even a second," I admit. "The work never ends."

"Looks like you've already accomplished a lot." Kat glances around the ranch and seems impressed.

I give them a quick tour by pointing. "We've got the coop finished, and the milking stand too. Now we just need some chickens and a milker."

"How in the world are you making do without them?" Kat asks.

"You can go a long way on powdered milk and dried eggs. I stocked up."

Kat wrinkles her nose.

"They're not so bad." I laugh, although I wonder if our poor diet might be contributing to my stomach troubles. "The fuel rations limit our trips into town. Without our horses here yet, we're kind of stuck." I search the distance for Bump as I lengthen the stirrups. The horses drink from the river, sipping around their bits.

"I'm so sick of this war," Kat sighs. "Too many rations and rules. Plus, all those posters in town pressuring every man to enlist. Uncle Sam expecting the women left behind to buckle up in overalls and buy a wrench. And now they've got me questioning every foreign face I see. POW camps and internment centers. It's as if we can't trust anybody anymore. I'm patriotic, Millie, I am. But I'm ready for everything to get back to normal."

"I'm sure it'll end soon." I test the stirrups and then pull myself into the saddle. Without a newspaper or radio here on the ranch, the war seems very far away to me.

"Let's hope," Kat says.

"I just need to tell Bump we're leaving. I don't want him to worry." I press my heels softly into the horse's side and pull the reins to the left, leading the chestnut in front of Kat's sorrel.

We keep our mounts at a slow pace, navigating the property

in hopes of tracking Bump. I call out his name and confirm he's not in any of the outbuildings. The truck is parked in the back corner of the pasture where he's gone to repair the fence. Even squinting, I can't see him. I'm just about to call out again when Henry yells, "There he is!"

Beneath the truck, Bump is lying on the grass. Two bony blue-jean knees jut up between blooms of wild scarlet paintbrush and orange sneezeweed. "How on earth did you see him there, Henry?" I ask. "Maybe I should change your name to Eagle Eye."

Henry giggles. Bump hears us and slides himself out from under the truck's carriage. His hat has fallen off, revealing a disheveled head of hair. A smudge of grease marks his chin, and his loose white shirt is stained with dirt. He greets us holding a wrench in one hand, a bolt in the other, as sweat makes him shine in the sun. How proud I am to call him mine. I'm not the only one to notice how handsome he looks. Kat holds her stare a second too long.

"Truck finally quit on me," Bump says.

"Good thing you know how to fix it." I smile. "Bump, you remember Kat and Henry."

Bump nods as they both say hello.

"I figured it wouldn't take you long to hit the trails." He gives my mount a few strong strokes and checks the straps, tightens the latigo.

Kat peaks her eyebrows, perhaps worried Bump won't like our leaving without him. I smile to let her know there's nothing to worry about.

"Sure you can handle it?" Bump asks. "Different from the trails you're used to."

"Are you worried?" I ask, surprised.

"A little. But you are a trick rider, I suppose." He turns to Kat. "I've seen Millie do things on a horse most people can't do on the ground."

I blush. "I'll be careful. You're the one who taught me to do this, after all."

"Just remember, this ain't Firefly." He rubs my leg through my jeans. I lean down to offer a kiss. Henry covers his eyes and Kat laughs. Then I follow Kat's horse to the trailhead by the river, the spot where we'll begin our climb.

"Watch out for lions!" Bump yells. He's teasing, but the memory of Sheriff Halpin's stuffed mountain lion keeps my eyes open as we head for the woods.

"I can't adjust to how dry it is," I admit to Kat. "Thank goodness you packed me a canteen." Barely gone a mile, and I've already downed half of my water.

"You'll never get used to it," Kat says. "I'm always thirsty, and I've lived here all my life."

"Never lived anywhere else?" I ask. The air smells sweet, like vanilla.

Kat pulls her horse to a stop, and Henry leans in to snap a piece of sap that has oozed and hardened through the bark of a giant pine. Then he pops the amber sap into his mouth and starts to chew.

"What's that?" I ask.

"It's a pitch tube," Kat says. "Henry likes the sweetness in it. We've got a bad beetle outbreak. Killing all the pines. When you see the sap oozing through like this, the tree has beetles."

I move my horse closer and break a sticky bulge of sap from the tree. I smell it, then the tree.

Kat laughs, so I explain. "Trying to figure out what smells like sugar cookies." Every smell seems so intense.

This makes Henry laugh. "Cookies?" Kat rubs his back and smiles.

"Everything is so different here."

"How?" Kat asks, smiling down at Henry.

I look at the dry southward-facing slope and try to describe Mississippi to a six-year-old. "Well," I say, "the trees, for starters. See how they grow far apart? Not much covering the ground between them."

Henry nods and looks at the trees as if he's seeing them for the first time, the bland gray tones of the young trees contrasting with the cinnamon bark of the older, more stately pines.

"In Mississippi, the trees stand close together, and there's hardly room to run through them." I smile, remembering the little girl who ran barefoot through the forests, slipping and sliding into deep ravines, chasing squirrels and gypsies and thunder.

"And the bugs," I continue. "Mosquitoes big as butterflies, and fire ants that sting the living daylights out of you. Not to mention snakes. Lots of snakes. Cottonmouths and copperheads. Mean ones."

Henry's eyes are as wide as silver dollars. Kat laughs. "Can't be that bad."

"Oh, but it is." Then I sigh. "And I miss it like crazy." I look around at the scrub brush and the big, gray boulders that project out from the mountain's side. "You know what these are, don't you, Henry?" I point to the boulders that line the trail. "These are warts on the giant's toes. If we don't hurry, he'll raise his foot and stomp us to bits!"

With that I squeeze my heels into my horse's side and lead the charge up the mountain, keeping a steady pace up the rocky incline. Kat and Henry stay behind, laughing and yelling for me to wait. But I'm having fun for the first time in a long time, and I don't slow down until the route ends at an overlook about two-thirds of the way up the mountain. I climb down from the saddle and drain the last of my water, noticing a ring of rocks that marks the trail. A smaller circle of stones forms its center.

"That was incredible," I say when Kat and Henry finally reach me.

"You scared me, Millie." Kat knocks back her long red hair. "You can't be too careful here. So many things could happen." She speaks with short, heated breaths. "Loose rocks. Cliffs. Plus the lions. You won't see them, but believe me, they see you."

I'm surprised she's so upset. "Do we really have lions?"

"Mountain lions." Kat nods. Henry tightens his grip on his mom and wrinkles his face with worry. "It's not just that. Anything could have spooked the horse and thrown you. Or us." Kat brushes her hand through her son's red hair with much more tenderness than she's dealt her own.

I move to the lookout and let Kat calm down. Soon she and Henry dismount and join me at the edge. The trees have become shorter as we climbed to higher elevations. We're surrounded now by spruce and fir, with a few mangled pines struggling to survive the harsher winds. Kat points to the peaks in the distance and gives each a name. "There's Estes Cone. Longs Peak. Mount Meeker." The softness returns to her voice, and I wonder if these might be the landmarks I spotted when we first stopped to see the mountains. They sure look more impressive from here. "Folks call Longs and Meeker the twin peaks," Kat explains, reminding me of my dream. "And if you look closely, you can see the profile of a beaver climbing the south side of Longs. See?"

I trace the outline of the beaver's tail and follow the shape up to the tip of his nose. She's right. The mountain really does look like a beaver. In the distance, a thick smoke rises.

"Fire," Kat says, following my gaze to the purple plume.

"Wildfire?" I take a closer look, remembering the spread of burned acreage on our own property. I worry we may lose the ranch to the fiery blaze.

"It's farther away than it seems," Kat says. Then she adds, "I'm sorry I snapped at you, Millie. I wish I could still be carefree. Like you. Wait until you become a mother. You'll see." She steps behind Henry as he tries to climb a boulder. "It's not easy. Especially by myself."

"I can't imagine." I track the large ring of rocks and wonder what happened to Henry's father. It seems rude to ask, so I focus on the stone circle and wait for Kat to continue. A few columbines work their way through the ring, a stunning mix of delicate purple and white petals climbing against the jagged rocks.

"It's a prayer circle," Kat says, following my steps. "Old Indian site. Some kind of sacred spot."

I look out at the magnificent view. "Perfect place for that."

Kat shrugs, and Henry slides down the boulder. We stay awhile and watch the smoke curling into thick, gray clouds. The columns rise, swirl, and spread across the horizon, bowing to the higher mountains that are still crowned with snow. Occasionally, a bird streaks across the blue, but otherwise, the scene is still, except for the smoke. Nothing but wilderness, as far as the eye can see.

One thing is for sure. I'm far, far away from Mississippi. From all the pain I wanted to leave behind. I stare out into the great beyond and offer a silent prayer. I thank God for this beautiful place. For Bump. For my new life. My new friend. For the mountains.

The three of us ride back down the trail at a slow, measured pace. I follow Kat's lead, and my horse thanks me by swishing her tail and relaxing her neck. The slow return is made sweeter by the songs of thrushes and warblers.

"I'm glad I met you, Millie," Kat says. "There aren't many women in this town who care much about getting to know me. And the men . . . well . . . most are off at war. All that's left are old, worn-out ranchers and the lucky few who were excused. I guess what I'm trying to say is, it's just nice to have a new friend."

I smile and don't admit how happy I am to have a friend too. I'm guessing the other women are jealous of Kat, and I hope my insecurities never get in the way of our friendship.

"Have you found the chokecherries yet?" Kat asks.

"Never heard of such."

"Follow me. Only a few places to find them this high." We steer the horses toward the river where Henry pulls a handful of small pink berries from the tree. "Don't eat them," Kat warns. Then she turns to me and explains, "They aren't ready until they turn dark. Then, if you spread some across a hot biscuit or bake them in a cobbler, they're divine."

The bubbling river tempts Henry, and before Kat can protest, he bounces into the shallow water. He wastes no time at all, climbing over rocks and dipping his head beneath the surface, until he loses his hat in the current. Then he pounds the water, sending a hard splash. "The bad man's gonna get it," Henry shouts.

"I haven't seen any bad guys," I tease.

Kat eyes Henry, and he ducks under water. "He's talking about that guy in the store."

"Fortner?" I ask.

Kat nods. "Just keep your distance, and you'll be fine." With that, she turns to ready her horse. "I better get Henry home. He'll be a beast if his stomach growls more than twice."

I get the hint and don't bring up Fortner again, but all the way home I think of this "bad man," the one who seems so eager to help us work the ranch.

Chapter 8

"Don't forget, Kat has invited us to supper tonight," I remind Bump over breakfast.

"Aw, boy. I did forget," he says. "What time, again?"

"Six." I laugh. I've told him many times since Kat invited us Monday.

"Can't we push it back a bit? I need every minute of daylight I can get."

"No, we can't push it back a bit." I break my smile to take a sip of coffee. "She's the only friend I've got in this place."

Bump shovels in another bite of oatmeal. "Well, in that case, I better get to work." He kisses me one more time. Then he steps into his boots and heads out for the day.

It doesn't take me long to wash and put away two bowls, two spoons, and two mugs. I cover the pot of oatmeal for tomorrow's breakfast and begin to list items needed from Sheriff Halpin's store. Then I pull on my boots and join Bump in the barn.

I spend most of the day knocking down wasp nests, creating a burn pile with old debris, and holding boards so Bump can nail them in place. We work together as a team, efficiently and effectively as we have each day. Today we fill the hours sawing, nailing, clearing, and scrubbing. We develop such a natural rhythm, we work straight through lunch. It's nearly four before I realize the time.

"I've still got to bake something for tonight," I announce, half panicked.

Bump doesn't blink. "Just bring cheese."

"Cheese?" I laugh and walk back to the house, hoping I can make something decent with the few provisions left in the kitchen. I decide to make biscuits and bring a jar of Oka's fig preserves, a wedding gift we haven't yet opened.

I turn a pie plate upside down inside a large black iron pot to make an oven, the way Sloth taught me. Then I load two new cuts of wood and light a fire inside the stove, careful to sweep up any ashes that escape. Blue smoke trails out the window as I roll dough on the table, my fingers coated in flour to prevent sticking. I cut round circles of dough with a glass, coat a second pie pan with butter, and place the raw biscuits around the pan before sealing the homemade oven with the pot lid and placing it on the warm burner. Sloth would be proud.

By 5:15, the biscuits are done. I ring the dinner bell, scattering bluebirds and chickadees from surrounding limbs.

By 5:30, I ring it again to call Bump.

By 5:45, I am hurrying to the barn, worried.

I find Bump covered in sweat, chopping down a lodgepole pine. "Beetles," he says. "It's sapwood, but still. Won't have no shortage of wood for winter, thanks to them."

"Bump. It's already a quarter till." I am not normally a complainer, but I really don't want to be late.

"Almost done." He swings the ax.

"Can't you finish this tomorrow?"

"Just gimme a minute." Another swing.

I return to the house and move the biscuits to a basket, covering them with a clean cloth with hopes they'll stay warm. I hang my cotton apron on the hook and freshen up before slipping into my nicest suit, one of the boutique outfits Diana bought me. Now the tailored fabric pulls tight around my waist. I make a mental note to eat less tonight, even though we've skipped lunch and I'm starving.

It's no wonder I've gained weight, despite our full days of sweat and labor. What started out as a nervous nausea has turned into a consistent unsettling. At first I blamed the altitude, even thought I had caught a stomach virus or eaten bad meat. But Bump says I've probably worked up an ulcer. While I'm not as sick as I was, I still spend many days moving back and forth between hunger and queasiness, never quite sure if my body would be soothed by eating or avoiding food.

By six, we are supposed to be arriving at Kat's ranch, but I'm still waiting in the kitchen for Bump to join me. I wish I could call Kat. No phone line. I'm so eager to go, I consider writing a note to tell Bump I've left without him.

I head to the porch to ring the dinner bell one last time when Bump hollers from the yard, "I'm comin'!" He runs through the front door smelling of hard work.

"You look nice," he says, walking past me to find what's left of the warm water in the reservoir of the stove. He removes his shirt and hurries to wash himself right here in the kitchen. "Grab my razor?"

I bring him his shaving kit and watch him lather up, without as much as a mirror to guide the process. It's a rough result, patchy at best.

The clock ticks. 6:20.

Bump lifts the cloth from the basket of biscuits and takes one, draws a big bite. I have taken time to arrange them perfectly in the basket, purposely placing the biggest, fluffiest one on top. It's now a crumbled mess in his mouth. I take the basket and the preserves and walk toward the door. "I'll be waiting in the truck." I let the door close hard behind me.

Kat's ranch is near ours, but it takes us ten minutes to drive there. We arrive after seven. Others might have another hour of daylight, but the sun bids farewell early here, diving down behind the mountains' silver spine like a child being tucked between deep pillows. Diana always warned me never to arrive late to a dinner party, and my stomach remembers this lesson with a spin. I am silent during the ride, and the darkening sky brings my mood even lower.

"You mad?" Bump asks.

I say nothing, figure it's obvious. It's not like me to be so bothered, but lately, every little thing seems to upset me. I've never been angry with Bump for anything, and I don't like feeling this way. I avoid looking his direction as Bump turns the truck onto a long lane and drives us through a grand entrance. Two stone columns base a high-arching wooden sign that welcomes us to F&F Ranch. The lane brings us between pastures, some with horses, others with cattle, until we reach a modest wooden home with a few vehicles parked in the drive. I'm a bundle of nerves, and I fear another attack of nausea. I don't really understand why the worry still gets to me most days. Life is better now, much better. I only hope the ulcer heals soon.

Bump opens my door for me and takes the jar of preserves.

"Is it too simple? I didn't know what else to make."

"They're delicious, Millie." He smiles. "You should be proud of what you can do with a woodstove and a sack of flour." Bump closes my door and extends his arm. Nervously, we make our way to the house.

I knock. Kat opens the door. Within an instant, I feel underdressed and ashamed of my homely basket of biscuits. Kat looks like a movie star, a redheaded Veronica Lake. She wears a long silver dress that flows loosely around her perfect curves. I think of Aphrodite, the goddess of love, beauty, and pleasure. A delicate loop of emeralds wraps Kat's wrist. Not the plastic cocktail jewelry most of Diana's friends flaunted at parties, but real stones. Just enough to show she's got money. "I'm so glad you made it." She welcomes us inside with a smile while I apologize for being late.

I was wrong about the house. The moderate-sized home that didn't seem imposing from outside opens into an expansive space once you get past the front door. What I believed to be a one-story abode is brilliantly stuffed into the mountainside, with the lower two levels exposed behind the slope. I want to whisper to Bump, "This puts Diana's house to shame," but I keep my thoughts to myself.

"Everyone's out by the pool," Kat says.

As we follow her through the majestic home, I mouth to Bump, "Everyone?" He holds his hat in his hands. His spurs clatter with each step, and I bet he's wishing he would have removed them before the party. I smile to help him feel at ease.

"Should I put these in the kitchen?" I ask Kat, hoping she'll let me ditch the biscuits and jam before we reach the other guests.

"Oh, yes," she says, lifting the linen as she takes the basket and adds, "Millie, you shouldn't have."

I bet she means it, because I, too, am wishing I hadn't bothered with the biscuits. In fact, I'm wishing I had followed Bump's lead, worked until sunset, and settled into a nice, comfy supper at home, just the two of us.

"How do you get electricity out here?" I ask Kat. Her kitchen is filled with all the modern appliances. There's no way she's running to an outhouse each morning. Indoor plumbing, lights powered by switches instead of oil. She's got it all.

"Daddy had this done before Mother died," Kat explains. "Took three years to get the lines out this way. Brought in a guy from Santa Fe to figure out the plumbing. Ended up renovating the entire house. Nearly had to start from scratch. Until then, our place wasn't much different from yours."

I can't imagine their house was ever anything like ours, but I do appreciate Kat's attempt to make us feel more comfortable. "I'm sorry about your mother." I don't tell her about Mama, or how she chose morphine instead of me.

"Thanks, Millie. We've had a few rough years, Daddy and me."

She still doesn't mention her husband. I figure Kat's about six or seven years older than I am, maybe in her midtwenties, closer in years to Bump than me. I've always felt older than people my age, and Mama used to say I had an "old soul," but here, in this house, I feel like a child. It's the way Kat struts in those heels, never losing her balance or missing a step. The way she smiles as she talks, drawing everyone's attention as if nothing more important could exist in the world. The way she flips her red hair with her wrist, letting her jewels dangle delicately down her arm. She may have seemed hesitant, even weak when we were on horseback, but here, in her home, she is ten times the woman I will ever be.

Bump seems to have noticed too as he holds the door open for her and watches her move. I find myself wondering if maybe I really am too young to be married, as Diana warned. Maybe Bump would be better off with a woman who is sure of her own worth. Someone like Kat.

"Daddy," Kat says, pulling my hand to lead us to the crowd. "Meet Millie and Kenneth Anderson."

"Sorry we're late, sir." Bump extends his hand. "Started a project and the time got away from me."

"Now, that I can admire," Mr. Fitch says, shaking Bump's hand and kissing me on the cheek before calling the others to meet his guests of honor.

One by one, Kat introduces us to the important people in her life, and it's not lost on me that they are all men. No husband. First, the youngest of the group. A balding, clean-shaven minister, Reverend Baker, who hopes to have a church built soon so he can stop holding Sunday service in the diner.

"And this is Dr. Henley," Kat says.

A slim man pushes his glasses up on his nose. "Call me Doc." He has a handlebar mustache, gray and perfectly balanced.

Next, the gruff store owner, Sheriff Halpin, whom Kat claims is her uncle on her mother's side. I see no resemblance. "I've met this little lady once before," the sheriff says.

Little lady? I try not to roll my eyes.

Bump jumps to my defense. "Don't underestimate her, Sheriff. Millie here can outride any man in this county. Outsmart 'em too."

"That so?" The doctor raises his eyebrows. "You a horse gal?"

I nod.

"I've got a set of mustangs back home," Doc says. "Nobody can do a blasted thing with them."

"Bump can," I say. "I've never seen a horse he couldn't break."

"That right?" Doc looks doubtful.

The sheriff jumps back in, eager to prove me wrong. "Those southern horses are easy to break. Up here, the horses have been living wild in the high country, bred to fight wolves. They'll just as soon buck you to high heaven. And take a bite out of you on your way down."

"Well then. Looks like we'll be having us some fun." Doc grins. "Welcome to Lewiston, Mr. and Mrs. Anderson." He raises a glass in our honor.

The laughter stops when Henry interrupts the crowd, yelling, "Mama, Mama. Look what I found!"

"What is it, Henry?" Kat is patient as ever with her son.

Henry hasn't yet learned to say his *r* sounds, so everyone smiles when he yells, "It's a bird! A baby bird!" He brings a tiny sparrow to Kat and sets it on the ground. "It's hurt, Mama. It's got a broke wing." Each *r* replaced with a *w*.

I look at Bump and figure he'll know what to do. "Bump's an animal doctor," I explain to Henry.

"You fix birds?" the boy asks, his red curls a mess of tangles on his head.

"Some," Bump answers. "Let's have a look."

The baby sparrow doesn't react in fear to Bump's touch. Instead, it cricks its neck quickly to look up at us, then releases a squeak.

"Looks like you've been very gentle with this little fellow," Bump says. "You'd make a good veterinarian."

"What's a vege . . . ti . . . narian?" Henry asks. Everyone smiles.

"A doctor who helps animals," Bump explains. "Like me."

"You feed them *vegetables*?" Henry senses the humor and grins too, exposing two deep dimples and some missing front teeth.

Gently prompting the bird with his thumb, Bump says, "Let's see what we can do." The bird hops around, letting one wing drop lower than the other, chirping its simple squeak. "Oh, see now, you've already cured her."

Kat crosses her arms proudly, and Henry stares as if he doesn't believe a word Bump says.

"You found her on the ground?" Bump asks.

Henry nods.

"See how she holds one wing lower than the other?"

"It's broke," Henry insists.

"No, sir," says Bump. "It's just weaker than the other one. She's learnin' to walk, and fly, and eat, and it'll just take her a little more time to figure it all out. She's called a fledgling."

Henry plays with the word in his mouth and then asks, "What can I feed her?"

"Well, that's somethin' she needs to learn to do on her own," Bump explains. "What we need to do now is get her back to the exact same spot where you found her. Then her mother can take over."

Bump scoops the bird from the ground and leads Henry on a mission to save the sparrow.

Kat watches them move into the woods. Then she sighs and tells me, "Got you a good man there, Millie."

I nod. I know I do.

Chapter 9

"Dinner was delicious," I tell Kat.

"Just steaks." Kat smiles. "Couldn't mess that up if I tried."

"Best meal I've had in weeks," Bump adds, then realizes his compliment is a direct insult to me. He's right, though. Powdered eggs just don't compare.

Kat thanks Bump and slices a homemade pie. "It's cherry. From last year's preserves," she says. "But fresh ones are coming soon." She stops Henry from licking his fingers. "I always make a trip to the Western Slope to stock up. Grant used to call me crazy, but I swear the harvest is better across the Divide. I take the train there each summer and sell preserves in my uncle's store year-round."

"Grant?" I seize the chance to ask the question that's been on my mind all night.

Kat looks surprised. "Don't you know?"

Bump and I exchange confused looks.

"Grant's my husband," Kat explains. "He's been overseas for more than a year. Navy. I thought I told you."

"Oh, Kat, I'm sorry," I say. "I had no idea."

She smiles. "Nothing to worry about." But she's obviously worried.

"Long time," Bump says.

"It sure is. I just hope he makes it home before Henry here leaves the nest." As Kat talks, the room stands still. The men are all at her mercy, clinging to her every word. Doc Henley leans in, over the table, to decrease space between them. Her father beams around her, obviously proud of his only child. Even her uncle, the grim storekeeper who turns animals into trophies, seems tamed by Kat's charm. There's a power about her, and I'm beginning to think the women here are smart to keep her at a distance. But Kat's the only friend I have, so I brush all insecurities aside.

"So tell me, Mrs. Garner." Bump focuses his attention on Kat. "What do we need to know about Lewiston?"

"Oh, goodness, Kenneth. Not much to tell about this old place. And please, call me Kat." She tells Henry to use his fork, but all I can think is how she made Bump's name sound when she said the word *Kenneth*. Bump must have liked it too, because he doesn't bother telling her to call him Bump.

I smile at Henry, whose cheeks are now streaked with cherry pie, and he says, "See, Mama. Mrs. Anderson don't care. She's nice."

Bump laughs and asks the group, "Y'all know anything about the Fortner place?"

Doc begins to fill us in. "Started as a homestead. Way back."

"That's right," Mr. Fitch chimes in. "Only 160 acres. Not much land for these parts." He interrupts the story for a bite of pie.

"But we've got five thousand acres there now." I am puzzled.

Doc takes the lead, pushing his glasses up again with fork in hand. "The Fortners lucked into prime land with all those springs along the river. Not like most homesteaders who got hoaxed into scrap. They had sense enough to make good of it too. Dug those ponds. Put in some sophisticated water systems for their day."

"Resourceful family," Mr. Fitch adds. "They'd find the most interesting ways to cash in. Carted timber down to Denver. Sold it to the mining companies. Then they'd pick up a load of coal from the city and deliver it to folks all around here."

"He'd sell mushrooms too. Hogs, milk. Honey. Pretty much anything you wanted. He'd find a way to get it to you for a price." Sheriff Halpin takes a turn.

"So they built that place up from a homestead plot?" Bump seems as impressed as I am, and I bet it's giving him hope for his own parents back in the Delta.

"Sure did." Mr. Fitch picks up where the sheriff left off. "But then we got hit with a few years of drought. Just when they had built up their stock and had everything riding on a good sale."

"It didn't help that the old man got influenza. He barely survived it. Wasn't able to manage the ranch like before. He bottomed out," Doc says. "But in the end, it was the drought that did them in."

Bump and I both give looks of disbelief. "When was that?" Bump asks.

Mr. Fitch gives Doc a look and says, "Maybe around 1889, if I remember right."

"Probably," Doc says. "Had a few bad years in a row. I was still a little thing. Always looked forward to seeing Mr. Fortner coming with his wagon or sleigh. Usually meant we'd get something good." This comment makes the sheriff grumble.

"They just left?" I ask as Henry steals a bite of pie from his grandfather's plate. No one else notices. I give him a knowing wink, and he laughs.

"Way I remember it, they tried to get help. Just to get them through the low points, but nobody had anything to lend those years," Mr. Fitch explains. "We were all in trouble."

"From what I've heard, the bankers got greedy," Reverend Baker pipes in. "Pinched everybody too hard." He's likely the only one of these men who is too young to know for sure.

"You can say that again. Fortners had no choice but to turn the place back over to the bank." Kat's father strokes his mustache as he talks. He's a handsome man, stately and composed. It's easy to picture him making political decisions with senators and the like.

"Unfortunately, they were one of many," the sheriff adds. He shoves a final bite of pie into his mouth, by far the roughest of the men here.

"I was there when they left," Mr. Fitch interjects. "Sad day. Mighty sad day. Mr. Fortner wasn't in his right mind by that point. His health had been bad, affected his mental state, but the bankruptcy drove him mad."

"It's been empty ever since?" I ask, trying to add the years in my head. "Such good land? Fifty-four years?" It doesn't make sense.

Kat and the others exchange looks. After fighting each other to tell the story, they all suddenly choose to remain silent, shifting in their chairs, intent on finishing their pie. Doc removes his glasses and polishes the lenses with his cloth napkin. Mr. Fitch looks into the next room, as if he's searching for an excuse to remove himself from the scene. The sheriff stares at me as if he wants to warn me about something.

What are you not telling us about the Fortner place? When is Kat's husband coming home? The line of questions I want to ask is long, but Kat suggests we move to the piano room, so we do what we all do best. We follow her lead.

~

We move out of the dining room as Henry weaves among the guests. Ducking behind legs and shooting a pretend gun, he launches a full attack against invisible villains. Kat snags him when he darts behind her. Then she plants a kiss on his curl-topped head. "Time for bed."

Tugging his grandfather's hand, Henry chirps, "Come with me, Grampy."

"I'll meet you there," Mr. Fitch promises, "as soon as you brush your teeth."

Henry bounds from the room at a gallop. The rest of us follow Kat and gather around a grand piano. I rub my hands along its intricate oak carvings and wonder how in the world they've managed to move it here.

Kat slides out the wooden bench, tucks her soft silver dress beneath her. The men give her their full attention as she strikes a few basic chords and clears her throat. "It's a little out of tune," she says, a suggestion to us all not to expect much. I already know enough about Kat to bet she'll exceed all expectations. "Sing it with me, boys." She smiles. Instantly, the men transform from rugged mountain ranchers to rosy-cheeked choristers. "*Would it be wrong to kiss, seeing I feel like this?*" She flirts with them all.

I can't help smiling as Bump exposes his playful side. It's nice to see him relax and have fun again. He's been working so hard since we moved to the ranch. Bump turns and sings the second verse to me, pulling me to his side. Kat watches, and I catch a certain flash of her eye. It must be hard for her, without a husband. But surely she can't be envious of me. The look leaves me unsettled.

Kat's father's voice brews loud and strong above the crowd, while her uncle's attempts fall short. The minister and the doctor provide harmony, and Bump's perfect pitch mixes with Kat's to create a stunning performance.

"Millie, you're next," Kat says as the song ends.

I don't know how to play. Or sing. I smile and shrug off the offer. "I can't possibly follow that performance." Everyone seems to agree.

"Daddy?" Kat tilts her head to urge her father to take a seat at the ivory keys.

Mr. Fitch shakes his head and holds his hands in the air. "I've got a little ranger waiting for me." With that, he excuses himself from the party.

"Kenneth?" Kat shifts the proposition to my husband.

Without hesitation, Bump slides into position. "I'm better on guitar," he warns. Then he bangs out a rapid ragtime, bringing the room to life. Everyone claps along to the peppy rhythm. I slip onto the bench and sit next to Bump as he plays. When he strikes the final note, I kiss him on the cheek and say, "I didn't know you could play the piano!"

He waves off the praise and says, "Mama took us to church every Sunday. We all learned music there."

"'Maple Leaf Rag'?" Kat asks, as if she doesn't believe he learned this song in church.

"We broke lots of rules."

Everyone laughs.

"Nothing more heavenly than Joplin." Kat bats her eyes. "Can you play 'Bethena'?"

"Not sure." Bump shrugs. "How's it go?"

Kat slides next to Bump and begins to tap out the melody. I stand to make room, but Bump stays seated. Soon he takes over, playing by ear. This song is different from Joplin's sprightly rag-times. A sad, lonesome tone. By the time the song is done, the mood of the entire room has dropped. Kat looks over at Bump and smiles. "I have to admit, Kenneth. You surprise me."

"Never underestimate a southern boy," he says, and Kat's laughter rises louder than the rest.

"We've had a wonderful time tonight, Kat. But we'd better get going." I pull Bump's arm and begin my round of good-byes.

"So soon?" Kat argues.

I give Bump a gentle nudge and hope he gets the hint.

"Millie's right," he says, wrapping his arm around me. "I sent word to a new ranch hand. He's likely to show up in the mornin'."

This is news to me.

"That right?" Sheriff Halpin prompts Bump for more information. I look to him for answers as well.

"Yep. Met a fella who seems awful desperate for a job. I sure can use the help."

He says "I" instead of "we," as if I haven't been at his side clearing brush, repairing stalls, and running fence lines from the start. Not to mention all the work I've done in the house. And in the yard. I hold my hands up to show the sheriff my blisters and calluses. "Here I was thinking he had help all this time." More laughter.

"No doubt." Bump corrects himself. "Millie's been workin'

nonstop, but fall will be here before we know it, and we gotta pick up the pace."

The sheriff grunts. "What's his name? This fella?"

"Fortner," Bump says. "Same family who started the place, I assume. I don't think you care for him much, though. We met him in your store."

The room grows quiet. I look at each person for a clue, but no one says a word.

"Somethin' we should know about him?" Bump asks, saying "we" again, as if he's finally remembering that it's the two of us here against a whole new world of strangers.

The sheriff pulls a toothpick from his vest and pops it into his mouth. Tells Kat, "Better pour me a double."

Reverend Baker frowns.

Doc speaks up. "You sure about that, Sheriff?"

I get the feeling it's not the sheriff's first dive into a double, but he chews on his toothpick and says, "The day that murderer leaves town will be the day I step away from the drink. Until then, don't lecture me about right and wrong."

"Murderer?" My stomach spins again.

"That's right," Sheriff Halpin says.

Doc Henley interrupts. "Now, hold up just a minute, Halpin. There's no need to get this nice young couple all worked up about nothing."

"I sure don't consider it nothing," the sheriff argues louder this time. "He murdered a woman, for God's sake." His face grows red with anger.

"No one knows for sure what happened," the reverend says to Bump and me quietly, as if he's trying to tame the tempers in the room.

"'Course we do," Sheriff Halpin snaps. "Where's my drink?"

Kat hurries to pour the bourbon, and the glass hits the bottle with a loud clink.

"If Fortner's a danger, I sure don't want him at the ranch," Bump says, his brow wrinkled.

"Exactly how I feel about my town," the sheriff answers. Sweat builds around his hairline.

"He's not leaving," Doc says.

"He will if I have my say." Halpin squeezes his hand together until his knuckles crack. His face is reddening, and I sense his rage is about to explode.

Kat hands her uncle a drink just in time. "Here you go." She smiles at him, trying to ease the tension. "Sorry it took me so long."

The rest of us are speechless. Sheriff Halpin empties the glass in one long drink before setting it down hard on the piano. The strings vibrate.

"If you know what's good for you"—the sheriff looks Bump in the eye—"you won't let that man anywhere near your place. Trust me. He's trouble."

We let the warning sink in, and the stress finally defeats me. My stomach roils in revolt. With only a matter of seconds to escape, I whisper, "Excuse me," and dart for the front door. I end the evening bent in the yard, sick again.

Bump finds me in the dark under the trees. The others stand huddled in the doorway, watching. Somewhere nearby, a skunk has sprayed, and the pungent odor is nearly more than I can stand.

"Let's get out of here," I murmur.

As we walk to the truck, I wave back to our hosts and offer, "Thanks. It was lovely." Then I fall against the seat. I've never been more embarrassed.

As Bump moves to the driver's side, Kat calls out, "Be careful!" The foyer light makes her hair glow, and the silhouette of her perfect figure is outlined beneath her dress as she waves goodbye. Bump gets into the truck, cranks the engine, and starts to laugh.

"I'm so ashamed."

"Nothing to worry about, Millie. You couldn't help it."

"Please don't," I say, slouching against the window.

"Don't what?"

I don't mean to sound snide, but there's a snap in my voice when I say, "Talk like I'm your child."

Bump says nothing, and we drive all the way home in silence. In bed, he reaches for me. I pull away and leave a cold, empty space between us all night.

Chapter 10

"No!" I yell. "Never again!" Then I wake at the same moment I have every time I've dreamed this dream. Covered in sweat. Breathing fast. But silenced, still.

"Nightmares again?" Bump comes into our bedroom carrying a bundle of yellow wildflowers. It's barely past dawn.

"Unfortunately," I say, rolling out of bed to accept Bump's gift, trying to forge past the fear. "These are beautiful. What are they?"

"Heck if I know." Bump passes them to me. "From out back."

"They smell like mustard," I tell him, surprised somehow by the rich, woodsy smell. It triggers hunger. Lately, I've been working so hard, I'm always hungry.

"I can't smell 'em at all."

"Here." I pinch the delicate fibers to release the fragrance. "Now can you smell it?"

He nods. "You have one heck of an amazin' schnozzle, my dear." He talks as if he's on the radio, making me laugh.

"What's the occasion?" I leave bed to place the flowers in water.

"Sorry I made us late last night," Bump says.

A man who says he's sorry? Who brings me wildflowers? Who

wakes me with a kiss? I smile and say, "Tell you what. If you can forgive my bad cooking, then I'll forgive your tardiness. Deal?"

Bump laughs and says, "Yeah, about that. I didn't mean—"

I cut him off before he makes excuses for telling Kat she served him the best meal he'd had in weeks. Then I repeat myself. "Deal?"

"Deal."

"Now, how about some leftover oatmeal?" We both laugh as I try to poke the brick of day-old slop, which has hardened to stone. "Breakfast in town?" I suggest.

"I reckon so," Bump answers. "It's time we stock up on supplies anyway, and we do need to find some hens."

"Thank you." I kiss him.

"Gosh, all I had to say was I'm takin' you to town?"

"See?" I tease him. "I'm not as complicated as I seem."

"*The* most complicated person I've ever known." He's probably being honest.

Bump tosses the oatmeal out the door, pot and all, just to make me laugh. It nearly hits Fortner, who is standing in our front yard. His black horse is tethered to the porch. Last night's warnings ring loud. This is the "bad man" Henry was hoping to avoid during our trail ride and the "murderer" Sheriff Halpin got all worked up about at the party. I know only enough to think him dangerous. Realizing I'm still wearing my thin cotton nightgown, I step out of view.

"Mornin'," Bump says, walking to Fortner for a handshake.

Fortner looks at me. I blush, showing my face from behind the door. "We're about to go into town," I tell him, hoping he gets the hint and leaves. "We're desperate to find something to eat." I point to the pot of oatmeal in the yard and laugh nervously.

"I cook," Fortner says.

Bump raises his eyebrows at me. He likes to eat breakfast as soon as he wakes up, and he's already been out picking flowers with an empty stomach. Fortner lifts the pot and eyes the oatmeal.

"Can't seem to adjust to the high altitude," I explain. "I burn most everything."

Fortner chose the perfect weapon to break down any hesitation Bump might have about hiring him. Food.

"Tell you what," Bump says. "I do owe my wife a trip into town this morning, but if you're eager to work, I can get you started on a job and join you when we get back. Sound reasonable?"

Fortner smiles, revealing a tamer spirit beneath his wild exterior. "Sure."

"Know how to prep a smokehouse?"

"Consider it done."

"Need anything from town while we're goin'?" Bump offers.

"Not a thing. I'll move my teepee down from the woods, if that's okay. Pitch it near the river there." Fortner points to an area not far from our house, and I'm surprised when Bump answers, "Sure. Maybe we can work out some kind of room in the barn before winter hits."

"Not a problem," Fortner says. "I haven't slept inside in years."

Just like that, Bump's hired a suspected murderer to help us on the ranch and given him permission to move his teepee within sight of our bedroom window. I'm still standing half-naked behind the front door, as if my concerns don't matter one bit. Closing the door, I move to dress. I'll have Bump's undivided attention during the drive into Lewiston. It'll be a good chance to tell him how I feel.

~

As Bump drives us off our ranch, I take in the landscape with wonder. Except for last night's dinner party, I haven't left the property since arriving in Lewiston a month ago. The road curves along vertical walls, with deep plummets dealt to anyone who misses a turn. It's a slow route, and even though we are less than ten miles from Lewiston, the ride takes more than twenty minutes by truck. The vehicle sputters up each peak, nearly running out of speed before we reach the rise, and by then Bump is already having to shift to low gear before we crest and begin the steep decline. I'm betting when winter hits, we'll be socked in for months. I can't even imagine managing these roads in ice and snow.

Only a few ranches are scattered between ours and the town, the nearest being the Fitch place. Despite the risks, Bump doesn't watch the road. Instead, he scans the valleys and the peaks for elk, deer, and sheep. I watch for lions. And fires.

"Gonna be a hot day," Bump says. It's barely nine in the morning, and he's already lowering his window. Spring in Colorado has brought a wild mix of hot, sunny days, and cold, windy snowfall, but we're finally hitting summer now. This week has been nice and warm, even though the higher peaks are still dusted with snow.

"Think we should talk about you hiring a murderer?" I start the conversation from the far end of the seat and leave my window up.

Bump looks as if he wasn't expecting this. "You worried?"

"Of course I'm worried. Aren't you?" Bump's trusting nature is what first made me fall in love with him, but it can also be infuriating at times.

"I don't know yet," Bump says. "The reverend didn't seem

too concerned. Doc neither. From what I can tell, the sheriff's the only one who thinks he's any danger."

"He's the sheriff, Bump. Maybe we should take his warnings seriously." I try to keep my voice calm. I sure don't want to reach those annoying pitches that Janine hits when she's trying to argue her opinion.

"Seems like a good-enough guy to me. I've seen much worse come through the rodeo."

I shrug. He may have a point, but I don't want to be around anyone who *might* be a danger.

"Maybe we should give him a chance," Bump adds. "Sometimes that's all a man needs."

I let this sink in for a while before responding. "You really think it's safe?" I wish he could say more to convince me.

"I don't know. But I promise, Millie. I won't let nobody hurt you."

I look out the window and say nothing.

"Millie." Bump calls for me to look at him. When I do, he says again, "I promise."

We ride for miles without talking, both of us taking in the new surroundings. The clean, thin air smells of evergreens, and even with the heat, there is a crispness to the day. It's not soggy and moist, like back home. In every direction, the mountains surround us, blocking out the past. I feel worlds away from Mississippi, as if that life belonged to someone else, perhaps a story I read in a book. A distant, fading memory. But still, I cower in fear when a man like Fortner poses a possible threat. No matter how many times I tell myself I am strong, brave, in control, it only takes a moment to be dragged back into weakness.

Bump finally breaks the silence when he slows the truck and points to a wild herd perched on the steep, rocky rise. "Bighorn."

I roll down the window for a better look. I'm mesmerized by the massive size of the sheep. The rams' horns are each as wide as my thigh. "How do they climb that?" I ask, impressed they can navigate the rough, vertical terrain.

The road, too, is rural and rugged. Bump finds a flat area and stops the truck to watch the sheep. It's rare to have quiet, still moments like this with him, whole segments of time when he isn't being fully active. He pulls my hand into his and whispers, "We're gonna be okay here, Millie."

I want so desperately to seize this moment, to convince him I can help make things okay. Be the wife he deserves, and not a damaged child he has to protect. *Call me Kat,* I think to myself, remembering Camille's transformation when she said, "Call me Ann." I mimic Kat as I move slowly into Bump and pretend I am a confident woman who can charm the toughest mountain man. I kiss Bump without thought of any of the men who have hurt me. I don't yield to him as I usually do. Instead, I am the one in charge. I deliver a kiss so intense, it excites Bump. We nearly forget we're in public when a horn sounds behind us. A long blue Oldsmobile Club Coupe swerves to avoid colliding into our parked farm truck.

We are startled from each other's arms and ride the rest of the route with our eyes on the road and a smile on my husband's face.

In town, we park in front of Doc's Place. We'll walk across the street to the diner before returning to Doc's. He's invited Bump to take a look at his mustangs, and Bump is more than eager to land a paying customer. Plus, he insists I ask the doctor about my ulcer, and I'm certainly ready to end the constant irritation.

"Bump. Millie." Doc comes around the corner of his house and greets us cheerily as we climb out of the truck. "I'm just about to have breakfast. Come on in."

Bump gives me a "please say yes" look, obviously eager to eat. I laugh and follow the men into Doc's Place. The walls are bare, no photos of loved ones. No signs of family. His home is orderly and stocked with only the bare essentials, even though I'm guessing he can afford luxuries. Doc's a decent-looking man. Certainly intelligent, and friendly enough. I'm a bit surprised to discover he lives all alone. Only a whole lot of horses in the paddock and a coughing patient or two in the adjoining room.

The doctor pulls on his glasses and says, "I sure enjoyed those biscuits last night, Millie. I'd never had figs before." We follow him into the kitchen where he unwraps a biscuit, layers it with a fresh spread of honey-colored preserves. "I asked Kat for the leftovers."

I raise my chin and give Bump a look as if to say, *See, I'm not so bad after all.*

Doc hands the biscuit to Bump, and my husband makes up for last night's insult. "Millie's one of the best cooks I've ever seen." I smile.

Doc spreads preserves on two more biscuits, one for me and one for him. We stand together in the kitchen, eating without even bothering with plates or forks. I find comfort in the doctor's casual nature, and even though my biscuits have nothing on Kat's pie, every bite tastes like home.

"I'd be mighty grateful if you could take a look at my horses.

Got that batch of mustangs I mentioned. Wild as bears. Can't get a whip-length within a single one of them. And I've got a Belgian who is head shy about the bridle. He'll be worthless if he won't pull a plow."

"Happy to help," Bump says, "but we want to ask you about Millie's stomach first. I think she might have an ulcer."

"Y'all go ahead with the horses," I say. "I've got a few errands I need to run before you put me in a bad mood." I smile, and the doctor does too.

With that, Doc points Bump to the door and our first steady income. I leave the men, promising to come back and talk about that ulcer. Then I make my way to the post office. I need to mail thank-you notes for our wedding gifts. Plus, I want to send the tumbleweed to Camille. If only I could see her face when she opens it.

Within minutes, the postman is helping me stuff a big box with Camille's tumbleweed. Then he stamps, *FRAGILE* and says, "Well, that's a first." He is built square, shoulders and hips as wide as they are thick, and he stands on a step stool to see over the counter. He wears a starched federal uniform and seems to take his position very seriously, even though the entire post office is the size of a small closet, including a telegraph station in the corner. The two of us nearly fill the room.

"You the folks living out at the Fortner place?" the postman asks.

"Yes, sir." I introduce myself, give him the information he seeks.

"Abe," he says, pointing to his name tag. "Got a package for you."

"You do?" I'm too excited to care what it is or who it's from. I follow Abe to a narrow area behind the counter where boxes are stacked as high as his head.

"It's down here on the bottom." We work our way through the stack until I see the label from Miss Harper, the librarian in Iti Taloa. I can hardly contain my delight.

"Books!"

Abe gives a quick dip of his chin and says, "It's heavy, all right."

I tear into the box and find it filled with discarded titles from the library. *For Whom the Bell Tolls*, *Gone with the Wind*, *The Yearling*, *It Can't Happen Here*. I flip through the top of the stack and nearly cheer from excitement.

"Need help getting that loaded?"

"No, thanks. I can manage." I set the box on the counter to pay for my stamps.

"So what're your plans out there with that old ranch?" Abe steps back onto his stool and makes change for me. I tell him about Mr. Tucker's goals.

"Well, I'm no rancher," Abe continues, "but I know there's a need for stock horses in these parts. Broncs too. Got a rodeo not too far from here. Down in Estes Park. I suppose you already know about that one, though."

"You compete?" I ask.

He shakes his head. "Not in this lifetime. But I do like to watch. The big ranchers all come out and their boys go against each other. MacMillan usually takes tops."

"MacMillan?"

"Yep, big cattle operation just past the Stanley. Over in Estes. You been there yet?"

I shake my head.

"It's nice. See it sometime. Take a ride in one of those old Stanley steamers. They still have a few they run for tours."

"Sounds fun, I admit."

Abe's face is dry and red, and when he smiles I fear it may crack into pieces. He looks as if he spends all his time standing in the wind. "You two have everything you need out there? It's awfully remote."

"We're just getting the place up and running, but we do hope to find a dairy cow soon. Get some laying hens while we're in town today. Got any idea where we should look?"

"You're in luck." Abe laughs and steps down again from the stool. He leads me to a line of holding pens behind the post office. Several scrawny horses and a donkey share a small pen. Another area holds four goats and a couple of pigs. "No one ever showed up to get these goats. I'm only required to hold them for three days. Been a few weeks already. Far as I'm concerned, they're yours if you want them. Two mamas, three babies. Still milking."

I'm blown away by our fortune. "Bump will be thrilled. Think they can stand the winters up there? We've got good shelter."

Abe shrugs. "Seem healthy enough." One of the kids cries, and it sounds as if she's calling, *Mama, Mama.* Abe pets the baby's soft ears and pats one doe on the head.

"If we can carry them in the truck, we'll take them home today. Would that work?"

"That's exactly what I want you to do." Abe continues petting the goats, careful to give each equal attention. I get the feeling he wants to find them new homes before he becomes too attached. "I don't have chickens, but there's an old Indian woman about a mile from here who always has more than she can handle."

I follow Abe back into the station where I write down directions to the lady's home and fold them into my pocket. "I almost forgot," he adds, "you got a letter too." Then he pulls an envelope from a wooden slat behind the counter and tucks it in my hand.

"Thanks, Abe. I'll be back for the goats." Eager to read my mail, I hurry away. The box of books lands hard into the bed of the truck before I rip into the letter. It's from Camille.

Dear Millie,

I miss you, Mabel misses you, and Mother is worse than ever. So many parties! She made Mabel clean the floorboards with a toothbrush! And when Daddy stepped on the rug with muddy shoes, Mother gave Mabel a spoon and said, "Scrape it up."

She'd die if she knew who came to our house. A GYPSY! He walked right up and asked about you. Quite a looker, sis. He played the harmonica for me, and he was very nice until Mabel told him you were married. Then he just walked away.

Please come home. Writing letters is hard.

With absolute devotion
and undying affection
(that's how I will sign
when I'm famous),
Camille

P.S. Remember the Screenland cover of Lana in May? Well, guess what? Mabel fixed my hair just like hers, and I'm about to paint my nails RED! Won't Mother be thrilled!? XOXO

I read the letter three times. Then I tear it into pieces and toss it into a trash can behind the general store before returning to Doc's house. Along the way, I don't think of Miss Harper's shipment of books, or Camille imitating Lana Turner, or Mabel scraping the rug with a spoon. Only one thought rises to the surface with every step. River is looking for me.

When I make it to Doc's, I'm no longer worried about a silly little stomach ulcer. And it's a good thing too. Doc's got no time to treat me because Kat has beaten me here, and she is crying. "What's wrong?" I ask, stepping lightly into the foyer that doubles as a waiting room.

"Come on in, Millie." The doctor stands to offer me his seat. Bump is sitting next to Kat, his arm around her, trying to console her.

"Kat?" I ask again. I fear the worst—that something has happened to Henry.

Bump looks at me as if he doesn't know what to say. He stands and lets me move to comfort Kat. She wipes her tears. Then she hands me a crumpled yellow telegram. It is moist where her wet fingers have gripped the paper. The top line makes it clear the message has been sent from Washington, D.C. I read it silently as Doc Henley brings Kat a warm, wet cloth for her face.

THE SECRETARY OF WAR DESIRES ME TO
EXPRESS HIS DEEP REGRET THAT YOUR
HUSBAND SEAMAN GRANT COLEMAN GARNER
WAS KILLED IN ACTION ON JUNE 5TH 1943 IF

FURTHER DETAILS OR OTHER INFORMATION ARE RECEIVED YOU WILL BE PROMPTLY NOTIFIED

All caps. No punctuation. Then the bottom line states the message has been given by the Adjutant General. I'm in shock. "What a cruel way to deliver this news."

"It's okay," Kat says. "There's been a mistake. I'm certain of it."

"Kat." I move closer to her, in case she wants a hug. She doesn't.

She takes the paper and stuffs it back into her pocket. "This isn't how they do it. They can't just post a telegram. He'll be back. Just wait and see."

I pour Kat a mug of coffee from a corner pot and hold it out to her. She stares at it but doesn't drink.

"Where's Henry?" I ask.

She looks as if she's going to cry again. "Daddy's got him at the store."

"Do they know?"

Kat shakes her head no.

Doc excuses himself and Bump follows. I assume they're going to find Kat's father.

"Oh, Millie. What am I going to do?" She covers her face with the cloth and cries. "I don't want to be alone."

I sit with her but say nothing. Instead, I wait. Listen. The only way I know to show I care.

Kat leans back, closes her eyes, and says, "Thank you, Millie. Thank you for being my friend."

Chapter 11

Kat finds me cleaning the coop for our new batch of hens. She carries a jar of jam and sets it on the ground for me while Henry struggles to climb a small scrub tree out by the river. It's the first time I've seen her since we read the telegram in Doc's office a week ago.

"Kat?" I rush to greet her. "Thank goodness. I've been so worried about you." I've wanted to check on her, but I was afraid I'd be intruding.

"I'm fine." She offers me a stiff hug, and I give her a look as if I doubt she's fine. I've seen this look in other people's eyes. A look of determined survival. "Really, I am. I won't believe a thing they say until I have proof."

"Proof?"

She pulls away, turns to look at the mountains rising behind us. "They say there are no . . . They weren't able to find . . . They have nothing to bury." She forces a smile and continues staring in the distance for a long time.

"We could talk to the reverend," I suggest. "I'm sure this kind of thing has happened before."

Kat watches the mountains, as if she hasn't processed what I've said at all. Then it's almost as if a switch has been flipped. She spins back in my direction, looks right at me, and smiles big, as if this has all been some sort of joke. She places her hands on my stomach, as if we've been friends our whole lives. I take a step back, confused. "Kat?"

"Something you need to tell me?" She asks this happily, as if we're chatting at a tea party. As if her husband hasn't been blown to pieces over a foreign sea. I can't imagine what she's thinking. "Don't you dare look at me like that," she teases. "I'm no fool, Millie."

"What are you talking about?" I honestly have no idea, and I'm worried she's losing her wits. The shift is so sudden, so drastic. I can only think of Diana and her polished ability to pretend herself an entire reality to suit her own needs. I've seen her dry her tears, give her head a few fast shakes, and stand with a smile, like a stage actress ready to play her part.

"I can't believe it's taken me this long to figure it out." Kat walks in a circle and counts on her fingers as she makes each point. "You were the first to smell the ponderosas, before we even made it to the glen. You've admitted yourself, you've been fighting an upset stomach, for-ev-er. You've said you've been feeling more tired than usual, and, forgive me for saying so, my friend, but your dungarees are a tad too tight."

I pull my hands to cover my waistline, ashamed she's noticed my weight.

"Don't try to hide it, Millie. Motherhood is a beautiful blessing. Believe me. The upset stomach, the noxious smells, even the expanding dress size, it's all worth it. I mean, just look at little Henry out there." She pauses, smiles at her son. "He's my whole life." She sighs. "Wouldn't trade him for the world." She says this as if she's trying to convince herself it's true.

"Kat, I'm not—"

"Are you sure?" Kat interrupts and crosses her arms. "You certainly have all the signs."

"Sure I do." I say this sarcastically.

"Indeed, Millie. You do." Then she whispers, "Are you . . . sore?" She motions toward her own breasts, and I blush at her frankness. Then I nod, admitting I am.

"Have you missed your monthly?"

"Several." I'm certain my face has turned hot-pepper red. "But that happens to me sometimes. It's no big deal. It's probably on account of our limited diet and all this hard work."

"I knew it." Kat snaps her fingers as if she's won a contest.

"Kat, you've gone mad. I had planned to see Doc last week before . . ." I can't look at her. I don't want to bring up her husband again. She seems determined to avoid accepting that she is now a widow.

"You're pregnant, Millie."

I laugh. "Honestly, you're wrong, Kat. Bump knows a lot about medicine from all that vet school, and he says I have an ulcer." I scoop more waste into a bucket for compost and try not to let the smell get to me.

"I don't care what Bump thinks, my friend. He's never been pregnant. I have. And I'm telling you, you're going to have a baby."

I don't know how to react. For some reason, this time I don't laugh Kat away as if she's speaking nonsense. Is it possible that I've known the truth all along? That I've just been waiting for someone to say it out loud? Could I have been so determined to leave my past behind that I've been swimming in denial? Just like Diana and Kat, I've been weaving my own reality. But now Kat has put things together. She's forced me to accept the ugly truth.

I hold my head in my hands and trace the path that led me here. I square months in my mind and disappear into a desperate counting of days. Kat yells for Henry not to go too high, and I sink away into a deep, black pit of disgust.

"Kat?" I grip my hands together as if begging. "Can you not mention this to anyone yet? Please? I want to tell Bump privately."

"Of course," Kat assures me. "I don't blame you, really. Once men find out, they treat you like you're contagious. The whole idea scares them out of their wits. On the other hand"—she winks—"you can use it to your advantage, and I highly recommend you do just that."

I am seventeen. Some girls my age wouldn't know much about pregnancy, but I've spent too much time with the rodeo to be a fool about how things happen. I've read Bump's veterinary books too, so I know all about how an egg drops, and a sperm swims, and a collision occurs, and how a split-second interaction can throw someone like me all off course.

I rub my hand across my belly. I feel faint. Kat must notice me whitening because she turns for the pump and says, "Sit down, Millie. I'll get you some water."

Maybe it's the sudden thought of being a mother, but my mind takes me back to Mama and her Bible stories. I'm betting the Virgin Mary didn't have to deal with nausea when she was pregnant. Surely no sour smell sent her spinning. I count again and again in my head. The vomiting started before our wedding. *Before* our wedding! One thing is for sure. I have no sacred seed growing inside of me. This baby is no gift from God.

Kat returns and hands me a glass of water from the pump. "Better now?"

I can't answer. Kat's words swirl around me, a warped warble, as if the sound waves aren't quite making it through. Kat laughs. "You better stay low to the ground for a while."

I lie back in the grass and stare at the trees. Above me, the monotonous shree of the waxwings reminds me of the fledgling sparrow Bump and Henry returned to the woods the night of Kat's dinner party. I wonder if the mama bird came back for her baby. Did she want it? Or had she abandoned it on purpose, leaving it for a cat to find? Like the mama mutt dog who swallowed her own puppies when I was a kid. Do I have it in me to do such things? To take life away from my own child?

I have not asked for this. I have been cursed. So who could blame me for ending my pain? For shouting to the heavens that I am done. This is my life. Mine. And I do not want this baby. I do not want to be the mother of Bill Miller's child.

It's early July and the heat has reached the ranch. Still, even when the temperature climbs, it's bearable compared to Mississippi's humid swelter. Bump has taught me to prime the water pump so the leather gaskets won't dry out. I take a long drink and then refill the jar so it's ready for the next prime. Then I move to the clothesline, draping the wire with wet clothes from the wash bin. I'm amazed to find they're dry before I hang the last of Bump's shirts. The white cotton sleeves shine bright like lights, reflecting the sun in waves against the wind.

It's been more than a week since Kat's last visit, but her words still echo in my head. "You're pregnant, Millie." How could I have been so stupid? I cannot believe Kat has caught on to my condition when I convinced myself I had a stomach ulcer, ignoring all the signs. Even the constant craving for beets, a vegetable I've never had a taste for until now. If Kat has discovered my secret so quickly, that means Bump will figure it out soon too. If he hasn't already. I've added the days, I've counted the cycles, I've calculated and subtracted and whipped the numbers every which way they can tumble, and still, there's no way around it. I am nearly four months pregnant. I am carrying Bill Miller's child.

Bump comes up behind me, pulls my hair back, and kisses me on the neck. "How's my beautiful wife?"

I jump, as I do every time he kisses me in that spot. It's a trigger, for some reason, and I can't stand the way I feel when touched there. I try to remember the way River's kiss would send a different kind of chill up my spine. I try.

"No reason to be scared," Bump says. "Nobody here but you and me." The same thing Bill Miller said to me in the steeple. My stomach churns. Bump kisses me again. This time wrapping his arms around my waist and pulling me into him. I stiffen. Try to focus on the way he smells of grain, sweat, and grass. Nothing like Bill Miller.

"Where's Fortner?" I try to hide any sign of worry in my voice. I'm not ready to tell Bump about this baby. Not ready to hurt this man I love so much. I should have been honest from the start. Then he might understand. But now the lies are too deep. The betrayal, too much.

"Braidin' ropes," he says. "He suggested I take a break. Reckon he's tired of my singin'?" Bump laughs, and I will myself into a better mood. He's here to flirt, to have fun, to take a break for the first time since we arrived. I owe him that much, at the very least.

"Well, well," I tease. "Is the hard-working rancher out of jobs to do?" I hope he doesn't sense the false tones in my voice.

The laundry flaps in the wind, and I have to raise my voice above the loud sound of the shirts being whipped like flags. I pull one from the line and fold it.

"Only one job I care much about right now." Bump pulls me back to him.

"Why didn't you say so?" I force a smile, handing him the laundry basket and pointing to the line of dry clothes waiting to be folded and ironed. I leave him with a twirl.

He drops the basket beneath the line, scoops me off my feet, and brings me to the door, laughing. "I just realized, I never did carry my wife over the threshold."

"Wife," I repeat. "I can't help smiling every time you say that word." I try to think of nothing else. Dip my toes back into the sweet, cold waves of denial.

Bump shows no shortage of romance, and for fleeting moments, I almost believe he can recover the part of me that was lost that cold day in March, when bells rang in the steeple. And my dress tore. And my soul shattered. Maybe, just maybe, with enough patience, Bump's gentle giving could bring me to a place so pure, so perfect, and so peaceful, that nothing else would matter. Not even the fact that I'm carrying the child of another man.

But in the end, I have to pretend again. Disappear into the mind of someone like Kat, a woman confident in her own skin, so sure of how to keep a man happy. What occurs to me is that Bump might be pretending I'm Kat too.

In bed, Bump runs his rough hand across the subtle rise of

my belly and gives me a look that makes me think he knows. I am barely showing, and for that I am grateful, but I need to tell him the truth. To let him know a baby will be born. A child who is not his. How unfair this truth—not just for me, but for the baby, for Bump, for all of us.

I struggle to work the words to the surface. How can I tell him? *Bump, there's something you need to know . . . Bump, I haven't been honest . . . Bump, please forgive me . . . Bump, I never meant to hurt you . . .*

"Bump," I hesitate. "I've been trying to—"

He interrupts. "Oh, I forgot to tell you. Mr. Tucker is comin' soon. He's already got a ground crew movin' the horses up from Mississippi. He'll take the train and hope to get here before they arrive. Says Janine's comin' with him."

"Are they bringing Firefly?" Suddenly, the weight of the world falls away, with just the thought of seeing my horse again.

"Yep," Bump promises. "Scout too." I sense he's as eager as I am.

"When?" I ask, sitting up in bed, barely able to contain my excitement, nearly forgetting the baby and the awful truth that must be told.

"September," he says. "Expects us to have a good start on the pastures by then and wants to beat the winter snow."

"How many horses?"

"Two dozen mares, plus their foals, so they'll move slow. Keepin' the others in Mississippi till we see how it goes. Plans on pickin' up more along the route, and hopes to bring a fresh stallion down from west of the Divide in the spring. Some work horse with great lines. He can spout off the whole pedigree, so don't get him started."

"Pick up how many more?" I want to know all the details.

"Didn't say exactly, but mentioned it could be a couple hundred or so. Some Texas rancher died. Good herd for good money."

I add this in my head and realize we're about to take on nearly two hundred and fifty horses in all, plus the new Colorado stallion, plus Doc Henley's mustangs and the rest of his herd, which he plans to rotate through our ranch. And cattle will be soon to follow. The fence lines still need mending, weeds cover the pasture, and we're still working out the kinks with the water system. Not to mention we aren't sure we'll have enough hay to get us through winter. Five thousand acres of grassland won't do us any good if it's all covered in snow. A ball of panic begins to bounce inside me as I think about all we have left to do.

"Don't worry," Bump says, sensing my anxiety. "It'll get done. It always does."

"Is Oka coming with them?"

"She sure is." Bump smiles. "Janine's worked it all out." And with that, he pulls me back down into bed and wraps me into him. I forget all about fence lines and hay supply and water pumps. I think only of this gentle man who loves me, and how I am running out of time to tell him the truth.

Chapter 12

"Knock, knock!" Kat calls. She and Henry find me in the root cellar where I've spent the morning cleaning out old, moldy food and preparing a space to store new goods from our gardens.

"Kat." I smile. "You're just in time to help!" I laugh because the thought of Kat helping me clean this filthy dugout is about as absurd an idea as Bump ever being lazy.

"I'll be happy to stock those shelves with all the fruit preserves you can stand, Millie, but if cleaning cobwebs is what you want, you're asking the wrong girl."

Henry, on the other hand, jumps right in with me and starts playing in the dirt.

"Figured as much," I tease. Then I shift to the serious subject Kat seems determined to avoid. "You doing okay?"

"We're fine, Millie. And I'd rather not talk about it. I came here for laughs, and I'll settle for nothing less."

"Well, in that case . . ." I try to hand her a pair of work gloves, and it does indeed bring laughs.

"As long as I don't have to clean this awful cellar." Kat steps out of the dank room, leaving prints in the floor. "Henry, why don't you run and check the coop? I bet you'll find eggs."

Henry leaps at the chance to have a real job.

"Fortner still here?" Kat asks. It's been two weeks since her last visit, and it sounds as if she expected he'd be gone by now.

I follow her gaze in the direction of Fortner's teepee. He's already arranged various tools, ropes, and hides in neat, organized stacks around his home. A rifle rests against a spruce next to his camp. "From the looks of it, he's not planning on leaving anytime soon," I say. "You think we should worry?"

Kat glances around, seemingly unsure about whether to share her thoughts with me. "I don't know. My uncle's convinced he's a murderer, but honestly, I've always had my doubts. Most folks just steer clear of him, so I always have too."

"What happened?" I don't look her way, hoping she'll continue to confide in me.

"Not sure exactly. But story has it—" Kat lowers her voice to a whisper to avoid the risk of Henry accidentally overhearing—"when the Fortners had to abandon the ranch, they left town and didn't take their son with them."

"You mean he stayed behind?"

"Yes, but he was just a boy at the time. Supposedly, he camped out in the woods and wouldn't leave."

"How old was he?" I ask.

"Not old, from what I can tell. Twelve, thirteen maybe? Folks say his family couldn't afford to keep him. His father was ill, both body and mind. He insisted the boy was old enough to make it on his own. Suggested he find a job in the mines."

"That's unbelievable," I say, turning my attention back to the pickled vegetables. I learned long ago not to put much weight on rumors.

"It gets even more unbelievable," Kat says. "Story goes, a new family moved in a few years later, tried to get the ranch working again. In a matter of months, the wife was dead."

"And people think Fortner killed her?"

"That's what they say."

"Why would he do such a thing?"

"I haven't the faintest idea, Millie. Most people say it was a big misunderstanding, that the boy was young, like you say, and he never would have done anything like that. Others got scared. Said the place was cursed. Either way, no one dared come out this way and the house has sat empty ever since. My uncle didn't buy into the stories. He's always suspected Fortner was guilty."

"But he's never been tried for it?"

"No, he was just a kid at the time. And besides, Fortner wasn't around much after that. He started working as a trapper and trader, kind of a middleman between the Utes down south and the ranchers up this way."

"That's why he dresses like that?" I think of Fortner, dressing like he's part of a tribe but moving through the world in skin that is paler than mine.

"I guess. I think he prefers their way of life to ours."

"I don't blame him."

Kat gives me a surprised look, as if she can't possibly understand why anyone would choose such a life. Then she looks around as if she's just remembering we use an outhouse and a hand pump and kerosene lamps. "Well, anyway, there's more to the story. Years later, there was a German woman, Ingrid, kind of big at the top, if you know what I mean."

We both laugh, and I continue cleaning the shelves with my work rag, suddenly aware of my own swollen breasts.

"Well, Ingrid took a liking to Fortner. Started asking him to help her with odd jobs when he came through town. Things the woman already knew how to do by herself. She was a tough one, I tell you. Skin a deer, clean a gun, sharpen a blade. It was obvious what she was up to, and the sheriff didn't like it one bit. She was keeping Fortner too close to town for my uncle's liking."

"Sounds like he might have been jealous."

"That's what most folks say, but either way, people started talking, and before we knew it, Ingrid was caught in the middle of a feud."

"Lovers' quarrel?"

Kat shrugs.

"Don't tell me people think Fortner killed her too." Now I'm getting chills. Could Fortner be worse than I fear?

"Well, supposedly, one night Uncle Halpin went to Ingrid's house, and guess who was already there?"

"Fortner?"

"You guessed it." Kat crosses her arms. "Uncle Halpin didn't take it well, and that's where the story takes two turns. Tempers flared. Shots were fired. And somehow Ingrid was the one who caught the bullet. Both men blame the other, and neither has changed his story in more than twenty years. Fortner started spending more and more time on the trails, until eventually he stopped coming through town at all. It's been nearly a decade since anyone I know has seen or heard from him. Until you showed up."

"Why?"

"People talk. Your boss bought the ranch from the bank. Fortner got word, I assume."

"You think he'll hurt us?" I look out at Fortner's stash of weapons and hides.

"I really don't know, Millie. I'd like to think he's just curious, sticking around long enough to make sure you'll take care of the place."

"But it sounds like he never cared about the place until now."

"That's what I can't figure. Uncle says he's evil, and he's not to be trusted. Says he's as wild as the Injuns, that he has no soul."

I take offense to this, and Kat seems to suddenly notice my dark complexion. "Oh, goodness, Millie. You're not . . ."

"Choctaw," I say. "My dad's side."

"I didn't mean—"

I cut her off. "So that's what your uncle thinks," I tell her, wiping dirt from another shelf as I try to ease the guilt she feels. It's certainly not the first time I've heard such things.

"Yes, that's right. Him, not me." Kat seems eager to prove she thinks I do actually have a soul.

I decide it's a good time to change the subject. There's something I've been wanting to ask Kat, and now's the perfect time. "So, on a lighter note, I've been finding a lot of berries around the ranch," I begin, carefully plotting my questions to disguise my true intent. I can't let anyone know my plan.

"Oh, yes," Kat says, obviously relieved I've let her comment slide. "Tons of wild strawberries in this range. Raspberries too. Have you found those yet? Might be too early."

"Not yet. I'm waiting for the chokecherries to turn dark. And I'm watching for blackberries. I've been looking for cuttings and wild herbs to train in my garden, only I'm not familiar with all the plants here."

"Are they that different?"

"They seem to be. In Mississippi, I could have told you the use for nearly every living thing in sight. Here, I just don't know."

Slow down, Millie. Keep calm. I avoid looking Kat in the eye and focus instead on the old jars of beets and rhubarb on dusty shelves. None of the food can be salvaged, but I'm hoping to reuse the jars for this year's canning.

"You seem to know everything about these parts," I continue. "Do you by any chance have a book on plants I can borrow? Something to help me prep the pastures before the horses arrive? Someone mentioned loco weed."

"Got quite a few, actually," Kat says. Then she adds, "How's the baby?"

I don't like hearing the truth out loud. I hold my hand to my lips to signal for Kat to keep quiet.

Kat's eyes pop wide with alarm. "You haven't told him?"

I shake my head. "Don't want to get his hopes up, in case things go wrong." Kat looks as if she's on to me. I stutter, adding a better excuse. "It's just so sudden. I don't think Bump's gotten used to having *me* in his life, much less a baby."

"That's ridiculous."

"I mean, we can barely handle all our work as it is." I scramble to make a better excuse. "If Bump knows I'm carrying, he won't let me help. It would be too much on him. It's just not time yet. That's all."

"Babies come when they're meant to, Millie. I was young when I had Henry. Believe me, I sure wasn't ready."

"But you make it look so easy."

"It's not. I certainly never bargained to do this on my own." Kat stands tall. "Being a mother changes everything. You may not know it yet, but believe me, this pregnancy isn't all about you."

I turn my back to Kat and drop a jar of old pickles a little too hard into the discard box. The bailing wire snaps, and the glass shatters into a million little shards. How dare she say this pregnancy is not about me? It's my body, isn't it? It's me who will risk my life by giving birth. It's me who will look this child in the eye, day after day, seeing only the man who violated me. It's me who may lose my husband, the one person in this world who loves me, when he learns the baby isn't his.

This *is* about me. It's not my fault I'm in this situation. And the choice should be mine. But I don't say any of that. Instead, I stare at the broken glass and regret the waste. Three jars ruined.

"Millie?" Kat asks calmly.

I don't look at her.

"Find the Indian woman, up in town. The one where you got the chickens. She might be able to get you some pennyroyal. And blue cohosh."

Now I look at her, confused.

"That's what you really want to know, isn't it? How to stop this?"

I say nothing as Henry returns with a bundle of eggs tucked in his shirt. Kat places them gently in the grass and gives her son a hug.

"They don't grow here. But I've known of women who . . ." Like me, she can't seem to say it out loud. Henry pulls Kat's leg, and she rustles his hair. Then Kat looks out toward Fortner's teepee and says, "Why, heck, Millie. You may not even have to go into town."

"Fortner?"

Kat nods. "He'll have what you want, or he'll know where to get it."

I've heard whispered stories of back-alley abortions back home. And once, when Mr. Sutton's farmhand was delivering Mama's brown paper bag of morphine, I overheard them talking about one of the young daughters of another hand. The man told Mama he had "fixed it." Mama asked him how, and he said, "There's a plant for everything." It wasn't until recently that I realized what he meant.

"Ready, Mama?" Henry asks.

"Sure am, baby." Kat looks me in the eye and says, "Millie?"

I can't hold eye contact. I'm too ashamed.

"Think it through," she tells me. "You can't change your mind once it's done."

Chapter 13

I've got no direct reason to fear Fortner, but he's been linked to two suspicious deaths, and one of them happened right here, on this ranch, to a woman like me. While Bump sings his praises every night, chatting about how grateful he is for the help, I've barely said two words to the strange visitor since he started working with Bump. I've purposely kept my distance, refusing to let any man other than Bump get too close, especially someone with such a violent reputation. I don't trust him, and I have no way of knowing if he'll help me. This entire idea seems crazy, but I have no other options. And I don't have time to spare. I have to risk it.

I find Bump and Fortner patching feed bins in the pasture, the hot summer sun burning the back of Bump's neck. When I brush Bump's shoulder with my fingertips, he turns, dripping with sweat, to greet me. "Think I could borrow Fortner for a minute?" I ask. "I need help lifting a crate out of the root cellar."

"I'll help," Bump says, giving me a salty kiss.

"It's okay. I thought Fortner could give me some tips on compost."

Bump senses I'm up to something. He knows how resistant I've been to giving Fortner a chance.

I tinker with the stall door to avoid Bump's eyes. "I'll bring him right back. Promise."

Fortner sets his hammer down on the bin and moves to follow me. He seems curious too.

I'm a bundle of nerves as Fortner walks with me to the root cellar. He doesn't wear boots, like most of the men around here. Instead, his steps are soft, nearly silent, in his moccasins. They extend almost to his knees, where a bulge appears beneath his pants. He must be hot, but he doesn't sweat nearly as much as Bump. It's hard for me not to stare as I walk beside him and struggle to find a way to start the conversation.

"Here's the crate." I move down into the cellar and point to the bin of old jars. "I figure we might just dump the old food into a compost pile. What do you think?"

"That much scrap? Probably just attract rodents. I'd save it. Use it for roughage. Chickens will like it."

I look at the shelves I've just emptied, frustrated that I've wasted all this time removing preserves I should have saved. Fortner senses my disappointment.

"How about I push it over here in the corner? That way it won't get mixed in with the new jars."

I'm relieved he's willing to help. I want so badly to do things right around here. Fortner eyes the pile of broken jars and spilled food. "I'm a bit clumsy." I laugh, but really I'm embarrassed.

Fortner sets the crate in the back corner and looks around for something to hold the broken glass. He settles for a sheet of milled wood, which he begins to use as sort of a dustpan, moving shards onto the rough plane.

I bend to help him. "Kat said you've been trading with the Ute for years."

"That's what Kat says?" He neither confirms nor denies the gossip.

"Says you know all there is to know about herbs and plants. Even medicine."

He looks at me now as if he suspects I've got bigger intentions than starting a compost pile.

"You sick?" he asks, looking at me with eyes the color of glass. They remind me too much of mirrors, revealing all my shame. I look away.

"Not sick, necessarily. Just . . . well . . . I need your help." My voice drops to a whisper.

He bends to move the smaller shards, working his way around the slimy food. "I'll do what I can, but first you have to tell me what it is you need."

"I need . . ." I can't say it. How can I tell this man I want to end the life of my own child?

Fortner looks at me. Waits.

"I need to put an end to something."

The teeth around his neck clank together against his chest as he stands. "You in a fix?" He looks at my stomach. Kat says I'm not showing nearly as much as I should be at this point, but it's only a matter of time before I can no longer conceal the swell behind loose shirts.

"I'm afraid I might be."

"And you aren't comfortable with that?"

"I don't think Bump should have to handle this right now," I say. "He's under a lot of pressure. Everything is riding on making this a profitable ranch."

Fortner crosses his arms and listens intently.

"A baby will get in the way," I continue. "It's not time. Not yet. I'm just trying to help my husband." I can't tell him the real reason I don't want this baby.

The silence between us feels thick. "I've never been comfortable with that sort of medicine," Fortner says.

"Kat said you'd know what to do. Pennyroyal maybe? Blue cohosh?" My speech spews fast, as if my whole life is riding on this moment. "She said nothing grows around here but that you could get it. You might already have it."

He ignores me.

"Fortner, help me? Please?" I reach out in desperation. "Help me."

He takes a step back and puts his hand on his hip. His thumb rests next to one of his pistols as he leans against the framed entrance. Even at his age, he is a striking man, rugged and worn in a way that brings out the strength of his spirit. He doesn't smile when he gives his answer. "I probably have what you want. And Kat's right, I could tell you what you need to know. But if helping you is what you want, then I have to tell you no. It wouldn't help anybody for me to end that baby's life. And believe me, if this ranch fails to turn a profit, it won't be that child's fault."

I turn my back to him. How can I convince him this is best for everyone? So many lies.

"How far along are you?" he asks.

I can barely say it. "Four months."

"It's too late. You'll risk your own life. Or deliver an unhealthy baby. Nothing I can do."

"That can't be true." I face him again.

"I won't be responsible for your life. Understand?"

"No, Fortner. I don't understand anything." My voice tightens as I fight tears, try harder to maintain control.

"What's there to understand?" Bump peeks around Fortner and looks into the cellar. "Everything okay?"

Fortner steps to the side to let Bump enter. "Wow, Millie. The cellar looks great."

I manage a nervous grin. "All ready for new preserves," I say. "Fortner says we should save this for roughage." I point to the crate of the old canning jars.

"Good idea," Bump says. "Need anything else?" He gives me a strange look, still trying to figure what I'm up to.

"Nope. Almost done." I add extra pep to my voice and hope Fortner doesn't tell Bump what we've really been talking about.

"Have you been crying?"

"No, no," I say. "I'm just tired. That's all." I look at Fortner for a clue about what he's thinking, but I can't read his expression. *Please, please don't tell him!*

Bump pauses before turning to Fortner. "Well then. You ready to move to the back spring? Need to install a pump and a trough."

Fortner says nothing as he steps back out into the sunlight. He walks away without looking back. Not even once.

The men have spent the morning chopping wood while the goats have kept me focused on work. Every time I drift, one of the babies jumps on me, or a doe gives me a nudge with her strong, bony head. I've trimmed the hooves and practiced milking, a process that seems much easier and faster than with the dairy cows I've milked in the past. Now I find Bump and Fortner bent over a scattered collection of metal parts, trying to fix the old windmill.

"Thirsty?"

Bump nods and Fortner looks at me as if I've just offered him a block of gold. It's been two days since I asked him for help, and still, no herbs. No sign he's changed his mind about helping me. I'm getting desperate.

"I'll be right back," I say. Bump smiles, and Fortner gives me the eye.

An ice-cold spring bubbles clear in the backyard keeping fresh water at the ready. We've rigged porcelain pipes to an underground cistern "so it won't freeze come winter," as Bump explained. For now, we're still in the full sweat of summer and the thought of anything frozen sounds good. As I bend to fill glasses, I can no longer ignore my bulging belly, and I'm certain Bump has noticed it too. Fortner's right. I've let this go on too long. Too long. I am such a fool for not realizing my situation sooner.

I'm four months into this journey, and I have found no way out. I have been tempted to drink the fermented contents from the root cellar. I've considered a brew of poisoned berries or a tumble down the stairs. Awful thoughts have rattled my brain, as though the Devil himself were braiding his way into my being. Yet here I am, moving from one day to the next with my belly blooming, ribs expanding, and womb swelling. Tiny bones form, new blood pumps, and a fragile soul sprouts within me.

It's nearly too late now to fix this, and yet it's all I think about.

The cold water runs through my fingers as I fill three glasses. An orange tabby cat greets me, one of several strays that have claimed the barn as their own. When I lean to pet her, my eye catches movement nearby. A branch bends. A twig snaps. Some leaves rustle. There's no doubt. Something is moving within the underbrush on the other side of the river.

Sloth trained me not to make a movement or a sound when trying to spot something. Now I am crouched low, curious, with all my weight on the balls of my feet. I can stay balanced only a short time before my toes go numb, but I hold the stance, challenging myself the way I would when I was a child. Looking for furred and feathered friends in the forest. I expect to spot a chipmunk. Maybe a shrew. I'm sure it's nothing big, like a bear, even though many of the trees around here are marked by claws, and we've spotted them foraging in the forests not far from the house.

The tabby cat purrs louder now as she rubs my legs, stepping on my boot and nudging me with the top of her head. She tells me I belong to her, marking me with her scent to warn other hungry cats away from this woman who shares scraps.

I scan the wood line, looking for contrast, for movement, for anything. But I see nothing. Hear nothing. "So much for new friends," I tell the cat. She meows, and that's when the leaves move again near the water's edge.

I look up just in time to catch the white tufted ears of a much larger cat, twitching. Not just a cat. A lion. A mountain lion, just like the one I saw displayed in the general store. I have no gun, no knife, no way to defend myself. So I sit still and stay silent. And I pray.

Please, God. Keep us safe.

The lion stares at me with her yellow eyes. Every part of my body fills with alarm.

Please protect Bump. And Fortner.

I pray in silence, hoping God can really hear my thoughts, the way Mama always promised.

Make this lion go away.

I remember Mama's story about Daniel in the lions' den. How his faith kept him safe.

Dear God, please. Please protect this baby.

As the words form silently in my head, I realize I have just asked God to keep this life inside me from harm. After begging Him to rid me of this baby, to give me a fair chance in this world before I become a mother, I am suddenly praying for this soul to be safe. Is it imaginable that I can love this child?

Focus, Millie. I can't think about that right now. I keep my eyes on the lion, repeating my prayer over and over again in my head, trying to keep the tabby cat from drawing the predator to us. There's no doubt, the lion's patience will outlast mine. My legs begin to cramp. A rise of needles spreads up my calves. I can't stay in this position any longer.

I have to make a move. Either I stand and face this lion, holding my ground, or I make a run for it. There's no question who would win that chase. So I stand tall, waving my arms and yelling as loudly as I can, hoping to intimidate the feral beast. I throw each of the three glasses at her, one at a time, and they shatter against two separate trees. It's nothing short of a miracle that together, the smashed glass, my loud threats, and the splashing water form enough of a warning to convince the lion I am not worth her time. She turns and takes three graceful leaps until she's out of sight, leaving me only with the sight of her long, curled tail slipping back into wilderness.

I stay in place long after she's gone, too afraid the slightest movement may draw her back to attack. Even the tabby cat gets bored and leaves to nap in the sun. Finally, I move with slow, cautious steps, hoping to reach the safety of the barn.

I'm within ten feet of the broad opening when the lion screams the loudest, fiercest sound I've ever heard. She sounds like a woman being murdered. It's a haunting, evil wail, one that draws Bump and Fortner running, but the lion runs too—full speed from out of the woods, straight toward me, faster than anything I've ever seen. Her tan coat a blur against the browns of the mountains, her padded feet pounding the ground with each rapid thrust. I make it into the barn just as Fortner draws his pistol and fires. I dart behind Bump, latching my nails into him so fiercely, I've likely drawn blood. Fortner fires again, and the ear-piercing echo slams against the hollow chambers of the barn. The whole world shakes.

Bump grabs me. I'm out of breath and trembling. "It's okay," he says, pulling me against him. "It's okay. We're okay." He brushes his fingers through my hair and holds my head firmly in his palm, trying to steady me.

"She's gone," Fortner says, holding his pistol out for another shot, just in case he's wrong.

"Gone or dead?" I ask.

"Gone," Fortner says, keeping his eyes on the woods. "For now."

My shock wears off slowly as I retrace the events for Bump. I have just gone head-to-head with a mountain lion. A lion! "I was terrified."

"Thank goodness Fortner's quick with a gun," Bump says.

Fortner's eyes are set in a pensive gaze. I wonder how many times he's used that gun to kill something. Or someone. With his buckskin pants and strand full of teeth, he's clearly an excellent hunter. Did he miss that lion on purpose? The thought terrifies me.

I want to know more about Fortner and the stories he has buried here. He's been living on our property, cleaning his guns mere feet from where I sleep, and I've never dared ask him anything about his past. "Kat says you left this ranch when you were a kid."

"Kat says a lot of things," Fortner answers. He paces the large opening in the barn and watches the woods.

I choose my words carefully, not wanting to sound like a gossip. I also don't want to make Fortner feel threatened. If I anger him, he could tell Bump about the baby. I can't let that be the way my husband finds out. "I don't mean to pry." I frame my words carefully. "But I need to know if lions are always a problem here or if this was just a once-in-a-lifetime scare."

Fortner walks out of the barn a few feet, still within view. He stares up at the house but says nothing. Bump and I stand in the barn, where we feel safer, and watch Fortner pace back and forth, gun still in hand. "I hated to see them lose this place." His soft voice is carried away by the wind.

Bump asks, "Your parents?"

Fortner nods. "I grew up here. Learned to swim right there in the river."

"I can't picture you as a child." I smile, trying to ease the awkwardness between us.

Fortner turns to look at me. He pulls his cowboy hat from his head. "Years can do a lot to a man." He returns the smile, a glint of boyish charm in his eyes. "Right here's where I learned to ride. Fish. Hunt. About killed me when they lost this place."

"What happened?" I ask softly.

Bump gives me a look as if I've crossed the line, but Fortner doesn't seem to mind my asking. "Bad luck, I guess."

"Was it the drought?"

Fortner seems surprised I know so much, arching his brows in a quick peak. "That and a few other things."

Bump turns to pull a pistol from the shelf and says to me, "Keep this on you. Scares me to think what might've happened."

Fortner eyes me taking the pistol. "I didn't kill her, if that's what you think."

Bump and I both wait for more, ready to hear the whole story from this man Sheriff Halpin warned us about. The one who just saved me from a mountain lion and who has spent every day helping us build this ranch back from disaster. The one who has kept my secret, although he still hasn't given me a way out.

Fortner comes closer and leans against the wall, his long legs crossed one in front of the other. His pistol still shines in his hand, the worn metal grip fitting tight against his dirty palm. I clutch my own gun, just in case. "I didn't kill her," he repeats. I don't know if he means Ingrid or the woman who lived here before us. But Fortner gives us nothing more.

After waiting through an uncomfortable silence, Bump finally breaks the tension and says, "How 'bout we get back to work."

"Thank you. For stopping the lion," I say to Fortner, trying to keep my voice from cracking on the word *lion*.

Fortner nods. "She'll be back."

Chapter 14

By August, the winds drive walls of dust across the pastures, swirling and twisting the currents into miniature tornado spirals that Fortner calls dust devils. The river is now barely more than a stream, the bright wild blooms have withered, and thin patches of grass bend in thirst, as if they bow on their knees and beg for mercy. Even the ponds have shrunk, revealing hard, crusted rims.

"I can't imagine what this place was like in a real drought," I say as I help Bump stretch strands of wire across another mile of fence line, careful not to let barbs pierce my leather gloves. Fortner is probably fifty yards ahead of us, clearing slash from the fence, but the bright sun sends his image to me in waves, a hazy blur blowing across the horizon. He hasn't brought up the alleged murders since the day in the barn, and neither have we. Bump's too grateful for Fortner's help on the ranch, and I'm too distracted by my own sins to worry about Fortner's.

"Millie? You awake?" Bump pulls me from a daydream, asking a second time for me to tack the next strand to the post. No matter how hard I try, I can't keep my mind on the work today.

I keep hearing Fortner's answer when I asked him for help. "It's too late."

"Can't believe we're usin' devil's rope. Worst thing for horses," Bump says, tugging the barbed wire and bringing me back to the here and now. He doesn't like the idea of fencing at all, much less barbed wire. Horses have been known to plow right through it in a stampede, resulting in painful injuries and sometimes deadly infections, but we need separate pastures for the stallions and round pens for the broncs, not to mention safe foaling pastures for the broodmares and pens for branding the cattle.

Bump has chopped wooden runs for large sections of fence, but we're also using coils of barbed wire we've found in the barn and strands we were able to salvage from the original fencerows. "Makes no sense to waste it," I say.

Bump nods but grumbles. He's not sure it's worth the risk.

At nearly five months pregnant, my stomach is nearly too swollen to hide anymore, even if I am, as Kat claims, "one of those lucky girls who never gets big." As I stand to hand Bump another width of wire, he stops and stares at my middle. "Millie?" he asks. "I can't ignore it no longer. Is there somethin' I need to know?"

I pretend I don't hear him. I reach for a hammer and begin to nail the wire to the wooden post, still half hoping this pregnancy will evaporate like the water from our ponds.

"Millie?" he asks again. I can't tell if his voice is tinted with anger or sadness or just a curious desire to get an answer. I fear the worst. What will happen if I tell him everything, right here, right now? Will he believe me? Will he leave me? Will he forgive me? Will he ever get over the hurt?

He moves closer to me and places his hands on my belly, smoothing my blue cotton dress tight across the swollen mound.

I've already outgrown all my pants, so I've resorted to working in housedresses. "Either you've been sneakin' seconds, or we're gonna have us a baby." He is smiling, and before I even realize what I'm doing, I start to cry.

"What's wrong?" he asks, moving his attention from my stomach to my eyes. "Aren't you happy?"

I can't pull words from my lungs. Instead, I lean my head against his chest and sob.

"It's a good thing," Bump assures me. "Faster than we planned maybe, but it's good, Millie."

My thoughts don't reach the wind. Every worry, every ounce of shame lies just beneath the surface. And Bump, my sweet, honest Bump, has no idea why I'm crying.

"I'm gonna be a father." He laughs, kissing me before he kicks the fence post with a burst of excitement. "I knew it, Millie. Why on earth didn't you tell me? I've been dyin' to ask you for weeks."

More than anything, I want to tell him. But instead of telling Bump the truth, as I should have done from the start, I do nothing but shrug.

"And tell me the truth, why are you cryin'?"

I shrug again, turn away.

"You're gonna be a real good mother, Millie. I got no doubt." Bump shouts down the fencerow to Fortner, "We're havin' a baby! A baby!"

Fortner waves his hat in the air and smiles.

It's just like Bump to have no doubts, no worries. But what if he knew how awful this really is? He pulls me back to him, puts his hand to my belly, and stoops down to talk to the baby. "You're gonna love it here, Little Bean. You got the prettiest, sweetest mother in the world. Just wait till you meet her."

He calls this child his little bean. Except for a brief moment of absolute terror when facing the lion, I've never thought of the baby as anything, really, but a curse. But as Bump speaks, I feel a rising bubble from my womb. The baby moves inside of me, and my body reacts. It's the first time I've felt this, the proof of life within me, and its power is indescribable.

I look down at my swollen middle, move Bump's hands over the rise, and imagine this child, this little bean, listening, reacting, and reaching up for us.

"Do it again," I tell Bump.

"Do what?"

"Say something. Talk to her. I think she hears you."

Bump drops to his knees. He leans close to my belly and says, "Of course you hear me, Little Bean. Your mama thinks you don't know what's goin' on out here."

The baby kicks again, a tiny, gentle swell of pressure, like a marble rolling beneath my skin. Nothing Bump can feel, but enough to let me know she is here, and she is fighting for me to give her a chance. In all my life, I have felt nothing like this. Nothing so strong, so real. I can only think of one word to describe this feeling. *Awakening.*

Bump's eyes are moist. I think he's about to cry too, but instead he stands and looks up at the rising mountains, down at my swollen belly, and says to me, "I sure never dreamed I'd ever be this lucky."

Chapter 15

September. It's been four months since we left Iti Taloa, and now we are waiting at the depot in Longmont for Mr. Tucker and Janine to arrive for their first visit from Mississippi. "Thank goodness Oka's comin' with 'em," Bump says. "We could sure use the extra help, especially when the baby arrives." He sounds tired, as if the hard work is finally getting the better of him. He's never once complained, but since he found out I was pregnant, he does everything in his power to stop me from lifting, climbing, or straining in any way, even though it means more work for him.

"They're bound to be exhausted," I say. "I think they had at least three transfers. Long ride on a train."

"Yep. Would have been too stressful for the horses. Let's hope they make the drive in good shape. Hot time of year to push 'em up from the south. Especially with the foals."

"When will they arrive?" He's told me a thousand times, but I want him to tell me every detail of the plan again and to promise me Firefly will be safe.

"Within a day or two, I'm bettin'. Week at most. Mr. Tucker

and Fortner will stay in town with me until the herd arrives. We'll help move 'em up to our ranch from here."

I try to imagine Firefly in the horse drive. "Hope they didn't push them too hard."

"Better than being shipped. They stuff 'em into those stock cars. Worse than a circus train. Minus the tigers and monkeys and gypsies." There is a bitterness to Bump's mention of the gypsies, a degrading tone as he insinuates River's people are the equivalent of circus animals.

This stings. Bump knows I chose him over River, and he knows it wasn't an easy choice for me. But it's the first time he's mentioned the gypsies since the day I made my decision and joined Bump for the Texas Stampede. His resentment seems to come out of nowhere. I don't know what he's thinking, or why, but the last thing I want to do is make him feel threatened by a memory. I ignore his remark and step forward to get a closer look at the station.

It's seven in the morning, and the air is already thick with dust. A small uniformed man pushes a cart toward the rails. With bent back and a heavy frown, he walks as if some weighty worry might drag him under the wheels of the train. He stops at the edge of the track and waits to unload bags. If he leans one inch farther, he'll be a goner.

It wasn't so long ago I felt like this man, and some days I still do. But now, despite a baby in my womb and the threat of mountain lions and wildfires and drought, plus a ranch hand who may or may not be a killer, I am learning to love the west. The way the air whips around me in currents, always blowing. How the sun shines bright with warmth, and the skies spread blue to the flat eastern edge of the horizon. Never a gray, sad day to be found. I have set my pulse to the slow, steady rhythms of the mountains. When the pale moon peaks beyond the rocky crown and the coyotes sing their night hymns, the blood within me steadies and I almost believe I am home.

I move back to Bump's side, shielding my eyes from the glare of the sun as we turn toward the sound of a screeching whistle. Children squeal, mothers tighten their grips, fathers adjust their hats, and the broken man at the rail's edge still doesn't move.

The black engine chugs and tugs my grandmother to us. Bump seems distracted. I bite my nails. He doesn't seem to notice.

I follow Bump's stare to a mother holding her baby. Unlike me, Bump grew up with a huge family, playing constantly with siblings and cousins, nieces and nephews. I don't have any idea what to do with a baby, but since the day in the pasture, when Bump called her his bean and our child responded with a soft dance, I have tried my best to put away my questions.

I went from begging God to strip my womb of life to crying a desperate daily plea for this baby's safety, but I still have uncertainties. When doubt creeps in, I remember Mr. Tucker's words to Bump, when he offered him this ranching job. "Ready as you'll ever be." And I try to carry on. When Bump calls this baby his own, I don't argue. I go along, pretending everything is right with our world.

"Millie?" Bump's voice sounds strange. It's clear he's got something on his mind. "How long has your stomach been botherin' you?"

Before I can answer, the train whistle blows again, closer, louder, and the brakes squeal as steel scrapes steel. Suddenly the empty platform is filled with travelers spilling from the passenger cars like ants. Those who have been awaiting their arrival swarm to offer a hug or handshake, a howdy or a hello.

Bump and I stay back from the crowd, tilting ourselves under the eaves of the depot, watching for Mr. Tucker, Janine, and Oka to enter our new world. We hear them before we see them, as Janine's signature shriek pierces the air. "Millie?"

I laugh and say, "Guess who?" hoping to get Bump's mind on a different track.

"Millie?" Janine chirps again, sweeping her high heels so quickly across the platform she nearly steamrolls a toddler in a white dress. I move to meet her as my mouth stretches into a smile so sweet, I ache from joy. I hold her in a hug until I have to let go. I am swollen with so many emotions, I nearly burst as Janine whispers, "We miss y'all so much."

"I miss you so much more," I tell her. I can't stop smiling as I reach to give Mr. Tucker a hug. Oka too. The way my grandmother holds me, close and long, reminds me of Mabel, of someone who knows how to care.

"Janine tell you the good news?" Mr. Tucker doesn't direct his question to either Bump or me. We both signal no, and he pulls Janine's left hand into the air. "This lil' gal's gettin' hitched."

Janine's smile is wide as she wiggles her fingers, showing off the biggest diamond ring I've ever seen. It's not the diamond I'm impressed with, though. It's how happy Janine and Mr. Tucker are as they announce their engagement. Mr. Tucker, who usually tugs his mustache with bravado or pulls a drag from a snipped cigar, puts his arm around his beaming bride-to-be. Janine barely reaches his shoulders, even in the highest heels she can find. She leans into him now after waiting years for him to take her hand.

Oka steps back a bit, remaining quiet. I smile to let her know I'm happy she's here, but her eyes droop with worry, fatigue.

"Tell 'em how you popped the question, honey." Janine sure hasn't dropped the honey, sugar, and sweetie from her speech, but it no longer bothers me.

"Took two weeks to plan," Mr. Tucker says, grinning at Janine. They act more like classroom sweethearts than middle-aged adults who've known each other for years.

"Two weeks?" I ask, impressed.

Oka sighs and nods, as if she's already heard this story several times. Janine adds, "You should have seen it, Millie! The entire arena was packed. Not an empty seat in the house."

"You proposed during the rodeo?" I take a second look at the stone. It's much too big for Janine's miniature frame. Just her style.

"Fourth of July. During the grand entry," Mr. Tucker says, beaming. "Right after the flags."

"He had it written out in flames, Millie!"

Oka raises her eyebrows as if she doubts this detail. I laugh.

"True," Mr. Tucker agrees. "I propped up that microphone, and I said, 'Janine, I've got something I've been meaning to ask you.' And then . . . all lit up across the floor . . ."

The couple talks in sync now, finishing the story as if they've rehearsed. "'Marry me.'"

With this, Mr. Tucker delivers a kiss and Janine giggles wildly. "I don't know if any of this would have happened if Bump hadn't tricked you into dancing with me."

Bump slaps Mr. Tucker on the back with a hearty, "You're welcome," but I catch his eyes drifting back to the woman and her child.

"Who're you kidding?" Mr. Tucker chuckles. "That dance

was my idea from the start." Then he gives us a wink and adds, "But enough about us. Poor ol' Mrs. Reynolds here has had to put up with this all the way from Iti Taloa. We best give the woman a break or else she might hightail it right back to Mississippi."

With that, the attention shifts to Oka, and I finally have a chance to give her a proper welcome. She's wearing the faded dress she wore to our wedding. Her hair is braided the same too, only now she seems more nervous and unsure. I figure it's probably the first time she's ever left Mississippi, and I want to tell her I know how she feels.

"I don't know how you survived the trip with these two," I tease, "but I'm sure glad you came."

Oka puts her hand on my stomach and smiles.

Janine notices. "Millie?" She is too stunned to squeal. "Looks like we aren't the only ones with a big announcement!"

Mr. Tucker rolls out a deep, heavy chuckle and pats Bump's shoulder. "Well, heck, boy. You sure didn't waste no time!"

Bump doesn't smile. Instead, there's a shift in his eyes, a subtle pulse in his neck, and a change in his stance. He looks down at my stomach and says, "Seems that way, don't it."

It isn't like Bump, to act so cold. Fear shoots through me. *Does he know?*

Mr. Tucker shrugs and says, "Should get our luggage."

Bump follows him to the cart, and I lead the women inside the depot. "Enjoy it while we've got it." I point them to the lavatories, trying my best to forget Bump's strange reaction. Oka smiles, but Janine doesn't seem to catch what I'm saying. I don't tell her that she'll be using an outhouse for the next few weeks. Despite our best efforts, we haven't had a chance to run water indoors. Something more important always comes up.

We take our time to freshen up before heading back outside to meet the men at the truck. Fortner has waited here, and we make a quick round of introductions. He stays quiet, offering polite handshakes and smiles. Oka smiles at him, but Janine eyes his bullets and bones, and it's obvious she isn't quite sure what to make of our strange ranch hand.

"Could take us a week or so to bring the horses in," Bump tells me. "You sure you'll be okay? Fortner can stay with y'all." Janine gives me a look as if to say there's no way she wants Fortner staying with us.

"I'm not worried," I tell Bump, trying to get my husband to look at me. He keeps his eyes on the ground.

"No boys allowed," Janine stresses. "We'll be living it up. I brought nail polish. Perfume. And chocolates shipped special. Not easy to get with the war. I plan to remind this girl what it means to have fun." She finishes with a wink.

Oka scoffs.

"Well, don't spoil her too much," Bump says, finally starting to thaw a little. "She'll be wantin' to run off to the city. Or join a band of gypsies." Another unexpected stab.

"Never." I smile, hoping he'll stop acting so standoffish. "Stay safe." I tug him to me. "And take extra care of Firefly for me, please."

Bump offers me a quick peck good-bye, while Mr. Tucker lays a passionate kiss on Janine. Oka steps back, uncomfortable with their open affection, and Fortner laughs.

"It'll be our first time apart," I remind Bump, hinting he might want to leave me with a better kiss than the one he offered. He doesn't. So I pull him into a final hug and whisper, "I love you." He leaves it at that.

We leave the men in town where they'll wait for the drovers to arrive with the horses. I drive the truck back to the ranch, struggling a little with the steep climbs and trying to focus on my guests while managing the constant shifting of gears. I'm so overjoyed to be with Janine and Oka, I try not to ruin it by worrying about Bump's behavior at the depot. "Just another hour or so," I promise. "It's just slow going on these roads. Is this your first time away from home, Oka?"

"Yes," Oka says. "First time." Her voice falls flat, and she sounds exhausted.

"It's different here, isn't it?" I try to make her feel more comfortable. I've been here an entire summer, and I still feel overwhelmed at times.

Oka nods and watches everything with wide and cautious eyes.

"I remember the first time I ever saw Colorado," Janine pipes in, pinning her hair beneath a scarf to block the wind. "I couldn't believe how dry and brown everything is here. It's as if the whole state is dead. Or dying. Or burning. Or burned." We cross a bridge with no water underneath. "See what I mean? They call that a river!"

I laugh, and Oka leans to examine the evaporated water route. "Just wait till you see the ranch. I promise, it's absolutely beautiful."

Oka keeps looking out the window, taking it all in, not minding the way the wind whips loose wisps of her hair. "Did you know Oka runs a store, over in Willow Bend?" I ask, shifting focus on Oka again.

"That right?" Janine asks.

Another nod from Oka. Janine struggles to continue the

conversation. "You sell clothes?" Her voice lifts, excited by the possibility.

"No," Oka says. But she adds no more information. I sense she is overwrought by Janine's rapid speech, her quick change of thoughts. Like all the Choctaw I've ever seen in Iti Taloa, Oka's conversations move slowly, her intonation stays flat, and her stories are rarely about herself. Janine is a complete contrast.

"It's an old trading post," I explain, trying to remember details Oka shared in the letter she gave me just before we left Mississippi. She enclosed it with our wedding gift, a list of things she wanted me to know about her family. "More of a general store now. Oka manages the whole place by herself. Fuel. Lunch counter. And everything else you could possibly need. Right, Oka?"

"My son help me. His boys too." She refuses to take the credit.

Oka has left her entire family for me. She has sacrificed so much to make this move. I feel a surge of guilt, even though she hasn't yet said how long she plans to stay. I can only imagine how her son must feel about her visit. I'm sensing Oka is having second thoughts, and I hope she doesn't decide to return home with Janine and Mr. Tucker in a few weeks.

"I think it'd be fun to run a store," Janine says. "Especially if I could sell clothes. I always say, there's nothing you can't handle if you have the right outfit. Most people could really use my help."

Janine keeps me laughing, but Oka doesn't react at all to Janine's rambling. It's as if she tuned her out hours ago. Janine doesn't seem to care, though. She goes from chatting about fashion to filling in details about her wedding plans to gossiping about the rodeo guys back home.

"How's Firefly?" I ask quickly when Janine finally breaks for air.

"Oh, she's been plumb pitiful without you, Millie. She mopes around, won't eat. Cauy ended up leaving her pastured at night. Couldn't take her in with the other mares because she was kicking the stall. Tore up her hooves. The farrier said it would do no good to shoe her. We were worried she'd do damage to her leg."

"Don't tell me she's gone lame!" I can't stand the thought of her being injured.

"No, no. Just stubborn is all."

"I can hardly wait to saddle up again," I admit. "It's been too long."

"You probably shouldn't ride in your condition, honey." Janine moves her hand onto my stomach, and I flinch. "I want to be a mother more than anything," she adds. "You're so lucky, Millie."

Shame overwhelms me. I drive the rest of the way in silence. Janine talks, but I barely hear a word she says. My mind is listening to another voice, a tiny, fragile bean that sings, "Here I am."

By the time we arrive home, Oka seems eager to escape Janine. She walks away from the two of us, taking in the scene. I leave her in peace, escorting Janine into the house and making three trips to carry luggage from the truck. When I finish, I find Janine staring at a chamber pot. "Please tell me you have indoor plumbing."

"I tried to warn you," I say, laughing. Janine isn't amused. "Sorry," I admit. "It hasn't been top on our list."

"Honey, nothing should top an indoor restroom. You're pregnant, for heaven's sake. I'll speak to Cauy about this."

"It's not so bad," I say, secretly hoping Mr. Tucker will indeed help us figure out how to get indoor plumbing as soon as possible. "We also only have one bed, so I'm afraid we'll have to make do."

"My goodness, Millie. I had no idea we'd sent you kids to the middle of nowhere with not as much as a bed to sleep on or a faucet to drink from."

"We're fine, Janine," I assure her. I can't imagine what she would have said if she'd seen the place before we fixed it up. "It's actually been kind of fun, living off the land like this. Every day I do something I never thought I could do. Everyone should get this experience."

"No, thanks!" Janine tilts her nose with disgust.

An hour later, Janine is calling my name from the outhouse. "How does this work?" She swats flies.

Oka shoots her a look from the porch, and I can't hold back my laughter. "You've never used an outhouse?"

"Never!" Janine says.

I smile and tell Oka, "At least she's had the sense to trade her high heels for boots."

Then I move to explain the lime bucket to Janine, who blushes when I show her the scrap paper. "Well, one thing's for sure," she says. "This day's been full of firsts for all of us."

I smile again, but inside I'm worried that Bump may be having a first too—the first time he realizes I am not the girl he thinks I am.

Chapter 16

Before I know it, a week has passed and the men are expected to arrive with the horses. "We'd better make extra," I tell Oka and Janine, scooping three more cups of beans into the pot to make sure we have enough for all the hired hands who are helping drive the herd to our ranch.

Just before sundown, the air fills with the sounds of hooves and the calls of riders. "Right on schedule." I smile.

"My goodness, it sounds like thunder!" Janine says, running outside to meet the men. Oka and I follow.

Bump, Mr. Tucker, and about ten extra hands lead the horses onto our property. It's a breathtaking sight, hundreds of quarter horses moving in against the red-ribboned sunset. Janine and Oka hold gas lanterns to light the fading path, while I dash around to open and close gates, trying to contain the anxious herd within the pasture's boundaries. Another four or five horsemen round off the back of the herd. Fortner directs that group.

Everything is running smoothly until a testy blue roan gets kicked by another who wants the lead. She panics and twists in the opposite direction, launching herself onto her front two hooves, throwing her two back legs up in violent defense.

I am in a bad position, pinned between the fence and the angry horse. I hurry to move to safety, but I'm caught. And I am scared. As the roan becomes more and more upset, the herd shifts from a controlled walk to a frenzied stampede, crowding me against the fence. It'd be different if I were on horseback, but I'm on my own two feet, a tiny, brittle being compared to even one horse, much less hundreds. I try to keep my stomach turned away from the herd, feeling an overwhelming maternal instinct to protect my baby at all costs.

I have no choice but to crawl between the slats of a closed wooden gate and find safer space inside the pasture, but at six months pregnant, bending and crawling is no longer an easy maneuver. I scramble to find the right position, while the roan continues to buck out of control. This time I am caught in her aim. Her right hoof clips my gut, slamming me back against the wood. Finally, she makes room and bolts away from the herd with aggressive jolts. About twenty horses follow her lead.

"Fortner!" Bump yells, breaking away to follow them in pursuit. No one seems to have noticed I got kicked.

Swinging his horse around, Fortner joins the chase. Two extra drovers pull out from back to help, while the others try to prevent the rest of the herd from following the runaways. Mr. Tucker keeps the lead. I pull myself off the fence, pumped full of adrenaline, and hurry to close the gate behind the last of the horses that stayed with the main herd.

Mr. Tucker begins counting the horses that have made it. The other cowboys turn to help Fortner and Bump, who are still struggling to catch the runners. They're too far away now for me to see them in the darkening dusk, especially with all the dust kicked up during the stampede, but I can hear their voices calling back and forth. "This way! Cut back! Here they come!" I sag against the fence as the pain swells. I clutch my belly, where a thin strip of blood spreads across my cotton shirt, and I hope the wound is only skin deep.

Within minutes, Fortner returns, leading the rogues back toward the pasture. Bump rides on the other side as I handle the gate. The other hands stretch across the back to keep them moving toward the opening. All but the roan move in. She resists, not wanting to move through the unfamiliar barrier. Bump has no choice but to throw a rope. He catches her with the lasso, causing her to snort and squeal, upsetting the rest of the herd even more, but somehow Bump manages to work her into the pasture, where I quickly pull the gate behind her. As soon as the rope is released, she bolts again, but this time the headstrong horse is safely contained. She doesn't like it, though, roaring almost as furiously as a penned stallion.

Emotions are high, and I don't dare call attention to myself in the midst of such an important moment for Mr. Tucker. For Bump. Our boss climbs down from his saddle and receives an especially warm welcome from Janine. Oka scoffs again at their display. Stepping toward the house, she says, "I go check supper." The hired hands dismount, removing their saddles and talking quietly about the pay that's due. We still have no barracks, but I'm sure they'll pitch tents here for a night or two before heading back south.

As the chaos begins to settle, I lean against the gate to catch my breath. I've seen others handle kicks before, but none of those cowboys were pregnant. I don't allow myself to consider the worst. Before the adrenaline has a chance to wane, I feel a nudge. I know, without looking, it's Firefly. She nickers softly to greet me, prodding for attention. I turn to her and she nods her head across the barrier, rubbing her face against my own. I tickle her behind her ears, her favorite spot, and kiss her tender nose.

"You found me," I whisper. Pain now spreads across my middle, but I will myself to ignore it. I focus only on the joy of seeing my favorite horse.

Firefly stomps her front hoof into the ground and neighs loudly. Her eyes are still wide with stress. I lean my weight against her and she supports me from across the fence, the closest thing to a hug I can offer from here.

Bump finds me with Firefly. "Big job," I say, removing his hat and running my hands through his hair. The other arm, I leave across my belly. I start to mention the kick, but then I stop. This is his moment, not mine. And he's so happy. I don't want to ruin it. Besides, it's probably nothing to worry about. It was hardly more than a clip, just enough to break the skin and leave a bruise, nothing serious. "Mighty proud of you," I tell my husband.

"Had good help." Bump shuns the compliment and kisses me. "Missed you like crazy."

"Missed you more." I kiss him again, relieved he's come home without the distant behavior he left me with in Longmont. He covers our faces with his hat and returns a long, passionate kiss.

"Don't worry," he says. "We'll make up for it tonight."

I give him a flirtatious shove and say, "We have guests."

"That's right. And they're hungry. You ready for supper?"

"I'll be right behind you," I say. "It's all ready. I just want a few minutes with Firefly. Would that be too rude?"

"Not at all," Bump says, kissing me again before heading to the house. "Don't blame you a bit."

"I'm glad you're home," I call behind him. He turns back and smiles before entering the house.

I move toward the gate and Firefly follows, soothing me with her earthy smells and deep bass sounds. Her tail is still clamped tight and her ears are stiff, twitching. I wait until she calms a bit more, relaxing her ears and lowering her head. Then I undo the latch and release her, closing it behind to make sure no other horses follow. I pet my sweet mare slowly, softly, moving from her black forelock down her sleek, muscular neck, across her smooth, firm back, and down her brown, bulging belly. Then I do it all again on the other side, offering gentle pressure to soothe her sore muscles and humming softly to ease her fear. She blows loud and rubs the side of her face against me, pawing the ground with her right hoof, an eager gesture to let me know she wants my full attention, as well she should.

Within minutes, she begins to relax even more, bending her back leg and swishing her tail slowly in the night breeze. I kiss the white blaze that runs along the bridge of her nose. "I think you'll like it here," I whisper. "Fewer bugs. Not as hot. Spring-fed ponds. Pretty good grass." I wrap my arm beneath her chin, letting my elbow bend back to the crest. Then I lead her slowly to the barn, where I've prepared new bedding in a stall just for her. Bump has tacked a sign to the door with her name burned into a strip of wood. Despite her long journey, she follows me into her new home without hesitation, with complete trust. A new start.

"Promise you won't kick the walls?" I tease her.

She neighs, and I laugh.

The stall is a bit smaller than the one she had in Mississippi, but it's clean and cozy and offers a private sleeping spot when she wants a little pampering. I show her the new water bucket and give her a fresh stash of hay. She drinks, eats, and makes a sound so unique she might as well be purring.

"I bet you're tired." I reach down low, where her legs are marked with black socks, and bend her left front knee, asking her to lie down. She responds, and I slide down with her onto the straw bedding, next to her warm folds. I mold my body to her curves and let my head rest across her massive chest, closing my eyes to let the steady rhythms of her breathing comfort me.

It's more than an hour before I wake in the dark on the floor of the stall, curled next to Firefly. Oka stands above me, holding a lantern, her face etched with worry. She says nothing, but stoops to take a closer look at me. My bones ache as I pull myself up. Firefly does the same, causing Oka to step cautiously out of the stall. Firefly would never intentionally harm anyone, but at nearly twelve hundred pounds, she could do serious damage. Oka seems respectful of this and keeps her distance. As soon as I stand, I feel a deep, heavy pressure between my legs.

"Millicent, you bleeding?" Oka lifts the lantern.

I hold my arms up for inspection, feel my face. A string of cuts from the fence stings across my back and neck, but it is my stomach that contracts in spasms. I try not to cry out in pain. "Oh, Oka," I cry. "The baby!"

"I get help," Oka says, turning to leave me in the stall with Firefly. I am gasping for breath now, holding my belly as cramps seize control. Before I know it, Bump is running to the barn with Oka, Mr. Tucker, and Janine all in tow. Thank goodness the extra cowboys haven't followed. I am angry at myself for putting the baby at risk. Ashamed for causing such a scene.

"Millie?" Bump calls. His temples pound with tension as he lifts me from the stall and carries me home. "What happened, Millie?"

"I got kicked."

"Firefly kicked you?" I've never seen Bump this upset.

"Of course not." I defend my devoted horse. "It was the roan. She spun around and kicked me before making a run for it."

"The roan," he says harshly. "Why didn't you say anything?"

"It wasn't a direct hit," I explain. "I didn't think . . ."

Bump pushes open the bedroom door and signals Janine to prepare the bed. He places me in the chair until extra linens can be draped across the mattress. It takes him awhile to calm down enough to speak, and still his words are fired with alarm. "You could have died, Millie. Did you think of that?"

No one mentions the baby, but as Bump moves me to the bed, Oka pulls hot water from the stove and Janine makes several trips back and forth with a bucket and towels. Bump works to stop the bleeding, to clean the hoof-shaped wound that oozes from my belly, to prevent the loss of a child he believes is his to save. I reach for the towel and try to help, but he snaps it away from me. "Let me handle this."

I give in, too numb to cry. Again and again I hear Jack calling Mama *pathetic*, *weak*, *useless*. Everything I don't want to be.

Fortner takes the truck to fetch Doc Henley, promising to come right back. Janine and Mr. Tucker stay in the living room to give us space. Oka chants in her Choctaw language, and even though I have no idea what she is saying, I know she is asking for help. Like Oka, Bump stays right by my side, bent in prayer, asking God over and over again to save me. To save our baby. I go even further than Oka and Bump. I beg for this child, this baby I didn't think I wanted, to be safe. But I also beg for forgiveness. I'm sorry for all I've done that led to this. "I'm sorry," I say aloud. To everyone.

As the minutes pass and the bleeding slows, Bump's anxiety begins to wane. Oka now sits on one side of my bed, deep in thought. Bump sits on the other side, his face a web of emotions. Within an hour, Doc arrives.

"The bleeding stopped," Bump stands and tells Doc Henley.

He places a large black satchel on the foot of the bed and says, "I should still have a look." Oka and Bump step aside.

"Stay," I tell Bump, reaching my hand out for him. His anger has diffused now, but still, there is heat between us, friction.

"You did all the right things," Doc praises Bump as he finishes the exam. "But this is serious." He continues speaking to Bump, not me. "If there's any chance at all of saving this baby, Millie needs to take it easy. Strict bed rest."

"Bed rest?" I try to remind the doctor I'm in the room.

"Yes, Millie. You need to stay off your feet."

"For how long?"

"Until the baby arrives." He begins to pack his supplies.

"Months?" I don't point out I'm actually due in December, long before anyone expects.

"You'll be lucky if you make it that far," the doctor states. "In fact, you'll be lucky if you make it through the night. We're probably looking at a placental abruption. There's really nothing more I can do, Millie. I'm sorry."

"There has to be somethin' we can do," Bump argues.

"Sure there is," Doc says. "Pray."

Chapter 17

It's been two weeks since I was kicked by the angry roan, and now the whole world is tinted gold. The aspen leaves have yellowed, blazing a stark contrast against their bright white bark, and the elk have shown up to compete for attention, slamming their antlers together with brute force as the rut begins. Wildflower season is nearly at a close, and except for a few remaining asters, the blooms have all blown away in the wind.

"Sorry you got stuck upstairs," I tell Janine, full of guilt that I've taken the only bed and left my guests scattered around the house on floor pallets.

"Nothing to worry about," Janine assures me. "Oka and I are becoming quite cozy as roommates." She laughs.

"I can't believe you're leaving in the morning," I tell her. "Seems like you just got here."

"I've been waiting to give this to you." Janine hands me a package. "It's from Camille." I take my time, careful not to ruin the pretty blue paper. Inside, I find a beautiful leather photo album with pictures taken from all around Iti Taloa.

"Scoot," Janine says, climbing into bed beside me. "This'll be fun."

"Where's Oka?" I lean to peek out the window but don't see her in the garden. Oka has not stopped working since she arrived. She cooks, cleans, gardens, and tends the goats and chickens while Janine keeps me laughing, telling stories about the rodeo crew and filling me in on life back home. "Working?"

Janine shrugs. "Where else?"

We flip the pages together, stopping at each image and laughing as a flood of memories fills the room. "I used to spend hours in that library." I show Janine a photo of the two-story redbrick building where I spent many a rainy day.

"Never been in there," Janine says. I shouldn't be surprised, but I am. I turn the page to find something Janine might recognize.

"Our family's cabin." I point.

"Yep, I was there, remember? The day you fell from the tree."

"That's right." I put the events back together in my mind, the ones that led me here.

"And that was Sloth's cabin." I flip the book sideways to show the right perspective.

"The Suttons' place sure is nice," Janine adds, tapping the photo of the big house.

I rub my fingers across the photo, remembering the swallows that nested above the wide white columns, the heavy wooden door with the brass ring I used for knocking, the box beside the door where I left eggs each morning. "I guess. Never was invited in."

"You're kidding." Janine looks shocked.

"Lived there my whole life and never was allowed past the porch."

"I'll never understand rich people." She sighs.

I snicker and tell her, "You are rich people."

"Well, I sure wasn't until Cauy proposed. Anyway, we don't act like rich people." She scoots closer.

"No, you just don't act like *mean* rich people." With that, Janine flips the page to a close-up of Sweetie, my sweet gum tree. Then the spot on Mr. Sutton's hill where my parents are buried, and the other one where Sloth is at rest with his wife. Then the rodeo arena, the carousel, and the town square.

The entire album is packed with memories, bringing me back to all my favorite places, but one photo in particular brings back feelings I'd rather forget. It's a snapshot of the Miller family's church. It shows the steeple standing tall against a cloudless sky, its stained-glass windows looking dark in the black-and-white image. I look at the photo and think only of the bells in that steeple room. The big black bells that witnessed the entire assault. I turn the page quickly and wonder if I'll ever be able to fully forget, or if the sound of church bells ringing will always sting my soul.

I stay in bed as Janine stands to pack the last of her luggage. "You sure you don't want to stay here with Oka and me?"

"Good idea," Oka says, and I can't help but smile as my grandmother joins us in the bedroom. Janine has managed to win her over, just as she did me.

"As much as I don't want to leave y'all, I admit I can't wait to get back to running water and an indoor commode. Roughing it is not for me. I don't know how you stand it."

"I'm used to it." I shrug.

"You too?" Janine looks at Oka as if I've lost my mind.

Oka laughs and says, "Not so different from home."

"Well, Cauy has already agreed. We're leaving y'all some extra funds to make things a little more comfortable out here.

And don't be afraid to spend it. I'll be ordering you some furniture for those empty rooms, and please, buy something nice for the baby. A pretty doll maybe. A couple of fancy outfits."

"Janine, you've already done too much." I sit straighter in the bed.

"Let me enjoy this, Millie. I want to spoil this little girl something silly."

"Why is everyone so sure it's a girl?" I ask.

"Just a feeling." Janine touches my stomach again. This time I don't flinch. I smile.

"You think it's a girl too, Oka?"

Oka nods.

"What should we name her?" I think of names I like. People and places that bring smiles.

"You mean you're not planning to name her after me?" Janine laughs.

Oka unpacks a shirt Janine has just added to the suitcase. She refolds it and packs it again, much neater and tighter than Janine managed to do. Janine gives her a smirk, and Oka laughs again.

"*Chahta* receive many names," Oka says. It's the first time she's brought up her Choctaw traditions, so I pull myself a little straighter in bed to show I'm eager to hear more.

"What's she talking about? I still don't understand anything she says," Janine teases.

Oka gives her a playful push. They've developed a peculiar relationship in the last few weeks, and they've sure given me tons of entertainment as a result. "We get one name when born. From parents. Birth name. Then later, we get second name. Something family choose. That name for our . . . skills. Things we good at, maybe hunting, swimming, or horses, or beadwork."

"What's your name mean?" Janine asks.

"Oka mean water. That my second name. I save my brother from . . . die in river." Oka imitates someone struggling in the water. She's learned to give us hints with movements when she lacks the English words to express her thoughts.

"You saved your brother from drowning?" I pull the covers over me and pat for Oka to sit beside me.

Janine closes the suitcase and latches the two clasps. Then she plops back down next to me in the spot I've made for Oka.

"Yes," Oka says, as if everyone has saved a life and it's no big deal.

"How old were you?" I prompt her to continue.

"Thirteen. My brother ten."

Janine crosses her arms, impressed.

I love that I'm finally learning more about Oka, and I don't want her to stop sharing. "So what was your name before that one? The one you were born with?"

"*Nahotama*," Oka says. "It mean caring, helping, strong-hearted." She pats her heart, causing mine to strum.

"That's beautiful," I say. "And it fits."

Oka smiles.

"It's hard enough for me to choose one name for the baby," I say, "much less two."

"When she born, you know what name to give her. God tell you. You see. That her birth name. And then she grow, and she learn, and she earn new name. Family name. And that come in time. And then she find her own way. She know herself. Then she find her true name. Her secret name."

"You mean there's a third name?" Janine asks. "For heaven's sake, this is confusing."

Oka continues, patiently explaining the tradition. "When I turn eighteen, I already marry, have babies, but *Ishki*, Mother, tell me, 'Go find true name. One true thing you know about you. Tell no one. Keep secret, between you and God. No one take that from you. Ever. It tell who you are.'"

"That's a beautiful idea," Janine says. "Did you choose a true name, Oka?"

"Yes." Oka makes herself comfortable in the corner chair.

"Well, what is it?" Janine begins to braid my hair, always trying to make me look my best.

Oka laughs. "I never tell."

"Oh, Millie. We have to do this!" Janine chirps. "What would your true name be?"

I rack my brain for a name, something to describe myself, something other than Millicent or Millie. I think of nothing.

"What would you choose? For you?" I ask Janine.

"This is hard, isn't it? I honestly don't know. Maybe, hmm. What do you think?"

"No," Oka says. "Only you choose true name. Secret. Remember?"

"Oh, there's nothing y'all don't know about me. I'm an open book. But . . . I'm going to think about this and come up with a really good one. Something sexy." Janine laughs. "That's it! Sexy!"

"Keep thinking." Oka rolls her eyes.

Janine, Oka, and I end the night painting our nails and rolling with laughter. Janine and Mr. Tucker will be leaving in the morning. There's no way around it: good-bye has come too soon.

After supper, Bump says good night and turns out the lantern. I tell him a little about Oka's names. "If you had to think of one name to describe me, what would it be?"

"Stubborn."

I laugh and elbow him in the ribs.

"Nah," Bump adds. "I guess if I had to give you one name, it would be Loved."

I fall asleep counting my blessings and let my husband hold me tight.

Janine and Mr. Tucker have barely left town when loneliness hits me. I return to the house while Oka heads out to milk the goats. She's managed to wean the babies so we can have fresh milk each morning. She may be still settling in, but I'm already so attached, I don't know how I'll handle it if she ever decides to leave. Janine leaving was hard enough. The house seems too quiet without her constant rambling. I put down my sewing and thumb through the photo album from Camille, looking again and again at the images of home.

My favorite part is the last section, where she's included photos of the people I love. Camille having a picnic under a magnolia tree. Mabel in Diana's kitchen, snapping a mess of string beans. Janine and Mr. Tucker smiling in front of a crowd of rodeo fans. Diana, bright with perfection, sipping sweet tea on her front porch swing. There's also a shot of the gypsy caravan rolling through town. In the right corner of that photo, with a glinting harmonica tip in his white shirt pocket, is River.

I've avoided looking at this photo in front of Janine and Oka, but now that I'm alone, I can't help myself. I'm curious. I wish I knew what became of River. What did he think when Mabel told him I was married?

A surge of excitement moves through me, and for the first time in a long time, I find myself yearning for a man . . . without having to pretend I am Kat. I didn't know I could still feel this way. I close my eyes and picture River, pressing his lips across the harmonica, laughing as we race through the woods. Within minutes, I begin to nod off. Here, in my Colorado bedroom, with a photo in my hands, I am reminded that somewhere each night, a long-haired traveler might still be singing to a heaven of stars, and to one star he named after me.

I wake late in the afternoon to sounds of laughter, light bursts that tip me back into hues of yellow and white, drawing me out of the blue-dark tones of my dreams. "Oh, Kenneth." Kat giggles. "You are some kind of funny."

My eyes open just as Kat touches Bump's arm and hands him a stacked sandwich. He smiles, takes a bite, and says, "Good stuff."

"It's not much," Kat says. "We'll all be happy when Millie can cook again. She makes the best biscuits." Kat passes a second sandwich to Bump and places her hand over his. He lets her keep it there. Smiles at her. She is hand in hand with my husband, calling him Kenneth, laughing and saying "we."

I shake my head, hoping this is nothing more than a bad dream. I am the We. Bump and Me. *We* are the We.

"Did Janine and Mr. Tucker get off okay?" I ask.

Bump quickly pulls his hand from Kat's and moves to my side. He kisses me, only on the head this time. "Yep. I just got back from Longmont. You musta' been in a deep sleep. You never heard me come in."

"Millie," Kat begins. "You're finally awake. I thought I'd come sit with you for a while, but Kenneth won't leave your side. Talk some sense into the man, will you?"

"That's very kind of you, Kat, but no one needs to sit with me. Really. I'm fine."

"You shouldn't have to be alone." She tries to adjust my pillow. I fix it without her help.

"Oka's been extremely helpful." I look around and ask, "Where's Henry?"

Kat waves her hand like she's pushing away the very idea of her son. "Daddy took him fishing, so I'm all yours." She looks at Bump when she says this. I can hardly believe she's flirting with my husband, right here in front of me. Oka would probably tell me it serves me right, since I was just dreaming about River.

"Millie's right," Bump says. "We've got it covered. But I *am* mighty glad you brought these sandwiches, Kat." He takes another bite. You'd think the room was filled with angels by the way he expresses his appreciation.

"Thoughtful man, Millie. Most would be complaining about the bed rest by now." Kat flashes her green eyes my way and takes me back to another childhood memory.

I was only about seven, admiring an afternoon sky tinted a spectacular shade of green, just like Kat's eyes. Sloth looked up and said, "Best be warned of that kinda sky." I asked him why. He said, "It'll trick you. Keep you lookin' at them pretty green clouds while danger be blowin' in the wind."

Later in bed, Bump is quiet. He doesn't kiss me good night, but instead turns his back and seems distant. "Deep in thought," I tell him. "What's on your mind?"

"The war." His voice stays low and quiet.

This surprises me. He's never mentioned anything about the war, even when his brothers were shipped out. "I'm glad you got exempt as a rancher. I don't know what I'd do if you had to leave."

"I guess. But I hate to hear of folks like Kat's husband," Bump says. "All those people over there losin' their lives. Makes me think I should be there too."

"You're needed more here." I roll my fingers along his back and try to get his mind away from Kat. "Even the government admits somebody has to grow our food."

"Well, I ain't doin' too good a job at that either," Bump says. "Can't believe those cows never showed up." He's been disappointed that a deal Mr. Tucker arranged never panned out. We should already have some cattle here, but we only have horses, hens, and goats. He turns to me now, rubs his hand across my stomach, shifts mood. "How's our Little Bean tonight?"

"She's been dancing all day. Here, feel." I move his hands beneath my nightgown and let him touch my bare belly. I slide them slowly across my swollen waist, and for the first time, I don't feel a rising surge of panic as his hand goes beneath my navel. I'm hoping he can feel the baby move, but she stays still.

"I think she's waiting for you to tell her a bedtime story," I tease.

"I don't know any." He doesn't sound like he wants to play along.

"Make one up." I speak gently. "You'll have to learn sooner or later."

"Yeah, I guess you're right." He leans his head against my middle and begins talking softly to our child. "Once upon a time, there was a princess. The most beautiful girl in the world, only she didn't know it. She was smart too. And brave."

I close my eyes and let him take me far away, the way Mama used to do when I would climb into her lap and listen.

"Unlike most princesses, this girl didn't have a good life. Her father was cruel. He made her believe she was nothin' special. And her mother was too sad to care. So every day the girl would stare out into the woods and watch the birds and the deer. She wanted to be like them—happy and free.

"As years passed, many stories spread about the princess. People said she was in danger, that her father had gone mad. Even worse, men were ready to battle for the beautiful princess, who was now old enough to marry. One day a young farmer heard the tale and decided to help her.

"That afternoon he snuck into the castle and gave her a choice. She was nervous, and she wasn't sure if she could trust him. But remember, she was also very brave. So she agreed to leave with the poor farm boy, hopin' he could help her be happy and free.

"She climbed onto the back of his horse and together they rode off into the sunset. They didn't stop until they reached the mountains, and there they lived, happily ever after."

Chapter 18

The cadence of our lives settles after Janine and Mr. Tucker return to Mississippi. Before I know it, it's been a month since Doc Henley told me this baby might not make it through the night. I've stayed in bed for nearly thirty days wondering why. Why don't I get up, run a couple of laps around the pasture, take a challenging mountain hike, ride Firefly across the fields at full gallop? Doc said the only way this baby might survive is if I rest. God gave me what I asked for—a way out. All I have to do is take it. Yet I stay here. Why?

At times I think God must be saying, "I'm sorry, Millie. You're right. You've been through enough. I take it back." Even before the mare kicked me, He had kind of offered me a choice by letting me know there were options, herbs, medicines. All along there were ways to bring a different ending to this tale. He has left it up to me. But there's cruelty in that too. I go back and forth, riding the rift between love and hate, forgiveness and fear. Sometimes I want to make it all disappear. But then I think about Bump, talking to this child, calling her his little bean, falling to his knees when he found out he would be a father.

And then I feel her move inside of me, tiny pulses and tugs as she dances against the pleats of my lungs. My heart swells with love for this sweet soul within me. And just as I start to believe we can do this, that Bump and I can make this work, I remember she isn't his daughter after all. And then I'm back to wanting it all to end. But then I imagine burying this child, and I'm sickened.

I am living a lie, and I don't know how to fix this. I don't know how to make this choice. Either way, someone gets hurt. So I just wait, and hope God chooses for me. That the burden will no longer be mine.

I'm deep in thought when Oka knocks on the door. "Millie? You awake?"

"Come on in, Oka," I say. "Can you believe . . . when we first moved here, I was so tired. All I wanted was to spend just one late morning in bed."

Oka laughs and says, "God give you what you want."

"He's got a wicked sense of humor," I say. "Surely He knows you're the one who deserves some rest. You never stop working." She's not only turned my starter rows into a well-fertilized garden, she's also become a master at trout fishing, spending long hours at the river catching rainbows, browns, and cutthroats. And she's been managing the flock of hens we brought from town. The chickens deliver fresh eggs, which Oka whips into delicious batters using butter she's churned from the goat milk. Now that the days are getting shorter and the hens lay fewer eggs, she's tricked them by hanging a lantern on their cage for an hour after sundown each evening. It's a brilliant solution, one she hopes will keep them laying long into winter.

This week she's been making a pair of moccasins to send

home to her grandson. I watch closely now, trying to learn the craft. As we sit together, I feel such love and acceptance from Oka, I am pulled to open up to her, to say things out loud. I need to put an end to all these secrets, and for some reason, I trust my grandmother more than anyone else. I'm hoping she can give me some good advice.

"Oka." I bite my lip in nervous pulses, "I know everyone's excited about the baby, but to be honest, I don't know if I want this." The words bring fire to my veins. Shame. I no longer consider this baby a curse, but I still don't know if I'm ready to mother Bill Miller's child. The emotions have been hitting me in waves, peaking and crashing. Love. Hate.

Oka nods but doesn't look up from her work. I've just admitted one of the most awful things a mother could admit, and she says nothing. Just keeps pushing her needle through the thick leather segments of the shoes.

"It's not what everyone thinks." I try to explain.

Her fingers continue to work the seam. Her way of listening.

"Bump . . . he's . . . he's not the father." My voice drops on the final word. I can't believe I've said this out loud. For months I've kept this secret. I've been terrified to set it free. But just like that—seven sharp syllables—it's out. I don't feel dizzy or shaky or hot or cold. I just feel numb.

Oka puts the moccasin down on the nightstand and takes my hand. "You wrong, Millicent."

"You don't understand." I figure the meaning has been lost in translation.

Oka squeezes my hand and speaks again. "I do, Millicent. I understand. But the start, it not matter. That past." She puts her hand on my stomach. "Now. Here. You and Bump. This what matters." Oka pats my stomach with two gentle beats. "You no different than others, Millicent. You think you not deserve this?"

Her words crush me. Of course I think I don't deserve this. Who would deserve this? But then I realize what she's trying to say. Bad things happen. Every day. To people everywhere. People just like me.

Oka continues to deliver truth, no matter my reaction. "This baby fighting to be yours. You, the mother she want."

"But what if . . . what if I don't want her?" I whisper. Words too heavy for my voice to hold.

"Hush now," Oka says. "Let this baby choose." She rubs my stomach gently. "This soul can change its mind too. You know?"

Oka has taught me to let the words sink in, to process my thoughts and let words roll from my tongue slowly. *Let this baby choose. This soul can change its mind too. You know?*

"Are you saying this baby chose me?"

Oka nods.

"You don't know, Oka. There's more to this story than anyone knows. This was not my choice, you understand? There was a man. He—" How do I explain what took place in that steeple?

She waits for me to finish.

"I'll never be able to look at this baby and see anything but a monster."

"Listen, Millicent. Listen close." She takes both hands now and leans over me for full attention. "My husband, he not a good man. But never, never, do I say my children a curse. They mine. They choose me. God give them to me. I never look at them and see Boone. I see only my babies. You understand?" She does not cry. She does not raise her voice or show emotion in any way. She simply tells me her tale, leaving it up to me to make of it what I will. "Understand?" she asks again.

"I understand."

"Want to show you something," she says, and then she leaves me alone again. Curiosity gets the best of me, so I leave the bed and follow her upstairs to her room where she pulls several photos from a Bible. She selects one picture from the slim set and hands it to me. Two young boys, shirtless and shoeless, peer out from the image. They wear big, broad, open-mouthed smiles.

"This Jack." Oka points to the boy carrying the other. I am mesmerized by the joy I see on my father's young face.

"This John." Oka touches the younger boy who rides on Jack's back. She may leave out a few letters and twist the verb tense. Even her vowels sound off-key, but Oka's meaning is clear when she says, "Jack take care of John. Of us."

Then she selects another snapshot. "This my favorite."

Jack looks about eight years old. He sits on the porch steps next to his brother, John. They are both looking down at a toddler who sits between them. Jack is touching the young girl's face. Even in the photo I can tell the touch is nurturing, loving. A touch he never once extended to me, his daughter.

"Who is this?" I ask, pointing to the girl.

"Choctaw never talk about our dead." Oka doesn't look up from the photo.

"She died?" I ask.

Oka nods and hands me the picture.

"Your daughter?"

She nods again.

"How old was she?"

Oka holds up three fingers. Her hands shake.

"Three years old?"

Another nod. Tears.

"Can I ask? How did she die?"

"Fever," Oka says, wiping her cheek with her sleeve. I hope she will tell me more, but she adds nothing.

"I don't know how you ever get over a loss like that," I tell her.

Oka is so quiet, I worry I've said the wrong thing. Then she says, "You know this Chahta story? How we carry bones?"

I shake my head and hope she'll teach me everything there is to know about being Choctaw.

"Well, long ago, before my time, when we walk to motherland, if Chahta die, the family wait for bone picker to come. Then we carry bones. We walk for years, and we carry bones, but bones get too much. Some Chahta make trips, back and forth, back and forth, to carry bones. And they heavy too."

She bends her back as if she's weighted down with a heavy sack. I nod to show I understand.

"Well, one day Chief call Chahta together. He say, 'This not smart. This burden too big. It time to make choice. Choose now. Which bones to carry. Which bones to bury.'"

The words hit me, and I know what she is trying to say.

"You see?"

I nod.

"Sometime, Millicent, our past too heavy to carry."

I sit on the bed and look at the photos for a long time. Oka sits beside me, letting it all sink in. Finally, she asks, "You pray, Millicent?"

I'm surprised by the question. "You know I do."

"No, not just for supper. I mean, you pray for other things?"

I nod hesitantly. "Do you?"

"I pray every day, Millicent. I pray for me. For you. For baby. Bump. Everybody."

"You pray for the baby?" I'm surprised to learn others are asking God to protect this child. Maybe I'm not the only voice He's hearing. Maybe that's why this baby still dances within me.

"Of course. Will be nice when she get here," Oka says, putting her hand on my stomach again. "Been long time since I have little girl to hold." And just like that, I know for sure, Kat was right. This pregnancy isn't all about me.

Chapter 19

It's Christmas week. Bump is already snoring as I finish the last of the gifts for his family. I've knitted scarves for the girls, socks for the boys, and stitched needlework patterns for the women. I'll be late getting them to Mississippi, but I'm glad the task is complete.

I've also made a blanket for the cradle Bump built. Oka's helped me sew a set of infant day gowns, as well as cut some small diaper cloths out of the softest cotton we could find. I expect to go into labor any day now. Since Doc warned us the baby could come early, I'm hoping no one catches on. I'm sickened by the lies I weave, and at the same time I'm sickened at the thought of my sweet husband ever learning the truth. There is no easy path. As the days have stretched into months, it's even harder now to know the right thing to do, if there is such a thing.

Our little bean has moved lower this week, and the pressure has been building within me for days. My breasts are swollen, I have no appetite, and I am always on full alert. Nothing goes unnoticed. Not a sound, not a smell, not a sight. I now understand the hesitancy of the mule deer as they try to cross the pasture with their fawns. Fear. Determination. A fierce and primal mothering.

Bump sleeps beside me while I toss and turn, my body readying itself for birth. As I try to imagine our child, I hope only that I can look at her, hold her, love her, without seeing those steeple bells above me. Maybe it's the cold winter winds, or the rise of the mother in me, but this week, something deep within has tilted. I am riled with energy, tethered to this fragile little soul.

The entire house sleeps as I spin thoughts, wide-awake. I'm not afraid of labor. Maybe it's because I've watched countless mares deliver. Even the first-time mothers seem to know what to do when the time comes. They never hesitate to clean the site, groom the foal, and nurse the baby before breaking for water or hay. Oka has been easing my fears as well, telling me stories about the Choctaw women who still give birth the traditional way. "Walk alone to quiet place in woods," Oka explained. There, they deliver their child with no help at all. Then they return to normal chores within a few hours, baby at their breasts. If they can do this, if Oka can do this, I can do this.

By nine p.m., my water breaks. I gather sheets and towels, bowls and buckets. A bottle of alcohol and another of saline. I work quietly, using only the light from one lantern and trying to stay close to the fire. I am careful not to wake Oka, who sleeps upstairs, or Bump, who needs his rest after another long workday. I could be in labor for hours, and I'd rather them both sleep while they can.

For a few hours, I walk through the contractions, counting my soft steps between bends, listening to the wails of the wind. The lonely moans of winter remind me that things change. That one day you can be soaking up sunshine, singing along with the songbirds of spring, flitting with the bees through fields of flowers. And then you turn a page, and you're all alone, in a blank, white desolate world, met only by bitter winds and hungry howls. You can never start to believe the spring will last.

What if Bump learns the truth? What if it's all more than he can take? What if he leaves me, and I'm left to care for this child all alone? What kind of life can I offer her? Have I made the wrong choice? Not just for me and for Bump, but for this baby?

As hours stretch, the pain worsens and my worries expand. The contractions fall heavier now. I begin to recite poetry silently, trying to stay calm. I force myself to breathe to the beat in my brain.

Inhale: I wandered lonely as a cloud
Exhale: That floats on high o'er vales and hills,
Inhale: When all at once I saw a crowd,

The pains become closer, stronger. My body tenses and tightens from deep inside. *Breathe, Millie. You can do this.*

Exhale: A host, of golden daffodils;
Inhale: Beside the lake, beneath the trees,
Exhale: Fluttering and dancing in the breeze.

I walk through the pain, reciting Wordsworth's poetry aloud now. I whisper each line, trying to pull myself from fear.

Continuous as the stars that shine
And twinkle on the milky way,
They stretched in never-ending line

Along the margin of a bay:
Ten thousand saw I at a glance,
Tossing their heads in sprightly dance.

My breaths become short and shallow. I focus on only one sound at a time, moving through the poet's field of dancing daffodils. As I reach the last lines, I am no longer able to breathe my way through the contractions. I think of the horses I watched give birth to their foals. I close my eyes and imagine myself in the pasture with Firefly. In my mind, as the next contraction takes over, Firefly picks up the pace. She runs faster and faster, galloping through the worst of the cramps, carrying me bareback across the prairie with the mountains at our side, the blooms below. She stays with me, running me right through the pain. I cling to the chair, pretending it's her mane. I squeeze my hands. I bend my back. I huff. I puff. We run.

The winter wind blows cold and fierce with a high-pitched scream through the gaps in the walls. With the fresh snow, there's no way we could drive to Doc's Place, even if we needed to. When this contraction hits, I let out a small cry. I hope I haven't woken Bump. He never complains, but it's easy to see the red threads that lace his eyes and the wrinkles that form under his hat. His hands are so chapped they bleed, and he barely finishes his prayers before he's sound asleep each night. I'll wake him when it's time. But for now, as much as I need him, he needs sleep more. When the pain gets worse, I remind myself again of the Choctaw women. I try to be brave.

Hours continue to pass as my muscles contract again, and again, and again. Each time with more intensity. Now I buckle in pain with each hit, letting the cramps crash like waves. As soon as I come up for air, I am slammed again with another heavy breaking crest. Breathe, cry. Breathe, cry. Try not to vomit. Cry. Call out for my mother. "Mama?!"

I don't know where it has come from, but suddenly, I want my mother. I wonder what she would be doing now if she were alive. Would she be here? Would she help me through this? Maybe I'd never be in this situation at all if Mama hadn't died. Or if Jack hadn't beaten her just as I was supposed to meet River. I would have left town with the gypsies, and I never would have met Bill Miller, and I wouldn't be giving birth now, in a cold winter cabin, at the age of seventeen.

But I also wouldn't have Bump.

I fall with another contraction, and this time I can't help myself. I scream in pain. Within seconds, Bump is at my side. "What on earth?" he asks, tripping over the stack of bowls I've placed beside the kitchen table. "Millie? Is it time?" Bump becomes a pile of nerves, bouncing around the house, accidentally knocking towels off the counter.

"Oka," I gasp. "Get. Oka."

Bump scrambles up the stairs yelling for my grandmother. Within seconds, Oka comes downstairs smiling. "I tell Bump to stay upstairs and go back to sleep."

"He . . . didn't listen." Another wave drags me under as Bump barrels past Oka on the stairway and jumps from the third step down to the first floor. I breathe hard and heavy with each rapid breath. And now no amount of poetry will stop the pain.

Oka sits in a chair and begins to work on a quilt. She knows the best thing she can do right now to help me is to be quiet and calm. Bump, on the other hand, stays right by my side, talking a mile a minute, and trying to gather his wits.

I think of Mama giving birth to my brother, John David. How unfair for her to have to go through all this, only to lose her baby in the end.

What if our baby is born blue, like my brother? Bump holds my hand and seems so tender. *Was Jack ever this kind of a man? Before he lost his family? And then his son? Could Bump ever be hurt so deeply that he would build a callused heart, like Jack?*

The next contraction hits, and this time I bite my lip so hard it bleeds. Then another, nearly as soon as the last one ends. And another, and another. As morning breaks, Bump insists I move to the bed. I squeeze Bump's hand hard, and he takes it. Firefly runs faster and faster in my mind, and before I can reach the mattress it's time to push. "Bump?" I half yell, half cry. "I'm pushing!" I lift my nightgown off the floor as Bump lets go of my hand and suddenly, Oka is right here, handing him towels. I brace myself against the wall. I close my eyes. I push. I pray. I push. I pray. With each rapid contraction, I push. I pray.

Before I've fully realized what's happened, Bump is laughing. "It's a girl!"

I collapse onto the bed. Bump shouts again, this time loud enough for Fortner to hear outside in his teepee, "It's a girl!"

The baby cries, and I can't help myself. I laugh, I cry. "Oh, listen to her! What a beautiful sound." Proof. This baby has survived.

"December 21," Oka says, noting the birthday. Mama once said I caused the world to do "an about-face" when I was born on the vernal equinox. Now my child arrives on the winter solstice, and just like that, the world is back in balance. Everything is okay.

Bump's veterinary training has served him well. He places this tiny, blood-streaked being directly to my breast and cuts the cord with a sharp, sterile knife. She nurses instantly, a gentle give-and-take between mother and daughter. There are no words. I have never known such love.

After so many hours of hard labor, I should be exhausted, but my body has been resting for months. I feel as if I could get out of bed right now and run the mountain trail to the prayer circle where I once rode with Kat. I am energized and ecstatic, fueled both by adrenaline and absolute adoration. As Oka helps deliver the afterbirth, I feel relief, release, renewal. And I realize, this is not an end, as I had feared, but a beginning. A beautiful new beginning.

Oka has boiled water, and together we gently clean the baby as she nurses. Her eyes stay closed, and she knows just what to do. "She is so peaceful," I say. "So perfect." How could I have ever, for even a second, not wanted her?

I rub my fingers across every inch of her. Her soft, round head blanketed with a coat of my own dark curls. Her flaccid, chubby cheeks, pumping for sips of colostrum, a word Bump taught me during the last foaling season. Her velvet skin, coated in fine white infant fur. She is strong. She is eager. She is ours.

I trace her tiny outline: protruded belly like a ball, miniature fingers bent round my own, tiny toes on padded feet. She opens her eyes and looks at me. She sees me. Knows me. Her dark blue eyes change within minutes to a deep black, like mine. Like Oka's. Nothing like Bill Miller's.

I am disgusted by my thoughts these past months. All the times I prayed for God to take her back. The plans I made to fake an accident. To drink poison, or worse.

All along, I knew I needed to heal, but I had no idea how to make that happen. Now, with this child in my arms, I think of a song Mama used to sing. *"It is well, with my soul."*

I kiss the top of her head, and *I am well*. It's how Oka said it would be.

"What are we gonna name her?" Bump asks, bending down to give each of us a kiss.

All these months I have avoided choosing a name, resisting that bond with her. But now, as her eyes hold my own, as her swift heartbeat erases all my scars, I know her name. I will never again hear church bells and feel the fiery flames of hell. "Isabel," I whisper, forming the word *bell* into something beautiful and innocent again.

"Isabel?" Bump asks.

"Isabel Anderson," I say, rubbing her soft curls.

"I like it." Bump smiles. "My sister will love it!"

His family is so large, I'd almost forgotten one of his sisters is named Isabelle.

"My mother said the name can mean two things: pledged to God, or God's promise. Either way, I like it." He kisses Isabel's head gently and she pumps her lips to drink faster.

"She loves you already," I tell him.

"She know her daddy," Oka says. And with that, the secret goes deep underground, like the box Mama buried so many years ago. Only this time, I hope no one will ever uncover it.

"I want to give her a Choctaw name too. What do you think, Oka?"

There is a long pause as Oka considers the answer. "How about *Hofanti*?" she finally says.

"Hofanti?" I toy with the sounds. "What's it mean?"

"It mean . . ." Oka thinks of how to say this in English. "It mean brought up, cherished, nourished. It mean protected."

I smile at Bump, and we both repeat the name. "Hofanti," he says. "It's perfect."

Bump and Oka work together in silence, bringing clean cloths until Isabel's small body no longer tints red, and her skin is dry and warm and swaddled in a soft white blanket on my chest. When the work is done, Oka grants us privacy.

Bump climbs into bed with Isabel and me. We lie here, in the quiet early hours after the dawn, looking at our daughter. *Our* daughter. Our perfect, our beautiful Hofanti. Isabel.

And then Bump looks at me. My eyes lock into his, and I feel the heat of tears. "Could there be anything better than this?" I ask him.

He kisses me. "You're already a wonderful mother, Millie."

Tears fall hard now, as the three of us pull together. A family. Bump, Isabel, and me. The We.

Chapter 20

The first few days Isabel nursed a couple of times each night, took several peaceful naps a day, and spent most of her time either sleeping or eating. Other than interrupted sleep, there was nothing hard about it. But by the time we celebrated her first full week of life, she had already begun to cry, a lot, fighting to end her hunger, biting hard when the milk would bring her pain. "Colic," Bump said. "Don't worry. She'll outgrow it."

I'm glad Bump has had medical training in vet school, but I don't always trust he knows as much about babies as he does about foals. This time he was wrong. It hasn't passed. Days have turned into weeks. Weeks into months. Isabel is now three months old, and still my head rings with her screams.

I place Isabel in her cradle for the third time tonight and hope she'll manage to get some sleep. I lie down next to my husband. Kiss him. Move my hands across his chest. Bump deals me a quick peck and then turns his back and pulls the covers. "Try to get some sleep before she starts cryin' again."

I can't remember the last time Bump showed any real desire for me. He's always too exhausted, or in a hurry, or needing to get a job done. Always stressed. I lie against his back, feeling the warmth of his body next to mine, wishing he would turn and kiss me. Touch me. It's not the kind of love I ever wanted from him before. In fact, I did everything I could to avoid being intimate. But now he seems so distant. So cold. I'd do anything to feel his love again, even if it *is* just physical. Instead, he keeps his back to me. I feel invisible.

Within minutes, Isabel's piercing cry startles us both. "Please . . . make her stop," Bump snaps. "She's been cryin' for three hours." He covers his head with the pillow.

"I don't know what else to do," I whisper. I, too, want to cover my head and tune it all out. I've tried everything. Rocking her, nursing her, singing to her. I've changed her diaper cloth, taken her outside in the cold, inside by the fire. I've placed her on her stomach, her back, in our bed. I've fastened her into the cradleboard Fortner made for me and walked her with every speed of stride I could manage, trying to find the perfect pace to calm her. I've placed her in the crib Janine ordered for us, curling up next to it, sobbing along with her. Still, she wails, and for me there is no escape.

"I can't stand it." Bump leaves the bed, taking a blanket and pillow with him.

"Again?" I ask. This isn't the first night Isabel's crying has sent Bump to the extra bedroom floor. I hold her in my arms while she screams herself hoarse.

"I gotta get some sleep, Millie. Headin' up to Estes Park tomorrow to meet with the rodeo producers and work out a deal to buy some cattle from MacMillan." Bump moves upstairs, and I try again to hush our baby.

I sing softly to Isabel, my voice cracking with tears as I rub her stomach in gentle circles. "*Little star, little star, shine, shine, shine. Little light, little light of mine, mine, mine.*" This quiets her a bit. Her bottom lip quivers and her eyelids droop. She's exhausted too. Lack of sleep is getting to all of us, but it seems to be affecting Bump most of all. His temper has flared, and he's said things he never would normally say. "Burned the food again?" or "What exactly *have* you done all day?" or "Would be nice to come in to a clean house once in a while." He seems to resent me now, as if his life would be better without Isabel and me always getting in the way. Just as I had feared.

I finally broke down last week to Oka. "It's not like him. He's so angry."

"Give him time," Oka said.

"But Isabel's already three months old," I argued. "Bump said she'd outgrow it by now."

I stroke her tiny belly, rub my thumbs across her miniature heels, sing every lullaby I know. What I didn't tell Oka is that Bump hasn't been intimate with me in months. No matter how I try. I remember his father's prayer, at our wedding reception. "When times get hard," Mr. Anderson had said, "as they will, and when marriage becomes strained, as it will, and when Kenneth and Millie are so desperate they want to give up and walk out, may they find strength in You, Lord. May their faith draw them back to one another, and at the moments when they need it most, may they remember the love they feel today."

"Please, please," I pray. "Let Bump remember the love he felt that day."

"I gotta send a telegram over to Mr. Tucker. How 'bout we go into town today?" Bump cracks a few nuts and tosses the shells on the ground from where we stand on the front porch.

I beam. "You think it'll be okay to bring Isabel?"

"I think so," Bump says. "We'll be quick."

I offer a kiss and clap my hands together with a surge of joy. I haven't left the ranch in months.

"Let me get Fortner set." Bump steps toward the barn.

"I'll be ready." I rush back inside to change into nicer clothes.

Oka laughs at me as I rapidly change into a dress. She says, "You look pretty."

I blush. "I'm fat, Oka. Admit it."

"No. Not fat. Mother. *Ishki.*"

I move across her bedroom and pick up a beautiful hand-woven basket. "You want me to bring some of your work to the store? See if Sheriff Halpin has room to sell it there?"

Oka shrugs. "Nobody want that."

"Oka, these are incredible. Nobody knows how to make these things."

"Lot of Chahta do this." She takes the basket from me and sets it back down on her floor.

"But look around, Oka. You're the only Choctaw in this town. People are starting to collect this kind of stuff now. And even if they aren't collectors, this isn't just art. It's useful. You could make a lot of money."

She eyes the basket and the pile of beaded necklaces, bracelets. "You think people buy?"

"I have no doubt." I smile and gather a few of the most intricate pieces. Oka helps me stack them in the truck, making sure they won't get damaged during the drive. Then she hands Isabel to me, and Bump takes us away from the ranch.

By the time we get to town, it's nearly noon. "How about we try that diner?" I suggest. "I'm starving."

"Good idea." Bump parks in front of Sheriff Halpin's store, and we walk the short distance to the restaurant. I recognize a few familiar faces across the room, and we make a point to stop and say hello to the reverend and Mr. Fitch who are seated together at a table for four. They gush over Isabel and she cries at the sight of these strangers, Mr. Fitch with a silver mustache, the reverend's balding head shining like a light.

"The new church looks like it's coming along," I tell the reverend.

"It sure is," he says. "Starting the roof tomorrow, if the weather holds out." I look outside at the wild spring weather. Snow is falling in the higher altitudes while the sun brightens the green valleys below. Here, we are caught in an unpredictable mix, with a constant wind to batter anyone on that roof.

"It's bigger than I thought it would be," I admit.

The reverend nods proudly as I struggle to unbutton my coat. Isabel squirms in my arms. "Maybe she can be the first to be baptized in the new building," he says, reaching his finger out for Isabel to touch. She pulls away instead.

Within seconds, Kat appears with Henry. "I hope we didn't keep you waiting." Kat looks like she's just come off of a pinup calendar, and the men respond, as always, to her magnetic pull. Standing next to her, I feel like a whale, which makes Kat a siren, a tall, glamorous siren. I latch onto Bump's arms so he doesn't swim away. I haven't seen her in a few weeks, and it seems she's become even more beautiful since our last visit. Kat smiles and taps Isabel's rosy cheeks. "Join us for lunch?"

"Oh, no, we—" I start to explain that we're spending the day together, just the three of us, but Bump is already pulling two extra chairs to the table. Henry climbs in next to his grampy while Bump holds one chair out for Kat. Then another for me. He sits between us, and I hold Isabel. We're all crowded together so close, it seems accidental when Kat rests her arm against Bump's. But I'm beginning to wonder.

Reverend Baker notices too. He clears his throat and shifts in his seat. Bump doesn't seem to mind. He leaves his arm where it is. "Came to post a telegram today. Have to give my boss the bad news that the cattle never showed." He's still disappointed because the deal Mr. Tucker arranged never panned out.

"You have good news to send too," I say, hoping everyone knows how much Bump has done on that ranch. "Bump's about to buy a stallion," I explain. "We'll be breeding by summer."

"Kat says you've already made a lot of progress," Mr. Fitch adds to my praise.

Bump smiles at Kat. "Mostly on account of Fortner. He might be old, but I never met a harder worker."

"Thank goodness Uncle Halpin didn't hear you say that," Kat says, tapping Henry's elbows to encourage him to move them off the table.

I put my elbows on the table just to make Henry laugh.

"Perhaps it's difficult for him to see Fortner content again," Reverend Baker suggests.

"With all due respect, Reverend, that sounds like a bunch of hogwash," Mr. Fitch argues. "Halpin is convinced Fortner murdered an innocent woman. Maybe two. He's not happy to have a killer on the loose when it's his job to keep us safe."

"Maybe so," the reverend agrees, but I get the feeling it's only for the sake of avoiding an argument. I'm guessing Mr. Fitch is the biggest donor to the church building fund, and the reverend would be a fool to risk those ties.

"One thing's for sure. Love can make a man do crazy things," Kat says. "Take the rut. Did you see the elk last fall? Smashing their heads together like they have no sense at all. Those bulls are a perfect example of how men stop using their brains when a woman's involved."

Everyone looks at Kat. No one knows how to respond. She's said exactly what we all think every time we see her. If anyone has the ability to make a man do crazy things, it's Kat. I'm hoping Bump has more sense than most men. But by the way he's smiling at her right now, I doubt it.

"I really don't think Fortner is dangerous," I admit, trying to draw Bump's focus back away from Kat. "I mean, he's nearly become part of our family. He shares meals with us, and he's pitched his teepee right behind the house. He's done nothing but help us from the start."

Mr. Fitch motions for the waitress and says, "Bump, you spend more time with him than any of us. What's your gut tell you?"

Bump speaks clearly, with not an ounce of doubt. "To be honest, Mr. Fitch, I think I'm more violent than Fortner, and I ain't never even hit a man."

The waitress brings water for each of us, which crowds the table even more. Henry accidentally spills his glass and Kat snaps, "Henry! I told you to keep your arms off the table!" Then she looks at me and says, "I swear I don't know how much longer I can manage on my own. Some days I'm tempted to enlist. It's bound to be easier than this." She laughs, but it's a tired laugh. Then she turns to Henry and tries to wipe his shirt dry.

Bump leaves the table to find more napkins. As he walks out of earshot, Kat whispers to me, "You're so lucky, Millie. To have a husband at home."

After lunch, Bump and I walk to the post office, where we find Abe hanging a new war bonds poster. He greets us cheerily and hands me a stack of mail. When he makes silly faces at Isabel, she cries.

"I'd like to post a telegram," Bump says. Abe motions for us to follow.

"I'll wait outside with the baby," I announce, sorry Isabel greets everyone with a wail. I bundle her beneath my coat before returning to the chilly air. Outside, I thumb through the letters, shielding them from the falling snow by standing close to the wall, beneath the eaves. The first note is short, with pink lipstick kisses stamped in every corner.

Dear Millie,

I miss you. Come home. NOW!

Camille

P.S. I'm wearing lipstick!

I laugh and open the second, a pink envelope that must have been sprayed with perfume. The sharp paper delivers a fine slice across my thumb, and a tiny line of blood rises through my skin.

Dear Millie,

Mother took all my makeup AND my magazines. I want to move to Colorado.

Love,
Camille

And finally, a third one, postmarked the very next day. The cold wind nearly blows this one away, but I hold tight until the gust weakens a bit.

Dear Millie,

I can't move to Colorado. Garrett Jenkins is now my BOYFRIEND! Has that cute gypsy found you yet?

XOXO,

Camille

At the bottom is a big heart, in which she's inscribed "Camille loves Garrett" followed by lots of *x*'s and *o*'s floating around the heart like stars. My emotions have been a mess throughout this pregnancy, and I'm still a hormonal wreck. The thought of Camille sitting on her bed drawing these tiny symbols nearly makes me cry. Instead, I tuck the letters into my purse with the rest of our mail as Bump joins me, suggesting we head to the store. We stop by the truck to grab Oka's baskets and beadwork, and then head inside to show off her talents. I set the jewelry on the counter and a woman with a flowery hat eyes it.

"What's this?" the sheriff asks.

"All handmade," I tell him. "My grandmother, Oka, is Choctaw." Bump holds up a few of the baskets. "Woven from Mississippi swamp cane," I continue. "Tight weaves, all very functional. Not just for decoration. And they're dyed naturally. All original designs."

Another shopper takes notice and asks, "How much?" She examines the baskets. Thankfully, Isabel stays asleep against my chest. Sheriff Halpin is all smiles as he negotiates prices for the goods. Bump and I stand in amazement, watching money swap hands. Within thirty minutes, two baskets have already sold.

"Think she can make more?" the sheriff asks.

"Absolutely," I answer. "She'll be thrilled!"

Bump paces the aisles, jiggling his keys and toying with the various items on the shelves. It's obvious his patience is wearing thin. "You're really not a shopper, are you?" I talk with a teasing voice as Isabel stirs against me.

"What makes you think that?" Bump juggles three onions.

I pause, thinking. "Why don't you go find something to do at Doc's Place? Doesn't he have a new colt for you to break?"

Bump drops the onions into the bin and gives me a relieved smile. "Thank you!" he says, then kisses me on the cheek. "You'll know where to find me."

Trying to remember everything Oka asked me to get, I load my basket with the items we need to bring home. Seeds. Jars. Some new fabric, a stash of sharp needles, and some basic staples for the pantry. Without Bump here to rush me, I take my time, enjoying being out of the house and doing something useful. By the time I finish, I've blown more than an hour in the store, chatting with townsfolk and working out the payment for Oka's goods with Sheriff Halpin.

The sheriff helps me load everything into the truck and tucks an envelope of cash for Oka into my purse. "I can't wait to see her reaction," I tell him. "She didn't think anyone would want to buy this stuff."

"As long as it's selling, tell her to keep it coming," Sheriff Halpin says. "I only take ten percent." Then he pulls my arm and speaks sharply. "You're being foolish, letting Fortner stay at your place. There's no line he won't cross. And when it happens, don't say I didn't warn you."

I find Bump and Kat riding horses together in Doc Henley's pasture. Instead of greeting them, as I should, I stand back behind the fence and watch, letting Isabel nurse beneath the warmth of my coat. Kat giggles and flirts shamelessly. She pulls her horse to a stop and swings her legs. "If I ride longer than ten minutes, I end up with pins and needles in my feet."

Bump climbs down from a dun gelding and moves near Kat. He proceeds to touch her legs, pushing them gently into the horse's side. "Now sit back, farther in your saddle." She does. Then Bump says, "Your stirrups are too long." He continues to shorten the length, touching her knee as he makes the adjustments. "Shouldn't go below your ankle or else your heels will be up and you'll lean forward. You want a long leg, so you can arch at the waist. Try it now."

Within seconds, Kat's galloping across Doc's pasture laughing at the top of her lungs. "And to think, it was that simple all along!"

I know good and well Kat didn't need Bump to show her where to place her stirrups. What I don't know is how they both felt when my husband touched her legs and placed his hands over hers. They're acting as if Kat isn't the only one without a spouse.

Kat circles around and notices me at the gate. She rides toward me, all out of breath. "Hi, Millie. Wow, Kenneth's really got a way with horses. In five minutes he's taught me all I've been doing wrong for years."

"That right?" There is no warmth in my voice. I move Isabel to my left and she continues nursing.

Bump walks our way. "Doc asked me to work a few of the horses. Kat asked for a lesson. Killed two birds with one stone!"

"All done, then?" I phrase it more as a demand than a question, much sharper than my usual tone. Bump looks at Kat as if he's sorry he has to leave. I stand here with my extra weight, my baby at my breast, fearing the worst.

"What's wrong, Millie?" Kat asks.

I don't even know how to respond. I look at Bump. I hope he'll take my hand and walk out of here with me, right now, before I make any bigger a fool of myself.

Instead, he says, "Maybe you've pushed yourself too hard today. Why don't you go inside and rest while I put tack away?"

Breathe, Millie, I tell myself. *This isn't like you. Your hormones are surging. Calm down.*

Kat jumps from her saddle and resets her Stetson, tucking her red hair underneath. "Come on, Millie. Let's go find some water."

For a second or two, I am tempted to tell Kat exactly what I think of the show she's been performing for my husband. But what if I am overreacting? I don't want to be that kind of wife. I leave the horses with Bump and follow Kat inside Doc's house, hoping she can convince me she's more interested in developing a friendship with me than with my husband.

When we arrive home, I can't wait to give Oka her money from the sale. I look through my purse for the envelope of cash and find the rest of the mail, unopened. "Oka?" I call as I sit on the new sofa Janine and Mr. Tucker ordered for us, a lush, navy love seat that provides a perfect spot to sit next to the fire.

"I come down," Oka calls from upstairs. Her footsteps sweep across the floor. A door opens, closes.

While I wait for her, I read a note from Bump's mother, a sweet letter, filled with lots of funny stories about the Andersons back home. Then I set it aside to show Bump when he comes in for supper.

I move to the next letter in the stack. It's addressed to me but has no return label. I don't recognize the handwriting. I open it to find a page torn out of Fitzgerald's *This Side of Paradise*. A quote is circled. "*The girl really worth having won't wait for anybody.*" It's what River told me, just before he left for good. I flip the page over. No personal note, but his intent is clear. He wants me to understand . . . he knows where I am.

"Have fun?" Oka moves into the room.

I tuck River's note back into my purse and find Oka's money. "I have something for you." I pass her the envelope of cash.

She frowns. "What this?"

"It's all yours, Oka. You should have seen the shoppers. Sheriff Halpin wants more. Says as long as it's selling, he'll keep ordering."

"Hmph," she says, as if this is the first thing that has ever surprised her.

"We did it!" Bump runs into the house. "We got a contract, Millie!"

I'm upstairs with Oka and can barely hear him over Isabel's crying. "I had just gotten her to sleep," I complain to Oka. I sigh and stand from the pallet where I, too, was trying to rest. Bump's shouting has startled us both awake. I step down into the kitchen, trying to calm Isabel in my arms. I'm too tired to smile, but I try.

Bump, on the other hand, is all smiles. He greets me with a kiss and says, "MacMillan just sent word. He's gonna work with us. We'll drive the cattle up here soon, move 'em back down the mountain come winter. Try to stay ahead of the snow. He's already got the buyers, knows all the stockyards. Clear route with friendly landowners. It's perfect, Millie. Perfect!"

"I knew you could do it," I tell him. Isabel twists in my arms and wails, rubbing her eyes.

Bump doesn't seem to notice. "He's sendin' some hands too. To help with the drive. Good ones. With lots of experience. We might need to build some barracks, but that shouldn't be too hard." He's so excited, he doesn't even stop at the door to take off his boots. A crumbled line of dried mud trails his steps.

I try to fix Bump a glass of water from the dipper, but Isabel pulls on it, spilling it onto the floor.

Suddenly, he's furious. "Can you just . . . boy, Millie, can't you put her down? Five minutes. That's all I needed!" He stomps back out of the house, leaving the door open behind him. Isabel's volume increases.

"Bump?" I call after him, but he doesn't look back. I carry Isabel outside and try to soothe her with the rock of the porch swing. The sound of the river. The coarse, thick fur of the goats. Still, Isabel screams, arching her back and rubbing her red face with her clenched fists. She almost flails out of my arms, and I tighten my grip, which angers her more. I have to do something.

I whistle for Firefly and lead her into the barn. I carefully put Isabel into a makeshift cradle Bump built in the tack room, a safe, high box where I can place her when I need both hands. "I've tried everything," I confess to my horse. "I need to calm down too, sweet girl."

I'm hoping some time grooming Firefly will help me relax. I move the brush in long, slow strokes across her firm brown belly. Then I work the comb through her mane and weave a thick black braid along the length of her neck.

But Isabel's wails echo around the barn, and Firefly neighs. "What do you think, girl? You think Isabel's ready for her first ride?"

Firefly ruffles her lips.

"I'll take that as a yes." I prep Firefly, adjusting the blanket, bridle, and straps, before pulling into the saddle with Isabel in one arm. The stirrups squeak, their leather tight from lack of use lately. "Now, see there? Better already." I laugh and direct Firefly out to the grass, managing the reins with one hand. Isabel rests quietly across the saddle, safely cushioned between my lap, the leather horn, and my arm. Her breathing slows a bit.

As Firefly walks, slowly and carefully, across solid ground, Isabel begins to calm. It's the first time I've seen her tune into something outside of herself without it triggering tears. She is focused and content. And I remember the first time I rode Firefly. How the same feeling came over me that now comforts Isabel.

By the time we reach the corner fence post, Isabel is sound asleep. I am so relieved to hear the silence, I don't dare do anything that might wake her. Firefly leads us along the pasture's edge, back and forth, for nearly two hours, until Isabel finally wakes, eager to nurse. I feed her right here in the pasture.

"Look at her," I tell Firefly. "She looks so happy. So peaceful." Then I say to Isabel, "I wish I could help you feel this way all the time."

Isabel kicks her chubby legs and reaches up for my face, touches my cheek, looks at me. I melt.

Chapter 21

May 1944

It's already been a year since Mr. Cauy Tucker handed Bump a set of keys and sent us on our way. We're celebrating our first wedding anniversary tonight, and Kat suggested we go see *Casablanca.* They're reshowing it in Denver since it won the Oscar for best picture. Of course, I only know this because of Camille's frequent updates. There's nothing she doesn't know about Hollywood.

Oka has been helping me sew a new dress with some fabric I bought on our last trip to town, a beautiful burgundy cotton that is soft and thin, almost like silk but much easier to handle. Now Oka helps me attach the last of the buttons and twists my hair up in the back.

"I feel like a movie star," I tell her. "Camille would be so proud of me."

"Pretty," Oka says, adding the last pin to my hair as Bump knocks on Oka's bedroom door. Isabel lies on the mat playing with her own hands, happy for the moment.

"Come on in," I say. Bump opens the door as I give him a spin. Isabel's five months old, and I am finally starting to feel like me again.

Bump whistles, which makes Oka laugh. "How did a guy like me ever land a girl like you?"

I give Bump a quick kiss on his lips and say, "I'm the lucky one."

We give a round of good-bye hugs and leave Oka in charge of Isabel for the evening. "You sure you can handle her crying?" I ask.

"Go," Oka says. "Have fun!"

"She should eat the pear preserves," I say, reminding Oka to mash them well. "If not, she may like the carrots, if you boil them and puree them. And there's always the oats. Remember, she likes to sleep on her back."

"I know. I know." Oka laughs. "Now go!"

I give Oka another big hug, kiss Isabel for the thousandth time, and wave good-bye as if I'm leaving forever. Tears well in my eyes as I climb into the truck with Bump.

"Why are you crying?" Bump laughs as he starts the engine.

"It's just hard," I explain. "I feel guilty. For leaving her."

He pulls me close to him on the seat and says, "She'll be fine." So this is the difference, I think, between a mother and a father. It's physically painful for me to leave my child, while Bump doesn't seem to mind leaving her at all.

It takes almost two hours to get to Denver, and my breasts are already swelling with milk. I focus all my attention on Bump, even though I'm a mess inside. I'm worried Isabel may be crying in pain. What if she's hungry and refusing to eat? I'm afraid she'll be too much for Oka to handle. But I try not to let Bump know how worried I really am. I don't want anything to ruin this night.

When we arrive in Denver, Bump walks beside me and holds open the doors. He makes me feel like royalty, especially when he offers to buy me a beautiful green dress I admire in a boutique window. "Try it on," he says, encouraging me to go into the store.

"We sure don't have that kind of money," I argue, smiling. I quickly add, "And I'd never have a reason to wear such a thing anyway. It'd be a waste."

"Come on, Millie. That dress was made for you." He looks as if he's imagining me in it. I blush.

"It's the last thing I need." Even though part of me wants to try it on, just for fun, there's no way I could ever spend that kind of money on myself when his parents are struggling to keep a roof over their heads. "I'd much rather you send the money home."

Bump nearly pouts. "Why won't you let me spoil you? Just once?"

I don't answer, but lead him instead to the next fancy window where we dream all over again. It *is* awfully fun to pretend.

As the evening continues, Bump is the perfect gentleman. He lets go of my hand only to open doors for me. And he insists on letting me order first at the restaurant, anything I want, no matter the price. I'm surprised when he asks the waiter to open a bottle of champagne. A very special treat. Then he raises his glass and gives me a toast. "To Millie. The girl I want to kiss every morning and every night." I am happy to give him that kiss. And then another. Diners watch and giggle, but I don't care. Nothing will stop me from having a good time tonight.

"To Bump," I add. "For making me the luckiest girl in the world."

We splurge on crisp green salads, fresh fruits, grilled trout, and sautéed vegetables. For dessert, a rich crème brûlée with a crispy, golden crust, "like they make in Paris," the waiter tells us, saying *Par-ee* as if he were French, even though he's obviously as American as the rest of us, with his sunburned skin and Clark Gable mustache.

"It's absolutely the most delicious meal I've ever had." I sigh and lean back in my chair, wishing we could eat like this every day.

Bump agrees, following his bite of crème brûlée with a second glass of bubbly.

"We should do this more often," I say, holding my hand up to decline a refill of champagne. I already feel light-headed and am afraid I wouldn't be able to handle another taste.

"You got that right," Bump says a little too loudly, grinning widely. I'm afraid he may not be able to handle his refill either.

After the meal, we settle in for the film, and Bump sits close against me. I am a girl again, with a tremendous crush on my husband. I lean my head onto his shoulder and love the way it feels to be this near him. It's been so long, too long, since he wanted me by his side.

The movie only adds to the romance. The entire effect is magical, as if we'd taken a voyage far, far away. As Ingrid Bergman moves across the screen, I pretend I'm Ilsa Lund. I'm feeling lighter, more graceful, beautiful even, until Annina and Rick shake me with their truths.

Annina: *Oh, monsieur, you are a man. If someone loved you very much, so that your happiness was the only thing that she wanted in the world, but she did a bad thing to make certain of it, could you forgive her?*

Rick: *Nobody ever loved me that much.*

Annina: *And he never knew, and the girl kept this bad thing locked in her heart? That would be all right, wouldn't it?*

Rick: *You want my advice?*

Annina: *Oh, yes, please.*

Rick: *Go back to Bulgaria.*

Bump's fingers lace through mine, and I hold his hand tightly, afraid to let go. He has no idea of the bad thing I keep locked in my heart. If I told him, would he forgive me? Would he understand that his happiness was the only thing I wanted in this world? Or would he tell me to go back to Mississippi?

The movie ends with me in tears and Bump praising the film. "I can see why it won an award," he admits. "I didn't know what was gonna happen, right up to the end."

As we exit the theater, I'm surprised to cross paths with Kat. She's dressed to the nines, wearing the gorgeous green dress Bump tried to buy for me earlier this evening. She's also walking hand in hand with a man we've never met.

"Millie! Kenneth!" Kat delivers each of us a quick hug and introduces her date. "Meet Samuel Brigg, an old friend."

"Nice to meet you," Brigg says, shaking Bump's hand, kissing me on the cheek. A charmer, this one.

"They're my neighbors," Kat explains. I can't believe she's come here tonight. She knew this was where we'd be spending our anniversary date. She's the one who convinced me to plan this whole event. Sitting on the porch swing with me during her last visit. She had held Isabel in her arms and said, "I think she should call me Aunt Kat." Then she went on and on about how happy she is to have me as her friend and encouraged me to take a night out with Bump. "Believe me, Millie," she said. "If I had Grant with me, I'd plan a big surprise to celebrate our anniversary. Take Bump to Denver. He'll love it." Now she's here, at the very same theater where she told me to come, acting as if she never expected to see us here. I remember Mabel telling me long ago, "There's no such thing as coincidence."

Then Kat asks, "What are y'all doing in the city?" Am I putting too much thought into this? Maybe it really is a fluke.

"It's our anniversary," I say, watching her reaction closely. For a second Kat looks sad, and I feel guilty that she will never celebrate another anniversary with her husband. "We just saw *Casablanca*, like you suggested. Did you see it?"

"Yes! Wasn't it wonderful?" Kat smiles at her date, and there's no doubt about it, she could easily be an actress on the silver screen.

Bump has said nothing, and I worry he's coming across as rude. He can't seem to take his eyes off Kat in that green dress. I nudge him with my elbow and say, "What'd you think of it, Bump?"

"Me? I don't know. Good, I guess." Not exactly the same response he gave when he was raving about the film in the theater.

"We're heading across the street for a drink. Join us," Brigg says. He's quite handsome, with straight, strong teeth. A subtle dimple on his left cheek. Tanned skin framed by light blond hair, a fresh trim as if he's just left the barber.

"Sounds fun," Bump says, accepting the invitation before I can make an excuse.

The last thing I want to do is spend my anniversary competing with Kat for Bump's attention. "We really ought to get back to Isabel," I explain. "I don't want to give Oka any reason to move back to Mississippi."

"Don't blame you a bit, Millie." Kat smiles. "Henry and I plan to stop by next week. I've got a new recipe and need someone to test it on."

"Come on by anytime," I answer. "You know you're always welcome. It's very nice to meet you, Mr. Brigg." I pull Bump's arm gently as we offer polite farewells. By the time Bump and I reach the truck, I am determined to make my husband forget all about Kat. I slide in close and thank him for the best date I've ever had.

Bump responds by paraphrasing Rick's character in the movie: "Of all the horse barns, in all the towns, in all the world, she walks into mine." Then he says, "It sure is nice to have you all to myself again."

I assume he means he's tired of sharing me with Isabel. I've heard husbands can get that way. "I know it's been hard on you, Bump. With Isabel waking us up all night."

He sighs. "I could deal with that. It's her cryin'. She never stops."

I understand how he feels. I'm worn out too, but I am also hurt to hear him complain about Isabel. "She's in pain, Bump. You said it yourself. You said she'll outgrow it."

"Yeah, but I never heard a baby cry so much. And she should be past it by now. I can't understand what's wrong with her. Doc doesn't know either. Says she's the most difficult child he's ever seen."

"Just think how she feels. The only thing that soothes her is a long ride with Firefly. And even then, I have to hold her a certain way in the saddle. She insists on looking out at everything around her, and I have to put pressure on her belly too. She just needs a little help calming down. That's all."

"Seems that's where you are every time I go lookin'." He shifts away from me.

"I've tried everything, Bump. No one knows how to help her. Even Oka and Fortner just shake their heads."

"I know. But it seems like . . ." Bump grows quiet.

"What?" I ask, although I'm afraid to hear the answer.

He swallows hard. "Like I've been alone in this. From the start. If it weren't for Fortner, I don't know what I'd do."

Of all the things I thought he might say, I did not expect that. "Bump, that's not fair. I know I had those months of bed rest, and now the baby takes a lot of my time. But I'm trying my best. I really am."

"I know," he says, finally offering a softer tone to his voice.

"I'm sorry," I say, taking his hand from the wheel to hold it in my lap. "I don't know what more I can do."

Bump lets me hold his hand for only a minute or two. He drives the rest of the way home in silence. By the time we arrive, my breasts are full and leaking milk. We've been gone too long. We open the door to find Oka in the living room, walking back and forth with Isabel. Our baby is screaming at the top of her lungs. Fortner sits in the kitchen, his head in his hands.

I pull my child from Oka's arms and try to nurse her. "I'm so sorry." I say this to no one specifically, just a general apology to everyone. How I wish I could make it better for them all.

"I've never seen anything like it," Fortner says.

Oka sighs.

Bump doesn't say anything. Instead, he goes to our bedroom and closes the door hard behind him.

Isabel arches her back and throws her head back, resisting the milk. I reposition her, try the other side. Nothing works. I finally give up, fastening Isabel into the cradleboard and carrying her out to the barn. I saddle Firefly and draw us both up onto my horse's broad back. We ride at a slow, soothing pace across the pitch-dark pasture. We ride and we ride, listening to the cries of the coyotes and the songs of the owls, until Isabel's tiny eyelids start to close and her voice begins to quiet, and finally, we find the peace we need.

Kat and Henry show up one week after our date night, as she promised. But this time they arrive during breakfast.

"Come on in," I tell them. "Plenty of biscuits. Sausage."

"Sorry we're so early," Kat says, handing me a pie. "Heading into town to meet the reverend. I promised Daddy we'd be there by nine."

I hold Isabel with one arm and put the pie on the counter for later. Then I fix two extra plates and set Kat and Henry a place at the table. Fortner stands until Kat is seated. Bump does the same.

Kat hesitates, looking at Fortner, then at me, as if she is surprised we really do welcome this man to our table for family meals. I shrug and smile, and that seems enough for Kat to take a chance on him. "Why, thank you," she says, nodding at each of the men. Fortner doesn't give her the attention she wants, but Bump gives her plenty. Except for our date night, which ended with us in separate rooms again, Bump hasn't looked at me like that in months, and I feel a pinch when he smiles Kat's way.

As Bump's eyes follow Kat, little Henry stares at Fortner, examining his belt of bullets and the pistols holstered on each hip. Unlike Bump and me, who always remove our guns at the table, Fortner stays fully armed at all times.

"Morning," Fortner says to Henry, whose red curls catch the morning sun.

Kat's son is too stunned to respond. He looks to his mother for assurance, and Kat signals for Henry to sit in the chair beside her. She scoots the seat beneath Henry's small frame, and the child sits without taking his eyes from Fortner. "Mama," Henry whispers loud enough for all of us to hear. "It's the bad man."

I shuffle my feet uneasily and pass Kat a cup of coffee. Pour Henry some milk.

"Is that what they say?" Fortner looks at Kat but speaks to Henry. "They tell you I'm a bad man?"

Henry nods, still intimidated by Fortner's reputation. We've been here a year already, but this is the first direct encounter Fortner has had with Kat and Henry. They visit nearly every week, but Fortner is always hard at work when they come.

Kat tries to laugh it off as a misunderstanding, but Fortner talks right over her, asking, "What else do they say?"

"That you kill people," Henry says.

Kat gasps. "Henry!"

Henry doesn't respond to his mother. Instead, he keeps his eyes set on Fortner. "You gonna kill me?" he whispers.

Fortner puts his hands on the table, two firm fists, and says, "Tell you what. Your name is Henry, is that right?"

Henry nods.

"Okay then, Henry. Can you do me a favor?"

Henry nods again, nervously.

"Next time somebody tells you I'm a bad man, or that I kill people, or something about me not having a soul, you look them right in the eye, just like this, you see?"

Another nod.

"That's right, you look right at them and you say, 'Eli Fortner is a good man.' A good man. You hear me?"

Henry nods. This is the first time Fortner has confronted the situation since the day the lion attacked, so we all pay close attention.

"Let me hear you say it."

Kat sits quietly, but moves her hand over Henry's shoulder now and draws her son near.

"Go ahead. Pretend I'm your uncle Halpin, jabbing on and on about what an evil man Fortner is. What are you going to say?"

Henry looks at his mother, then back at Fortner, and he says, "Eli Fortner is a good man?"

"No. You have to say it like you believe it. Won't mean a thing if you don't believe it's true."

I give Henry a gentle smile. Try to put him at ease. He turns to Bump, who suddenly says matter-of-factly, "Eli Fortner *is* a good man." No one knows how to respond. Fortner looks at Bump as if he's been pardoned. As if God Himself has come down and declared him a saint right here at the table. Then Bump says it again, louder this time, with complete conviction. "Eli Fortner is a good man." Not a speck of doubt.

Henry looks at his mother, but Kat frowns and says nothing. So Oka jumps in, announcing, "Eli Fortner is a good man." But Oka says this to me, as if she's still trying to convince me it's true.

Fortner's eyes have become misty, and his hands are no longer set in fists on the table. Instead, they are folded together, and they shake. He looks at Oka with a deep, wrinkled brow and partly opened lips, the look of a beggar who has just found unexpected kindness on a cold and crowded street.

Then I take a chance, and I say it too. "Eli Fortner is a good man." And as the words reach my ears, I am convinced they tell the truth. I finally understand what Bump and Oka have known all along, that Fortner really is one of the good guys. Fortner looks at me in such a genuine way, with such unconditional love, that all seems right with the world.

We all look at Henry, but Henry says nothing. Kat sighs and says, "That's enough."

Henry eyes Fortner a little longer, looks back at his mother, at each of us, as if he's trying to decide where he stands. Then he sits straight and says boldly, "Eli Fortner is a good man."

We all smile and Bump says, "Amen!"

Kat whispers to Henry and tries to get him to focus on his food.

"That's right, Henry. Now, if you can do that, well then, why in the world would I kill you?" Fortner extends his hand. "Do we have a deal?"

"Deal," Henry says, returning the shake. Then he pokes the tip of his pinky finger into his biscuit and makes two holes for eyes, one for a nose, and four for a happy smile. I offer him a grin and fill his happy-face biscuit with blueberry jam. He tickles Isabel's toes and she smiles at him.

"Weather's warmin'," Bump says, bringing us all back to a normal conversation. "Pass open yet?"

Fortner shrugs. Then adds, "If not yet, any day now."

"Is everything set for that sale?" I ask, finally taking a seat with Isabel in my lap. I pull a biscuit and break a small bite for her.

"Need to make some calls. Still plan to settle on twenty to one," Bump says, explaining his plans to move twenty young mares across the Divide to trade for one pedigree stallion. Despite many opportunities to purchase other stallions, Mr. Tucker insists this one will give him the breeding lines he's after.

Fortner questions, "Twenty of our best, I assume?"

"Plus some cash," Bump says between bites. "Mr. Tucker's been working this plan for years. Ever since that meeting back in '40, when Denhardt opened the stud book."

Fortner takes a long drink of coffee and says, "Must be some stud."

"Prized descendant of both Steel Dust and Billy." Bump wipes his mouth.

I've learned enough by now to recognize those names as two of the best quarter horses since the breed took root.

"Still plan to push them up?" Fortner asks, passing the pan of biscuits to Oka and Bump before taking another for himself.

"Yep. I don't care none for the trains." Bump butters a second biscuit. "Mr. Tucker agrees. Says the natural way is best."

"You're going to drive them across the Divide?" Kat asks. She still hasn't touched her food.

Bump nods.

"I've never made the route on horseback. Sounds fun." Kat waits as if she expects Bump to invite her to join them. Everyone's attention is pulled from our plates at the same instant, and we all look at Kat as if she's lost all reason.

"Are you sayin' you wanna join us?" Bump looks surprised, maybe a little impressed.

"Why not?" She smiles. "You don't think I'm up for it?"

We all laugh. I must not be the only one who finds the idea absurd.

"What's so funny?" Kat asks. "Fortner knows the pass, right?"

Fortner nods, chews his biscuit.

"And you'll need help moving the herd." Kat continues her plan.

"Fortner and I can handle it." Bump take a swig of coffee, hiding his amusement, and I pray he doesn't allow her to go.

"Aren't you going, Millie?" Kat asks, turning everyone's attention to me.

"I'd love to," I admit. "But I need to stay here with Isabel." Bump gives me a look that makes me feel as if I've disappointed him. I try again, wording it a different way. "Oka and I will be holding down the ranch."

"How long will you be gone?" Kat asks Bump, still not taking the hint.

"Month at most," Bump says.

"Well, that's not too long. Millie and I can both go," Kat says. "We'll help you move the horses west, and then, when you come back with the stallion, we'll split off for the cherry fields. Take the train back." Then she turns to me. "We must spend at least a day at the vapor caves."

"Kat, you're not talking sense. As nice as that sounds, Isabel's still nursing, and I won't leave Oka here to do all the work while I'm soaking in hot springs." I also wouldn't want to leave Isabel for a month, but I don't admit that.

"Millie's right." Bump takes my side, and I smile. "It's too much for one person to handle, and I need Fortner with me."

Oka looks relieved.

"You don't know what you're missing," Kat says. Then she picks up her fork and adds, "I'm not going to let this go so easy. I'm betting by summer, we'll all be in Glenwood Springs."

Bump laughs, and we let Kat have the last word. Just the way she likes it.

After finishing breakfast, I walk her to her car with Henry.

"So what do you think of Mr. Brigg?" Kat asks before starting the engine.

"He seems nice," I answer, unsure of what I should say. "Handsome too."

"You can't blame me, Millie."

"I don't blame you, Kat."

Henry climbs back and forth over the front seat. At the moment, he is upside down with his two small boots sticking up in the air. I don't want to say too much in front of him, but I'm wondering if Kat has finally accepted Grant's death. I whisper, "Have you decided to have a service?"

Kat blows air between her lips. "I won't believe a single thing they tell me. Not until I see proof. For all I know, he's still out there, Millie. Trying to find his way home to me."

"Then why Mr. Brigg?" I ask, perhaps crossing a line.

"Because, Millie," she answers. "Because I'm still out there too."

Chapter 22

A fresh pot of tea steeps as Oka pours us each a cup, something to break the chill of this spring morning. May in the mountains can mean many things, but today the weather is perfect. It won't take long for the sun to turn this into a beautiful, warm day. Outside, Bump carries feed buckets to the pasture trough. I watch him work while I sip tea and set my breathing to his long, even stride. Isabel sleeps in her crib while I write letters home to Bump's mother and to Camille and Mabel, trying to explain how wonderful our little bean really is.

The morning light catches Oka's face. My first impression of Kat was that she was such a beautiful woman, but now I know Oka possesses the true beauty. I can't take my eyes off her, with her scars, and her wrinkles, her gray hair and crooked teeth. She has become the most astonishing woman I've ever seen.

"Oka." I am scared to ask her about Jack, so I get it out before I stop myself. "What happened that day? When Jack killed Boone?" I have no right to intrude, but I need to know. I need to understand what happened to transform my father, Oka's sweet son, into the abusive man I feared.

Oka keeps looking out the window as the wind rustles the curtains. She stays quiet for a long time before answering. "My husband, he not good," she begins. "He believe I cheat. With another man." She turns to face me, shifting her weight to relieve her bad hip. "It not true. But Boone never believe me. He hear about Chahta woman, cut here, in her ear by elders, to show she cheat. Another woman cut across here." She points to her cheek. "Marked. Sign to all she not be trusted. Boone not Chahta. But he say I should be cut too. He drink too much and he hold me down, knife to my face."

As her emotions peak, her voice becomes strained and her English more broken. "Jack sixteen. He yell. So Boone turn on Jack. Chase him with knife, curse. John younger. He hide in corner and cry. I hit Boone with chair. Hard on head. But it not stop him. He grab me. Here." She puts her tea on the table, next to mine, and her hands shake so hard, she spills it. Then she gestures as if she's being choked. "Jack see this. Then Boone begin to . . ." She mimics the act of stabbing. "Again. Again. Fourteen times." Now a tear falls.

Oka pulls the long sleeves of her dress up to reveal raised scars, thick bubbled skin where a blade has been. Pulls her collar to the side to show marks on her neck. It is hard to look at, the proof of such a vicious attack. I am flooded with memories of my mother, broken and bleeding on the floor, and I, too, fight tears.

"He too big. Too strong. Then I hear gunshot. Boone fall. Blood everywhere. On wall. On me. What happening? I not move. Jack run to me. Hold me. Say, 'I love you, *Sashki.* Don't die. Please don't die, Mama.' Last thing I know."

Oka and I sit together for a long time. Quiet. Staring out at the bright green birth of spring. Like Jack, I listened to my father beat my mother and leave her for dead. I begged my mother not to die. I hated my father for what he had done. Turns out, we were not so different after all, Jack and me. Just two terrified kids, hoping to save our mothers.

Isabel cries, and I stand to tend to her.

"She outgrow this soon," Oka says.

"Let's hope," I reply, pulling Isabel into my arms. "Not sure how much longer Bump can stand it." I think of the way Bump turns from me in the night. How distant he seems. Is it really that he's tired? Sleep-deprived? Or is it something more? At first it was me resisting intimacy. Now it's him. We never seem to be on the same page. I might expect this after years of marriage, but so soon? I worry he regrets bringing me with him to Colorado. Or worse, regrets the wedding, the baby, the whole idea of us. There's no doubt his life would be much easier without the strain of a child and a wife.

By the time I finish feeding and changing Isabel, Oka has moved to the porch and I try to focus my thoughts back on good things. "Beautiful day!" I tell Isabel as we pass outside to join Oka. It's the first warm day we've had since winter, and I'm eager to enjoy every second of sunshine.

Oka sews as she glides gently on the porch swing Fortner made for us.

I spread a blanket for Isabel in the yard and return to watch as Oka's hands move in slow, even strokes, pulling and pushing the needle through dark green fabric, one small stitch at a time. She's teaching me to make a traditional Choctaw dress.

There's no pattern to follow, nothing to buy in stores, so I pay careful attention and try to remember every step. I hope to teach it to Isabel someday, so she'll understand what it means to be Choctaw.

It has taken nearly six yards of cotton—a splurge even without a war—but Oka insisted she use earnings from her basket sales to give me this gift. For weeks, I've watched her slowly transform the cloth into a beautiful gown, with three rows of loosely flowing ruffles across the bottom of the skirt and long, full sleeves to balance the weight.

Oka chose the green fabric, saying, "*Okchamali*, green for earth." Now she's adding contrasting white lines to trim the ruffles, the neckline, and the bottom hem. "Lines," she says as she embroiders the elaborate pattern, "like a river. See?"

I nod and pay careful attention.

Next to Oka sits an unfinished apron and collar, both cut from white cloth. Oka passes the dress to me now and encourages me to continue her series of perfectly symmetrical triangles, "half diamonds" she calls them, all lined up with a white borderline both above and below. It's an incredible work of art. "They look like mountains," I say.

"Road of life," Oka explains, again tying every part of the dress to something meaningful. "In life, Millicent, you take path. You try to stay on path. But sometime, you make mistake." She turns the half diamonds so the peaks point down, showing me that's not the way we want to go. "Make it right, you back on road of life."

"How do you make it right?" I ask, remembering Bump's belief that we could move mountains.

"Do good things, like for Isabel, or sick person. Help people."

She rotates the half diamonds again so the peaks point toward the sky. "Go right way."

Now Oka looks out at the pasture. Bump and Fortner are trying to break one of Doc's mustangs. Bump gets bucked off the horse, and Fortner reaches a hand down to help him. Oka laughs and says, "They make good pair."

"Yep," I admit. "I'm not sure we would have made it here without you and Fortner."

"I not do much," Oka says.

I laugh. "Oka, please. You do more in a day than most people accomplish in a lifetime." I begin to list all her strengths, ending with, "And you grow the biggest vegetables anyone's ever seen."

"Magic." Oka laughs. The truth is, she mixes straw with horse manure to fertilize the garden, adding ash to improve the soil. "But even magic not grow swamp cane. Not in mountains."

Oka uses the cane to make her baskets. No matter how hard she tries, it just won't take in this climate. Fortner showed her some ribbon grass mats, suggesting she look for other options, but she insists nothing works as well as swamp cane.

"It's nice of your friends to send you the cane." I rub my fingers across the beaded medallion Oka has made for the dress.

"They like money." Oka laughs. She's started paying them with part of her earnings, which keeps the cane coming her way from Mississippi.

I've learned to weave a bit too, but it's a slow process, one I have little patience for. I can dye the cane, though; I do enjoy that part. We gather berries and blooms when possible and create vibrant shades of blue, yellow, and red. Now Isabel stirs on her blanket in the yard, and I picture her sitting with me when she's grown, choosing just the right shades.

"My eyes tired," Oka says, standing to stretch. She pulls her sleeves up to check strips of cane in a bucket. They soak in water with slices of deep-red sugar beets. "Almost," she says, letting the cane steep a little longer. Her scars run thick across her arms, permanent reminders of wounds delivered long ago by a violent man.

Oka steps to the next bucket. I have watched her for months, moving through this world with grace and compassion. She doesn't seem to hold any bitterness, and even she was able to trust Fortner before me. I can't understand how she has managed to live a happy life after such a brutal attack. "Oka," I ask, moving to take a stick away from Isabel before she pokes her eye. "How did you forgive Boone? For what he did to you?"

Oka stays bent over the buckets of dye and works a forked branch through the solution, pulling strips of cane to examine the results. She takes time to answer. "Forgive? It not easy, Millicent. But I must forgive. Even if he never say he sorry. I do my part. Leave Boone's part to God. That not for me to control. So, not for me to worry about."

I let her message soak in, as if I'm a strip of cane in the bucket of beets. Like the cane, I hope to be changed.

"You know Chahta story about potato famine?" Oka asks, sensing my struggle.

I sit on the blanket next to Isabel and pull her into my lap. I shake my head and wait for Oka to tell the tale.

"You know *Nahollos*—white people—make Choctaw leave Mississippi, motherland, and go west."

I nod while I silently play peek-a-boo with Isabel, making her erupt in beautiful bursts of giggles every time I reappear from behind my hands. I'm hoping we've seen the worst of her colic and that Bump can sleep better again soon.

"It start 1831. Three years they send Chahta to new land. Now call it Oklahoma. Thousands go. Thousands die."

I'm ashamed to admit I don't know the whole story of the Trail of Tears, only bits and pieces I overheard from Jack.

"What happened?" I ask.

"Some starve. Or freeze. Disease. Many children stuck in hard winter. No clothes. Think, Millicent, you with Isabel, air more cold than ice, nothing but small blanket. No food. No shoes. No shelter. Nahollos tell you, 'Keep moving.'"

It's hard for me not to feel conflicted. Sad for the Choctaw part of me, ashamed of the other part. Mixed. I'll always be mixed. "But weren't you born in Mississippi?" I ask, not sure why Oka's family didn't head west with the others.

"Small group stay behind, try to keep land. My grandfather, he stay."

Isabel pulls my hair into her mouth, and I remove it. She cries.

"My grandfather work with missionaries. Help build school. Church. Back then, most white man and Chahta good friends. Work together. Marry too. Peace. Not like new nahollos who come with money and make us leave. Our friends try to help us. But even good nahollos not stop bad treaties."

"So what happened?" I ask, finally solving the mystery of the old letter with the perfect penmanship. The one Oka mailed to my mother's parents when she learned Jack would be marrying Mama. When Mr. Tucker gave it to me, I had very little information about Oka. I pictured her as well-read, educated, and proper. Now it makes sense. Oka must have had one of the English-speaking missionaries write the note for her.

"Chahta break apart. Families go away. People die. Bad

times, Millicent. But we hear of famine in Ireland. We feel bad. People suffer. We care."

"Ireland's pretty far away."

Oka continues. "Hunger is hunger, Millicent. We understand. We know this . . . suffering. So we send money from Oklahoma. From Mississippi. We try to help."

"You sent money to Ireland while you were still suffering over here?"

Oka nods. "Always can find someone who have more pain, more hurt than you. Always can find someone who need help. And you always have something to give. Even when you think you have nothing."

Isabel pulls my braid back into her mouth, and this time I let her chew it. Oka moves to the next bucket of dye and continues working. She pulls a batch of red cane and says, "Perfect," a broad smile stretching across her face.

Later, in bed, I rub Bump's sore muscles and snuggle next to his warm body. This time he pulls me close and holds me. I no longer flinch when he touches me, even when he traces the back of my neck, a spot that used to be a certain trigger for panic. Isabel has changed me, in more ways than one. Oka has too. I am softer now. Maybe not completely healed, but healing.

"You okay?" I ask. Bump's muscles are tense.

"Just worried, I guess." He stares at the ceiling and seems deep in thought.

"Worried about what?" I move my fingers through his hair.

"You wouldn't understand." He sighs.

"Try me."

"I don't know how to say it, Millie. I guess . . . I've been poor all my life."

"And I haven't? This isn't Kat you're talking to." I smile encouragingly, not sure where he's going with this. We're both better off here than we've ever been.

"I gotta get this right. With the stallion." Bump finally looks at me, and I smile.

"You will." I rub my fingers down his arm, circling his wrist.

"But what if I don't? I saw my folks bend too many times. They never could stand up to those greedy planters." He's never talked so openly about this before, and I don't want to say the wrong thing.

So I listen. Move my hands across his chest, feel a scar across his right side where a horse bit him earlier this year.

"I worked too hard to get out of that life. I ain't goin' back."

"Is that what you're afraid of?" I whisper. "Being poor again?"

"You ain't never been a sharecropper, Millie. It ain't no way to live. And tenant farmin' ain't much easier. I just wanna do more. For you, for the baby, for us. And for my folks back home. For Mr. Tucker too. I got too much ridin' on this to mess it up."

"You're not going to mess it up, Bump."

"One bad move, Millie. That's all it takes, and we could lose everything. We'd never get to start that clinic. We'd go home no better off than my folks. Worse maybe."

"Look how much you've already accomplished, Bump. You're the first person in your family to go to college. You finished vet school. You've started a ranch from nothing. And you're taking good care of a family on top of all of that. I'm proud of you," I say, kissing him gently.

"You are?" His voice quavers.

"I am."

Bump rolls over and unbuttons my nightgown, one small clasp at a time. He bends and caresses me softly, slowly. I close my eyes as he moves with such tender, honest desire. I am overcome with emotions. He touches me in ways he's never done, and I respond openly, without restraint or fear. Together, we enter into a beautiful, sacred giving. In the end, we are both near tears, safe in each other's arms. In love.

Chapter 23

Isabel wakes this morning happy and calm, and I'm feeling as if we're all moving into better days. After breakfast, I pull a stack of books to the bed and read random passages aloud, a treat for both of us. First, I skim *Winesburg, Ohio* by Sherwood Anderson. One passage makes me think of Kat and her search for the perfect fruit.

> *Into a little round place at the side of the apple has been gathered all its sweetness. One runs from tree to tree over the frosted ground picking the gnarled, twisted apples and filling his pockets with them. Only the few know the sweetness of the twisted apples.*

Hemingway reminds me who I am, and my anger swells unexpectedly.

> *Going to another country doesn't make any difference. I've tried all that. You can't get away from yourself by moving from one place to another.*

I trade *The Sun Also Rises* for *The Great Gatsby.* One line makes me think of Diana and Bill Miller: *"I married him because I thought he was a gentleman. . . . I thought he knew something about breeding, but he wasn't fit to lick my shoe."*

I give up on the male writers and turn instead to Louisa May Alcott. She soothes me with softening words the men could never offer: *"Some people seemed to get all sunshine, and some all shadow."* I stick with *Little Women*, losing myself in the world of the March sisters.

"Millie!" Bump calls me from outside, his anxious voice carries clear through the open windows. I leave the books on the bed and quickly bring Isabel to the pasture to meet Bump. I find him leading one of our new boarding horses to the fence—a massive three-year-old Percheron draft horse that was proving difficult for her owner.

"What's wrong?" I ask, relieved to see Bump isn't hurt.

"Take a look at this." He lifts the head of the horse and points to the lymph nodes beneath her jaw. "Look swollen to you?"

"Hard to tell." I rub my hand under the jawbone, along her neck. "Sure feels swollen."

"Strangles," he says. "I'm separating her from the others. We can't share supplies. This is very contagious."

"What's strangles?" I shift Isabel out of reach of the horse. I've still got so much to learn.

"Bacterial infection," Bump explains. "Attacks the respiratory tract."

"Is it serious?"

"Yes," Bump says. He seems extremely worried. "Bring me a halter?"

"Sure." I rush back to the barn with Isabel on my hip. We

gather a halter and a lead rope. As we're returning to the field, Fortner drives up from a trip to town. He parks the truck and greets me politely.

"Bump thinks we have a horse with strangles," I tell him.

"That's not good," he says, taking the tack from me as we head Bump's way. When we reach the smaller pen, where Bump has moved the horse, Fortner asks, "She the only one?"

"Far as I know. But we need to bring 'em in and have a look."

"No abscesses?" Fortner examines the draft horse.

"Not yet," Bump says. "But feel."

Fortner agrees the nodes are swollen. The horse's nostrils ooze a yellow-colored pus. It's obvious she isn't well.

Within twenty minutes, I've got the draft horse isolated in a stall, and the men are heading out to the back of the property on horseback. They plan to bring the herd in for examination. I scrub my hands thoroughly and come back inside with Isabel, who is straining to see everything in sight. "You're such a strong-willed child," I tease her. "And I wouldn't want you any other way." I cover her with kisses. She giggles, and my heart explodes with joy.

I start a pot of elk stew and try to get Isabel settled into a nap. Working my way through the rest of the books, I find a copy of River's favorite, *This Side of Paradise*. I've avoided this one, refusing to let myself spend too much time thinking of River. During all those months of bed rest, there were certainly days when I wanted to sink into the story River loved so much, but I always pushed it to the bottom of the box, thumbing through the rest until something else called to me.

Today it is another Fitzgerald favorite that catches me, one I brought with me from Mississippi and have read too many times to count. *Tender is the Night*. I pull Isabel to me, and she cuddles in my arms while I read aloud. Within a few paragraphs, the words stir chords in me. I am filled with vibrations of desire. The sentences hum from the pages, as if River himself were here playing notes on his harmonica, smiling at me, singing to me. As much as I love this author's ability to paint pictures in my head, I can't risk missing River, of giving in to my wondering about where he is and who he's become and when he may send me another letter.

I stuff the book back into the box and pull out a collection by Faulkner. I choose *A Rose for Emily.* I put Isabel in her crib and read aloud to her some more, sharing this story of Mississippi. At least Faulkner makes me laugh.

Eventually, Isabel falls asleep, and I put the book away to focus on supper. I also use the time to clean the windows and wipe the sills, sweep the floors and pull laundry from the line, iron our shirts and water the garden. The hours pass quickly, and before I know it, everyone is coming in for supper.

Bump kisses me and asks, "Where's Isabel?"

"Can you believe she's still sleeping?" I ask. "I'm getting worried, actually. I thought she was just worn out from playing in the sun, but it's long past her regular nap time." I go back to her crib, the tenth time I've checked on her.

"Bump?" I call, trying not to sound alarmed. "Bump, can you come?"

He hurries. "What's wrong?"

"Feel her. She's burning up."

Isabel is covered in sweat and her thin cotton gown is soaked through. She lets out a weak cry. Bump pulls her to him, presses his lips to her face, and says, "Fever's high, 102. Maybe 103."

"She was fine before I put her down," I say. "All morning she was playing, laughing. She never acted sick for a minute." I trace back through the day and can't remember a single sign that anything was wrong. Now she's too weak to support her own head, too feverish to even give a full cry. "What can we do?" I look to my husband for answers and hope he knows how to make this better.

Bump looks into Isabel's mouth and says, "It's red. She's got an infection." Then he examines her for a rash. We find nothing. I change her diaper. Bump moves into the kitchen to fix a cold wet cloth. I follow, and he washes Isabel down, hoping to cool her. Then Bump adds powdered aspirin to a pureed mush of beans. I hold Isabel and bring a small spoon to her mouth, urging her to take a bite. Isabel twists in my lap and refuses the bitter food. She cries, and my muscles tighten with angst. "I don't know what to do," I admit to everyone.

"I might have something," Fortner says. He leaves the house, and Oka follows. It angers me that I don't have the skills to heal my own child. Isabel struggles in my arms. Her dark locks, a wet mess atop her head; her eyes, glossy and blank. *Don't cry, Millie. It won't help anything.* Finally, Fortner and Oka return, and I meet them at the door.

"Pink root," Oka says. "Good medicine but strong power. Not time yet."

"You'll have it if she gets worse," Fortner adds, "but I need to weaken it."

"Is it dangerous?" I sure don't want to give Isabel anything that could hurt her.

"It's important to get the dose right." Fortner draws a ladle from the drinking bucket and fills a glass with water. Then he pours a few drops of the pink root mixture from a brown bottle. "Sugar?"

Bump passes the sugar bowl, and Oka says, "Just enough to sweet it."

"I'll leave this fixed for you," Fortner says, pushing the mixture to the corner where it won't spill. I look at Bump with wide eyes, suddenly remembering he's supposed to head out in two days to cross the Divide. Bump reads my mind. "Let's see how she is in the morning. Got five buyers wantin' that stallion. If I don't show up on time, he's likely to sell to the first guy with cash in hand."

I don't respond. Of course I want Bump to stay home until Isabel is better, but I know what's on the line if we don't get this stallion.

"Supper?" Oka asks, trying to keep a normal routine. She fills four bowls with stew and places them on the table. Fortner helps her, filling our glasses with water from the scoop. I bring Isabel to the table and hold her in my lap while everyone is seated. Then I lead the prayer, asking, begging, for God to keep her safe.

I haven't slept at all in two nights and neither has Bump. We have kept Isabel in bed with us, trying not to let the heat of our bodies raise her temperature but too afraid to put her in her crib. "I need to hear her breathing," I explain. Bump agrees. She's still running a fever, refusing to eat. I've tried nursing her, but she no longer wants my milk. She won't drink anything at all.

The slightest thought of losing Isabel makes it hard for me to breathe. She coughs a wet, gravelly cough, and my bones grind from the sound of it. I watch her weakening body, feel her rising fever, and fear overwhelms me. "I wish I could take away her pain," I tell Bump. "What if she can't beat this?"

"Shh." Bump kisses me and says, "She's got a little infection, Millie. She'll be fine. I promise."

Her skin is hot to the touch, and her cry is hoarse. It breaks into tiny short bursts, and all I can do is hold her and pray silently. *Dear God, I'm sorry. I'm sorry I ever asked You to take Isabel away. I want to be her mother, more than anything. I love this child. And I am grateful for her. Please, please, help her get well.*

Bump heads to the kitchen where Oka is already brewing coffee. I sing to Isabel, tenderly stroking her soft skin. I change the words to build happy endings. "*Rock-a-bye baby, in the tree top. When the wind blows, the cradle will rock. But the bough will be sturdy and strong. And safe will be baby, all the day long.*"

What a cruel and beautiful mystery, this mothering. The ache, the love. It's all too much. And I'm betting no mother comes out unchanged. Not just physically, but spiritually. Stretch marks of the soul.

Bump still plans to leave today for the western slope. He made the calls from town and arranged everything with the owner of the stallion. There's a short window of time to make it all work because the rancher has given us two weeks. No excuses.

"We have to seal this deal," Bump says. It's the hinge to his business strategy. The one important piece that will keep everything else working as planned. "I can't mess this up."

I try to ease Bump's guilt about leaving while Isabel is sick. "So many wives have sent their husbands overseas to the battlefields. I'm lucky to have you here at all. You need to go."

"Sorry," Bump says. He holds my gaze, and I know he means it.

Fortner jumps in. "Let me go without you," he suggests to Bump. "You stay here with Millie and Isabel."

Bump has been wrestling with this idea all night. He's

talked it over with me and explained all the reasons why this won't work. In order to stay here, he'd have to rely on Fortner to handle not only Mr. Tucker's mares but the prized stallion as well. It's not that he doesn't trust Fortner; he's trusted him from the start. But if anything goes wrong, it won't be Fortner who has to account for it. It'll be Bump. And me.

"I can do this," I assure them. "Oka will help me with the jobs. Isabel will be fine. I promise. I won't let anything happen to her." I try to sound convincing, but I'm struggling to believe my own words.

After breakfast, Fortner heads out to prepare the horses, and Bump puts on his boots to follow.

"Bump?" I ask. He leans, kisses me, and waits for me to finish my thought. "You haven't had any sleep. What if you get sick while you're out there? Isabel may be contagious. You'll be too far out to get help."

"Never been sick. Not once in my life," Bump says. "And I can catch up on my rest tonight. I always did dream well next to a campfire. It'll probably be the best sleep I've had since Isabel was born." He laughs. I don't. It's no time to joke.

He senses my concern. "We'll cut back through town, and I'll ask Doc to come check on Isabel. Maybe he'll know what to do."

"Thanks," I say, kissing him one last time.

Bump pulls himself into the saddle. "You know how to manage the strangles, right?"

"Drain the abscesses, dry the wounds."

"Keep 'em clean, if you can. Check the temp four times a day. And remember not to contaminate anything. We're lucky it hasn't spread. Need to keep it that way."

"I'll do my best." Bump is counting on me now, more than ever. I can't let him down.

With that, Bump signals Fortner to follow. Before I know it, they are heading west. Bump rides Scout, and Fortner trails on his black gelding behind the mares. I fight tears as I watch them ride away.

Chapter 24

Oka presses her lips to Isabel's forehead. No doubt, she's as worried as I am. Neither of us says what weighs heaviest on our minds. That Oka's young daughter died of a fever. While she never has put a name to the illness, we both know Isabel's condition could have the same result.

I spend the day handling the chores with Oka. We take turns caring for Isabel and managing the ranch. Oka collects eggs, milks the goats, and refills feed and water bins in the time it takes me to drain the wounds of the sick draft horse. The smell of infection gets to me, and I think of the illness raging inside Isabel's tiny body. She's so fragile. Any little thing could take her from us.

I'm topping the haystacks in the pasture and making rounds when Oka finds me. She holds Isabel and walks near a group of horses, something she never would have done a few months back. I remember her initial reaction in Firefly's stall the week she first arrived. "You could run this place by yourself," I say.

Oka shrugs. "Not hard."

I latch the last gate and take Isabel from Oka just as Doc Henley arrives. I race to meet him.

"Bump sent me," Doc says.

"Thanks for coming," I greet him. "We don't know what's wrong with Isabel. She's so weak, she can hardly hold her head up." I hold her limp body against my chest and look down at her as if to say, *See?*

The doctor takes her from me and moves inside. Oka and I follow.

"Her fever's been getting worse. It started two nights ago," I explain. "And she won't eat."

Doc listens to her heart, her lungs, pinches her skin, lifts her eyelids, looks into her ears, then her throat. "It's rare to see this in a child so young," he says, taking another look into her throat, "but these blisters in her mouth make me think it's bacterial."

"So what can we do?" I want answers.

He places a thermometer in her mouth and watches the mercury rise. "It's 103.8," he says.

I'm shocked. "That's the highest it's been."

Oka eyes the doctor carefully, and I get the sense she doesn't trust him.

"I have a feeling we're looking at strep. Usually works itself out in time. But her fever is exceptionally high. The bacteria could have spread. Could lead to rheumatic fever."

His words stop my breath cold. "What's that mean?"

"Probably nothing. Worst case, might attack her heart."

Oka sits on the bed and pulls her hands together. She exhales a breath so long and so loud, I imagine her lungs have completely deflated. I pull Isabel to me and try not to cry. I refuse to believe my child might die. I don't care what Doc says. Isabel will be okay. She will.

Doc Henley packs his things and prepares to leave. "I don't

want to worry you. As I said, I've never seen strep in a child so young. I could be wrong. Either way, I'm certain she'll be fine. She's already survived more than most."

"She sure has," I say. If he only knew the half of it.

"Be sure to give her lots of fresh air, and keep trying to nourish her. Don't let her get dehydrated. Some folks chew licorice root to ease the pain, but she's too young for that."

I pass Isabel to Oka and follow Doc out to his car where he holds up two glass quarts. "It's nearly impossible to find oranges anymore, but I've got this." Orange juice. "Packed with vitamins. Might strengthen her system, but it won't feel good on her throat. I honestly don't know what more you can do."

I take both bottles and thank the doctor. He gets into his car but sits for a minute on the shiny black seat. Then he gets right back out and says, "You know, Millie, there may be a better option."

Hope. My whole body reacts with a lift. "I'll do anything. Anything!"

"Over in Longmont. They've converted the sugar beet factory to a POW camp. Got Germans and Italians housed there. Maybe some Japs too. You might have seen them. Working the fields since we're so short on labor."

I shake my head. I haven't noticed.

"Well, some arrive sick or injured, as you can imagine."

I nod, anxious to hear how this relates to helping Isabel.

"I've been reading about a new kind of drug for the last few years. Penicillin. They've been using it in the military for a while now, and I heard they just shipped a batch over to Longmont. Not available on the general market yet, with a few exceptions, but so far, it's shown to be very effective."

"How can we get it?" I am desperate.

"Might be tricky," Doc warns. "But I'll head there straightaway. I'll do everything I can, Millie."

With that, he sits again, cranks the engine, and heads down our lane. Oka waits with Isabel on the porch, so I hand her the juice bottles in exchange for my child. I walk Isabel around the pasture, taking our time to watch Firefly, the woodpeckers. I dip her fingers in the cool spring and wet her lips with fresh water. She no longer cries or coughs, just lies in my arms with her mouth open, struggling to breathe.

By dark, Oka and I come together again for supper. I find her at the stove, already cooking. "Your specialty." I smile. Tiny white moons blossom above the skillet of hot oil, releasing a smell that brings hunger. "You know I love your fry bread."

Oka puts her arm around my waist and says, "And you know I love you."

I fight again to get Isabel to swallow aspirin powder, this time in a serving of applesauce, her favorite. Her tiny body is covered in chills, and I go back and forth between cooling her off and wrapping her in blankets. "Just a bite," I beg, urging her to swallow.

After dinner and dishes, I carry Isabel outside again. I hold her in my arms and walk her all around the ranch. As we roam, I label everything. "Garden, horses, barn, river." I name the flowers, moon, mountains, stars. Leaf, stick, tree, grass. I show her the many wonders of this wonderful world, proving she has much to live for. "Fight, Isabel. Your mother needs you here." I tell her she is loved. Hofanti. Cherished. Protected. I tell her she is a promise from God.

We find Firefly circled with her herd. I whistle, and she meets me at the fence. A few of her friends follow, and she nudges Isabel's blanket. "You've settled into quite a peaceful life here, haven't you, girl?" I rub below her jaw and am relieved to find her lymph nodes are not swollen. She's now a pasture mare, no longer worked, but part of me thinks she misses the training as much as I do. "You'll be a mother soon too," I tell Firefly. "Then you'll understand how I feel." Bump's decided it's time to let her have a foal since there are no expectations for us to compete again. She'll be bred when the new stallion arrives. Our trick-riding days are over. I'm a mother now. I just want Isabel to be okay.

All through the night, Oka sits up with me. We take turns carrying Isabel outside for fresh air. We rock her into the wee hours of the morn, and we try everything to get her to swallow liquids, but she pushes her tongue, using what little energy she has left to twist and turn away from anything we try to give her. She barely nurses, and my breasts have become full and painful. Hours drag, and as the stars give way to sun, Isabel's fever still burns. The exhaustion and the worry finally defeat me. I cry.

The photo of Oka's three children sits on my dresser. Oka takes it now and tells me more about her daughter, the one stolen by fever when she was a child.

"She look like you," Oka says, touching my shoulder and handing me the photo. She has never spoken her name.

I take a closer look at the portrait. Oka's right. Her daughter does look like me. Like Isabel.

"You choose your secret name, Millicent?"

"Not yet," I answer. Not one single name has come to mind.

"It not too late." Oka takes Isabel into her arms now. She

sings softly and kisses her forehead. "She choose her own name someday, Millicent," Oka says. "Wait and see."

"I can't accept anything less," I confess.

"Time for you to have Chahta name too." I assume she means the name my loved ones give me once they know my personality, my skills.

"You have something in mind?" I try to let Oka take my mind away from fear.

Oka puts her hand on my heart and says, "*Ihanko.*"

"Ihanko?"

"Yes, Ihanko. Strong. You strong, Millie. Strong mind. Strong heart. Strong spirit. *Ihankot tanna.* Woven strong."

"Most of the time, I don't feel strong at all." Tears still sting my eyes. I don't tell Oka about the old gypsy Babushka who gave me the name *Krasnaya* and told me I was strong, red, beautiful. I don't tell her about River explaining that Millicent is an old English word that means strength. Instead, I thank her, and try to convince myself I am really as strong as everyone seems to think. That I can help my child overcome this illness, my husband succeed with this ranch, my family survive all these dangers.

"Know your truth, Ihanko. Live your truth," Oka says. "Then you will know great peace."

When the sun rises, I find the bottle of pink root on the counter. "Should we try it?"

Oka shrugs and says, "Risk with baby. Might work. Might make worse."

I leave the bottle on the counter as a last resort. Instead of taking my chances on pink root, I take my chances on God. I spend most of the day on my knees, a place I've spent a lot of time since Isabel was born. In between prayers, I tackle the indoor chores, mending clothes, cleaning the house, scraping ashes from the stove's firebox, anything that will keep me within arm's length of Isabel. I go outside only to tend the sick horse. Her lymph nodes have ruptured now, oozing thick green pus from crater-sores bigger than quarters, and I have to clean them several times a day. Between tending the horse and Isabel, watching them both in so much pain, I feel frustrated by my own limitations. I want to make each of them better, take away their suffering. But all I can do is love them. And care for them. And pray. And hope that's enough.

Doc returns just after lunch, as the hens are all stirring up dust. Oka and I greet him with hopeful hearts. "Good news," Doc says, easing our worries right from the start. "They broke the rules."

"Oh, thank goodness." I release a deep breath and kiss Isabel on the forehead. We all move into the house.

"She'll be a test case," Doc explains. "They want to see if it works on children this young. Are you comfortable with that?"

I feel Isabel's skin, burning hot with fever. "What choice do we have?"

Doc nods. "Think you can give me a hand with this?" He clears a spot on the bed to work and immediately begins trying to insert an IV into Isabel's tiny arm. She's so dehydrated, it's tough to find the vein, and by the fifth stick I am nauseated from watching her cry out against the needle's sting. I hold her still as she screams. Finally, the vein gives, and a backflash of blood spills out. Doc shows me how to keep air from getting into the line and how to manage the flow, keeping the bottle hanging high from her crib.

Isabel pulls at the site, and I struggle to keep her contained. Soon her eyelids begin to droop again and she nods off. "We included something to help her sleep," Doc explains. "And extra fluids to help with the dehydration."

"Is that safe?"

Doc nods. "You might need to keep her restrained for a day or two." He hands me a set of white cotton straps, but I set them on the bed. I hope it doesn't come to that. "Think you can monitor this drip without me? Four times a day."

The medicine falls, one slow droplet at a time from the glass bottle into the line. "Should be fine." I try not to sound as nervous as I feel.

"If this works as well as they say, we should see improvements within the next twenty-four hours. Two days at most."

"That quick?" I look at Isabel lying listless on the bed and hope the doctor's right.

"That's what the research shows. This is being called a miracle drug, Millie. I don't want to get your hopes up, but if anything can help . . . this is it."

There are no words to express how grateful I am for Doc's help. "Stay for supper?"

"I'd love to, Millie, but I must get home to the horses. I'll check back tomorrow," he says. "They want me to publish this. I'll be expecting a positive report."

Oka smiles and says, "Good doctor." She's obviously had a change of heart. It's clear she trusts him now. We both wave goodbye to this kind man, and I whisper another prayer to the heavens. *Thank You.* And *Please.*

~

In the evening, Oka joins Isabel and me on the porch. I hold the bottle of fluids that slowly drip into Isabel's weak body. We watch the sun set behind the mountains, bright orange and red stripes that make me think of blood, and blisters, and the burn of a feverish child. Horses gather for their evening circle, and I try to soothe Isabel with a cold damp cloth. She's had half a day of the medication, and I keep waiting for signs of improvement.

The minutes tick away, and the flaming sky cools, turning dark with a million speckled balls of light peeking out from the great beyond. "It's something to see, isn't it? How beautiful the night sky is behind the mountains." I wonder if somewhere out there, a mother sits like me, holding her child, hoping, praying for a miracle.

"My mother say . . ." Oka turns to me. "She say, the stars always there. Always shine. But you not see the light until it get dark."

Isabel's tiny face shines up at me with clearer eyes and I am reminded of her birth, how she arrived on the longest night of the year . . . a bright light to end the longest dark. Oka's story soothes us, the stars shine beyond the mountains, and Isabel comes out of her feverish haze.

Chapter 25

Isabel sits in her crib, giggling and playing with her blanket, pulling it over her face and then off, again and again, laughing at the contrast between light and dark, not bothered a bit by the line of medicine attached to her arm. The morning sun paints the room with a bright, clear grace, as if to say, *Good morning. Welcome to a brand-new day.* It makes me feel as if maybe God has given us a new beginning. A fresh start. A chance to make things right. With the sun's rise, we have risen too, from the dark death of sleep to discover we are not simply alive, but in a sense, reborn.

I bring Isabel to the kitchen and start a pot of coffee, breakfast. Just as I sit to feed Isabel, Oka joins us. "You should have stayed in bed," I tell her. "She's all better now. You can catch up on your sleep."

"You the one who need to sleep." Oka kisses Isabel's head. Then mine.

"I couldn't sleep if I tried. Payback for months of bed rest."

Oka laughs. I hand her a cup of coffee and motion for her to sit. I serve her warm cinnamon-sprinkled oatmeal and two scrambled eggs. We eat together, both too tired to talk. Outside, the horses gather around the haystack, and I can't put off morning chores much longer. The draft horse will be hungry, and her wounds will need tending.

Isabel babbles from my lap, grabbing the spoon from my hands each time I reach for a new scoop of breakfast. After days of avoiding food, she now tries to satisfy her ravenous appetite. I feed her two scrambled eggs and half a bowl of oatmeal before she slows, more food than she's had in an entire week. I help her sip Doc's orange juice and laugh as her mouth purses at the harsh taste. Finally, her hunger wanes. I remove her IV and pass her to Oka. Once I've cleaned the dishes, I look down and say, "Okay, little Isabel. Ready to go outside?"

She reaches for me to lift her, and we head out for the day. The sick draft horse is still separated from the herd, stalled in the barn where she can't contaminate the others. Her abscesses look worse today, large, oozing open holes beneath her jawline. The pain must be immense. I put Isabel in her barn crib and fasten the strap, but she's having none of it today. Eager to move, she wrestles the restraints. "Well, that's not going to work, is it?" I laugh at my daughter, so grateful to see her well again. I've been thanking God ever since her fever broke, my life a continuous prayer.

She hasn't cried once today. Not when she woke, not when she ate, not even now, as she struggles to escape her crib. It's as if she, too, is thankful just to be here. I lift her from the box and move back to the house to find Oka.

Just as we reach the porch, the steady sound of hooves rises up from the valley below. A wave of brown cattle swells against the new green grass. I stand, holding Isabel on my hip, and wait for the sea of livestock to reach us. Isabel squeals and kicks, pointing to the approaching herd.

As the cattle draw near, I'm relieved to see a healthy, hearty batch of strong black Angus. The trail boss rides ahead and greets me. He's a solid, muscular middle-aged man wearing the typical rancher's work rag and hat. "Mrs. Anderson?" he asks from his saddle.

"Millie," I say. "You must be with MacMillan?" I remember Bump telling me the plan for MacMillan to drive his cattle here in the spring, back down to his lower fields come winter, but I certainly didn't expect them to arrive while Bump was on the western slope.

"Call me Dutch. Where you want these cattle, ma'am?"

I look out into the pastures. The dividing gates have been left open for the last few weeks, so the horses could have access to all four sections of fresh grass. There's no empty section for the cattle.

"I'm sorry. I wasn't expecting you," I tell Dutch. "Can you give me time to clear the southern pasture? We'll put the cattle in there."

Dutch looks out to the section I've indicated. The part we see has at least sixty horses scattered as far back as the property stretches, but that seems to be fewer than the other pastures. The trail boss nods. "I'll stall the cattle and get some help."

"Thanks," I say. "Let me get my daughter settled. I'll be right back."

Oka takes Isabel off my hands without complaint, and I rush to prep Firefly. She's never been trained to do real ranch work, but she's so conditioned to follow my commands, she does as I ask. The problem isn't Firefly. It's me. Since getting kicked by the roan during my pregnancy, I am hesitant to pin myself into a pasture with a moving herd. So I opt to do it on horseback. The thing is, I've never had to move a herd through a small gate by myself, especially not in a hurry with others watching me work. I assess the situation and try to figure how to do this without making a fool of myself.

The trail boss hollers at his men, directing them to hold the cattle. I can't mess this up. We are relying on this contract to turn a profit this year. I may not have been a rancher my whole life, but I do know two things about the horses. Their natural inclination is to follow their leader, and they will usually come to food. So I fill a bucket with oats and pull myself into Firefly's saddle, struggling not to drop the heavy pail.

I lead Firefly to the southern pasture where I call out to the horses, shaking the bucket to let them all know I have what they want. The oats are a nice treat compared to the grass and hay they eat every day. The lead horse heads my way, aggressively nudging Firefly, trying to come to terms with the fact that Firefly is in charge of the food despite her lower rank in the pecking order. I lead Firefly ahead, and the dominant horse doesn't like it. The others gather, and tensions build. I try not to think about the last time I was cornered by the herd, the night the roan kicked me into the fence. I continue shaking the bucket, leading Firefly out through the open gate into the adjoining pasture where other horses join the commotion. I hold the food high, out of reach of the determined animals, but the bucket is heavy, and my arm shakes from bearing the weight too long.

If I can just reach the trough, I can spread the feed and let the horses work it out on their own. *Stay calm, Millie. They won't hurt you.* Just as my arm is about to fail me, Dutch rides out to join me. "Well, that's one way to do it, I guess."

I smile and pour the oats into the trough. The horses circle and devour the feed. "Grab that gate?"

"Sure thing," Dutch says. And just like that, we've cleared the southern pasture. Firefly and me.

With the crew of cowboys, it doesn't take long to move the herd of Angus into the field. They've got plenty of green grass, several big haystacks, and fresh water. They are a docile bunch of cattle, happy and well-fed, and they quickly settle into their new home.

When the work is done, the trail boss huddles his crew of hands together and offers congratulatory pats on their backs. Then he gives me a flirtatious smile and says, "I assumed your husband would be here. You out here all alone?"

The last thing I want to tell this group of strange men is that my husband is across the Divide. That Oka, Isabel, and I are the only ones here, and that there is no help anywhere in reach if they decide to test us. I adjust my stance and move my hand to my hip. I make sure they all see my pistol at the ready, the one I've carried with me since the lion attacked. I refuse to feel threatened in my own home. With that one strong gesture, the men understand I'm not one they want to challenge.

"We aren't set up for guests," I say matter-of-factly. "You're welcome to use the well, and I can give you some dried fruits to take with you."

Dutch eyes me. Then looks back at his men. Then looks at me again. He's brought eight hands, each with their green-broke broncs along for training. The boss rides a strong, young circle horse and seems at ease in his saddle.

"If you head out now, you can make it to Lewiston in plenty of time to find rooms," I add. "You could probably make it all the way back to Estes if you hurry."

"All right then," Dutch says, smiling. "Boys, fill your

canteens." He rolls his arm to direct his crew to the water pump. A couple move their saddles to the greener mounts.

"I'll get the fruit," I say, turning for the house. When I return, I hand Dutch a stack of fruit leather and let him divide it among his crew.

"Mrs. Anderson?" The trail boss sits on his horse with great confidence. He's got a strong jaw, deep-set eyes, and just the right amount of roughness to convince me he could handle anything the mountain throws his way, while at the same time releasing a smile that lets a woman know he can be tender when it counts. I stare at him and wait for him to continue. "We'll be back before winter to move them down. Hope you'll have a place for us to stay by then. I do look forward to seeing you again." He holds eye contact a little too long, and I look away, embarrassed. Other than my husband, I haven't had a man flirt with me since River, and Dutch is certainly doing his best. "Until then," he says, tipping his hat and leading his men back down the mountain.

I round back through the gates, making sure they're all firmly fastened. It might take me a few days to forget the way Dutch looked at me, and I'm hoping Bump is home the next time those men arrive. The crew has just moved out of sight when Kat surprises me with a visit. I fill her in on the adventurous day, skipping the part about the handsome cowboy. I almost laugh to myself imagining the sparks that could fly if Kat and Dutch ever got together. What a pair that would be.

"I'm just dropping in to say good-bye," Kat says.

"Good-bye?" Typical of Kat's conversations, I have no clue what we're discussing.

"I'm leaving. In the morning. Heading out for the western slope," Kat explains, following me to the barn where I continue to care for the sick draft horse. Her fever is dropping, but she's got a long road before she's completely healed. "I'll be there for the summer," Kat adds. "Daddy plans to keep Henry, and I'm going to work at the orchard. Teach some classes on baking, making preserves, general things like that."

"You're leaving Henry for the entire summer?" I can't imagine anything taking me away from Isabel that long.

"Don't judge me, Millie." Kat says this with a snap in her voice. It's obvious I've offended her.

"Oh, Kat. I'm sorry it sounded that way. I'm just surprised, is all. Tell me more."

"It's a wonderful opportunity for me," she says, smiling. "I'll be staying at the orchard, in the main house, and teaching on-site."

"Will you be back before fall?"

"Yes. Early August at the latest."

I guard my reaction, trying not to seem critical. "We'll all miss you."

"I'll miss you too, Millie. Check in on Daddy, will you? I don't want Henry to be too much for him. I'll be going to the hot springs a few times, no doubt. Sure wish you'd join me."

I laugh. "Sounds wonderful." I'll miss Kat's frequent visits, but I'm half hoping she falls in love with some orchard worker and returns home with a husband of her own.

I send Kat away with a stash of dried fruit, just like the drovers, and she waves out of her window, yelling, "See you when the leaves turn gold!"

Chapter 26

In the garden, Oka and I work at weeding and watering our transplants. It's been almost four weeks since Bump set out with Fortner to buy the stallion. I have bitten my nails to the quick. No matter how I try to shake it, I keep hearing Bump's complaints play again and again in my head: "I feel all alone in this, Millie." I hope I've loved him enough, given him reason to come home.

I try to put it all in perspective and not waste my energy worrying about the "what-ifs" and "I wonders." The important thing is our prayers have been answered. Isabel is better, eating again and regaining strength. That's all that matters.

Isabel is the first to hear the hooves, and my, how she squeals.

"Oka! Oka, they're home!" I pull Isabel into my arms and run to greet my husband.

Bump jumps from Scout's saddle and hugs Isabel and me in one giant grab. He's smiling so big, my emotions overtake me. He's safe. He's come back to us. He is home.

Bump and Fortner work together to move the stallion into the side pen, separated from the rest of the herd. Standing at nearly sixteen hands with a tight, muscular tone, he is a chesnut quarter horse of stellar proportions. "Now I see why Mr. Tucker wanted this one," I say, moving closer so Isabel can get a look at him. I don't get too close, though. He is agitated, storming back and forth against the fence line, calling out to the mares in heat. He doesn't need to bother putting on such a show. They've already noticed him, as they begin to answer his calls and move toward his pen.

Bump watches, impressed. "He's already hooked the ladies," he teases. "But he's got good cow sense too, Millie. It's as if he knows what the cattle are gonna do before they do it. And he can turn on a dime. Never seen a stallion so workable." I almost point out that Firefly is surely smarter, but I let Bump soak in the glory, unchallenged.

"How'd he do on the trip?" I switch hips. Isabel's nearly six months old now, and she's eager to crawl. Holding her is more of a struggle than it used to be, and my arm muscles show the proof.

"Never spooked, Millie. Not even once." Bump leans against the fence and points to the stallion with pride. "I'm tellin' you, this is one good horse."

I'm so happy Bump's home, I can't stop smiling. "Have you sent word that he's here? The stallion?"

"Not yet." Bump removes his hat and wipes sweat with his shirtsleeve. "Figure I'll get him settled before I start celebratin'. You should see him run, Millie. Fastest horse I've ever seen."

I laugh. "I've never seen you so excited. You must have had a really good trip."

"Hard work, but worth it, don't ya think?" Bump grins at the new horse. Then he closes the gate and removes his gloves. He has accomplished what very few men have: transferred a herd of mares across the Great Divide and returned with a feisty stallion. "Wait till you see what he produces. I can't wait to start breeding."

As soon as the stallion is settled, Bump takes Isabel from my arms and holds her to the sky. "She's okay?" he asks. "She's really okay?"

"All better," I promise. "I'm convinced nothing will ever stop our little bean." Later I'll fill him in about Doc Henley's heroic efforts to save her. There's so much to catch up on.

"What's that?" Bump finally notices the black Angus cattle in the southern pasture.

"MacMillan's crew showed up." I smile, still proud I was able to handle the situation without Bump or Fortner here to guide me. I'm tempted to tell him about Dutch, just to see if I can make him jealous, but I let it go. Bump moves to examine the cattle. The rest of us follow.

"They look good," Bump says. "Any trouble movin' 'em in?"

"Nope. Turns out, Firefly's more than just a trick horse. She knew just what to do."

Bump draws his head back in surprise and then moves to the barn to check the draft horse. "How's this lady?"

"She's doing great. Few small sores left, but she's a fighter. Just like our Isabel." Bump passes Isabel to Oka so he can examine the horse.

"Didn't spread?" He turns the horse's head to check the nodes. Oka and Fortner turn all of their attention to Isabel, making silly faces and even sillier noises. Isabel erupts in laughter.

"Not at all. I've kept her stalled, but I started pulling her out for ground work last week, just to get her moving again. She seems to be feeling much better."

Bump smiles and kisses my cheek. "I never doubted you, Millie, but now I'm thinkin' you don't need me at all around here."

"Not true," I say. "I missed you every single minute."

"What about me?" Fortner jokes.

"Yes, Fortner. We missed you too. Did Kat track y'all down?" I ask, teasing. "She's been on that side for the last few weeks. I just knew she'd sweep you off to the vapor caves."

Fortner gives Bump a look and Bump turns back to the draft horse, avoiding me.

"What is it?" I ask Bump, lowering my voice. "Don't tell me she went after you." I laugh, but it is a nervous laugh.

"Maybe. A little." Bump shuffles his feet and looks at the ground.

"What does that mean?" I laugh again, hoping this is all a joke.

"I don't know, Millie. It's nothin'."

"You have to tell me, Bump." I touch his arm, a hint for him to look at me.

Fortner and Oka leave the barn with Isabel, giving us room to talk.

"She's just lonely." Bump lowers his voice. "Grief changes people. You know that."

"I don't understand what you're saying. Were you . . . *with* her?" I say it a little too loud and Oka looks back at us.

Bump shuffles his feet. "Not exactly."

My pulse is racing. "It's either yes or no, Bump. Which one is it?"

"Millie, don't be that way. You know how she is." Bump moves to hug me. I pull away. I remember what Bump told me the day we left Mississippi: "I only want a girl to kiss me." Real, unrestrained intimacy. Something I'm finally learning to give. But maybe I'm too late. Kat's ready to fill in the gaps. Give my husband the attention he craves. I leave Bump standing by the stall and join the others back at the fence. Bump doesn't follow.

"How could Kat do that to me, Oka? How could Bump let her?" I force the words through tears, trying to compose myself as I find Oka at the river.

"I never trust her," Oka says, watching her line and trying to land enough fish for supper.

I shake my head. "I saw it happening. I knew all along she was after him, and I did nothing to stop it."

"Men," Oka says, as if they aren't worth the trouble.

As much as I want to blame Kat for everything, I can't believe Bump had no part in the whole situation. Since he told me she met him across the Divide, I've spent hours imagining the long conversations, the quiet campfire evenings, the darkest hours. Oh, I hate this. My mind goes off in a million directions, constantly crafting different outcomes, each one worse than the other.

"Bump insists it's nothing. But I don't know if I believe him, Oka. Fortner knows what happened. You've got to ask him. I need to know."

Oka looks at me as if it's not a good idea.

"Please?" I am desperate. I have to know the truth.

I must look as pitiful as I feel because Oka puts down her fishing pole and says, "I try."

She leaves me at the riverside with Isabel. My daughter can scoot anywhere now, and it's all I can do to keep her out of the water. Without Oka to help me watch her, I give up, move Oka's pole against a tree, and take Isabel for a walk. By the time we return to the house, Oka is cleaning five fish over a cutting board in the yard. "You can outfish Fortner now," I tell her.

Oka laughs. "True."

"Did you talk to him?"

Oka nods.

"And?" I set Isabel on the grass to let her play. As much as I want to know, I'm also afraid to hear it. What will I do if she confirms my suspicions? If she says my husband had an affair with my only friend?

"She a beautiful woman, Millicent." Oka points her knife as she talks.

My nerves burn. I know Kat's beautiful. What I need to know is how my husband responded to this beautiful creature when she showed up to seduce him on the other side of these mountains. I gesture for Oka to tell me more.

Oka shakes her head, as if the truth is too awful to say out loud. "He just a man. A good man, but still, just a man."

My head begins to spin, and my vision blurs. I feel as if I'm losing my footing. "That's enough." I hold up my hands to stop Oka from continuing. I can't stand to hear anymore. I pace back and forth a few quick turns, but then I keep walking. I leave Isabel at Oka's feet and head for the pasture to find Firefly. I saddle her for a ride. She doesn't resist, doesn't even hold that extra breath Bump warned me about when we first met. She knows me well enough to understand, right now, I need to get away.

I lead her to the mountain path. She's careful with her step, even though we hurry, and we don't stop until we reach the top of the trail, the same lookout where I once rode with Kat and Henry. The place I first thought I had found a friend. When Kat admitted the women here had no interest in getting to know her. Now I know why.

I stare out into the valley where the whole world rests below. Stepping down from the saddle, I hold Firefly's reins. We trace the rock circle, walking around the sacred spot until I lead her to the center, where the smaller circle forms. Oka told me this represents a hole in the sky, the route to happy hunting grounds. I'm reminded of my childhood desire for Sloth to reach down from the heavens and take me with him. I stand in the hole to heaven and try to clear my head, try to forget all about Kat and Bump and what might have happened on the other side of these mountains. I focus on thoughts much older and bigger than me.

"Can you picture them here?" I talk to Firefly. "All the people who walked this trail before us?"

Firefly nickers. The wind is fierce, a loud and constant roar slicing across the mountain's edge. For a moment, there is nothing else. No birds. No chipmunks. No crying baby. No cheating husband. There is only Firefly. And me.

A bird nest has fallen to the ground beneath a tree, an empty bowl made of twigs and hair, with a tiny brown feather resting beneath its rim. When I move to cradle the nest in my palms, it breaks. The wind takes most of it away, scattering the pieces across the mountain. "You see?" I ask Firefly. "Just like that, it can all fall apart."

I loop Firefly's reins to a branch and return to the center of the prayer circle. I sit on the ground, cross my legs, and open my hands to the sky. I close my eyes, tuning in to the sounds of the wind. *Erase. Erase. Erase.*

One thing's for sure. I'm not the first person to sit in this spot and seek help. I'm not the first to feel pain, to know loss, to fall to the earth and look to the heavens for answers. I'm not the first to feel broken, lost, alone. The wind wails, and the sun burns, and the trees fight to stand strong against the mountain's steep slope. "God?" I ask. "What now?"

I look out into the distance. How vast these mountains are. How small I am.

~

By the time I get home, everyone is coming in for supper. I hurry, leaving Firefly saddled and tied to the porch. Isabel is in Oka's arms, crying. Bump responds with a sarcastic complaint. "I see one thing hasn't changed." He laughs as if it's funny, but I do not.

"You haven't seen her in a month, and that's what you have to say?" I'm too sad to be angry. I take Isabel outside where Firefly waits. I hold my daughter with one arm and pull up, placing Isabel in front and holding her safely against me. Firefly follows my signals. This time we take a long, slow ride, staying near the fencerow out past the pasture. The sky is dark, and the coyotes squeal in the distance, their frantic, high-pitched yelps an eerie warning for us all.

Isabel babbles and swings her feet, pumping her arms with glee as she points to the moon, the stars in the freckled sky. I pull Firefly to a halt and look with Isabel into the heavens. "What do you see up there, Isabel? See the stars? See the big, round moon?"

Isabel follows my point to the heavens.

"That's right." I reward her with a kiss. "Moon."

Firefly swishes her tail as if she could brush away all the secrets. All the lies. All the choices that led us here, tonight. But even Firefly can't tell me which sins outweigh the others.

Chapter 27

Wildfires have been burning for weeks, coating the sky with a thick blue haze. Thankfully, the flames have remained twenty miles to the east of the ranch, but that's not nearly far enough for me to relax. Bump assures me this is part of nature's process, that dry summers, lightning strikes, and high winds lead to fires. That twenty miles is a safe distance and there's no reason to fear. Still, I am grateful to look onto a clear horizon today. "Maybe it's a sign," I tell Isabel. "Maybe the worst is over."

I carry my sweet Hofanti to the woods for a quick morning hike. At nine months of age, she's growing by the day now and more determined than ever to move through this world on her own, crawling, exploring, putting everything in her mouth. I spend most of my time trying to keep her safe, removing sharp objects, blocking dangerous drop-offs, pulling her tiny hands back from the pecking beaks of the hens, and keeping her out of reach of the horses' heavy hooves. We're planning to spend the next few days in Estes Park for the Rooftop Rodeo, so I'm trying to give her extra playtime before we leave. It'll be a challenge to keep her with me in that crowd.

"Beautiful day," Bump says, taking Isabel from my hip and sliding his left hand into mine. It's been two months . . . two months since he returned from the other side of the mountains, two months since I learned Kat had met him there.

Since then, I've resisted every time he's touched me. He's tried, so many times, to get close to me. I couldn't. So we've danced circles around each other. He'd move forward, I'd move back, trying to keep a distance, avoiding the tender places that drew pain. Now we walk side by side through the woods, where the summer leaves provide shade and sparrows flit from tree to tree. Isabel notices everything. And I try, like her, to see the beauty, not the brutality, of the world.

"She reminds us, doesn't she?" I ask Bump softly. "What really matters."

He is quiet at first. Then he launches right into it. He speaks quickly, as if he's trying to get it out before I can stop him again. I've instantly put an end to our conversations every time he's tried to explain. The difference is, this time he starts with an apology. I wait. I listen. "I'm sorry, Millie. Kat shouldn't have met up with us."

There's nothing I can say without sounding bitter.

"She was at the ranch when we got there. I didn't know what to do. I didn't want to make a scene. Couldn't risk losin' the stallion."

Nothing about Kat surprises me at this point, but this seems extreme. The nerve of her, not only to track down my husband when she knew I was miles away but to find him during such a crucial moment for our business. I listen, trying to give Bump the benefit of the doubt, hoping he'll say what I need to hear. That he wasn't with Kat.

"I shoulda seen it comin'." Everything about him says he is sorry.

"Everybody else saw it." My voice gives away my hurt, the deep burn of betrayal that has blackened acres of my soul.

Bump stops and looks at me. "Maybe it's 'cause everybody else was lookin' at Kat, while I was lookin' at you."

I fight the urge to roll my eyes. I've seen him looking at Kat on more than one occasion, looks I would have loved for him to give me.

He tilts my chin up to meet his eyes. "I love you, Millie. You. Not Kat. And I can't stand this anymore. You gotta believe me. I stopped it. Maybe a little too late, but I stopped it. I don't care about Kat. Not one bit. You. Isabel. This is my life. You, Millie. You are my life."

Doves coo from a tall ponderosa, and I let Bump pull me into him. Kiss me for the first time in months. "I don't like feeling like this," I tell him. "Like I'm losing you."

He kisses me again. "You ain't never gonna lose me, Millie. Never."

Isabel wraps her arms around Bump's neck and says, "Dada!" Clear as can be.

"Did you hear that?" Bump asks, smiling ear to ear. "She just said Daddy!"

"Dada," Isabel says again. Bump covers her in kisses and says, "That's right, Little Bean, you're the only person in the world who gets to call me Daddy."

Later, back at the house, Oka and I prepare supper while the men breed the last of the mares with our prized stallion, hoping for a full pasture of marketable foals come spring. It's a little later than our normal July cutoff, but given the circumstances, Bump doesn't want to wait. I watch the stallion, who barely rests before moving to another mare.

"I want to believe him, Oka. I want to think he stopped it, but you know as well as I do . . . men bow to Kat. What makes me think Bump's any different?"

Oka dredges venison strips in egg, then flour. "You know about Code Talkers?"

"Let me guess . . . you have a Choctaw story." I laugh.

Oka laughs too and says, "Sure do." Then she continues. "You already know how this government tell Chahta we not citizens. This government hurt us, kill us, cheat us. But then new war start. World War I. And Chahta have to choose. We choose to fight with this country. We choose to help this government who hurt us."

I try to imagine Choctaw men in U.S. uniforms, going to battle with the same men who had betrayed them. I can't imagine how hard that must have been.

"Then," Oka continues, "it 1918. Big, important battle against German." She looks at me as if she wants me to tell her the right way to say it.

"Germany?" I ask.

Oka nods as she starts again. "Chahta soldiers use our language to bring secret message. German not break that code, and that why we win. Very important. Might have different country now without Chahta. You see?"

"You're saying the Choctaw Code Talkers helped us win World War I?" I peel potatoes.

"Yes." Oka browns venison in the skillet and the entire kitchen fills with the sound of sizzle.

"Sorry, Oka, but . . . what does that have to do with Bump and Kat?" I start a pot of water to boil, trying to steer clear of the blistering oil from Oka's pan.

Oka flips the meat. "Bump hurt you. That true. But now you have a choice. What side you on, Millicent? Who you fight for? Who you die for? Who you risk everything for? You choose."

~

"Did you know Lana Turner was here in '41?" Bump asks, reading the pamphlet for the Rooftop Rodeo. We've just arrived in Estes Park, where we hope to sell some of our best stock. Get Mr. Tucker's name in sync with high-quality broncs and ranch horses.

I look at the small arena surrounded by a few hundred seats and assume Bump's trying to fool me.

"Says right here." Bump taps the program. "She'd been shootin' some fancy magazine cover, and they talked her into bein' the Rodeo Queen. They even got Humphrey Bogart to be Parade Marshal."

"Can't be true." I smile.

"It's true," Bump says, brushing his fingers through Isabel's dark hair. "Maybe you'll be queen someday, Isabel." She smiles up at him and offers pure, unfiltered love. I try to do the same.

"Camille would be thrilled to know I'm sitting somewhere Lana Turner once sat. I can't wait to write her."

"Did you know the Millers want to buy a horse for Camille?" Bump asks.

"What about Poison?" Bump basically assigned the black pony to Camille and spent hours training her how to ride. By the time we left Mississippi, Camille was about as attached to Poison as I was to Firefly.

"Sold her," Bump says, clicking his tongue and shaking his head as if he can't believe Mr. Tucker would have done such a thing.

"What?" I'm shocked to hear Poison isn't at the barn anymore. "When?"

"Month or two back, I think."

"How do you know all this?" Isabel leans stiffly, but I can't put her down on the ground or she'll be trampled in the crowd. I pass her to Bump just long enough to give my arms a break.

"Called Mr. Tucker from that ranch out west. When I purchased the stallion. Had to connect him with the breeder, finalize the deal. He mentioned the Millers were interested in Firefly."

"Oh, Bump. I can't--"

"Don't worry." Bump interrupts me. "Mr. Tucker said she wasn't for sale."

I exhale. The very idea of losing Firefly brings panic. I consider the options. "What about that paint pony?" I point to the pen of sale horses. "She's a good horse. And no one up here seems to want a paint."

"True." Bump looks out at the pen. Only one paint. Ours.

"Mr. Tucker doesn't have anything down there for her?" Isabel pulls at Bump's hat and I smile.

"Been reducin' his stock, movin' everything good up here and sellin' off what's left. Poison was the only fit for Camille, even when we were there."

"Why'd he sell her?" I give Isabel the pamphlet, and she tries to eat it. I pull it from her mouth.

Bump shrugs as a man approaches us, hands in pockets,

black Stetson tilted crooked on his head. He has no spurs, and an old-fashioned pocket watch hangs from his vest pocket. My first impression is that he has money. "You Mr. Anderson?"

"Yes, sir." Bump extends his hand and the man returns the greeting. I take Isabel from Bump and step back a bit so the men can talk without Isabel reaching for them.

"You own that batch of quarter horses? Branded with a circled arrow?"

"Actually, my boss, Cauy Tucker, owns them. All work easy around the catch rope. All for sale."

"Mind if I take a look?" The man tilts his head, a gesture that makes me think he's interested in buying what we've got.

"Sure thing." With that, Bump leaves Isabel and me to wander the event grounds. We weave our way through groups of families, musicians, cowboys, and girls hoping to win some guy's attention. It seems strange to think I once competed with Firefly. As much as I love to ride, I no longer have any desire to perform in front of a crowd. I'm content watching the show, holding my daughter, celebrating when others win. I'm surprised Jack never outgrew his need for the crowd's cheers, and I'm happy I no longer crave that kind of affection.

As the announcer's voice breaks the air, the fans make their way to the stands for the start of the bronc competition. I move along with the spectators and find a seat, holding Isabel in my lap. She squeals with excitement when a sponsor girl circles the arena, flag waving in the wind. I remember how disgusted Jack was when the rodeo started letting sponsor girls be a part of the events. He thought it cheapened the competition by turning it into a show. I scan the crowd for signs of Fortner, hoping Oka can find her way back to me. I'm watching a little boy dip his finger into his sister's lemonade when I hear Kat's voice. My entire body tightens. *Please don't let her see us.*

Before I can turn away, our eyes meet, and Kat smiles awkwardly. I'm not sure I can bite my tongue if she stops to talk. She waves. I turn my head to look for Oka.

Henry runs toward me. "Hi, Mrs. Anderson!" He's full of energy and happy as usual.

"Hello, Henry." I return the smile. I can't blame him for his mother's actions. He tickles Isabel under the chin. "Tickle, tickle, tickle." I laugh, and Isabel does too.

"You better get back to your mom." I pat his back and add, "It's getting crowded."

"Bye!" Henry shouts behind him as he runs back to Kat's side. I don't look at her. Still, she doesn't get the hint. She moves down my row and sits next to me.

"Millie, it's so good to see you. I just got back last night. Feels like I've been gone for ages." Kat talks with a chipper pep, as if we're still friends. As if she can make the whole world work exactly how she wants. "My goodness, look how beautiful Isabel is. She's grown so much!"

I don't respond. *Please, Oka, hurry.* I shade my eyes with my hand and search the distance for Oka's dark braid.

"She looks just like you," Kat says, touching Isabel's hand. I shift my weight to pull Isabel away. I hope Kat doesn't make a scene. It's important for us to make a good impression here today. The business depends in great part on the deals we make at this event.

"I'm glad she's well," Kat says, still trying to engage me.

I don't give her what she wants. She's just like Bill Miller, too used to getting her way.

"Millie? Is something wrong?" Her voice squeezes into an annoying whine.

I look at her now. My temples pulse. "Yes, Kat. Something is very wrong."

With this, a flash of shame crosses her face. She finally accepts the fact that I know.

"Oka!" I yell, finally seeing my grandmother walking toward the stands. "Over here!"

Kat and Henry move up to the next section of seats as Oka finds her way to Isabel and me. *Don't do it, Millie. Don't you dare cry.*

"Want me to handle her?" Oka whispers, shooting Kat a look that could kill. She's obviously trying to make me laugh. It works.

The announcer delivers the opening prayer just in time, and the competition begins. Isabel, Oka, and I all cheer. Below us, Bump points out our best horses to the potential buyer. Instead of worrying that Bump might see Kat, I do what Kat would do. The same thing Diana would do. I pretend Kat doesn't exist, that my world is perfect, and that nothing can steal my joy.

Chapter 28

It's Christmas week, and Isabel turns one today. I've baked a pound cake to celebrate. Now I add one tiny white candle and strike a match. Fortner plays his beat-up guitar while we all sing "Happy Birthday." Oka claps and kisses Isabel from head to toe.

I pause for a moment and try to capture the scene: the way Isabel's curls brush beneath Oka's small fingers, the sound of Oka's laugh, deep and hearty and true. The flickering flame of the match reflecting in Isabel's dark eyes. The sun-kissed back of Bump's neck as he bends over the cake and says, "Make a wish!" The lemon smell of the browned batter, the white sugar icing drizzled thin across the top. Fortner's callused fingers strumming six strings, his soft humming as he tunes his guitar. The way the sun colors the room a shade of pinkish-yellow, a hue that knows no name, and the particles of dust swimming through the air like fairies, like the floating dandelion seeds scattered on our wedding day, when Janine also said, "Make a wish." I take photographs with my mind and file these memories, these simple gifts of grace. I never want to forget.

Isabel flaps her hands and squeals, "Daddy!" as he helps her turn the spark to smoke. Not Dada this time, but Daddy, clear as day, as if there's no more debating. As if she's telling the whole world, *See this man? This man right here? This man is my* true *father.*

I slice the cake and pass a piece to everyone. Isabel tears into hers, coating her face in sticky white icing, much to the delight of us all. Once I've cleaned her hands, I help her open presents. Janine has sent a set of wooden horses with a card from Mr. and Mrs. Tucker, proof she's fully embraced her new role as a wife. Isabel pulls each miniature pony from the box and puts them straight into her mouth for a taste. "Oh, look," I tell Isabel, trying to teach her how to play with the horses. "Here's a cowgirl to ride them."

Isabel takes the doll and tries to imitate my movements. She places the girl on one of the toy horses. "Oh, she likes this one?" I ask, pointing to the black stallion. Isabel nods.

We play horses until her attention drifts. Then Fortner hands Isabel a handmade leather ball, small enough to cup in her hands but too big to swallow. Isabel throws it into the air and laughs as it bounces three times on the floor. Then she does it again. And again. And again.

"That was very thoughtful," I tell Fortner. "She loves it."

Fortner's cheeks go pink, and he gives a bashful smile.

"She's awful lucky to have an uncle like you." Bump slaps Fortner's shoulders in the way men do when they really want to offer a hug. I remember when I was angry with Bump for hiring Fortner, too afraid we were putting our family in danger. I also remember Bump's response, telling me, "Sometimes all a man needs is a chance." Fortner rolls the ball back to Isabel, and she throws it again, erupting in laughter at her ability to send an object propelling so far and so fast.

Next, Oka brings Isabel a hand-stitched doll, soft and squeezable, filled with fabric scraps. "Baby!" Isabel squeals, hugging the doll tight. She brings her new baby around to each of us, and we all respond by giving the doll hugs and kisses. "Baby," she says each time, so proud of her new toy.

"You're a good mama," I tell Isabel.

"Baby," she says again, kissing her baby doll's head.

"That's right," I tell her. "Love the baby."

"Your baby sweet," Oka tells her.

"And loved," I add. "Just like you." I tap Isabel's nose, and she giggles.

Isabel tries to put her baby on one of the toy horses from Janine. "Too big," I say. So she puts the horse on top of the baby, and everyone laughs.

"I can't believe how fast this year has gone," I announce to no one specifically. "It seems like Bump just yelled, 'It's a girl!' And now here she is. All grown up." Bump puts his arm around me, and we watch Isabel playing with her new gifts. Together, with Fortner and Oka, we all celebrate the life, the light, that Isabel has given us.

Bump takes the guitar from Fortner, strums a few chords, and says, "Ya mind?"

"Not at all," Fortner says.

Then Bump plays a slow tune, one I've never heard before. The melody is lovely, sweet in a way that feels honest, innocent like a lullaby. After a run-through, he begins to sing to Isabel.

I'll find you a place, a place you can rest.
I'll sing down the moon. Build a soft, feathered nest.

I'll carry you there, in my arms through the night.
I'll find you a place, call it yours, call it mine.
I'll give you a home, a whole world away,
And I'll love you forever. Plus a day.

By the end, I'm in tears. "That's beautiful," I tell him. "What's it called?"

"Just a little thing I made up." Bump puts the pick between his teeth and repositions himself for another song.

"You wrote that? For Isabel?"

That crooked grin spreads across Bump's face and he bends to kiss his daughter, my daughter, *our* daughter, our Isabel.

We are all laughing and talking and singing when we suddenly hear a scream. A horrifying, haunting cry behind our home. The same one I heard last year, seconds before the mountain lion launched her attack and sent me running into the barn.

"Lion," Fortner says, standing and signaling for us all to be quiet.

We hold still, waiting for another sound to confirm our fears. Then we hear it again. There's no doubt, a mountain lion is outside, probably in the woods behind the house. Fortner moves, pulling a pistol from his belt. Bump joins him, reaching for the rifle. But then he stops. Says, "No. Not tonight."

"The lion won't care that we're having a party," Fortner argues.

"True," Bump says. "But I do. We don't get many moments like this. Now where were we?"

Fortner gives Bump a long look, worried he may regret his decision. Bump pulls Isabel and me both into his arms, and says, "Keep the music comin', Fortner. I want to dance with my girls."

With that, Fortner trades the pistol for the guitar. He sits next to Oka and begins to play a lively "Cotton-Eyed Joe." We all dance together around the living room as Fortner moves from one cowboy song to the next.

Isabel wiggles from my arms, pulls herself to her feet, and takes a step. Then another. Bump pulls away and calls to her. She takes two more steps before falling bottom first.

"Did you see that?" Bump cheers. "Our Isabel is walkin'!"

"Not walking," Oka says. "Dancing."

Isabel giggles wildly, and we all clap. Outside these walls, predators stalk, cats prowl, unjust men do awful things, but in here, right now, we focus only on the celebration of life, refusing to let the constant threats break us.

Chapter 29

I hurry to the post office while Bump delivers another stash of Oka's baskets to the store. "More letters," Abe says, passing me my mail. "Nice day out there."

"It's gorgeous," I answer. It's one of those perfect mountain days, when the autumn colors burst forth and the summer sun yields to cooler winds. Three seasons have swept through since Isabel's first birthday. She's nearly two years old now, a feisty little thing. It's hard to keep her contained, and she cries every time I bring her inside. If she could manage it, I have no doubt she'd spend her days climbing trees, running through the woods, and exploring the creek beds, just as I did when I was a girl. It's only a matter of time before her body catches up with her will to be wild. Now Isabel reaches for the envelopes, fussing when I don't give in. "I knew better than to bring her to town today, with her teething," I say. I thank Abe and hurry out the door before my temperamental daughter breaks into a full tantrum. I thumb through the letters while Isabel wiggles in my arms.

I am heading back to the truck, pointing out the elk to Isabel, when the sight of Kat stops me in my tracks. She is talking to

Bump, right here, in the middle of town. It's been more than a year since I saw her at the rodeo in Estes Park. Since that awkward confrontation, Kat hasn't stopped in for a visit. Not even once. We haven't bumped into each other in town. And no one has mentioned her name. If anyone still talks about the whole situation, they do it behind my back. I was just beginning to feel a safe distance from Kat. And here she is. Again. Going after my husband. Isabel is squirming, whining, as I approach them.

"Millie," Kat begins. "I need help." She looks frantic. Henry is not with her.

Isabel cries harder now. "What's wrong?" I ask.

"It's Daddy. He's hurt." Kat's voice breaks, and her eyes dart in all directions. It's clear she's afraid.

I immediately soften toward her. "Oh, Kat. Where is he? I'll fetch Doc Henley."

"I had to leave him at home. He couldn't walk."

"What happened?" I ask, trying to soothe Isabel by giving her one of the envelopes.

"He fell from a ladder," Kat explains, speaking quickly. "Hit his head, and I think he broke some bones. Doc's down in Denver and Uncle Halpin's gone to Fort Collins with the reverend. I didn't know what else to do. So I went to your place."

I don't know how to react. Kat must feel very desperate to turn to me for help.

"Oka said you had come to town," Kat continues. "She was sending Fortner over to sit with Daddy while I came for help." She's on the verge of tears now, her voice tense. "Please, Millie?" She grabs hold of my arm. "Please. We need to hurry!"

Bump says nothing but looks at me, and I know he's thinking he can help. "Go," I tell him. "I'll meet you there."

"Thank you, Millie," Kat calls as she runs to her car. Bump grabs his vet supply bag from the truck before jumping in the passenger side of Kat's Oldsmobile. They speed away, and even though I'm the one who sent them off together, my heart squeezes tight.

By the time I start the truck, Kat and Bump are already out of sight. I drive carefully, with Isabel playing on the floorboard. The vibration from the road seems to take her mind off the pain from her teeth, so she's quiet for the first time in hours. The drive takes longer than it should because the elk have started their rut again. We have to stop and wait while a large harem blocks the road, their impressive bull filling the air with grunts and calls, still trying to attract more mates. Isabel climbs into my lap to watch the display. The bull walks mere feet from our window, his massive antlers spanning wider than my outstretched arms. Isabel bangs her tiny hands against the glass and the animal warns us with a snort. I'm reminded of the day we ate lunch with Kat in the diner. "Love can make a man do crazy things." I honk the horn and try to weave through the herd. Finally, we break through.

When we reach Kat's family ranch, Mr. Fitch is propped in bed. Kat is at his side. "I think he's going to be okay," she says, her shoulders slumped in relief.

"He'll still need to see Doc," Bump warns.

"Of course," Kat says, her voice quavering. "But thank goodness you were here. What would I have done?"

Mr. Fitch's eyes are closed, and I can't tell if he has passed out cold or if he's trying to block out his surroundings. "Have to run some stitches," Bump tells me. He begins to work a row of sutures through a patch where Mr. Fitch's silver hair has been shaved. A damp cloth rests over Kat's father's mouth, and I assume Bump has used ether. A sign that Bump has probably been doing something much more difficult than simple stitches. Resetting bones, perhaps. I shudder to think of the pain Mr. Fitch has suffered.

"Where's Fortner?" I ask.

"Just left," Bump says.

"I was hoping I could send Isabel home with him." She fusses and tugs my leg. As soon as I pick her up, she whines to be put down again. "Teething," I explain. No one answers. It's obvious we have brought more stress into the room.

"You better get her home," Bump says, not looking up from his work.

"I'll come right back." I lift Isabel again as she arches her back in protest, squealing at the top of her lungs.

"It's okay. Just go take care of Isabel. I'll take one of Kat's horses home as soon as he's stable." Bump kisses Isabel's forehead and she jerks back, splitting my lip. I taste blood in my mouth. "Look in my bag," Bump adds, returning his attention to the stitches. "Give her some aspirin."

"Will do," I call. I see myself out, a stab of worry in my throat. The last thing I want to do is leave Kat with my husband, together in a bedroom, but I know Bump's only here to help. *Right?*

Hours pass, and still Bump doesn't come home. Oka, Fortner, and I eat beans and bread without him, while Isabel chews on everything she can find, trying to work her teeth through the gums. By bedtime, I am worried Mr. Fitch might have taken a turn for the worse. I also worry that Kat's had time to sink her claws into Bump again.

"Think I'll run some supper over to Kat's place," I announce. "Mind if I leave Isabel here? I'll put her to bed before I go."

"Go on," Oka says, smiling. "I can handle it."

I give Isabel a kiss—Oka too. "Thank you," I tell her. She knows a seed of doubt grows wild within me.

In a hurry, I pack food and head out. I drive carefully along the dark roads to Kat's house where I pull in next to her Oldsmobile, parked crooked in the drive. I knock on the door. I wait. No one answers. I knock again, louder this time. No response. I test the knob, cold against my palm. It's unlocked, so I enter.

I am afraid to call out, might wake Mr. Fitch. So I bring the food to the kitchen and make my way to the master bedroom where Bump was treating Kat's father. When I reach the open doorway, I find Mr. Fitch sound asleep in the bed. His head is propped on pillows; his mouth is open, and he drools. I move quietly into the room. Bump sits on a love seat in the reading area, his head tilted back, snoring. Kat sleeps too. Her long body stretched out across the love seat. Her head at rest in Bump's lap.

I stare at them there, together, her red hair spilling down his legs. His hand across her ribs. It's clear to me now. Whatever started on the western slope, it isn't over.

What should I do? Should I wake him? And if so, what do I say? There's nothing I can do without making a fool of myself. They'll both act as if they haven't done anything wrong, as if I'm the one who is out of line, overreacting, a jealous wife who doesn't trust her husband. Bump's a grown man. He can make his own choices. And if Kat is his choice, then I don't want to force him to come home with me. That's not the kind of life I want.

I stand and watch them for another minute or two, trying to reason all the ways this could be more innocent than it looks, but in the end, I can't see any other truth. It's in the placement of his hand, just beneath her breasts, the fall of her hair, as if he's brushed it back as she leaned into his lap. I can't make any more excuses. I leave the food in the kitchen and my husband sleeping next to Kat. I drive home to Isabel, alone.

~

It's the first night I've faced an empty bed since Bump's trip across the Divide, when Kat went there to find him. All night I pace the floors, imagining the worst. Isabel wakes several times in pain, and I soothe her gums with a whiskey-soaked chew rag. I fight the urge to dull my own pain with whiskey as well. I'm exhausted, but sleep never comes. I am haunted through the long, dark hours, knowing my husband should be here, sleeping next to me. Finally, the sun rises, and I can wait no longer. "Mind watching Isabel again?" I ask Oka. "I'm sorry to ask, but I really need to check on Bump."

Oka takes Isabel's hand and smiles as she says, "Help me garden?"

"Dig!" says Isabel, and I'm relieved not to leave her crying.

I drive faster this time, whipping the truck into Kat's drive. Her car is no longer parked where it was last night. I sprint to the front door where a sign has been tacked. It reads, "Millie," in bold, black letters. Kat's writing, not Bump's. I take it down and unfold the letter. "Daddy in trouble. Took him to Longmont. Kenneth with us. Uncle Halpin has Henry. Tell Reverend."

I rush inside to the telephone. "Reverend Baker, please," I ask the operator. "Lewiston."

I hold the line. "No answer." The operator responds flatly, as if the world still makes perfect sense.

"Can you try the sheriff?" My voice hits a frequency of panic.

"Hold please." Her monotone voice still shows no emotion. "No answer."

I thank the operator and hang up the phone. Then I walk to the bedroom where I last saw Mr. Fitch. A pool of blood has stained the unmade bed, and a few bottles of morphine stand in the windowsill. A reminder of Mama and how badly we can hurt the ones we love. I step over a glass of water that has been knocked to the floor, the shattered glass proof they left in a hurry.

I leave the Fitch place and head for Longmont. I'm betting they went straight to the hospital, and I figure it should be easy enough to find. I will go there, and I will bring Bump back home with me. Where he belongs. But I don't get two miles down the road before I stop the truck. I sit and watch the last of the summer fires burning in the distance, a reminder that nature takes its own course and that sometimes the best we can do is get out of the way. I wipe my tears and straighten my spine. Then I turn the truck around and go home.

Just before nightfall, Reverend Baker drives down our lane. I'm sorting Oka's colorful beads on the porch with Isabel. My stomach drops when I see him. I'm relieved when Oka joins me as the reverend approaches. "Millie, Mrs. Reynolds." He removes his hat and nods in greeting. "I've just received some bad news."

My heart plummets. I fear the worst. That something terrible has happened. That Bump may be hurt.

"Mr. Fitch has passed away," the reverend says.

I'm stunned, and I'm betting the look on my face reveals my surprise. "What happened?"

"The head injury was more severe than they thought." I sit down next to Isabel and put my head in my hands. He was such a healthy, vibrant man. I look at Oka for answers, but she has none. She sits on the swing and motions for the reverend to have a seat too. He continues to stand.

"Your husband did everything he could, Millie. Everyone appreciates that." The reverend must know what I'm thinking. I can only imagine how awful Bump must feel. He's already felt like a failure on the ranch, with the delayed arrival of cattle at first, and then the late breeding season with the stallion setting us back. Not to mention the guilt he feels for not enlisting in the war, especially now that the men are returning home, broken and bulleted. And now, when it matters most, he wasn't able to save Mr. Fitch. I ache for him. For Kat too. As angry as I am with her, she must be in so much pain. And for little Henry, a boy who has already lost more than most.

"Are they still in Longmont?" I want to be there for Bump. He needs me.

"Yes. Kat's not taking this very well." The reverend rubs his smoothly shaven chin. "It's a lot for her to handle, especially after her husband. And her mother."

"Of course," I say. It's certainly not fair. Now I understand why Kat wants Bump. Except for Henry, she's lost everyone she's ever loved. She's drawn to Bump for the same reasons I am. He's safe. He's an anchor.

"She relied on her father for everything," the reverend continues. "Not sure how she'll manage without him, to be honest."

I nod. I agree.

"Bump asked me to let you know the situation. He had no other way to reach you. It sounds as if Kat's quite fragile right now, so he plans to stay awhile longer. Give her the time she needs."

I sink. He's telling me my husband is spending more time with Kat. Out of town. "Has she been admitted?" I remember how the hospital staff handled Mama's grief when Jack died. How their flawed attempts to help led to her death too. I don't trust doctors to handle these things. On the other hand, I hope Kat is in the hospital because if they aren't staying there, they might end up with a room somewhere. The thought sends my blood to a boil.

"I'm not sure, Millie. Kat insisted I stay here." The reverend finally sits next to Oka, and the swing creaks. "She wants me to plan the services. And help with Henry."

"I should go. I'll take care of Kat, and Bump can come home to manage the ranch." I look at Oka, and she nods in agreement. She knows what I'm thinking.

"I suggested that too," the reverend says. "But Bump feels responsible. He wants to make this right."

I try not to reveal how this makes me feel, to know my husband has chosen to stay with Kat, after all that's happened. The reverend surely wouldn't understand my concern. He knows nothing about Kat chasing my husband across the mountains. "Well then, how can I help?" I try to ignore the warning flares my nerves are sending. "Henry's welcome to stay here, of course. And I can cook. Just tell me what you need."

Isabel spills the bowl of beads, and I lean to collect them, trying to catch as many as I can before they roll through the cracks of the porch.

"Thanks, Millie. Bump said you would understand. I'll let the sheriff know he can bring Henry here. He'll appreciate that."

"You sure I shouldn't go to Longmont?" I pass the bowl of beads to Oka, hoping to keep them out of Isabel's reach.

"No need. They'll be heading home soon, I'm sure. You'd probably pass them on the way."

"You'll let me know if anything changes?" I say this to the reverend, but I look at Oka, hoping she'll tell me what to do.

Oka has sat quietly through this entire conversation. Now she gives me a look that says, *I'm sorry.*

"Of course." With that, the reverend stands to leave. I stand too.

"Stay for supper?" I ask. "Venison chili. Plenty to share."

"Sure sounds good, but I need to head on over to Halpin's place. Check on Henry. Figure out the plan."

"I'll send enough for all of you," I insist. He follows me inside where I scoop him an oversized serving bowl before he heads on his way.

"Well, one thing's for sure," the reverend says. "With food like this, Bump won't stay gone long." I sigh, knowing what Kat offers Bump is much more tempting than food.

Little Henry plays with Isabel in the yard, rolling her birthday ball all around her. She reaches to grab it. Misses. Laughs. Tries again.

"When's the last time you heard from Kat?" I ask the sheriff. He's taking me up on my offer to keep Henry. They've just arrived, and now he places a bag of Henry's clothes on the porch swing.

"She called two days ago." Halpin kicks at a post. "Didn't sound too good."

"Did she say when they were coming home?" I still haven't

heard from Bump, and my patience is wearing thin. I can't count the number of times I've almost gotten in the truck and driven to Longmont. I probably would have done just that, if I wasn't afraid of what I'd find when I got there. It's now been nearly a week, and he's still not home.

"She just said 'soon.'" The sheriff avoids eye contact, and I'm certain he's having the same fears as me.

"Did you talk to Bump?" I try not to sound as desperate as I feel.

"Afraid not." He spits off the porch and leans against the post, crossing his arms.

I've already imagined every possible scenario. "What if they ran off the road?" I ask. "They could have driven off into the canyon."

"I'm sure they're fine, Millie." He doesn't say what everyone is thinking. That my husband has run off with Kat. That they're never coming back. That they're long gone. "This came in last night for you." He pulls a telegram from his shirt pocket. "I read it. It's from Bump. You understand."

I take the paper and read it aloud. My voice shakes. So do my hands. "'Need more time in Longmont. Be home soon.' That's it?"

"Just what it says there, I'm afraid." The sheriff shrugs, as if even he can't reason this.

Oka and Fortner have noticed the sheriff's car and are making their way toward us from the barn. "You know where they're staying?"

Halpin shakes his head. "No, but I'm going to find out. This has gone on long enough."

Fortner and Oka move to the porch and ask for an update. I

read the telegram again, aloud. "Kat need to come home to her son," Oka tells the sheriff. She's trying to defend me, by putting the blame all on Kat. But I know better. Bump's to blame too.

"From the looks of it, he's not missing his mother all that much." Fortner pushes the sheriff a bit too hard with this comment, but as we all look out and see Henry playing happily with Isabel, there's no denying the truth. Kat has put Henry on the back burner since learning the news that her husband had died. We all know he hasn't been her priority for a long time.

The sheriff lets Fortner's comment slide, lowering his voice and saying instead, "He won't stop asking for his grampy. I don't think it's my place to tell him. It'll break his heart."

We all watch Henry playing with Isabel, and I wish I could shelter this child from yet another loss. "I'm going with you," I tell the sheriff. He's right about one thing. This *has* gone on long enough.

"Best you wait at home," Halpin says, the same tone he used at Kat's dinner party, when he called me little lady. "I'll start at the telegraph office in town and track back from there. I'll send Bump home as soon as I find them."

"But I can help," I argue. "I should go."

"If you really want to help, stay here and keep Henry."

Chapter 30

"Kat's bound to come back for Henry soon," I tell Oka over breakfast. Henry waddles into the kitchen with messy morning hair and a sleepy smile. He doesn't ask for Kat, but he does say, "Where's Grampy?"

Oka looks at Henry but says nothing. We both know Kat left him for the whole summer without a single tear. I'm kidding myself to think he's enough to bring her home. I'd like to believe there really was a time when Henry meant the world to Kat. But as Bump said, grief can change a person. And Kat has been dealt more than her fair share of loss, that's for sure.

"I have to go to Longmont," I say. Then I lower my voice to a whisper, turn my back so Henry can't hear me. "I can't just sit here while she steals my husband."

Oka shakes her head as if this whole situation is a sorry, pitiful scene.

"I'll take care of breakfast. You should have plenty of soup left for supper. I'll keep the kids busy this morning and leave when I put them down for a nap. They should be able to play this afternoon without being too much trouble for you."

"It no trouble." Oka waves her hand.

"Thank you, Oka." I give her a hug and thank her again in Choctaw. "*Yakoki.*"

After breakfast, I bring Henry and Isabel outside. I can't stop moving. I've paced the entire fencerow, carrying Isabel in spurts when she's too tired to toddle behind. Henry manages to keep up, barely. I've convinced him we're on a hunt for dinosaurs, looking for footprints, bite marks, scratches, and scrapes. Anything to take Henry's mind off of his grandfather and my mind off of Bump.

My questions are endless. Has Bump worried about the ranch at all? Does he care that I haven't slept? Has he thought about little Henry, crying for his grampy? Or Isabel, crying for her daddy? Nothing about this situation makes any sense, and as the minutes turn into hours, and the hours become days, I am losing faith in my husband. I'm afraid to accept what everyone else is already thinking. That Bump has chosen Kat. My emotions shift from fear to rage, and from sadness to disbelief. I am a wreck.

"Maybe Firefly can help us catch a dinosaur," I suggest. "Let's go ask her." I lead Henry and Isabel to the barn. There we brush Firefly before draping the saddle blanket over her strong, muscular back. All I want to do is ride away, as fast as Firefly can take me, but I'm here, taking care of Kat's child, while she's the one who breaks free. With my husband.

I pull the saddle over Firefly's back and adjust the stirrups to fit Henry's short legs. I'll lead him around the pasture, let him pretend he's a dinosaur hunter. Then I'll put them down for naps, and I'll drive straight to Longmont. No more delays. I have to find my husband. I'll start at the hospital. Someone's bound to know something.

I've just tightened the last saddle strap when Oka finds me. "Millicent?" she calls. "Someone here to see you."

The sun shines in from outside the barn door, blocking my view, so I move to greet our guest. By the time my eyes adjust, my hand is in his, and chills are tracing my spine.

Oka leads the introductions, "Mrs. Anderson—Mr. Greene." Dark hair, rough beard. Can it be?

"Pleased to meet you, Mrs. Anderson," he says. My knees buckle. It's all I can do to stay upright. There's no question about it. This is not just any Mr. Greene. This is River Greene. River. It's River. He has found me.

"Likewise, Mr. Greene," I answer. "How can I help you?" His shirt is dirty, his nails too. He doesn't quite match the perfect image I've carried in my memory. But still.

"I'm here about the yearlings. Heard you had the best in the region." That voice—the same one that quoted Fitzgerald to me beneath the clouds.

"In whole country," Oka corrects him.

"Says a lot for you, Mrs. Anderson." River smiles at me, and I am sixteen again. In a field of flowers, at a gypsy camp, falling away from the fires and onto the silvery trail of a magic moon. I am in braids and bare feet, a lonely girl in need of love. And this man in my barn is the boy, River, a loner among a traveling clan. We are mending together under the stars, talking of dreams and stories and faith. He is kissing me. My first kiss. Telling me he'll return. For me.

"Millicent?" Oka draws me from my daydream, and I stutter.

"Y-yes. Let's go see about those horses." I quickly unsaddle Firefly and leave her in the stall. The dinosaur hunt can wait.

I lead River out to the pasture and Oka follows. Henry and

Isabel trail behind. River walks with us as if this were any normal situation. Perhaps he doesn't recognize me. Maybe he hasn't yet figured that I'm the same Millie of his youth. I should tell him to come back when my husband is home. I should leave him with the horses while I surrender to the solitude of the house. Somewhere safe from the mystery.

"I knew a girl named Millicent once," River says. "I called her Millie." And just like that, there is no more wondering. I know why he is here.

I go through the motions, letting River test a few colts and fillies before he asks if we have a place for him to stay the night. "We're not really set up for guests," I say. I haven't looked River in the eyes yet, and I can't bring myself to do so.

"I have a tent." There's always been something about the way he smiles . . . makes me weak. "I'd rather take my time, watch the horses for a day or two before I decide."

"I guess it's okay," I answer. Oka gives me a look. She knows it isn't like me to let my guard down with strange men. "Out there. On the other side of the fencerow, if you don't mind." I point to a distant field.

"Of course," River answers. "That's where my horses are. That's where I'll be."

The empty house swallows me, and the seconds scrape away. No matter how many times I tell myself to get in that truck and go after my husband, I haven't left for Longmont, as I had planned. It's taken River years to find me. How can I just drive away?

I rub my hand across Bump's empty pillow and wonder when

he's coming back. If he's coming back at all. It's not like him to be this irresponsible. This inconsiderate. Even if he doesn't care about our marriage anymore, surely he cares about Isabel. About the ranch. I can't shake the feeling that something is wrong. I also can't stop picturing him with Kat. Anger consumes me.

The night songs seem especially loud tonight. The coyotes wail at the full moon, its light too bright. I twist my fist into the sheets, worrying. What will tomorrow bring? I pray. I count sheep. I read. I tumble in bed for hours, hoping to escape into sleep. No luck. No release. I can't stand this anymore. I'm going mad.

I finally give in, grab my coat, pull on my boots, and go outside. The autumn nights have brought a chill, and my breath forms clouds as I walk. Fortner's teepee is closed, and I move far downstream, careful not to disturb his sleep. As the sky wraps itself around me, I feel starfields away from Bump. I spread a blanket near the river and hope the water will sing me to sleep. I am just dozing off when River finds me.

"What are you doing out here?" River asks softly. Part of me is surprised to find him here. Part of me expected just that.

"Couldn't sleep." I turn to look at him. He stands above me, lit by the moon, and all my anger melts away.

"Me either." River motions toward the blanket, asking permission to join me.

I make room for him to sit beside me. Could his nerves be surging like mine?

He tosses a pebble into the water, and it is carried away. "It's been a long time."

"It has," I answer. Long pauses stretch between us, but neither of us seems to want to rush this. We let words fall as they may.

"A lot has changed." He clears his throat.

"It has," I agree again. Yellow leaves rustle in the wind. Water surges over the rocks. The ranch sleeps. And here, under this barrel-bellied moon, River is with me. After all this time. "I didn't think I'd ever see you again."

"I always knew I'd see you." The weight of his words makes me shift position. Try to regain balance.

I have to let him know we can't do this. "I'm married, you know. I have a child."

"And are you happy?" River looks directly at me now, and I am captured in his flint-black eyes. The eyes that took time to see me, the real me, when no one else bothered to look.

I don't answer.

"Why are you alone?" There is a tint of accusation in his tone, and I feel defensive.

"It's not what you think." There's no way to explain everything that is happening. It makes no sense.

"You seem lonely." His voice quiets.

I roll my fingers through the grass. "I'm not. Not at all."

He says nothing to this, and I feel pressured to prove my point. "I have a wonderful life here, River. I love my daughter. My husband." I try not to think of the empty bed, the nights Bump and I have slept apart, even in our own home, the fact that my husband is miles away. With Kat. But I don't have to say it. River hears the uncertainty in my voice.

"Why did he leave you?" He leans closer, and I shift away.

"He didn't leave me." I want to believe what I say, but it comes out sounding abrasive. Too harsh. My walls are up.

"I wouldn't leave you," River says, tilting his head to make me look at him again.

"You did," I shoot back.

"Greatest regret of my life," he says. "You can bet I'd never make that mistake again."

Tears sting my eyes. I can't believe any of this is happening. Bump has chosen to stay with Kat in Longmont, without any real explanation. And here I sit with River. More than three years after I made my choice and sent him on his way.

"I don't recognize you anymore, Millie." River tosses another pebble into the running stream.

I don't point out all the ways he's different from what I remember. We've both aged a lot in just a few years. Hard livin', as Janine would say.

"What happened to the girl who wanted to see the world?" he asks. "Who laughed and danced and raced through the woods?"

"She grew up." I weave the corner of the blanket through my fingers. Anything not to look back into River's dark eyes.

"She got stuck," he answers. "Your husband's off doing all the things you want to do. And you're stuck."

His words carve through me. *Stuck.*

"Bet you never did see the sea."

He still phrases his thoughts like poetry, and I soak in each sweet syllable. "All you had to do was ask twice that day," I say. "Our lives would probably be very different right now."

"I should have, Millie. I knew it the minute I walked away. I should have turned around and begged you to leave with me." He touches my shoulder, and I yield to him. My body ignites with his touch. Is this what Bump feels when he's with Kat? Then River adds, "I should have fought for you."

"I can't do this," I tell him. "I'm married. I love my husband." I turn my back to him again. Watch the river swell and fall. Try to focus on the water and not let myself cry.

"I didn't fight for you when I should have. But I'm here now, Millie. Asking you again."

I should tell him there's nothing he can say to convince me to leave my husband. But I think about Kat convincing Bump she needs him to stay with her in Longmont. I picture her head resting in his lap, his arm tucked beneath her breasts. I remember all those times when Bump stayed back, whispering with Kat, laughing, and flirting. The way he embraced her when she got the telegram about her husband's death. The trip across the Divide, the talk when they returned. Kat saying things to me like, "I don't want to be alone," and "You've got what women like me only wish we could have," and "I'm still out there too." The fact that she's the only person in town who calls him Kenneth.

At one point, I believed joining the rodeo might allow me to tour the country, competing with Firefly in front of cheering crowds. But then I married Bump, and we moved here to Colorado. Before I knew it, Isabel came along and one day became a month, became a year, and then another. And now I'm the mother of a girl who will quickly outgrow me. The wife of a man who has left me behind. The rancher of an operation that isn't even ours. What if River's right? Bump is gone, I am here. *Stuck.* Such a sharp little stab of a word.

"Look, Millie," River adds. "I'm not here to break up a family. If you're living the life you want, then I'll go. No problem. But I had to find you. Had to make sure you were happy. Because if there's any chance you're not, if this guy doesn't realize what he has in you, then we can leave, together. Millie, I can set you free."

I never do fall asleep. Instead, I stare at the sky until the stars fade and the sun spreads, and still I am afraid to move. Afraid to find River again, telling me he is here to rescue me from my pitiful life.

I try to convince myself it was all a dream, but I have spent the night tossing River's words in my head. Trying to remember the last time Bump made love to me. *Is* this the life I wanted? Is *this* what I imagined when I dreamed of heading into the free? Am I *stuck*?

I shake the blanket into the wind, wishing all of my troubles could blow away too. Then I collect two dozen eggs from the coop and move inside to start breakfast. Brown the sausage in an iron skillet. Fry eggs in the grease. Toast bread with butter. Rinse fresh berries in a bowl. I ring the bell from the porch. Fortner doesn't come, but River does. He says with his eyes, his endless eyes, that I can leave all of this today.

I cannot believe River is in my house, sitting at my kitchen table, putting his mouth against the same glass I drink from, one of my forks to his lips. My first love has come back for me, ready to fight for me. All I do is serve him breakfast and try to ignore the flames he's reignited. As tempting as it is, I refuse to feed this fire.

I save a plate for Fortner and figure he'll find it when he's ready. He's probably out for a morning hunt. When dishes are finished and everyone's belly is full, I busy Isabel and Henry with a block of clay and say, "Well, Mr. Greene. I guess we best settle this sale so you can hit the road." He needs to leave. Bump needs to come home. And everything needs to fall back in place.

"I watch them," Oka says, offering to take Isabel and Henry while I negotiate the trade.

As soon as we're a safe distance from the house, I question River again. "What do you want from me?"

"Isn't it obvious?" River answers, as if he doesn't care who hears.

"I'm not the girl you knew in Iti Taloa. You said it yourself. I've changed. I'm tired."

He laughs. "You shouldn't be tired."

"But I am, River. I'm so tired." One warm tear slides down my cheek, and I wipe it with the back of my hand.

"Come with me, Millie. Life is too short for this." River reaches for my hand.

"For what?" I step away from his touch.

"For . . ." He pauses. Thinks. "For anything less than what you really want."

"This *is* what I want, River. This, right here." And part of me means it. I love this simple, stuck life. Don't I?

"Then why are you shaking?"

I fold my hands together and try to still them. "Why did you come?" I turn and walk toward the barn, and then I swing around and face him. Words string together like bullets. "Do you think it was easy for me? To make this choice? Do you think I don't stare at those stars and wonder which one you named after me? You think I haven't dreamed of you, traveled with you in my sleep? I have, River. All of it. And I've missed you. It's been three years since I was supposed to meet you at your camp, and I've spent every day wondering, 'What if?'"

"There you have it," he says. "That, Millie, is exactly why I'm here."

I shake my head. "But it's too late, River. I made my choice. And I can't change this."

"But now you're getting to choose again," River says.

I don't respond. How do I explain everything on my mind? How I love my husband, but he's run off with Kat. How if I didn't have Isabel, this choice might be easy. My stomach twists and turns with disgust. This whole situation is more than I can take.

"Is your choice the same, Millie? Knowing now what you didn't know then?"

"It's not that simple, River. I have Isabel. She's . . . she's everything to me. I can't explain that to you. How it feels to be connected. Really connected. To a family. A place. A home."

"That's not fair, Millie." He looks away, stung.

I move to him. Touch his arm. Try to ignore the sparks. "I'm sorry." River looks at me, and my heart races against my ribs. "You're right," I continue. "That wasn't fair. I know you lost your family." I don't mean to hurt him. "I'm just trying to say . . . you're completely free. Untethered. Have been for a long time. And I can't live like that, River. I need this trap, if that's what you want to call it. I'm secure here. It's not perfect, but things will get better. They will."

He listens to me. Time has been kind to him, even though his face shows lines of worry now, and his eyes are sad. He has no harmonica in his pocket, no guitar on his back, and he's a rougher cut of the man I remember, no coins around his waist. But he still melts me with his gaze, and I have no doubt he could still work wonders with his hands. Everything about him tempts me, and in spite of my strong words, I can't avoid feeling his pull.

"Do you remember when we raced through the rain?" he asks. "And Babushka gave you that key?"

"Yes." I lean against a spruce and remember the way River once kissed my ankles, pulling me down from the branches. I shiver.

"She told me something that day."

"What?"

River looks into my eyes, holds his gaze. There is nothing I can do to stop my body from reacting with desire. I force myself to think of Bump. But all I can see is Kat's head in his lap. His arm around her. The telegram that announced he was not coming home. The knowing, sorry look on Oka's face when we got word.

"She told me you were not mine to keep," River says.

I am surprised. "You never told me that."

"I didn't want to believe her. Everyone said she had the gift. That's why people would wait all year to have her read their palms."

"She never read mine," I say, wondering what she would have seen. Could she have warned me about Bill Miller? And if so, would I have changed that event if it meant I would have to lose Isabel?

I leave River standing in the yard while I still have the power to pull away. I go to Firefly, a reminder of the love I have for Bump, for Isabel, for this life.

Chapter 31

I put Isabel and Henry down for a nap and take Firefly out to my favorite trail, the one that takes me deep into the woods and high up the mountain. Away from River. Away from the ranch. Away from Kat's abandoned child and Isabel's constant needs, a missing husband and an endless list of chores. I follow the trail away from loneliness. Away from fear. Away.

I ride up to the lookout and watch the whole wide world unfold below me, pockets of golden aspens burning bright against the pines. The sky is an eerie shade today, almost green. And the winds are unusually still. I am swallowed by a solemn silence, one that reminds me how empty life can be. I close my eyes, seeking release, until I am distracted by the sound of movement. My first thought is lion or bear, but Firefly hasn't reacted, so I know not to worry.

I watch the woods and wait for a sign. It is River.

"How'd you find me?" I am not disappointed. Just surprised.

"Followed you," he says, just as he did when we were young. Now we are here, far away from my daughter, my home, my grandmother. My real life. I pat the boulder. River sits beside me. The length of his body touches mine, but this time, neither of us pulls away.

He offers small talk, comments on the view, and then he tells me what he came to say. "I can live without you, Millie, if that's your choice. I'll leave today and move on, as I've been doing for years. But it won't change anything. I'll always love you."

River does need to leave, but there are things I need to tell him first. Things I should have said years ago, when I sent him away. I begin, hoping to fill in the gaps, trying to bring the closure we both crave. "I wanted to meet you that morning, at your camp, like I had promised. Something happened. I couldn't come."

"Was it Jack?" River leans closer, and my body absorbs the weight of him. Even my bones are hungry for more.

"Worst ever. I couldn't leave Mama. Not like that."

River takes my hand. I let him.

"And then she died, River. Jack too. It happened so fast. I was all alone and you were gone and I had no way of finding you. All I could do was wait. I marked days on the calendar. Watching for spring. For you to come back for me. And then . . . then, there was Bump." I do not mention the rape that left me numb on the very morning of River's return.

River throws a stone off the cliff and it disappears. *Erase. Erase. Erase.*

"And other things," I add.

"I should have stayed," River says. "It's my fault for leaving in the first place."

"It's no one's fault," I tell him. "We were kids. What did we know?"

He shakes his head. "I knew. I knew even then."

The way he says this fills my body with warmth. I think of Bump and try to ignore the flames River sets in me. "I've missed you, River. I have. But choosing Bump was the right thing to do. And I love him. I love my husband very much." I don't sound very convincing.

River turns my chin, leans in, and touches his lips to mine. I pull away, but not fast enough. I taste him first. Feel the soft, tender pressure of his lips, and allow myself to remember the passion I felt back in that first-kiss field. Then, and only then, do I stop him. I stand and turn quickly for Firefly. "I can't do this." I face him again. "You're making this too hard for me. I love you, River. I do. But Bump is my life."

"Then where is he?" River stands, moves close to me.

"He'll come home." I refuse to cry. Maybe if I say it enough, it'll come true.

"Sit down, Millie." River speaks softly to me. "I'm sorry." The light within him is fading.

A long pause spreads between us before I finally break the silence. "Sing me a song?"

River laughs.

"I'm serious. I want to feel alive again, River. I want both of us to feel alive again. Tell me what books you are reading. Where have you been? Tell me everything. Let's give each other this day. And let that be enough. Can we do that?"

River draws me back to the boulder. And then we begin again. He tells me how he left the gypsies, choosing to make it on his own. Started trading horses, in search of the Cauy Tucker ranch in Colorado, hoping to work his way across the country, one trade at a time, until he found me. He tells me Babushka is buried in Iti Taloa, in Hope Hill cemetery, where River and I first met. Where Babushka told stories and made me long for a tribe of my own. A place to belong. A family.

I tell him about mothering and Oka and Firefly. I let myself rest against him. He holds me close, his strong arms wrapped around me. He sings a song to me. A gypsy song he translates: "*The moon will shine, the stars will sing, and here with me, your heart will heal.*"

I tell River more about what happened with Mama and Jack. "Have you seen the cabins?"

"Still there," he says. "New tenants in all three. Kids were playing in the yard."

"And Sweetie?"

"A girl was climbing her limbs. Just like you."

This makes me smile. The thought of Sweetie still offering safety and hope to a girl from that cabin. "It's funny, isn't it? How life can shatter into a million shards. And circle back around again."

River brushes my hair from my face, a gentle touch.

"Ever miss Mississippi?" I admit I get homesick sometimes.

"I guess," he says. "You know what Fitzgerald says?"

I smile. "Tell me."

"He says, '*With people like us, our home is where we are not.*'"

I'm relieved to hear him quoting books again. It's one of my favorite things about him, his knack for language, his ability to capture a feeling, a mood with a single phrase from another story, another place and time. It makes me believe I'm not alone in this world. That it's not up to me to figure it out all by myself.

People like us. There will never be another who knows me like River does. The thought frightens me, and I stand quickly.

"Isabel and Henry are probably up from their naps," I say. "I need to get back." No matter how much I want to, I can't slow the passing of time. "Thank you," I tell him, "Thank you for finding me. And for giving me this choice. And for letting me go."

"I'm glad we have this," River says. "This day." And then he kisses me again. Only this time, I don't resist. I don't hold back. I let him take one last gift from me, a kiss, unhindered.

"Millie?" It's Bump. He's found us. River and me. How long has he been standing on the trail? What has he seen?

"Bump? Oh, Bump! You're back!" I rush to him, color flooding my face.

"What are you doin'?" he snaps.

River stands and holds out his hand. "You must be Mr. Anderson."

"That's right," Bump says, giving River a long, hard stare. "And who are you?"

"River Greene," he says. "Came to take a look at your yearlings. Brought some broodmares to trade."

"Don't look like you're doin' much tradin' up here," Bump says. His teeth bite hard on the words.

"Where have *you* been?" I bite back.

A starched silence stills us all. No one seems to know what to say. So I begin to lead Firefly down the mountain path. River and Bump walk ahead. It's an awkward trio, and neither man tries to make the other feel more comfortable. Tension builds with each step.

"River Greene," Bump says slowly as we follow the trail. "Seems like Millie knew a River back in Iti Taloa. Wouldn't by chance be the same River, now, would it?"

"As a matter of fact, that's me. I happened by here on business, and we were catching up on old times."

"So that's what you call it?" Bump's face is red and his hands are clenched.

"There a problem?" River asks calmly.

"Problem?" Bump swings around to face River. "You show up when I'm out of town and don't waste any time sneakin' up here with my wife." I pull Firefly's reins and back away.

"Oh, please," I interrupt. "If anyone here has explaining to do, it's you, Bump. For all I knew, you were never coming back."

He whirls toward me. "Are you kiddin' me, Millie? For God's sake, when are you ever gonna learn to trust me?"

I hold up a hand. "No. Don't do that. Don't turn this around on me. You left, Bump. With Kat. And you know what everyone was thinking."

"I wasn't *with* her, Millie. I was never *with* her. Not out west. Not in Longmont. Never. More than I can say for you." His eyes flash fire.

"Don't talk to her like that," River says, closing in on Bump as if I need someone to protect me. Before I know it, Bump rears back and slams his fist hard into River's face, and within seconds, both men are throwing punches.

"Bump! Stop!" I shout. "River, back off!" They don't listen. They are too busy bleeding and panting, tumbling on the ground, wearing out their resentments. It doesn't matter how much I yell or throw myself between them to block the fighting, they don't stop until they've exhausted themselves completely.

Eventually, River stands and spits a mouthful of blood. Bump looks worse. The first time he's ever hit a man. Bump says nothing as he turns and walks down the trail. I pull Firefly, and we follow. River stays behind. I look back only once. He wipes his bloody nose with his sleeve and gives me a look as if to say, *So that's your choice.*

When we reach the ranch, I stall Firefly quickly and find Bump at the well, bloody and bruised. I can't bear to look as he washes his face with water from the pump. I dip my shirt in the water and help clean his wounds. He lets me. "I thought you were gone," I tell him. "For good."

He says nothing.

"I'm glad you're back."

"Coulda fooled me." He turns and walks away, leaving me standing at the well. Alone.

Within minutes, Oka meets me in the yard. "Bump find you?"

I nod. It's all too ridiculous to say out loud, and my mind is swirling, trying to process everything that has happened in the last hour. The kiss. The fight. Bump telling me he was never with Kat. Asking when I would ever learn to trust him. It's what he's been trying to teach me all along, since I first started working with him at the rodeo barn back in Mississippi. Maybe a marriage isn't all that different from riding a horse. It only works if I trust Bump in return.

"He tell you?" Oka asks.

"Tell me what?" I'm distracted. My mind shoots thoughts in every direction.

"Why he stay in Longmont?" Oka says, looking hard at me, trying to get me to focus.

I shake my head.

"He stay to surprise you. Pick up special guests." She points toward the house.

"What are you talking about? Is someone here?" Maybe

Janine is waiting for me in the house. She'd be just the one to put this all in perspective for us, make us all laugh again.

"Mr. and Mrs. Miller," Oka says. "They come to buy horse. For Camille."

"Diana and Bill Miller?" The world tilts off axis, and I nearly fall to the ground. "They're here?"

Chapter 32

Supper is tense. Earlier today I prepared a large pot of chicken gumbo, so there's plenty of food for everyone. I pass bread to Fortner with shaking hands and keep a close eye on Bill Miller at the other end of our table. He sits between Diana and Oka, smiling his banker's smile, asking about investment potential with horses. "You raise any racehorses?" he asks Bump.

I place my hand on my pistol, a cold, hard handle of steel against my palm. I could shoot him. Right here. Right now. No one could stop me. I could put a bullet between his eyes, shatter his skull with one quick pull of the trigger. In a matter of seconds, I could put an end to the man who held me down with the bottom of his shoe and laughed as he tore into me. I remember Jack holding Mama down, pressing a silver knife blade to her neck and saying, "I could kill you, Marie. I could."

"So, Millie, how do you like living on a ranch?" Diana asks, smiling, trying her best at small talk.

I keep my stare set on Bill Miller and say nothing. He turns to look at me. He gives me a smirk, a quick little wink, a sign that he still has all the power.

"Millicent?" Oka repeats my name, but all sound is muffled, as if I'm underwater.

"I like it just fine." I answer Diana's question sharply, staring at Bill Miller, trying to imagine if he would die instantly, or if I would have time to stand over him first and tell him not to be late for supper.

Diana clears her throat, uncomfortable with my rudeness. I want to tell them all the truth. Say it isn't me who is making dinner so awkward. It's Bill Miller, this horrible man, who dares show up in my house, smiling, laughing, eating my food, acting as if he has every right to march into my life with his expensive suit and his wallet full of money.

"Camille sure won't be happy when she finds out we came without her," Diana tries again. "I warned Mabel not to let on. I want the horse to be a big surprise."

I know I should smile at Diana, answer, do something to make her feel better. But I don't. Instead, I turn my attention outside and stare through the window. River has not come in for the meal, but a lantern in the distance suggests he's still camped beyond the fencerow.

Fortner notices my gaze. "He should wait till tomorrow to break camp," Fortner tells me. "It's too dangerous for him to head out this time of night."

Bump shows no sympathy for River. No one mentions the fight.

"Plenty extra," Oka says, passing me another bowl of gumbo.

"Go on and take him the food, Millie," Fortner says. "Tell him to wait for sunup."

I look at Bump. There's so much to say, and we're stuck here at the table with a house full of guests, including Bill Miller. I've done just what I always said I'd never do. I've become my mother, choked by a web of secrets and shame.

I take the bowl of gumbo and announce I'll be right back. Bump holds Isabel and says nothing. I am happy to escape this house. I close the door and make my way to River's tent.

"You all right?" I hand River his supper.

He nods, standing to meet me. He takes the bowl and says, "Thanks." He has built a small fire, and he pats a log for me to join him.

We sit together under the stars, looking at the lanterns lighting the house. Their flames flicker, making the windows move in waves against the night. I take it all in. The horses in the pasture. The cattle huddled tight against the trees. The bubbling spring that feeds the river. Behind us, an owl calls. *Who cooks for you? Who cooks for you all?*

"I'm glad you came," I tell River, "but when morning breaks, you need to leave."

"I know," he says. "You can't blame me for trying, though. I had to find you. I had to see."

"I have a good life here, River. If I haven't ruined it all. I have a family. A home. And I wish the same for you."

Winds have begun to howl, suggesting a storm is brewing, something to soothe the spirits, soften the pain. I wait with River, side by side, sitting beneath the moon, until Fortner drives the Millers back to town. They've insisted on renting a room with "proper facilities." Seems having an outhouse is a good thing after all. As the truck leaves our ranch, and I know it is safe for me to return, I stand to offer a final farewell.

"Just think," River says. "If Jack hadn't banged up your mother. If I hadn't left town without you. If Bump hadn't swooped in with flowers at just the right time. It might all be different now."

I touch his face and smile. "Wait till sunup. Okay?"

River watches me walk back to the house. I stop on the porch and look back at him standing in the distance. He is still a powerful presence. I think about all we've talked about today, and my life lines up in series, like dominoes. One tile falling into the next. An orchestrated turn here, a rising crescendo there. And yet, somehow, it's all connected. Every single person. Every choice. This string has purpose—it all adds up to me.

Later, in bed, Bump and I both lie on our backs, staring up at the dark, blank ceiling. Our bodies don't touch, and the empty space between us feels as big as the sea. We say nothing. Isabel sleeps soundly in the corner crib. I pray silently to the heavens, and hope my husband can someday forgive all the hurt I've caused.

There's no doubt now, it's Bump I want. Not River. Maybe it was the fact that Bump finally fought for me, or that I now have the closure I needed all along with River. Maybe it's because Bump made it clear he was never with Kat. Or maybe it's the fact that Bill Miller showed up and reminded me how bad things could really be. Whatever the reason, tonight confirmed my choice in a new way, and I'll never doubt my love for Bump again.

Outside, the elk call to their prospective mates beneath the night moon glimmer of the aspen leaves. Their loud bugling hits three main notes with each trill, piercing the skies with a message that sounds much like "I choose you! I choose you!"

Bump takes my hand in his, and tears fall. Our bodies stay

parallel, our eyes looking up, and I'm afraid to move. I don't want him to let go of my hand. "I'm on your side, Millie," he says. "Don't you understand? I've always been on your side." I fall asleep to the sound of Bump's breathing. *I choose you.*

Chapter 33

River is gone. I will likely never see him again. Diana and Bill Miller spent the night in town, but now they're back with Sheriff Halpin, who has come to pick up little Henry. Thankfully, Kat hasn't joined him.

As Oka welcomes everyone in for breakfast, a gray mood swarms the kitchen and no one tries to cut it. We let it weigh us down as we focus on eggs, sausage, milk. When I can't stand it anymore, I excuse myself, pretending Isabel needs to be changed. I don't have it in me to be polite. I'm sure Diana wonders why I've been so rude. It's not her fault, and seeing her here, now, with such a beast for a husband, I feel sorry for her. But nothing can excuse Bill Miller walking boldly back into my world, my life. I refuse to give him the power he craves. Control.

Instead, I do everything I can to steer clear of the Millers. I move through the day one task at a time, breaking sweat. Hardening calluses. Building blisters. And keeping Isabel as far from them as I possibly can. By late afternoon, clouds sprout, lightning forks, and the rain brings everyone inside. But I don't join them in the house. I head for the barn.

The rain falls hard for more than an hour, causing Isabel to miss her nap and giving me plenty of time to think. By the time Oka finds us, Isabel is fussing with a vengeance. "Millicent?"

"Back here," I call to Oka from the tack room. She shivers as she enters, the damp autumn chill getting to her. "Where's Bump?"

"At the house," she says. "We have guests."

I sigh. "I know."

"You not happy they here?" Oka raises her shoulders and angles her chin in confusion.

I'm tired of feeling afraid. Sick of Bill Miller feeling free to do as he pleases. It's time for the truth. "Oka, you remember I told you about Isabel. How her birth wasn't planned?"

"Yes," Oka says, taking Isabel from me now and trying to comfort her. "You glad to have her now, though. See? Oka was right."

"You were, Oka. Thank goodness you talked sense into me."

She kisses Isabel and rolls her fingers through my daughter's soft black curls.

"Remember I told you . . ." I lower my voice and try again. "Remember I told you Bump wasn't the father?"

"Hush, child," Oka says, rocking Isabel in her arms and covering her ears.

"Oka, he raped—" My voice cracks on the word, and every cell in my body screams out, a violent eruption from within. I will keep this silent no longer. I say, loud this time, nearly a yell, "He raped me!" All the emotions I've kept capped for so long burst free, exploding. Finally, I have found my voice. My body shakes. My knees grow weak. I try not to, but I begin to cry, more from the tremendous feeling of relief than any real sadness.

Oka steps back, her brow furrowed, as if she doesn't understand what I'm saying.

I say again, even louder, determined to finish this. "That man in there." I point, shaking. "Bill Miller. He held me down in the steeple of his church and had his way with me. And now he's here. I don't know what to do." I am sobbing now, crying so hard I can barely breathe.

Oka pulls me close and holds me against her chest, next to Isabel, until I finally manage to soften the sniffles that fuel my tears. "My sweet, sweet Millicent." She rocks me back and forth. "Shh. I take care of you."

Bump has brought the Millers to the pasture for a final look at the paint pony he selected for Camille. I guard Isabel from a distance as my husband explains what to look for in a good horse. Waves of words follow the wind: "well-collected," "full rear quarters," "good saddle back." Isabel and I scratch shapes into the mud with sticks as I teach her the words *circle, square, triangle.*

Bump mounts the horse bareback, proving the pony is full broke. He commands her to trot. Canter. Turn left, then right. He backs her. And gets her to spin. All with just a little pressure using his hands and heels. Bill Miller seems impressed; Diana, distracted. She surveys the surroundings and heads in my direction. It's too late to escape.

I draw an *A* in the mud and shift from teaching shapes to working on letters. "Up. Down. Bridge across." Isabel tries to copy my lines.

Diana approaches. She bends and rubs her hand through Isabel's hair. I bring my daughter to me, an impulsive reaction. *Protect her, Millie.*

"Millie?" Diana stands quickly, as if she's been stung. Then she turns to watch the men in the work pen. She waits a long time before continuing. Too long. Surely she is upset with the way I've been acting since they arrived. I sense she is about to walk away. Instead, she speaks. "I heard what you said. To Oka."

I pause, say nothing. I'm not sure what she means.

"About Isabel," Diana goes on. "About my husband." She shields her eyes from the sun and directs her stare toward Bill Miller. "I heard what you told her. In the barn. I know."

Surely she doesn't mean *that* conversation. "You know?" I stand.

Now she turns and confronts me eye-to-eye. "Yes, Millie. I know." The pitch of her voice is unsteady, and I can't tell if it's a result of anger or disgust. She stares at Isabel as if she's looking for proof that Bill Miller is her father. I step between them, hoping to shield my child from any threat. "Truth is—" Diana gives a long and desperate sigh, as if she's trying not to cry—"in a way, I guess I've always known. I knew when you didn't come home from church that day. Bill Miller was late for supper." Her voice breaks. "He's never late for supper."

Now Diana's gaze settles back on her husband in the pasture, the monster who fathered my child. "I knew when he wouldn't let me search for you. I knew when you snuck your suitcase out the window and never looked back."

Neither of us speaks, and the silence seems to stretch for days. I struggle to find a single thing to say. Such phrases don't exist. So I stick with the closest terms English offers to express what I am feeling.

"Diana, I'm . . . I'm so sorry."

Her body folds in on itself, as if she's a balloon and all the air is leaking out. I don't know what else to say to her. I just want to get away. Get Isabel away.

Finally, she speaks again. "It's not your fault, Millie. I couldn't accept it. You understand? I couldn't . . ." She cries now, and for the first time, I see the real Diana. Vulnerable and afraid. I want to hug her, but I don't.

"I couldn't accept he would do such a thing. Not my husband," she continues with her eyes kept down, focused on the hard dirt ground. "But now I see it all. He was never the man I thought he was. Was he? He lied from the start. About your mother. About you." She wipes her cheeks, trying to gather herself.

I want so badly to reach out to her, to do something, anything, that would take away her pain. Instead, I catch Isabel and head for the trail. Escape.

I can't get Isabel far enough away from Bill and Diana, but I also don't want to frighten her. So I carry her on my back, moving quickly up the trail until we reach a safe distance. Only then do I slow our pace, letting her take the lead. She walks intently, listening, smelling, touching, seeing. I try to be like her, to capture the creation, every sacred inch of this mountain, and to tune in to what really matters. To block out the rest.

We walk between yellowed aspens, their white bark based beneath the singing leaves. Below, in the valley, the elk sing love songs. The rivers run without pausing. The forests breathe. One thing is for sure: the mountains don't care about Bill Miller. His presence hasn't changed them at all. Oh, how I want to be strong, like these mountains. Unbreakable.

When we reach our prayer circle, I pull Isabel into my lap. I make a wish on a small stone and toss it to the winds. Isabel does the same with a tiny pebble. Then she plays on the rocks, laughing and singing. How can I protect her innocence? How can I keep her happy? Safe? Sheltered from men like Bill Miller?

The twin peaks stand in the distance, watching over us. I think of Bill Miller, traveling here to find a horse for Camille. Sitting at my table. Giving me a wink. He acts as if he has every right to intrude in my life, as if he wants me to know that no matter how far I go, I'll never really get away from him.

I think of Diana, overhearing the conversation between Oka and me. Learning of her husband's betrayal. This makes me even angrier with Bill Miller. Not only has he hurt me. Now he's hurt Diana too, and that will hurt Camille. The damage has no end.

But that's what would happen, isn't it? If I took revenge on Bill Miller, it would only hurt Diana and Camille. To them, he is a husband, a father, a much-loved man who is the provider for their family. I wish Diana hadn't overheard our conversation. I wish the truth was still buried. I wish the burden was still all on me.

I pull the pistol from my hip, rolling the weight of the weapon from hand to hand. Then I aim out into the nothing, imagining Bill Miller standing over me when I was a girl. As I cock the hammer, I am reminded of the green wall of quotes Miss Harper kept in her library. I memorized the words when I was younger, and one comes to mind now, an ancient quote from someone named Calcott or something. "*He that has revenge in his power, and does not use it, is the greater man.*"

Strength. Ihanko. Power. The greater man. Krasnaya. Red. Millicent. Strength.

Isabel tires, and I am reminded of how frail life can be. I release the hammer, without firing the gun, and put the pistol back into my holster. Then I pull my child close to me. Isabel's tiny lids grow heavy, and soon she is napping on the sun-warmed boulder. While she sleeps, I think through the choices Mama and Jack made in their lives. The bad decisions that drew us all into a spiral of chaos and pain. Now it's me who makes the choices. How do I fix all that is wrong in my life? How do I save my marriage? Build the family I always wanted? Give Isabel more than I ever had?

As the sun begins to sink into the afternoon haze, my daughter stirs. It's a late nap for her, and she wakes hungry. I pull her onto her feet and we turn for home, following the trail back into the trees. I'm hoping by the time we reach the ranch, the Millers will be long gone. Then I will tell Bump everything. It is time for him to know the truth.

I try not to let Isabel feel my tension. None of this is her fault, and I will not allow the hurt to trickle down to her. We stay the path, singing simple songs together as we hike, hand in hand. *"London Bridge is falling down, falling down, falling down."*

As we make a bend in the trail, I stop cold in my tracks and warn Isabel to hush. Just ahead of us, a pale mountain lion crouches on a ridge. This time a cub lies at her side. The tip of the mother's tail twitches, the only thing that gives her away. I lift Isabel into my arms and warn her again to be quiet. She listens.

I pull the pistol from my hip again, its chamber still warm from my time in the sun. It's likely the lion has seen us long before I ever spotted her. She is no more than three feet from us now, perched in prime position for an attack. Fortner told me they keep a large territory, so she's probably the same one who chased me into the barn when we first moved to this ranch. If that's the case, she's already shown she can be aggressive. And while an attack on a human would be rare, our odds are worse because her cub is tucked close.

My heart pounds heavy against my chest and my teeth buzz with alarm. "Run!" the signals tell me. "Get away!" But we don't stand a chance. The lion would pounce before I finished a single step. I know this. All the fears of our last encounter come back like hot coals against my skin. There's not a cell in my body that isn't screaming loud and clear: "Danger! Danger!"

But I hear Oka's voice too, reminding me of my Chahta name. "Ihanko," she says. "Strong."

Isabel wraps my hair around her tiny fingers, and my thoughts turn to Mama. I picture her now, yielding to the forces against her. Refusing to stand up and protect me. Refusing to protect herself.

With the gun in my hand and my eyes on the lion, I feel Isabel wiggle in my arms. Her soft, plump cheek rubs against my neck. She has survived so much already. This can't be how it ends for her. I won't allow it. This lion will *not* hurt my child.

The mother lion remains in place, still moving her tail with random, irregular tics. She's trying to make me flinch. Scare me into movement. But I refuse. I breathe in. Out. Maintain my stare. Isabel seems aware of the tension. She, too, stays quiet.

I set the pistol but can't get a clear shot. All I can really aim for is the tail. That would do more harm than good. I could try to fire a warning shot to scare her away, but it's too great a risk. If the threat caused her to lunge at me instead, she'd slash my throat before I could fire a second shot. I have no real option. So I wait, gun at the ready, and I rely on the one thing that has always seen me through. I pray.

With Isabel pressed against me, I don't stop praying, even when the lion turns her head to the sound of footsteps down the trail. In the distance, leaves crunch hard and loud beneath fast feet. I keep my eyes on the lion while I monitor the approaching noise. It could be Bump. Or Fortner. Or Oka. I have to warn them. "Stop!" I shout, afraid my voice will draw the lion, but she doesn't move an inch. Instead, she stares down the trail, waiting, just like me. *Oh please, Bump, don't come any closer.*

Just as I'm about to yell out "Lion!" Bill Miller's head arcs over the rise, and as hard as it is to believe, I am suddenly being stalked by two kinds of predators. I hold Isabel close in my arms and tighten my grip on the pistol. I don't know which is worse, the lion or the man.

He's talking before he reaches me. Shouting angrily, "How dare you!"

Diana must have finally found the strength to confront him with the truth. But if that's the case, did she tell Bump the truth too? *Think, Millie. Don't panic.* I need to get to Bump, but I've got to get past a lion and Bill Miller first.

I try not to show any reaction to Bill Miller's anger because that would give him two things I don't want him to have: power over me and fuel to feed his temper. I learned long ago how to navigate a safe path around an angry man. I focus on trying to breathe slowly, hoping to keep Isabel from crying in distress. I avoid looking him directly in the eye, just as I do the lion, trying to observe without signaling a challenge. As he shouts louder, the lion's ears tuck back and she draws her mouth back to bare sharp, yellow teeth. It's clear she's agitated, threatened, with her cub against her side. I hold my own child, understanding how the lion feels.

Bill Miller is completely unaware that he is approaching a mountain lion. She is well camouflaged by rocks and brush, perched on a ridge above us, tucked beneath the trees, watching cautiously as the man moves closer in his city clothes, yelling, "You think you can make those kinds of accusations?" He stops to catch his breath, struggling with the climb and the higher altitudes. With hands on his knees, he bends a bit, looking down and breathing heavily. But by the time he lifts his chin, he has managed to collect himself. I am sickened by the way he stares hard at Isabel, as if he can control her too.

I lift my arm and point the gun directly at his chest, nothing but air between the chamber and this man. When he realizes I am armed, a flash of fear crosses his face. Only for a second, but that's enough to make me hold my fire. I don't shoot, and my hesitation calms him. In a matter of minutes, his behavior has shifted from red-faced shouts to a winded break for breath to a moment of sheer panic in the face of the gun, but now he offers a smug smirk, as if he's certain he has the upper hand.

"So she's mine," he says, looking at Isabel with a vile twist of the eye. The corner of his lip rises.

Again, my instinct is to run. But if I do, the lion's predator-prey responses might be triggered. So I stand still, hoping to outlast both beasts. Hoping to keep my daughter safe. Praying for God to pay attention. To send help. My heart bangs hard against my ribs, and my lungs sting with the understanding that each breath could be my last. But one thing is for sure; I refuse to be silent anymore. I refuse to give in to any of his threats. If it's a fight Bill Miller wants, I'm ready.

"You have no right," I say to this man, each word a punch. "You will never lay a finger on her. Not one dirty little finger." I try to steady my shaking hand as I cock the gun with my thumb. It's hard to do with Isabel in my arms, but I manage. I don't want Bill Miller to think I don't know how to handle a pistol. How to make a good shot.

As I reset my aim, the snide banker releases a hissing sound, as if he's got no intention of listening to anything I say. As if he'll do exactly what he wants, when he wants, and no one will ever stop him. Not even a girl with a gun.

He takes two quick steps toward me.

I stand my ground and reposition my weapon. "Not another step." I try to say this with conviction, but my voice quavers.

Isabel squirms in my arms, tugging my shirt. Bill Miller watches her with a strange look, and I'm not sure how to read him until he says, "If she's my blood, you can't keep her from me."

Breath leaves me with force, as if I've been pierced in the gut. This man doesn't care one bit about being Isabel's father. He's only trying to hit me where it hurts the most. It works.

"You can't do that," I say. I am shaking harder now, but I refuse to whisper, to stutter. Refuse to give in to this man ever again. I will stay strong. He will hear me.

"You better believe I can. You're nothing more than half-breed trash. No judge would think twice." His laugh is a high-pitched rattle that causes the lion to flinch. Still, Bill Miller doesn't see her. He takes another step, reaching his hand out to touch Isabel's cheek. I pull away before he makes contact, but this brings me closer to the ridge where the mother and her cub are perched. Bill Miller shrugs his shoulders, to show he's not the least bit concerned with what I think. Then he lets me know his plan: "Diana always did want another child."

In that one sentence, I see the bigger picture. This man would try to take Isabel just to spite me. Just to put me in my place. But he forgets. I have a choice too. *Pull the trigger, Millie. End this now.* My fingertip slides across the trigger. One quick pull. That's all it would take. But then I remember the lesson from Mama's story about Cain and Abel. The choice. I have a choice.

Please, please, God. Help us. The wind stirs leaves around our feet, bringing me back to my senses. Bill Miller looks away, and I exhale.

Isabel leans to be put down. She doesn't fully understand our danger. She only wants to catch the swirling leaves. As the limbs above us bend and sway, I remember my sweet gum tree back home, Sweetie. How I watched from those limbs as Jack pressed a knife against Mama's throat. How I wanted, more than anything, for Mama to stand up and fight for her life. To fight for mine.

As the yellow leaves wave above me, I slowly gain composure. I look Bill Miller right in the eye and say, "You know what I just realized?" He curls his lips down as if he doesn't care to know, but I continue anyway. "I'm the one with the gun. I could pull this trigger right now, and there's not a single thing you could do about it. I could leave you bleeding on this trail and I'd never have to worry about you hurting anyone ever again."

He cocks his head and grins, obviously finding me amusing. "You don't have it in you. You're too much like your mother."

"You think I'm the weak one?" I almost laugh. "You? Bill Miller?" I say this condescendingly, shaking my gun for emphasis. "The rich boy who didn't get his way? Still pouting because my mother told you no?" His smile fades. "That's right. I know who you are, Bill Miller. I see right through your fake smile and your fancy suits. I may be a half-breed. I did grow up poor and you can call me trash all you want, but the truth is, Mr. Miller, you're the pathetic one. Having to force yourself on a young girl just so you can feel like a man."

With this, an evil overcomes him. He gives me the darkest, angriest look I've ever seen, and I've seen plenty. But I don't back down. For some reason, I'm no longer afraid of him. The power has shifted. "You know what else, Mr. Miller? You're not even worth this." I twist my wrist, letting the gun tilt a bit, releasing my aim. "You aren't worth the worry I would carry with me if I did shoot a hole through your heart. You're the bad guy. Not me."

Bill Miller stands for a minute or two, staring at Isabel and me. The lion still sits no more than two arm lengths above me, watching cautiously, trying to remain hidden. She must realize she's outnumbered, as she tries to protect her cub who now tugs her mother's tail with her teeth. But that doesn't change the fact that with one quick pounce, we're their next meal. Diana's husband still hasn't noticed the animals, and this doesn't surprise me at all.

"Now, Bill." I drop the family name to prove he's no better than me. "Here's what you're going to do." I talk while moving my hand, letting the barrel of the gun add weight to my commands. "You're going to turn around and walk right back down that trail to find Diana. You're going to tell her you are a pathetic fool and that you'll do anything she wants for the rest of your life, if she'll even consider forgiving you. Then you will head straight for the depot and catch the first train back to Mississippi. If you've got a lick of sense, you won't look back."

With this, I send the heavens another silent plea. *He's all Yours. Please help me walk away. Keep Isabel safe. Please.* I hold my daughter in one arm, my pistol in the other, and give one last look to the mother lion before stepping slowly away from all these beasts.

I try to move in a broad arc around Bill, but the trail is narrow here, with a steep rise to one side, a drastic drop to the other. I have no choice but to step within reach of this man. As we pass, he lunges to grab me. His arm catches mine, causing my foot to slip on a slice of stone. Then Isabel's weight shifts just enough to throw me off balance and send us both to the ground.

When I slam against the trail, my grip tenses and the gun fires. Isabel screams.

In a panic, I drop the pistol to the ground and search my daughter for any sign of injury. I'm frantic, terrified I may have shot my own child. Danger stalks from all directions, but Bill Miller no longer matters to me. Neither does the lion. I lift Isabel's arms, her legs, turn to examine her back, until I finally realize there is no blood. She hasn't been hit by the bullet. She's not hurt. Just terrified.

When I finally turn my attention back to Bill Miller, his feet are standing only inches from us. Those same shiny shoes that left me in that steeple. Only this time, they are dusty, just like mine.

Bill leans over us now, victory in his grin. He has grabbed the gun from the ground and is preparing it to fire again. He cocks the trigger as I clamber across yellowed leaves and dry, brittle broken branches and slivers of sharp-edged stone, scrambling to stand.

As I regain my footing, I quickly pull Isabel to me, determined to shield her from the gun. Then, with my daughter in my arms, I run.

I've made it only five or six steps when Bill Miller fires the pistol from behind us. By the time the sound hits me, I know the bullet has already been released, but I don't stop running. If the bullet has hit me, I don't feel any pain. I am driven down the trail by a determined mothering, a force greater than any amount of ammunition.

Obviously, the lion feels it too, because just as the gun fires, I hear another sound. Not so much a scream as a pitiful plea for help. I turn my head back toward the noise, trying to get a look as I run, afraid we're now being chased by the mother and her cub. But then I see.

The mountain lion has leapt from the ledge, but not to chase Isabel and me. Instead, she has claimed Bill Miller as her prey.

I stop running now, covering Isabel's eyes to block the view. Behind us, Bill is pinned facedown, struggling to get away from the lion, begging me to help him. She must weigh ninety pounds, maybe more. I bend to grab rocks, to throw them at the lion, but I don't release a single stone. If I try to save the man who threatened us, Isabel could be in danger. The lion could come for my daughter. And if not the lion, then Bill Miller. I can't risk either.

There's no doubt I despise this man, but still, it is not easy for me to leave him here begging for help. I try to move my feet again, but the command doesn't register. Nerves and muscles disconnect. I am too stunned to move.

The lion looks up at me and holds her eyes in line with mine. Her shoulders are hunched over her victim and her jaws stay low, ready to sink her teeth into the man who struggles beneath her sharp claws, but she doesn't give me the stare of a predator to its prey. Instead, she offers me an almost sympathetic gaze, as if, somehow, she understands. As if she's letting me know she is on my side. That we're safe now. Isabel is safe. Her cub is safe. And Bill Miller will get what he deserves.

Then she lowers her jaws and clamps them around the neck of this man. Diana's husband. Camille's father. Weakness overcomes me, and stars swarm. I nearly drop Isabel back to the ground. Numb from shock, I will myself to turn my back and take another step toward home. And another. And another. Until I no longer hear the sound of scream and bone.

Isabel's tiny fingers squeeze my skin as we move toward safer ground. Like me, she is terrified, pale with fear, but with each step, her cries soften until she only releases swift gasps and sniffles. "Shh," I whisper. "We're safe now."

I say it again and again, but I still find it hard to believe. Are we really safe? Or will the lion change her mind? She could easily catch up with us and launch a second attack. *Hurry, Millie,* I tell myself. *Keep walking. Find Bump.*

As we move quickly toward home, my fear begins to wane and calmness claims me. With it comes Mama's voice, riding softly on the wind. *Millie,* she says. *Listen.*

"Mama?" I call out, crazy as it seems, half hoping my mother has come back to me, as Sloth did after he died. I turn all directions but see no one. Not Sloth. Not Mama. Not the lion or her cub. Not Bill Miller. No one. Then I hear my mother's voice again, not from the woods, as I had thought, but from my own heart. Seeping through from the lessons she planted deep within me. She tells me the story of Daniel and the lions' den, the one she shared time and again from the kitchen, and the ironing board, and the squeaky porch swing. But this time, one of the verses stirs my soul. *"My God hath sent his angel, and hath shut the lions' mouths, that they have not hurt me: forasmuch as before him innocency was found in me."*

Innocency was found in me. I stand on the mountain, hold my child to my chest, and hear my mother speak my secret name. I have struggled to choose this title, not yet knowing enough about my own self to give myself a name. But now I hear it. The one thing Mama never managed to give me while she was alive. *Truth.* The only secret I will keep from now on. My name is Truth.

Someday I will tell my daughter everything, the truth of who she is, from start to finish. I will tell her she is Choctaw, with deep roots in Mississippi, the deepest possible, and that the land is her mother. And that there is nothing stronger than a mother's love. I will tell her she is a Miller, but that she has only the good parts, like Camille. I will tell her she is a survivor, Ihanko, strong, and that she is loved. Through and through. And I will remind her that no matter what led to her being here with us, she is and will always be an Anderson. Bump is her true father, and nothing will ever change that.

I will tell her the meaning of her name, Isabel, and that she is a promise from God. And I will remind her of her birth name, Hofanti, and tell her she is cherished, nurtured, protected. Then I will give her a second Chahta name based on her own special gifts. And when she is ready, I will teach her to choose a secret name, one just for herself. I will give her the truth. And, as Oka taught me, the truth will set us free.

Chapter 34

We don't make it to the end of the trail before Bump finds us. He slows his running. "I heard shots," he says, short of breath, full of worry. "And screams." As he pulls Isabel from my arms, his panic-white eyes perform a rapid scan, searching us both for wounds.

"She's okay," I tell him. "We're not hurt."

"What happened?" he asks, still trying to accept the fact that Isabel and I are both safe.

"Lion," I say. It sounds unreal, and part of me wonders if it happened at all. I can't fully accept what I saw.

Bump knows the fear I've had since the first time a mountain lion came after me at the river. "Let's go," he says, pulling me down the trail quickly, trying to add distance between us and the dangerous animal.

I follow him a few steps before I can get the words out. As much as I loathe Bill Miller for the things he has done, I can't just leave him on the trail. There's a slim chance he could still be alive. I have to send help.

"Bump, wait," I begin. "Bill Miller. He's up there."

"Alone?"

I nod my head.

"Well, we gotta warn him," Bump says, turning to move back up the mountain. He doesn't understand what I'm saying.

"Wait," I say, pulling him to a stop.

He is anxious, eager to hurry. Determined to save Mr. Miller. "It's probably too late," I say. "She got him. I didn't know what to do. I had to get Isabel out of there."

"You saw the lion take him?" Bump asks. Lines of disbelief mark his face.

I say yes only with my eyes, but he understands. Then I add, "It didn't look good."

Bump spins in a circle, as if he doesn't know how to react. Should he try to get to Bill, or should he get Isabel and me home to safety. He looks up the mountain, but the scene of attack is out of view. Then he looks down toward home, the roof barely visible through acres of trees.

"Was he alive, Millie? When you last saw him, was he still alive?"

I nod my head. I've never seen Bump so unsure. "I gotta help him, Millie. You should keep movin'. Get in the house. And send Fortner. Make sure he has his rifle." With this he heads quickly but cautiously up the trail toward Bill and the lions, scanning his surroundings for signs of danger. I haven't moved, so he yells back to me, "Go!"

"There's something else," I yell, stopping him again. He turns back, agitated.

"Not now, Millie. Hurry home!"

"No, Bump. Listen."

It's clear he's worried, and he wants Isabel and me to get to safety.

"She had his neck," I tell him.

With this, he finally holds still, sending a long breath into the air. A surrender. He understands. Lions are known for snapping the spine of deer. We can only assume they hunt humans the same way. "You can't go up there alone, Bump. Let's get Isabel down, and then we'll all go together. You, me, and Fortner."

"There's no time for that, Millie. I can at least stop her from . . ." Even Bump can't say the words out loud. She's probably chewed her way through his ribs by now. Predators always go for the heart.

"Bump, you're not thinking. She's still pumping adrenaline, fueled for attack. And you know she'll try to guard her prey. Plus she's got a cub. It's not safe. We have to go as a group. There's nothing you can do."

He seems to be thinking this through, trying to figure a way to save us all.

"Come down with us," I beg, hoping I can talk sense into him. "We'll get Isabel to safety."

He shakes his head at first, still determined to find a solution, but eventually reason wins. He gives in. "Let's hurry." He takes my hand, and we don't speak again until we reach the ranch.

There we find Fortner at his teepee, sharpening his knives. I rush to take Isabel to the porch where I leave her with Oka. My grandmother senses my concern, drawing back as if to question me.

"Mountain lion," I say quietly. I look around for Diana but don't see her. "It attacked Mr. Miller. We're going back to try to help. Don't tell Diana yet. It'd do her no good to see what we might find."

Oka nods and takes my daughter into her arms. I kiss Isabel's forehead and give Oka a long look, as if to say, *In case something happens, take care of her.* Then I race back out to find Bump and Fortner. As we make our way up the trail, Fortner struggles to match our fast pace, and for the first time, I see the old man in him.

By the time we reach the scene of attack, the mountain lion has dragged Bill's body into thicker brush where she has covered his legs in dirt. I am too horrified to look as the mother and her cub both devour their feast. The mother stops long enough to display a string of growls and hisses, warning us to stay back from the prized meal.

"Don't kill her," Fortner warns. "Just scare her away."

Bump quickly fires his gun, aiming at nothing but space up the trail. Fortner does the same, finally convincing the muscular cat that she is outmanned. She retreats quickly, and her cub follows, but the men reset their guns, just in case. They move closer to Bill Miller.

As the lions run deep into the woods, my view of Bill expands. I fall to the ground, horrified. I can't breathe. Bits of rock slice my knees as I crawl through the leaves, trying to reach Bump. "Stay back, Millie," Fortner shouts. "Stay back!" I can't reason what he says. I just keep moving forward, scrambling on all fours, like some kind of wild animal.

Even from a distance, I see the body. His head angles hard into the ground with eyes open, as if to say, *I see*, and a thin ribbon of blood slips from the mouth where his cheek falls slack against chipped teeth. The air is filled with the smells of gunpowder and blood.

My brain can't process what it sees. I am hit with waves of confusion. "Is he dead?" Sounds stick as they string together. Tongue tangles. Mind fogs. I try again to squeeze the folds together in my throat, move wind through chapped lips, make voice. "Is he dead?"

"Yes" is the last of the sound before silence swells, blocking all understanding. In an instant, I am sinking into a thick, gray, numbing blanket of shock, and everything else disappears. He is dead. He is dead.

I come to as Bump and Fortner are discussing what to do.

"Should we bury him here?" Bump asks Fortner, keeping his back to the mangled body.

"I imagine his wife will want a proper burial," Fortner answers.

I nod from where I sit on the ground, still weak from fainting. I can't imagine how Diana will take this news. I don't know how we'll tell her.

"They can send the remains back to Mississippi by train," Fortner continues.

"We gotta carry him down," Bump acknowledges. His brow wrinkles as if he's trying to reason all that has happened. Trying to fix something that can't be fixed.

"I'll go get a horse," Fortner says. I don't fully understand his plan. When he hunts, he quarters the elk before loading it on the horse in leather sacks he's made. Surely he has a better idea for Bill.

"You shouldn't go alone," I argue. "The lion is still out there."

Fortner doesn't seem worried a bit about the lion. "She's had her fill for now," he says. "She knows we could have killed her. And her cub. She won't forget."

With this, he turns to make his way back down the trail. Confident. Calm. Certain he will make it back to us without harm. He's barely out of view when Bump says, "I shoulda kept a better eye on him." He is pacing back and forth, taking full blame for the attack on our guest.

I wait for him to calm, trying to seize the perfect moment to tell him the truth.

"I don't understand," Bump says, his face puzzled. "What was he doin' up here in the first place?"

"He came to find me," I admit, biting my nail to the quick.

"But why? Diana seemed upset. Did something happen?"

"Not exactly." What will he do when I tell him?

"You sure haven't been very welcomin', Millie. I thought you'd be excited to see 'em again. Granted, I figured Camille and Mabel would come, but still—"

"Bump," I interrupt. "Listen." I should have done this from the start, but I won't make him go another minute without the truth. He deserves to hear it now. From me.

"If this is about Kat—"

I interrupt again. "It's not."

He keeps talking as quickly as he walks. "I had to stay in Longmont, Millie. I tried everything to help Mr. Fitch, but I couldn't save him. You should have seen Kat when they told her the news. I couldn't leave her like that. It was my fault he died, Millie. You understand?"

"It wasn't your—" He cuts me off before I can finish. He is determined to say what he wants to say.

"And then the Millers were supposed to be comin' in two days, so I just waited in town. I didn't know until dark that their train got delayed a day. Then another, and another, so I kept waitin', each mornin' expectin' them to arrive. Each night findin' out about another delay."

"Why didn't you tell me?" I ask. "You should have sent

word." I feel so ashamed about River. The kiss. None of this would have happened if Bump had been honest with me. If he had told me the truth. All this time, I've been convinced he had chosen Kat.

"I didn't tell you because I didn't wanna ruin the surprise. I never thought you'd . . ." Now he stops walking and looks at me. "I should have let you know what was goin' on. I wanted to surprise you. That's all. It got out of control."

"Shh." I reach for his hand, but he doesn't take it. "What I have to say is worse."

"River?" His voice drops.

"Worse than that." My hands tremble. Bump notices. Fortner is long out of sight. Too far to hear us now.

"What could possibly be worse?" Bump stops and leans against a spruce. Two squirrels chase each other around another ragged trunk.

I inhale a deep breath and brace myself for the fallout. "You deserve the truth."

Bump looks at me with open eyes. "Whatever it is, Millie. Just tell me."

"It's about Isabel," I begin. *Please, God, don't let this hurt him.* "When I was pregnant."

Bump holds up his hand to stop me. "I already know," he says.

He knows? I'm confused. Has Oka told him about the rape? Diana? "What do you mean you already know? What do you know?"

"Kat told me what you tried to do, early in the pregnancy." Bump makes a quick survey of the woods, then looks back at me. "The herbs."

"Of course she did." I hate to think I ever considered her a friend.

"This mornin' I asked Fortner if it was true. He wouldn't say, but from what I can figure, he likely talked you out of it."

"Bump, let me explain—"

"It's okay, Millie." He gives me a look of understanding.

"You're not angry?" I look at him, amazed by his ability to forgive.

"I'm no fool, Millie. I studied medicine, for goodness' sake."

My mouth drops open. "You knew she wasn't—"

He holds up his hand to stop me. "Don't say it, Millie. Don't ever say that. Isabel is *my* daughter. Has been from the start."

"I'm so sorry, Bump." I start to cry. "I couldn't tell you. I never meant to . . ."

Bump shrugs and smiles gently, as if he's already come to terms with all of this. "I figured you'd tell me when you were ready. But I never bargained on him showin' up here. That about killed me, Millie. To find you with him. I never thought—"

"You should have told me they were coming. I would have stopped you from bringing him here."

We suddenly realize our conversation no longer makes sense.

"What?" we say, in sync for the first time.

"Millie, are you sayin'—" Bump stands straighter now, pulls away.

I do the same. "You thought it was River?"

"Who else would it be?" His voice grows louder. Angry.

"Bump, no. This has nothing to do with River. I would never have done that to you."

"What are you gettin' at, Millie?" His temples pulse.

I release a long breath. Think of Isabel. Try to get this out the right way.

"It wasn't my fault." I close my eyes and wish I could make this all go away.

But Bump wants more. He takes both my hands and makes me look at him. "I'm not mad, Millie. Tell me the truth."

"Bill Miller." I cry harder now. Every time I say his name, it gets me.

Bump's teeth clench. He looks back at Bill's limp body, and then he says, "Explain."

I tell Bump everything, starting from the beginning. How I went to church that morning with the Miller family. How I asked to stay, spend some time alone in the sanctuary. How Diana's husband found me later, in the steeple, and forced himself on me, taking all I had, leaving only a seed. "I wanted to tell you about the . . . the steeple, before the wedding, but I was afraid."

"You should have trusted me." He paces quickly, a bad energy filling him. He looks back down the trail, but Fortner has yet to return.

"I didn't know I was pregnant, Bump. I would have never trapped you like that." I follow him, begging, pleading for him to understand.

"You didn't trap me." His voice is flat. I've never seen him so . . . consumed.

"At first I didn't know. I realize I should have, but I guess I was in denial. Kat's the one who finally made me accept that I was carrying, back when I thought she was my friend."

Bump says nothing to this.

"She told me which herbs I'd need. Said Fortner could help me. But he refused."

Bump kicks the trunk of a tree.

"I wouldn't have gone through with it." I think of Isabel and feel disgusted by the plans I once had. "I'm so sorry, Bump. I never meant to hurt you. I was afraid. Afraid I'd lose you. Or that you wouldn't understand. And I thought maybe I couldn't be a good mother to her, after all that had happened."

"I gotta let this sink in," Bump says. He takes a few steps, then turns back to me. "All this time, I thought it was River."

The woods have grown quiet now. Even the wind is holding its breath.

Bump spits, as if the truth is more than he can swallow. He walks to Bill Miller's mangled body and gives it a hard, angry kick. Then another. I wince with each blow. Then Bump stands over the man who raped me. He holds his gun above Bill Miller's face. "Well, one thing's for sure," Bump says, spitting again, this time onto Bill's face. "This monster got what he deserved." Then Bump shoots him, right between the eyes.

Chapter 35

Fortner sits at the table, his arms crossed. Oka sits in the corner, rocking Isabel. I sit next to Bump on the sofa, his arms tight around me. He knows not to let me go. Every time he does, I cry. I still can't believe we're alive. That Bill Miller is dead, and that my family is safe.

Sheriff Halpin stands in the doorway. "All right," he says. "You first, Bump. What happened?"

The sheriff has seen the body. He knows the lion did a lot of damage, but what he doesn't know is whether the bullet entered Bill's head before or after the lion took her share.

Oka passes Bump a glass of water, a sign of support.

"Bump didn't kill him," I say for the third time since this interrogation started. But my voice cracks and I worry the sheriff may take that as a sign of stress. Of dishonesty. He doesn't believe a mountain lion would attack a grown man for no reason. They tend to try to avoid people, not pounce on them. Especially when there are plenty of deer to catch instead. The sheriff looks around the room, trying to read the faces of everyone present.

Then he turns to Fortner, and a flash of satisfaction crosses his face. Halpin may have finally found his chance to lock him away.

Fortner looks the sheriff in the eye but says nothing.

"Let me guess. You're going to deny this one too?" It's clear Halpin wants to blame the shooting on Fortner, even if the bullet had nothing to do with Bill Miller's death.

"What difference does it make?" Fortner says.

Bump speaks up, defends Fortner. "As excited as that idea must make you, Sheriff, Fortner did nothing wrong."

"From what I can tell, he fired his gun." Halpin gives Fortner a cold, hard look, while talking about him as if he weren't in the room. "Seems a likely story that Fortner killed this man, hauled his body into the woods, and left him there for the lions to find."

"Fortner did no such thing. He was only there because I asked him for help," Bump explains. "The lion killed Bill Miller. Whether you believe it or not, it's the truth. Millie saw the whole thing. She can tell you. We moved the body down the mountain, not up."

I nod at the sheriff, who still looks confused.

"But both guns were fired," Halpin says.

"We shot to scare the lions away," Bump explains. "He was already dead when we found him."

"Then why shoot the man?" Halpin asks Bump. "If he was already dead, as you say, then you weren't trying to put him out of his misery. What made you put a bullet in his brain before you retrieved the body? What am I missing here?"

The room swells with silence.

"Seems to me, somebody's not telling the whole truth." Sheriff Halpin continues to glare at Fortner.

"Maybe somebody's not asking the right questions." Fortner

walks toward the window and points outside. Diana sits on the porch, head in her hands, crying.

Sheriff Halpin opens the door. "Mrs. Miller?"

Diana looks up. She's white as a sheet, with makeup rolling down her face. Her entire body shivers from shock. She cries, "What have I done?"

Sheriff Halpin looks back to Bump for an explanation. I nod, giving my husband the permission he seeks to tell everyone the truth. Bump exhales, squeezes my hand, and starts at the beginning. He spills years' worth of secrets and shame. But I don't care anymore who knows. It doesn't matter what the sheriff thinks of me. Bump is safe. Isabel is safe. That's all that matters. We will deal with the rest in time.

Dishes clatter, feet shuffle across the wooden floors, and the smell of morning coffee stirs me from sleep. Oka must be cooking breakfast. Bump is still in bed with me. Isabel too. It's the first time we've ever slept in together, letting the chores take last priority. Bump brushes my hair from my face and looks long into my eyes. Isabel stirs between us.

"I love you," he says. And never did the words hold more meaning.

I kiss him softly. Freely. The room is heavy with emotion.

"I'm sorry, Bump. I've made so many mistakes."

"Shh." He kisses me again. "We both have."

I rest against him, finding no words for what I feel. Finally, Bump speaks. "Sheriff's decided to stay with Diana. He's going with her all the way to Mississippi. She's too upset to travel alone. Especially with the remains."

"I'm so worried about her. And Camille." Now the tears start to fall again, despite my best efforts not to cry. Because of me, Camille has no father. Diana, no husband. Bill Miller may have been a monster to me, but now they're the ones who will pay for his sins.

"They'll be all right," Bump says. "They've got Mabel." An angel there to catch their fall.

I think about that row of dominoes. One choice leading to another. "This is all my fault."

Bump pulls me closer. "Nothing about this is your fault, Millie. That man brought this on himself. He got what he deserved."

"But if I had told the truth, from the start—"

"Shh," he says again. "It's all over now."

When we finally crawl out of bed, we find Oka and Fortner sitting in silence by the fireplace, as if the whole world has been placed on pause. Bump and I move to the love seat, and Isabel jumps into Bump's lap. Now that everyone knows the truth, Oka wants more. She confronts Fortner, direct as always. We are all tired of secrets and surprises.

"You really kill two women?" Oka asks.

Fortner gives her a look of understanding, as if he realizes she's only trying to free him too. We wait to hear his story. He clears his throat and looks down to his moccasins.

"Halpin shot Ingrid." Oka nods, as if that's all she needed to hear, but Fortner continues to argue his case. "You think for a second he'd let me go if I was really the one to blame?"

"Why'd he do it?" Bump asks, bending to stoke the fire. Isabel moves from his lap to mine.

"He didn't mean to hurt her," Fortner explains. "Not his fault any more than mine, I suppose. We brought it on ourselves. Ingrid just got caught in it."

"Sounds like you really cared about her," I say. The coffee percolates, and Oka heads to the kitchen.

Fortner looks out the window, nods, and says, "I did."

Oka pours a cup of coffee and brings it to Fortner. No sugar. No cream. He motions for her to sit beside him again on the hearth. She sits, letting silence soothe his scars.

No one asks about the other woman, the one who lived here at the ranch. The one folks say he shot when he was a young boy. But Fortner knows it's what we're all thinking. Like me, he's ready to bury the burden. He is ready to tell the truth. He starts with a sigh, and then allows the secrets to surface.

"I was just a kid," he begins. "Living in the woods after my folks left. I came and went those first few years, hopping trains, working the mines. Made it all the way to California by the time I was fifteen."

It's hard for me to imagine a boy so young, all on his own. But then I realize I was sixteen when I became an orphan. Oka was already married with children by that age. Bump was working to support his family long before then. Survivors, all of us.

"I came back through town, looking for work," Fortner continues. "Found a new family living here on the ranch, and I thought they might hire me. I knew this land like no one else. It was my home. I had a horse by then. A sound mare that looked just like Firefly." Fortner looks at me, and I smile. "Best horse you could have asked for. I let her lead me through the woods, to make camp, but it was getting dark, and I couldn't see." He gets upset now. Stops talking.

"I didn't see," he says again, as if he's trying to convince us.

"It's okay," I tell him. I know how hard it is to say things out loud. I don't want him to feel forced to do this. Oka moves closer against his side and touches his knee. Her kindness gives him the courage to continue.

"She stepped in a trap," Fortner explains, clutching his cup as the coffee steams above the rim. "It clamped her leg tight and there was nothing I could do. Best horse, I tell you. The best horse."

His voice cracks. It's clear he's fighting tears. He blows on his coffee and takes a sip before continuing.

"I was all bent out of shape," Fortner admits. "Had no choice but to shoot her. I was still a kid. Just a kid. And that horse, well, she was all I had."

Oka wipes tears from her eyes. I do too.

"The family must have heard the shot. They all came out with guns, ready to fire. They circled me in the woods, threatening me, demanding to know my name, where I'd stolen the horse from. I was furious. It was their trap. You see? They had done this. Not me."

He stands again. Paces now. His voice is tightening.

"I fired a shot. I did. I yelled at them, and I shot straight into the air. I threatened them too, but I didn't kill that woman." Fortner sounds desperate now, ready to leave all this behind him. Ready to release the blame.

"We believe you," Bump says calmly. "I know you don't have it in you to do such a thing."

Fortner faces the wall. I assume it's his attempt to hide his tears.

"But the woman die?" Oka asks, still trying to put the pieces together.

Fortner nods.

"If not you, then who?" I ask.

"Her son," Fortner answers, finally turning back to face us. "He was small, even younger than me. But he was aiming right at me. The woman moved just as he pulled the trigger. She was trying to stop him from shooting me."

I pull my hands to my mouth. "He shot his own mother?" I can't imagine anything worse.

Fortner nods. "They didn't want to hang it on him. What else could they do?"

"They blamed you?" Bump asks.

"They blamed me."

Later, at night, I crawl into bed next to my husband. I sink into Bump's strong hold and hope he never lets me go.

"Bump," I say. "There's something I still need to know."

He waits. Runs his fingers through my hair.

"I came back to Kat's house that first night. I saw you there, with her asleep in your lap. I know it's all over now, but if there's anything else you need to tell me. Any more secrets . . ."

"Millie." Bump kisses me softly, his lips lingering long on mine. "I was never with Kat. I promise. I was a fool. That's all. I stayed because she asked me to. She said she was afraid to be alone, scared somethin' might happen to her father after I left.

And she was right too. I sat on the sofa to wait it out. Just to monitor him until I was sure he was stable. But then Kat started talkin', tellin' me everything about her mother, the cancer, the day her husband left. She went on and on, Millie. I tried to stay awake and listen, but I kept noddin' off. Next thing I knew, the sun was comin' up. I woke hours later to find her head in my lap and Mr. Fitch not breathin'."

Whether his story makes any sense or not, I believe him, and for the next several moments we hold each other tight, whispering words of forgiveness. Then Bump moves his finger slowly across my neck, tracing the line of my collarbone, down into the subtle dip of my throat. My body fires, and in this moment, I feel the passion for my husband that I have always felt for River.

My hands explore him, and every nerve within me sizzles with heat. He turns gently over me, and I don't tense up. I don't spin away. I don't pretend I'm Kat.

"I told you, didn't I?" Bump runs his fingers through my hair. "When we moved here."

"You told me lots of things," I say. "That Fortner was no killer. That you'd never let anyone hurt me. That we could turn a profit with this ranch."

"Was I right?"

"You were right." I kiss him.

He smiles. "And I said we'd be okay here. That everything would work out."

The house is dark. Quiet. Isabel sleeps soundly in her crib. I look into Bump's safe blue eyes, kiss him once more, and say, "I really am the luckiest girl in the world."

The next morning we stay in bed, with Isabel climbing between us. We talk, we read, we snuggle. Outside, the air cools, the colors shift, and the elk sing.

I've twisted and turned in bed as we've laughed and played, trying to revive our spirits, treating Isabel to tickles and pillow fights. In all the commotion, I've ended up backward, with my head falling over the edge, and that's where I notice the twin peaks in the distance, the very ones I've stared at through this window for years. The ones we first saw when we moved to Colorado. When I pointed them out and asked Bump if he really thought we could move mountains.

"Bump?" I ask. "Come here."

"Again?" he teases. "You gotta go easy on me, Millie."

I laugh and tell him to behave. "I'm serious. Come see."

He moves next to me, his head hanging over the foot of the bed like a child. Isabel climbs over us and does the same, laughing. "You see what I see?"

"Um . . . mountains?"

"How many?" I ask.

Bump looks confused.

"Look again. You see the twin peaks? The ones from my dream?"

He looks where I point but says nothing.

"They've moved." I release a laugh.

"What are you talking about?" Bump twists to get a better look from my angle.

"See? From here, it looks like they've finally come together. They stand as one. Just like you said they would."

Bump moves closer and brushes my hair from my face. "But that's not really what happened at all, is it?" Bump says softly. "The truth is, Millie. It's you who had to move. And me too."

I take in what Bump is saying, thinking long and hard about the real message of that verse his mother taught him: "*If ye have faith as a grain of mustard seed, ye shall say unto this mountain, Remove hence to yonder place; and it shall remove; and nothing shall be impossible unto you.*"

I remember the traditional Choctaw dress Oka made for me. The one with the half diamonds that represented mountains, the road of life. Maybe Bump is right. Maybe that's what Oka was trying to say all along. The only way we can really change anything is by changing ourselves.

Bump wraps his arms around us and calls us his girls. Outside, the mountains stay strong. In here, I feel strong too. Strong. And brave. And safe. The three of us. Bump, Isabel, and me. The We.

Chapter 36

It's been three months since Diana returned to Mississippi to bury her husband. The sheriff returned to Colorado once he knew she was safely surrounded by loved ones. Tomorrow we will celebrate Isabel's second birthday and another swift spin around the sun. But for now, I am sitting by the fire with my daughter, rereading a letter from Camille.

Dear Millie,

Every spring when the clovers bloom, I make crowns, just like you taught me. I keep them in a special box in my room. I wore one to Daddy's funeral so I would feel brave. Then I made a wish, and you know what? I think Daddy heard me. He sent me a rainbow, all the way from heaven. Mabel says that was a sign that everything's going to be okay. Mama says Mabel's right. She also says we will come visit you soon, maybe for Isabel's baptism. I made a crown for her. I hope she likes it.

I love you, Sis.

Camille

I place the letter back in its envelope, an oversized plain white business casing, nothing pink or perfume-laced this time. Then I pull the clover crown from the package and place it on Isabel's head. She reaches up and feels the tiny white blooms. "You are brave," I tell her.

Isabel does her best to repeat the word, saying, "B'ave."

She looks at me and smiles.

"And loved," I add, covering her with kisses.

"Love you, Mama," Isabel says. I cry.

Bump joins us on the sofa, and I show him the letter. He reads it silently, then kisses the top of my head. Isabel's too. "There's another letter," I say, handing him an unopened envelope addressed from Janine and Mr. Tucker. "Read it to me?" I'm still drying my tears. It's hard to believe I have any left to cry.

Bump scoots close against me and begins to read aloud. The note has been written by Janine.

> Dear Millie,
>
> Cauy says to warn you. We'll be making a trip there in the spring, and he expects a bed to sleep in. Also, I refuse to suffer another stay with an outhouse. Mark my words, hon. If you don't have a flushing commode, I'll be staying in town, and I'll be dragging you right up there with me. Heaven knows you've served your time.

I laugh and roll my eyes. I miss Janine like crazy. Bump continues.

> Give Isabel a kiss from me. I can't wait to teach that girl how to play dress-up. I'm bringing tons of treats for

her! I worry you've got her wearing some dreadful dungarees or something.

Cauy also says you've done a great job with the ranch. He's been pleased as punch at the profits you've made. Hard to believe it's been almost three years already! Have you decided what you want to do next? Cauy says it's completely up to you. Stay and continue what you're doing. Or start that veterinary clinic Bump always talked about.

Tell Oka I'm looking forward to her fry bread. And tell her I finally thought of my name . . . but it's a secret!

See y'all soon!

Love,
Janine

Bump and I are both laughing, sharing stories about Janine and Mr. Tucker, when Oka and Fortner join us in the living room.

"What's that?" I ask, pointing to the bundles in their hands.

"Cedar," Oka says. "Picked from east side of tree."

"We bundled it with sinew," Fortner says proudly. "The traditional way. We've given it plenty of time to dry, and now we can do a proper smudging. I even found eagle feathers up at the keyhole of Longs Peak."

I take a closer look at the bundle of small cedar branches wrapped tightly together to form a stick of sorts.

"What's it for?" Bump asks. He looks as confused as I do.

"Time to cleanse this house," Oka says. She leans over the fireplace and lights one end of the tightly bundled cedar. Then she begins to chant in her native tongue. She lifts the bundle and pulls the smoke from the smudge stick over her head. Next she moves the smoke in slow strokes across her arms, her legs, and last, her body. Then Oka turns in what appears to be a pattern. First she faces the east and continues her chant. Then she faces north. Then west. And finally south, repeating the same series of sounds, the same movements with the smoke in all directions.

"What's she saying?" I ask Fortner.

Fortner doesn't speak Choctaw, but he seems familiar with what Oka is doing. "It's a prayer," he explains. "She's giving thanks to the spirits of each direction and asking them to be with us, to watch over us."

Then Oka moves her stick toward me, continuing her ceremony by moving smoke above my head, my legs, my arms, my body. Then Bump. Then Fortner. And then Isabel. We each remain still and reverent, carefully observing Oka's every move.

Next she makes her way through the house, using eagle feathers to wave the sweet-tinged smoke through every room. She walks in the same counterclockwise order of directions, east, north, west, south, until she has circled through the entire house with her smoldering bundle. The process is slow and soothing.

Now Fortner explains further, "She's ridding the home of bad spirits. This breaks the negative energy. Gives you a fresh start."

"Erases the past?" I ask.

"In a sense, yes." Fortner smiles.

I catch Bump's eye and reach for Isabel's hand. Together, we watch as Oka rids our world of all that came before. She's giving us each a chance to start anew. Kind of like Mama's idea of being "born again." *Erase. Erase. Erase.*

As Oka completes her ceremony, Fortner lights his bundle of sweetgrass. The smell is sweeter, like a cornfield at harvest, a natural, earthy, pleasant scent. "Like it?" Fortner asks.

I nod. As the smoke covers us, I feel protected. Clean. Forgiven.

"This will surround you with goodness, sweetness," Fortner explains.

Oka dips her smudge stick in water to kill the flame. Fortner fills the air with his own sweet smoke. Bump moves closer, and I lean against him, pulling Isabel into my arms. We all circle together, and I am reminded of the prayer circle resting on the mountain above. I'm reminded also of the row of dominoes, all lined up, tipping over, one at a time. Not so long ago, I was foolish enough to think the tiles all added up to me. That the line had an end. But now I know better. The circle continues, each choice leading to another. Each ending, a new beginning.

As the smoke clears and Bump grabs the guitar, I offer a silent prayer to God, my own way of requesting forgiveness. Mercy. Grace. Somehow, whether through smoke or through song, passages or prayers, I believe our message gets through. We forgive. We are forgiven.

Discussion Questions

1. Do you think Millie makes the right decision by marrying Bump? What makes some marriages stick while so many others fall apart, and what would you advise a young couple wanting to get married today? If you are not married, what do you expect of marriage and a spouse?
2. What do you think about Millie's decision not to tell anyone about the rape? So many victims of sexual violence never report the incident, and like Millie, many victims feel as if they have no voice. Why do you think this is the case? What can we do as a society to support people who become victims of violent acts?
3. When it's time for Millie and Bump to leave Mississippi, Millie realizes she is loved by many: Janine, Mr. Tucker, Mabel, Camille, even Diana. Who are those special people in your own life? Is there someone you know who might need such a person in his or her life?
4. As Millie enters her new marriage, she struggles to develop a fully open and trusting intimacy with Bump. She also resists the urge to tell him why this is the case.

Although Millie has been determined not to repeat the mistakes of her parents, how is she continuing certain cycles of dysfunction? Have you ever hurt someone you loved when your intentions were to protect them or shield them from a truth you thought would hurt them more? Is there anything your loved ones could tell you that would make you love them less?

5. In Colorado, Millie and Bump are met with many challenges. How does this experience bring them closer? Tear them apart? What are some of the most challenging situations you've ever had? Have you missed big opportunities because you were afraid of change or afraid to fail?
6. When Kat and Millie become friends, Millie admires Kat and wants to be like her in certain ways. Do you have a friend you admire? Have you ever been jealous of a friend? Have you ever been deceived by a friend? Eventually Millie realizes Kat is not a good friend after all. Millie is hurt by that betrayal but still does the right thing when Kat needs help. If you were in Millie's situation, would you have sent your husband to help Kat?
7. Millie becomes convinced her husband is having an affair with her only friend. What's the worst thing your partner or friend has ever done to hurt you? Were you able to forgive? And likewise, how have you hurt the ones you love? Have they forgiven you? If you haven't had to deal with infidelity, how do you think you would handle learning your spouse is having an affair?
8. Millie's grandmother, Oka, serves as the voice of reason in this book. Do you like Oka? What did you learn

from Oka's character? What did you learn from her Choctaw stories? How important is the grandparent/child relationship in your family?

9. Millie admires Oka's strength, beauty, talent, and wisdom. How has Oka managed to survive traumatic events in her life and still have such a sweet, genuine spirit? What does Oka teach Millie about forgiveness and grace?
10. When Millie first meets Oka, she notices Oka is Catholic when she makes the sign of the cross after her prayer. Oka mentions she grew up around the missionaries, as did many who are members of the Mississippi Band of Choctaw. Do you think Oka is a Christian? How do you think her faith impacts her life, and what do you think of the smudging scene at the end of the book? Do you think we may have more in common across varying religious practices than we sometimes believe?
11. Throughout the first section of this book, Millie is forced to make a terrible decision when she learns she is carrying Bill Miller's child. What would you do if you found yourself in such a situation? What if your young daughter was in that situation? Where do you stand on the issue of abortion, and what circumstances might make you feel differently? Have you ever had an abortion? How would you handle the situation if you were put there again? Have you ever adopted a child in need of a family?
12. At one point, Millie feels as if there is no right choice at all. Any route she takes brings pain to someone. We like to divide life into black and white categories, but sometimes life is messy and there is no perfect solution. Have you ever been in such a situation? Have you ever made a

decision you regretted? How have you forgiven yourself for a bad choice? And how have you learned to move past that mistake and make the most of your new situation?

13. Near the end, Millie is given a second chance to choose her first love, River. Were you glad when River showed up to fight for Millie? How did you feel when Millie kissed River? How did you feel when you realized Bump saw this kiss? Were you glad when Bump finally fought for Millie too? Have you ever had to choose between two loves? What would you do if you were given a second chance to choose again?
14. What do you think about the way the book ends? What is the significance of the mountain lion throughout the book? How does nature have its way again and again in Millie's life?
15. In the end, Bump tells Millie he has always been on her side. Do you have someone in your life like Bump, who loves you through and through? Does such perfect love exist outside of a novel? Why do you think so many people struggle to find healthy relationships?
16. What do you think will happen next for Millie and Bump and Isabel? What will happen to the other characters?

Writing Prompts

1. When writing this book, I actually wrote six or seven different endings before settling on this one. Pretend you are the author. Write a different ending to this story.
2. Pretend you are one of the characters in this book. Write a journal from that point of view. Now choose another character and repeat. How do the entries compare/contrast?
3. What would you want to happen next to the characters of this book? Write the first chapter of the next book in this series.
4. Choose one crucial scene in this book and rewrite it with a different result. For example, rewrite the wedding scene so that Millie and Bump do not end up getting married. Or the root-cellar scene so that Fortner agrees to give Millie what she wants. Consider the birth scene, the scene at the fencerow when Bump learns of the pregnancy, the confrontation with River, etc.
5. Write a letter to the author about your reaction to the book. I love hearing from readers.
6. Discuss the theme of nature, faith, forgiveness, or love from the book.
7. Compare and contrast character pairs from *Into the Free* and *When Mountains Move*. For example, how do Mabel and Oka compare? Diana and Kat? River and Bump? Sloth and Fortner? Mr. Tucker and Sheriff Halpin?

Find more ideas for book clubs, teachers, readers, and more by visiting www.juliecantrell.com

Acknowledgments

Writing this novel has been one of the most intense periods of my life, stretching me in all sorts of new ways. Thankfully, I've been surrounded by supportive people through it all, so here is my attempt to thank them publicly for that crucial encouragement. The truth is . . . I'll never be able to thank them enough.

First, I thank my family for letting me give this writing life a go. You deserve special recognition for tolerating me as I struggle to find enough hours in a day to do all it is I love to do. Nothing, and I mean nothing, means anything without you. I only hope at the end of my life people will remember me, above all else, as a good mother and a worthy wife. If not, I will have failed completely.

Thanks also to my friends, who didn't stop inviting me when I said, "I can't," and who showed up with homemade meals just when I was ready to toss in the towel, and who loaded me up in a car and took me away on a girls' trip, where we laughed and talked and danced and celebrated all that is wonderful in life. My life is SO good, thanks to you. Big hugs!

To everyone who went out of their way to make my launch of *Into the Free* such a special, beautiful night of my life, and to everyone who has taken a chance on that debut novel since its release. Words will never be enough to express my gratitude. Letting Millie's story be shared has been the most terrifying thing I've ever done. You gave me the encouragement to see it through. Thank you. Thank you. Thank you.

My favorite part of the entire publishing process is the research. I love hitting the road, meeting new people, and asking way too many questions. I have enjoyed getting to know every single person who touched this book, and I hope their spirit shines through these pages. Please remember, any mistakes are mine and mine alone. Any stroke of brilliance probably came from someone listed below.

Particularly, I thank my dear friend Robert Pritchard. One day, when I was at my end, Robert booked us a flight to Colorado and said, "Let's go!" There, we explored the Rockies with our pal Claire Ferrell Von Dedendroth, who welcomed us into her stunning mountaintop retreat and introduced us to her beautiful world. From the hut of a Peruvian sheep herder to swanky Vail author events, we did it all, and that week will forever be one of the highlights of my life. Robert and Claire, XOXO and thank you!

As I left Robert and Claire west of the Great Divide, I was delighted to join more families on the Eastern Front Range. My sweet cousins Connie and Bobby Masson, my dear old college friends Vinita and Jean-Noel Lemercier, and my closest buds from my Colorado days, Gina and Ron Beltz. Thanks to your tremendous hospitality, I was able to extend my stay to do the research needed to finish this book. Your friendship and your generosity will forever top my gratitude list. (That includes you too, Mama Joyce and Papa Dean Glorso!)

I considered my first book, *Into the Free*, my love song to Mississippi. This second book is my love song to Colorado, a place that is near and dear to me for so many reasons. My return visit was a remarkable journey, personally and spiritually. I came away with a deeper appreciation for the men and women who founded our western frontier and for the real cowboys, ranchers, and livestock professionals who continue to live life on the edge today.

Thanks specifically to Mark Howes, the most authentic cowboy I've ever met. He's the owner of Double H Ranch Saddle Shop in Fort Collins, Colorado, and if you're ever looking for custom-made tack, he's your man. Thanks also to Jesse Freitas, Madame Vera, and Bonnie Watson at The Stanley in Estes Park. They took time during their busiest day of the year to entertain me with remarkable stories of early settlers and to direct me to locals who knew the history. Thank you all.

Also, big thanks to the entire staff at Wind River Ranch, particularly Becky Ball, Molly Chretien, Nick Herald, Luke Lamar, Rob Luttrull, and Vanessa O'Neal. My day hiking with you through the snow and learning all about the early ranches of the Estes Park area will forever bring me smiles. The ministry you have at Wind River is extraordinary. You make this world a better place.

Also thanks to Don LuMiller, who welcomed me into his home with a big, warm smile and showed me a photo of him skydiving for his ninety-sixth birthday. What a man, what a spirit, what a lifetime of stories. Thank you, Don, for sharing your old ranching tales with me. There are pieces of you all through this book, and I hope you enjoy discovering them.

Thanks also to the incredible researchers with Colorado State University Equine Reproduction Laboratory in Fort Collins. I spent the day with Dr. Patrick McCue and Kathy Lachenauer, and what a fascinating day it was. Thank you for teaching me so much about horses. I was impressed beyond belief by what you all accomplish at your state-of-the-art reproduction facility and honored to be given the personal tour.

I also am extremely grateful for the knowledge and expertise of many Colorado outdoor enthusiasts who helped me build a believable world for Millie and Bump. Specifically, I thank Lyn Murdock and Larry Frederick with the National Park Service, as well as Joe Roller, Jeff Birek, and Nathan Pieplow, three Colorado Field Ornithologists who went out of their way to help me add the background to this story.

This story is, of course, a Colorado story, but the whole tale has its roots in the South. I thank the Lauderdale County Department of Archives and History in Meridian, Mississippi, where the research began years ago for *Into the Free*. In particular, I thank local authors and historians Leslie Joyner and Richelle Putnam, who helped me discover dusty file cabinet drawers and too many buried secrets to share. I owe tremendous gratitude also to the Mississippi Band of Choctaw, who welcomed me into their tribe and shared such inspirational stories with me. Specifically, I thank Dianna Albertson and her husband, Glenn Gibson, MBCI. I'll never forget the day I arranged to get into the car with a total stranger whom I knew only as Di. It was one of the scariest things I've ever done, and I'm betting Dianna felt the same way. But now we have a friendship that will last a lifetime. Thanks for taking a chance on me, Dianna, and for making me feel a part of the beautiful Choctaw culture.

Also thanks to Priscilla Williams, SPM/Immersion Trainer with the MBCI, and Dr. Kenneth York, Tribal Historian and Language Consultant. Priscilla read early drafts of this book and helped me with the Choctaw language, never laughing once at my silly questions and showing tremendous patience as I strove to get every detail as accurate as possible. Her beadwork is second to none, and I strongly encourage you to support the MBCI by investing in their original, handmade arts and crafts.

One of the best adventures that came along with writing this book was a day I spent in Frankie Germany's Talented and Gifted (TAG) classroom at the Choctaw Tribal School. Her fifth- and sixth-grade students and Dr. York gave me a tremendous history lesson. Then they helped me name Millie's baby and gave Oka her original name. I also was treated to a Thanksgiving feast with these students, and they ended my visit by singing "Amazing Grace" to me in their native language. It was such a moving day for me, one I will cherish forever. Thank you all!

The Choctaw Nation of Oklahoma was also instrumental in helping me shape this book. In particular, I owe tremendous gratitude to Presley Byington, traditionalist on the advisory board for the CNoC, who also read early drafts of this book and helped me with the details and language. And also to Sarah Elisabeth Sawyer and her mother, Lynda Kay Sawyer. The Sawyers are authors, filmmakers, and Choctaw storytellers who strive to preserve the Choctaw culture. Also thanks to James Parrish, Andrea Pavlovsky, and Eleanor Caldwell, whose assistance with *Into the Free* continued to shape this sequel.

In addition to Priscilla, Presley, and Sarah Elisabeth's help with early drafts, I owe big thanks to early readers and critique partners: Marie Barnard, Alicia Bouldin, Mary Ann Bowen, Lynne Bryant, Carol Langendoen, Patricia O'Sullivan, Cindy Perkins, and Lisa Wingate. I hope you all already know how much your encouragement and your advice has meant to me along this journey. Thank you!

Thanks also to Haley Fairbanks Bishop and her brother Jared Fairbanks for helping me research the finer details of old cars and trucks. Jared is a master at all things automotive, and I highly recommend him if you need anything to do with vintage vehicles. The dude knows his stuff. (And if you are interested in artwork featuring vintage vehicles, you must see the beautiful paintings of Dean Glorso.)

I also got to meet many talented veterinarians while researching this book, including the wonderfully kind and hospitable Dr. Steve Shideler, who welcomed my daughter and me into his father's home (Dr. Bob Shideler) where we were treated to a day of stories and artifacts from Colorado in the forties. Your kindness will always be greatly appreciated, and if anyone is looking for a good vet in Mississippi, the younger Dr. Shideler runs a clinic in Sardis. I also enjoyed chatting with Dr. Thomas M. Ellis, Veterinary Medical Officer, USDA, when he came to inspect my family's own herd of sheep. Sometimes a person with all the answers just walks through your door. That was Dr. Ellis. Thanks to all of these fine doctors for sharing their knowledge with me.

Thanks also to Dr. Cletus P. Kurtzman and Dr. Steven Vaughn with the National Center for Agricultural Utilization, ARS, USDA, who taught me about the history of penicillin in our country. Both of these researchers currently run labs in Peoria, Illinois, at the same facility where penicillin was discovered. I enjoyed taking a peek into their bright minds and learning about the birth of antibiotics.

Also thanks to Adam Burns with AmericanRails.com who helped me map the train route from Meridian, Mississippi, to Longmont, Colorado, in 1943–46, and to my dear friend Kathy Haynes, who always answers all sorts of random questions about horses anytime I ask and who never rolls her eyes at her clueless writer friend (well, actually, Kathy, sometimes you do roll your eyes, but you give me the answers anyway, and for that, I thank you!). And thanks to Laura and Ken Parkinson for helping me with many details for a plotline of the book that was later cut. Unlike those details, I hope our friendship outlasts life's edits.

I'm also grateful that Elizabeth Monteith placed the winning bid at a charity auction to support Regents School of Oxford. Her generosity enabled her to name a character in this novel. As Mabel says, "There's no such thing as coincidence," because Elizabeth gave me the name Isabel. I knew as soon as she said it that she had named Millie's baby.

Thanks also to two friends and counselors, Lucille Zimmerman (author of *Renewed*) and Ken Murray, of Clarksville Family Therapy. Both have answered questions, offered advice, and blessed me with their beautiful friendship. For this, I will always be grateful.

Of course, I owe BIG thanks to my fellow educators and students at Bramlett Elementary School in Oxford, Mississippi, who have given me room to try this writing gig while still letting me keep one foot in the world I love so much. My students bring such light to this world and such joy to my heart. I am honored to play some small part in their lives. It's also a blessing to work with such inspiring, dedicated, generous coworkers. Specifically, thanks to Brian Harvey, SuzAnne Liddell, and Suzanne Ryals for your support and flexibility. In every language, I thank you.

None of this would have ever happened without a few fine men taking a chance on a nobody writer who dared to submit her book for publication. Thanks to Greg Johnson, literary agent with WordServe Literary, and to John Blase and Don Pape, with

David C Cook. There will never be words to express my gratitude to each of you for allowing me to live this dream. And to the entire team at David C Cook, particularly Renada Arens, Ingrid Beck, Michael Covington, Ginia Hairston Croker, Nicci Jordan Hubert, Amy Konyndyk, Nick Lee, Karen Stoller (Oh goodness, I cannot say enough about sweet Karen!), Mike Worley, and to my publicist, Jeane Wynn (I still can't get used to the fact that I have a publicist . . . wow! But an even bigger WOW because I get to call you my friend.). I say it again and again, but because I get to work with you, I feel a bit like Millie . . . the luckiest girl in the world.

I may never have believed I could write a story, and I may never have given it a try if I had not crossed paths with one special teacher many moons ago. Linda Purcell, I owe it all to you. Thank you for being the kind of person who said, "Of course you can!" instead of the kind who says, "No, you can't."

Thanks also to the many "real authors" who have offered unconditional support and friendship and who have given me some of the most incredible adventures of my life. There are too many of you to name here, but you each hold a very special space in my heart. THANK YOU!

Finally, thanks to every single person who chose my debut novel, *Into the Free*, from the shelf, and who came back for a second helping. And to the teachers and the book clubs who keep the discussion going (especially all you Pulpwood Queens and Kathy L. Patrick of Jefferson, Texas!). And to the booksellers and librarians who find room for this story on your shelves. You have given Millie a voice, and that has given voice to Millies everywhere.

Thank you all for letting Millie inspire you to reach out, to lift up, and to love one another.

Notes

Chapter 1

"Who Wouldn't Love You?" © 1942 Kay Kyser.

"There Are Such Things," lyrics by George W. Meyer, Stanley Adams, and Abel Baer © 1942 Warner/Chappell Music, Inc.

Chapter 3

"Dearly Beloved," lyrics by Jerome Kern and Johnny Mercer, from the film *You Were Never Lovelier*, directed by William A. Seiter (Los Angeles: Columbia Pictures, 1942).

Chapter 4

"Taking a Chance on Love," lyrics by Vernon Duke, Ted Fetter, and John Latouche © 1940 EMI Music Publishing.

Chapter 7

Tender is the Night © 1934 F. Scott Fitzgerald, originally published by Charles Scribner's Sons.

Chapter 9

"It Can't Be Wrong," lyrics by Max Steiner and Kim Gannon © 1942.

Chapter 19

"I Wandered Lonely as a Cloud" by William Wordsworth, originally published in 1807.

"It Is Well with My Soul," lyrics by Horatio G. Spafford © 1873.

Chapter 20

This Side of Paradise © 1920 F. Scott Fitzgerald, originally published by Charles Scribner's Sons.

Chapter 21

Casablanca, directed by Michael Curtiz (Warner Brothers, 1942).

Chapter 23

Winesburg, Ohio © 1919 Sherwood Anderson, originally published by B. W. Huebsch & Co., New York and London.

The Sun Also Rises © 1926 Ernest Hemingway, originally published by Charles Scribner's Sons.

The Great Gatsby © 1925 F. Scott Fitzgerald, originally published by Charles Scribner's Sons.

Little Women © 1868 and 1869 Louisa May Alcott, originally published by Roberts Brothers.

Chapter 31

This Side of Paradise © 1920 F. Scott Fitzgerald, originally published by Charles Scribner's Sons.

Chapter 33

Thoughts Moral and Divine, Wellins Calcott, originally published 1761.

An Excerpt from The Feathered Bone

Part 1

Love is the child of freedom, never that of domination.
—Erich Fromm

Chapter 1

Friday, October 29, 2004

The Day

A magic moves the day as if anything could happen. Perhaps it's the pulse of jazz in the air, or the rhythmic churn of the riverboats, or the warm winds that swoop the levee, but there's a hint of mystery surrounding us. Something has charged the marrow walled within my bones. *Pay attention*, it says. And so I do.

It's the week of Halloween—not the best time to bring a sixth-grade class on a field trip to the Big Easy. But three rain delays pushed back the date, so here we are in New Orleans, where thick, milky fog rises from the river like steam. It nearly blocks our view of a shiny white tugboat and her long string of barges nosing their way through the coffee-colored currents.

We wait at Mardi Gras World, the famous tourist trap where my daughter, Ellie, and her classmates have come to learn the history of carnival season. Unlike the cars that buzz across the Crescent City Connection, or the boats that linger lazily beneath the bridge, we are landbound. We're also surrounded by mermaids, each elaborately carved and painted by Blaine Kern's studio artists.

Around the sculptures, a festive crowd filters through. They are free spirits, wearing rainbow face paint as they scuttle for a better view of the Mississippi. "A cape?" my friend Beth whispers. "Cute."

"Getting that party started early." Raelynn eyes the most flamboyant tourist before taking a seat beneath the pergola. "Argh, it's wet." She pulls beads around her neck, adjusting the plastic pendant that serves as our admission ticket for the guided tour.

Across the waterfront patio, a brass band pipes through scratchy speakers. Potted palm trees dance in the breeze. From the river, a dull horn bellows, causing our students to roar. The raucous tourist swings by again, her cape whipping wildly, her cheeks all aglitter. While this scene might be expected during Mardi Gras, it's unusual for a Friday morning in October.

My daughter shuffles through the crowd, staying close to her best friend, Sarah. A heavyweight redhead wearing dollar-store fangs jumps in front of them with a deep and masculine "Boo!" Ellie startles, and the jokester jolts away, laughing. This leaves our students wide-eyed, the chaperones on edge.

"Let's go ahead and get the children back inside," Miss Henderson instructs. She is young and not yet burned out from the never-ending demands of public education. Even now she remains pleasant as she taps one of her more rambunctious students on the shoulder, nudging him down from the railing where he's at risk of falling into the dangerous currents.

"Girls?" Beth and I both call for our daughters. In response, Sarah and Ellie skip into line, their arms laced together, their steps in sync. As they prance beneath a strand of purple and green party lights, Sarah's blond hair catches a glow, exaggerating her angelic complexion. Her innocent blue eyes twinkle with a sort of naïve joy not normally associated with raucous Bourbon Street celebrations. I whisper to Beth, "She could model for American Girl dolls."

"They're both beautiful." Raelynn drags behind. "The only problem is, which one will get to marry my Nate?"

"Yuck!" they protest, and Miss Henderson laughs, closing the double doors behind us.

Inside the gift shop, students explore rows of spirit dolls and voodoo pins, while Sarah and Ellie move to the collection of intricate masks. They have just begun to dance in disguise when a shopper steps up from behind. She's older than us. Close to fifty, I'm guessing. At thirty-five, fifty is sounding younger to me by the day.

"They sisters?" She asks this while watching Ellie and Sarah giggle in feathered face gear.

"Might as well be," Beth answers. "Born on the same day. Best friends since birth." She doesn't bother explaining that our girls are without siblings and have learned to rely on one another to fill that role.

"Figures. My daughters wouldn't have been so nice to each other at that age." She looks at me a little too long, and I shift away, adjusting my heavy backpack. It's crammed with first-aid gear and water bottles—just in case.

The woman leans closer. "You're from Walker?" She points to my bright-green shirt, the one Miss Henderson designed. It shows a school bus surrounded by classic New Orleans symbols: Mardi Gras masks, musical notes, and the traditional fleur-de-lis. At the bottom it reads *LP to NOLA 2004*, suggesting we've all traveled more than an hour east from rural Livingston Parish to explore our state's most famous city, "The City That Care Forgot."

I nod. "We're here for a field trip. You?"

"Albany," she says. "You may not remember, but are you a social worker? In Denham Springs? Amanda Salassi?"

My heart sinks. *Is she one of my clients? Why can't I place her?*

I scrape my brain, trying to pull this file—her round face, the gnawed fingernails, the tiny Hungarian hamlet of Albany known for its strawberries and quiet way of life. I draw nothing but blanks.

"You go out on call sometimes, with Sheriff Ardoin?" She keeps her voice low, hesitant.

Chills rise. I remember. She weighed at least a hundred pounds less when I last saw her, but her soft voice, something about that thin smile. "Mrs. Hosh?"

She nods, and we offer one another a warm glance.

"I'm sorry I didn't recognize you. Your hair was a lot longer. And brown."

"Yeah." She says this with a half chuckle, reaching up to feel her short blond crop.

It's all coming back to me now. The tight-knit settlement. The protective way her kinfolk circled, unwilling to let me in. Her late-night calls to my home phone, in secret, asking to talk.

"I want you to know"—she dabs her eye with the back of her finger—"I couldn't have survived it without you. Knowing you cared. And you didn't judge. Getting the others to call me. That helped. More than you can understand. Just knowing they had survived it."

I gesture for Beth to watch the girls. Then I lead Mrs. Hosh to the side. "You're here," I whisper. "You survived it too."

"One breath at a time. That's all I can do."

"That's all you have to do," I tell her, drawing her into a gentle hug. "Just keep breathing."

She holds me close, so tight her shoulder clamps against my throat, but I don't dare pull away. It doesn't matter that we are in a public gift shop, surrounded by chaperones and strangers. Or that my daughter and her friends watch us as they toy with touristy trinkets. All that matters is that this woman, right this moment, needs a hug. So that's what we do. We hug.

After the emotional exchange with Mrs. Hosh, I hurry to catch up with Ellie's class. They are following a cheerful tour guide into the theater, where he instructs us to zip sparkly costumes over our clothes. I grab four hangers, each with a long satin shirt that's been studded with sequins. Ellie chooses turquoise, her favorite color. It works well with her olive complexion and dark curls, which she inherited from Carl's Italian roots. In contrast, Sarah snatches hot pink, a bright anchor to her blond ponytail.

Beth and I settle for the leftovers, while Raelynn snags a set for Nate and crew.

"Choose a hat." Beth points to a stand filled with plush velvet caps. We select a few and hurry to the back of the room, where a three-dimensional Mardi Gras mural has been built for photo ops.

Sarah waves her hand like a princess and stands straight. "I'm the Queen of Endymion."

"And I'm the Queen of Bacchus," Ellie adds, bending her knees in a dramatic curtsy. I snap her photo, certain it will make the cut for this year's scrapbook.

Just on the other side of the wall, a café keeps our space swirling with scents of chicory coffee, a temptation that is becoming hard to ignore. "Man, I need a cup of brew," Raelynn admits. She rushes past us with her group of boys, a motley crew of hunters and fishermen who would rather be on a boat or a four-wheeler than anywhere near a city. But they are being good sports, pretending to fight over which one of them gets to wear the pastel pink shirt for the photo.

Before the students get too hyper, the guide takes over again. "All righty. Parents, please put the costumes away while I start the film." He speaks with enthusiasm, dimming the lights.

The students quickly pass the gear while black-and-white images begin to flicker, bringing us back to the early 1800s when Creoles held lavish masquerade balls. Eventually the parties spilled into the boulevards, and revelers began to toss special treats to onlookers. Then came the first floats, lit with flambeaus—an elaborate party-on-wheels.

"When will they pass out the king cake?" Raeylnn asks, causing the students to look our way.

Beth puts her finger to her mouth, the way a mother would

tell her child to hush. Then she sweeps soft curls from her forehead, revealing a thin streak of gray at her crown. Raelynn's brightly dyed locks and tattooed wrists mark a stark contrast to Beth's conservative style. And yet we've grown up a tried-but-true trio. The "three amies" as Raelynn likes to call us, a play on her Cajun tongue.

The film ends, and we make our way into the café where our guide begins doling out the cake, a braided sweet dough topped with confectioner's icing and sprinkled with colorful sugar crystals. Miss Henderson prompts, "Do any of you know why we eat king cake?"

Sarah, teacher's pet and usually the first to raise her hand, draws a blank and turns to Ellie for backup. But my daughter, too, seems to have no clue. Either that or she's too shy to answer.

One of the boys shouts his guess. "Some kind of voodoo thing?"

The guide chuckles. "A lot of people do associate New Orleans with voodoo, you're right. And some in these parts still practice, but we're mostly a Roman Catholic culture. So if you grew up in Louisiana, you probably already know the story of the three wise men."

Seeing we are from Walker, a rural sidekick to Baton Rouge and the kind of place that has more steeples than graves, the guide must realize he's safe with this religious topic, even if we are a public school. "Twelve days after Christmas, on January 6, we celebrate the wise men's visit with the Feast of the Epiphany. And we keep the party going all the way through Fat Tuesday, which in French is called . . . what?"

"Mardi Gras!" A handful of students are proud to know the answer.

"That's right. It's the day before Ash Wednesday, which of course launches the Lenten season—when Catholics give up our favorite treats and focus on being good." He laughs before adding, "Well, as good as we can be down here in New Orleans."

Then he steers off course a bit. "I'm sure some of you are Catholic." About half the class raise their hands, including Nate, one of the many CCD kids who has spent his Wednesdays riding the catechism bus to Immaculate Conception. "Anyway, to honor those three wise men, or *kings*, we make the cake round—like a crown—and we only serve it during carnival."

Ellie takes a bite, dusting her lips with green sugar sparkles, just as Nate cheers, "I got the baby!"

"Figures," Sarah says, eyeing the small plastic token in Nate's hands. "He wins everything."

When offered a piece of the dessert, Beth holds her perfectly trim waistline, saying, "I'd better not."

Raelynn then woos the guide into giving her Beth's forsaken slice. "Score!" She turns my way, beaming.

I nibble my cake and stay with the girls as our guide leads us into the massive warehouse—one of many owned by the business-savvy Kern family. Here, they design and decorate floats, while storing the oversized parade trailers.

We are led past giant replicas of everything from anime characters to zoo animals. At our first stop, a woman stands on a ladder, coating a massive sea monster in papier-mâché. Strip by strip, she covers the sculpture with brown craft paper, patiently building a smooth surface for the next round of artists to coat with primer.

"They must not know your trick," Beth says, wafting the air as if she can't bear the odor. She knows I add cinnamon to our glue at home, where Ellie and I are always working on some kind of art project.

"I want this job," Ellie says, now admiring a half-painted prop. The artist dips a thin brush into a pool of pink and drags it across the lips of a goddess.

"Seems like a fun place to work." I roll my fingers through Ellie's dark curls. She tolerates my touch for a second before easing away, moving from childhood through tweendom, closing in much too quickly on the tipping point of thirteen.

"I wish I could draw." Sarah's praise causes my daughter's cheeks to turn pink.

"What do you want to be?" I ask Sarah.

"A missionary," she says. "Somewhere far away. Like what my parents did."

Beth responds with affection, recalling her brief stint in Ghana where she fell in love with Sarah's father—the laid-back Cajun youth minister known only as Preacher.

Before Beth gets too deep in reminiscing, the guide redirects our attention to another artist, this one drawing a corset around a tiny waistline, exaggerating the voluptuous figure. The painter holds a feather and examines her work.

"What do you call that thing she's wearing?" Sarah asks.

Beth stiffens. "We'll talk about that later."

Sarah blows her cheeks and accepts defeat, but the artist turns and with a grim expression says, "It's a corset."

I'd guess she's in her sixties, with thinning gray hair and skin that hasn't seen the sun in decades. Her clothes, wrinkled and paint-stained, give her a look not so different from the homeless men we saw on our way through the city this morning.

"What's the feather for?" Our guide points to the brilliant blue plume in the painter's hand.

After a heavy sigh, the woman grimaces. "Well, a long time ago, women used to wear these corsets under their fancy dresses. Some people called them *stays*. Girls had to start wearing them when they were very young. Maybe eight years old." She looks at Ellie. "How old are you?"

"Twelve," Ellie answers, nibbling her fingernail. It's a habit she's trying to break.

"Twelve," the woman confirms. "So, if you lived in the eighteenth or nineteenth century, you'd be wearing one of these. Your ribs and your lungs and your stomach would all be pinched up tight beneath the stays." She tweaks her face at the thought of it.

"Why?" Sarah asks. Not a speck of hesitation.

"That's the question." The artist smirks. "Why do you think?"

No one comes up with a guess.

"Because women were slaves."

Beth scoffs.

"It's true!" The artist comes closer. "Slaves to fashion. To society. To culture. The men wanted women to have tiny waists, and we gave them what they wanted." She points her feather at our tour guide, the only adult male in the group. "Sometimes, if a man was looking for a wife, he would line up women and wrap his hands around their waists. If his fingers could touch, she might stand a chance."

The girls begin to wrap their midlines, measuring their own worth according to waist size.

The artist notices. "Women were expected to wear these corsets all the time, so they could train their bodies to have this wasp shape."

"Why?" Sarah asks again, leaning in for a closer look.

"Because most women couldn't work, remember? They needed someone to provide for them. Many even slept in these corsets, tightening the straps more and more each day. Some schools would measure their female students, making sure waistlines were shrinking. Like those foot-binding traditions in China. Ever hear of that?"

Ellie looks back at me, her eyes wide with curiosity. "Later," I whisper.

"The things we do to our girls. Torture, I tell you." The painter shakes her head. "Good thing I wasn't alive back then. Put me into one of those things? Might as well wear a straitjacket."

Beth whispers between her teeth, "I'm thinking she could use a little time in a corset."

It's the meanest thing I've ever heard Beth say. I raise one finger, just enough to catch the artist's attention. "I'm still not clear. What's the feather for?"

"Oh yes. I got sidetracked. Sorry." Her eyes light up. "For years, the corset boning was made out of hard, rigid materials. Rods. Reeds. Whalebones. Can you imagine? Being caged into that every day? Even at night?"

Girls peak their brows. Boys shake their heads. Parents sigh.

"But in the late 1800s a man named Edward K. Warren had a store up in Michigan. Dry goods, they called it back then. His customers complained about the whalebone corsets. They were too expensive, too uncomfortable. They didn't seem to hold up. So when Mr. Warren was buying supplies over in Chicago, he noticed a factory that made feather dusters—you know those old-fashioned dusters?" She waves her feather as if dusting the corset. "Y'all ever seen those?"

Miss Henderson promises she'll bring one to class next week.

"Well, anyway, Mr. Warren noticed that the factory threw away big piles of feathers. He thought he might be able to use them to make corsets. And he was right. He patented his idea. Earned himself a fortune. People loved his new featherbone corsets. You know why?"

Blank stares.

So she continues. "They were less expensive, for one thing, but mainly the featherbones allowed women to bend." She bows the feather, demonstrating her claim. "So in a way, Mr. Warren helped women break free from bondage. You see? This was the beginning of their—emancipation—so to speak." She stresses this word. "Anybody know what that means?"

Nate pipes up from the back. "Set them free?"

"Exactly!" The artist's face softens, and a warm smile stretches her mouth. "So when I got this assignment to examine women's fashion, I decided to give these nineteenth-century women some breathing room. Kind of my own little act of rebellion."

She looks at the group of children with a tenderness now, then toward the ceiling where birds flitter between the roof beams, serenading us. "Girls, promise me this. Every time you see a bird flying around with her beautiful feathers, I want you to think of all the women who strapped themselves into corsets against their wishes. Think of all the women who fought to break free from those restraints. And then remind yourselves to never again become slaves. In any way, to anyone. You keep yourselves free. Understand?"

The girls whisper as we leave the woman. "Who would want to look like a wasp anyway?" Ellie asks.

"I'm glad we don't have to live like that. In a cage!" Sarah says. She squirms as she reaches behind her back. "Now if only we could stop wearing these."

They both giggle, and Beth pulls her lips tight, still recovering from our recent shopping trip when we bought the girls their first real bras.

I put my arm around Beth's shoulders. "If only we could slow the world for them," I say. "Keep them young, and safe. And free."

The story continues in *The Feathered Bone* by Julie Cantrell, available wherever books are sold.

About the Author

Author photo by Andew McNeece

Julie Cantrell is the *New York Times* and *USA Today* bestselling author of *Into the Free*, the 2013 Christy Award winning Book of the Year and recipient of the Mississippi Library Association's Fiction Award. Cantrell has served as editor-in-chief of the *Southern Literary Review* and is a recipient of the Mississippi Arts Commission Literary Fellowship. Her second novel, *When Mountains Move*, won the 2014 Carol Award for Historical Fiction and, like her debut, was selected for several Top Reads lists.

Visit her online at www.juliecantrell.com
Facebook: juliecantrellauthor
Twitter: @JulieCantrell
Pinterest: juliecantrell